*This book is dedicated
with love
to Gladys Allison,
who started me off
many years ago*

*And grateful acknowledgment is due Etta Barrit, Guy Dolen, Lucy Gaston, Lynn Contrucci, Lola Peters, Michael McNamee, Claire Zion, Maria Carvainis, Sterling Lord, and my fairy godmother, Elaine Koster.

But most of all to those who could not see this labor to fruition: Thomas E. Hill, "Oma" Maria Peer, and Rhea Gallaher, Sr., who gave unstintingly of their love and support to the very end. Rest in Peace, Friends. You are sorely missed.

LOVE-MAKERS

JUDITH GOULD

A SIGNET BOOK

SIGNET
Published by the Penguin Group
Penguin Books USA Inc., 375 Hudson Street,
New York, New York 10014, U.S.A.
Penguin Books Ltd, 27 Wrights Lane,
London W8 5TZ, England
Penguin Books Australia Ltd, Ringwood,
Victoria, Australia
Penguin Books Canada Ltd, 10 Alcorn Avenue,
Toronto, Ontario, Canada M4V 3B2
Penguin Books (N.Z.) Ltd, 182–190 Wairau Road,
Auckland 10, New Zealand

Penguin Books Ltd, Registered Offices:
Harmondsworth, Middlesex, England

Published by Signet, an imprint of Dutton Signet,
a division of Penguin Books USA Inc.

First Printing, March, 1996
15 14 13 12 11 10 9 8

 REGISTERED TRADEMARK—MARCA REGISTRADA

Printed in the United States of America

PUBLISHER'S NOTE
This is a work of fiction. Names, characters, places, and incidents either are the
product of the author's imagination or are used fictitiously, and any resemblance
to actual persons, living or dead, events, or locales is entirely coincidental.

BOOKS ARE AVAILABLE AT QUANTITY DISCOUNTS WHEN USED TO PROMOTE PROD-
UCTS OR SERVICES. FOR INFORMATION PLEASE WRITE TO PREMIUM MARKETING DIVI-
SION, PENGUIN BOOKS USA INC., 375 HUDSON STREET, NEW YORK, NEW YORK 10014.

If you purchased this book without a cover you should be aware that this book
is stolen property. It was reported as "unsold and destroyed" to the publisher
and neither the author nor the publisher has received any payment for this
"stripped book."

CONTENTS

From *The Forbes Four Hundred Fall 1982*

Elizabeth Anne Hale

Inheritance, real estate, hotel business. N.Y. 88. Twice widowed. One daughter (two daughters, one son deceased), one grandson, one great-granddaughter. Current matriarch of America's most powerful hotel family. Born in Texas, orphaned as a child. Strong-minded, dominates family business. Owns over 400 hotels, 695 motels worldwide. Sold 100 hotels for reported $520 million 1979. Made first fortune during 1929 crash. Lives in penthouse of privately owned hotel, is driven around in 1921 Rolls-Royce (also inherited). "Fortunes are easily made if you live to be my age." May be the world's richest woman. Minimum net worth is $1.9 billion.

REQUIEM

QUEBECK, TEXAS
ॐ

August 14, 1985

1

THE big Lincoln Continental ate up the asphalt miles between Brownsville and Quebeck. Seated beside her husband on the maroon leather seat, Dorothy-Anne Cantwell stared out the windshield with a blank expression on her face. Everywhere she looked she saw the wide-open spaces of Texas, expanses of irrigated fields and citrus groves dotted with occasional monotonous little towns. Not even towns, she thought, just clusters of sad houses, peeling and dirty and baked by decades of harsh sunlight. The sky, heavy and gray, loomed oppressively over the landscape. Traffic was light, and they saw only an occasional car or truck. The landscape was monotonous and hypnotic. And it was worlds away from Manhattan.

She glanced sideways at the big urn on the seat beside her. It was not the usual crematorium urn, somber and plain and poured from a mold. This was one of a kind, the sterling silver intricately hammered and fashioned in a rococo pattern of auricular scrolls and hand-rubbed to a high-gloss finish. The sides flared out into twin handles terminating in deli-

cately fluted ivy leaves which were repeated in swirls around
the leaf-footed base.

Buccellati had done themselves proud.

Slowly she reached over to touch the urn. She half-expected
it to radiate the warmth of her great-grandmother, Elizabeth-
Anne Hale, but the metal felt smooth and cold. The urn
weighed at least seven pounds, but the handful of gray ashes
in it was weightless.

Only three days ago her great-grandmother had been alive.
They had talked and she had smiled at Dorothy-Anne, kissed
her. Only three days ago.

Now she was ashes.

Dorothy-Anne turned away, her eyes blurring with tears.
She found the dampness soothing to the grittiness three sleepless, grief-filled days had left in her eyes, but she knew she
couldn't give in to tears. If she wept now, she wouldn't be
able to stop for a very long time. And, first, she had a job to
do.

She felt a stirring within her belly, and wiping her eyes
with a knuckle, she carefully shifted the weight of her body,
swollen with the baby she carried.

If only Great-Granny had lived long enough to see this
child, she thought sadly. The baby was due in just three
weeks. Closing her eyes, she felt for the movement within her
womb: a sharp kick, then another, followed by an ever-so-
slight shifting of the child. Usually the kicking filled her with
a warmth and closeness for the child. But now, in her exhaustion, her body seemed strangely alien and detached. She
felt her baby move, but wondered if it was in someone else's
body.

"Honey? You all right?"

Startled, she opened her eyes and turned to her husband,
Freddie. He kept glancing between her and the road, a concerned expression creasing his face.

"I'm fine," she assured him softly. She smiled and reached
over, placing a reassuring hand on his arm. He knew she
hadn't been able to sleep since her great-grandmother's death,
but she didn't want to alarm him by letting him see how
drained and weak she felt now. "Don't worry, honey. I'm

okay. Just tired.'' And then she let her head fall back gently on the headrest.

A few more weeks, she thought. Just a few more weeks and then I'll give Freddie his child. But that thought awoke a nagging worry which wiggled in the fog of her exhausted mind like a worm. What if it wouldn't wait a few weeks? What if it were sooner? What if the baby came tomorrow or even today?

She shifted again slightly, shaking her head to dispel the moment of panic. She shouldn't let Dr. Danvers worry her like this. He might be a doctor, even one of the best in the field, but he was just being overprotective when he advised her not to make the trip to Texas. She was, after all, still three weeks away from full term. And Dr. Danvers didn't understand the importance of her great-grandmother's last wish.

It had been a small enough thing to ask that Dorothy-Anne scatter her ashes in Quebeck, Elizabeth-Anne's home. Dorothy-Anne understood the request and knew she had to fulfill it as quickly as she could. That's what Elizabeth-Anne had wanted, and what Dorothy-Anne needed to do. She had to know Elizabeth-Anne's soul was finally at rest—the rest she had waited so long for, and so fully earned. Dorothy-Anne knew she was at the end of her rope, that she had pushed herself as far physically and mentally as she dared—but this was something she had to do now.

Dorothy-Anne closed her eyes, again trying to ease her sense of restlessness and anxiety. But she knew these feelings wouldn't fade. They sprang from a grief so overwhelming, a loss so profoundly deep, it was physically painful. She didn't know if she would ever be able to get over it.

And then she had a thought that brought a tentative smile to her lips. After all, how could she forget a great-grandmother who had given her a thirty-million-dollar birthday present?

That had been on her ninth birthday, almost eleven years before. Dorothy-Anne felt she would be able to turn the clock back to that day if she lived to be a hundred. . . .

October 17, 1974. Autumn, and she was looking out her bedroom window in the big house in Tarrytown, her chin resting on her crossed arms. Below, the gardeners were out in full force, raking the fallen golden leaves. But she wasn't watching them; she was on the lookout for Great-Granny's car. It would come from between the tall clipped hedges which stood guard at the far end of the curved driveway.

She had been dressed and waiting for over an hour. Nanny, her governess, had allowed her to wear her favorite red dress, with its starched lace collar and glittering tiny rhinestone buttons. After all, it wasn't every day that a girl celebrated her ninth birthday, or that Great-Granny came expressly to pick her up and drive her down to the city to celebrate it in style.

Dorothy-Anne glanced again at the china-shepherdess clock on the windowsill. Her heart skipped a beat. It was twenty-seven past one. Just three more minutes, and Great-Granny's car would appear. Dorothy-Anne knew this for a fact; Elizabeth-Anne Hale was never late.

Dorothy-Anne sat poised to leap up, watching the second hand of the clock make three last graceful sweeping revolutions, and then at precisely one-thirty she jumped forward and pressed her nose flat against the glass, her breath making a little halo of fog. Her eyes lit up.

There it was, the majestic yellow-and-black Rolls-Royce. The shiny hood with the chrome grille and the big bug-eye headlamps was just nosing out from between the hedges.

Jumping to her feet, she ran from the room and raced down the long carpeted hall. When she reached the head of the stairs she got up on the sleek banister with a well-practiced backward hop. She balanced herself carefully and then let go, beginning the long smooth slide down the wide staircase.

As she slid down to the first-floor landing, she saw Nanny looking up at her with stern disapproval. Immediately Dorothy-Anne clutched the banister so that, with a squeak of burning friction against her palms, she came to an abrupt halt. Slowly she slid off the banister and walked down the rest of the way with ladylike dignity.

She smiled shyly up at Nanny, but the smile wasn't returned. She didn't really mind. Nanny wasn't a bad sort, even if she wasn't much given to smiling. Dorothy-Anne was fascinated by Nanny's looks. She was over fifty, with gray eyes and hair, and in profile her body looked remarkably like a silhouetted map of Africa. The stateliness of her bust and buttocks beneath the black dress she always wore was especially surprising in contrast to her thin and shapely legs.

Nanny looked down at Dorothy-Anne and without speaking held out the tan cashmere coat and helped her into it. Then Dorothy-Anne stepped back and awaited inspection. She could almost see Nanny tick off the items on her checklist with her critical glance: hair combed and neat, dress buttoned, hem straight. Now came the final test.

Nanny stepped closer and leaned down so that her pointed face was not two inches from Dorothy-Anne's.

"Breathe," she ordered.

Dutifully Dorothy-Anne opened her mouth and sighed right into Nanny's face.

Nanny's eyes flickered. She straightened, reached into her dress pocket, and produced a rock-hard white candy. Dorothy-Anne accepted it, unwrapped it from the clear cellophane, and handed the wrapper back to Nanny. She then popped the mint into her mouth and with a practiced flick of her tongue pushed it into the hollow of a cheek. The menthol taste was sharp and mediciny, but she refrained from making a face.

Nanny leaned down again and began to button Dorothy-Anne's coat from the bottom up. "Now, don't you forget your manners," she warned sternly. "When you get into the car, say, 'Good afternoon, Great-Grandmother. It was very lovely of you to invite me.' "

Dorothy-Anne nodded solemnly.

"If you receive a gift, open it *slowly*." Nanny gave her a meaningful look. "Don't tear the wrapping to shreds. And don't forget to say, 'Thank you, Great-Grandmother. I'll treasure it always.' "

Dorothy-Anne nodded again. The mint was making her salivate, but she refrained from swallowing. That way, the awful menthol taste didn't spread.

She then followed Nanny to the main entrance and stepped

aside as the huge mahogany double doors were pulled open by the butler. When she stepped outside, the fresh air felt cool and good against her face. A brisk wind was blowing down the Hudson Valley, scudding the white clouds overhead and doubling the work of the gardeners, who were still busy raking leaves.

As soon as she heard the door shut behind her, she leaned over the balustrade, turned her face sideways, and spat the mint behind the clipped yews, where it joined a pile of others. Then she wiped her lips with the back of a hand, and letting out a whoop of joy, raced down the steps to the waiting car.

Forty minutes later, the big car rolled to a stop under the yellow canopy of the Hale Palace Hotel on Fifth Avenue. Both of the doormen came rushing down the red-carpeted steps, practically falling over each other to open the passenger door. Dorothy-Anne slipped carefully out on the street side, pushed the door shut with both hands, and came around the car. Wide-eyed, she stared at the doormen. They were identical twins, dressed in pale blue uniforms with glittering rows of brass buttons and braided gold epaulets on their shoulders.

Max, the chauffeur, went wordlessly around to the trunk and lifted out Elizabeth-Anne's collapsible wheelchair. Max was the biggest man Dorothy-Anne had ever seen. He was Japanese, carried his huge shoulders and enormous paunch with pride, and had once been a sumo wrestler. Dorothy-Anne thought Max was a funny name for a sumo wrestler, but Great-Granny had explained that her first chauffeur had been named Max, and thereafter, she had called all the others Max too.

During the drive down from Tarrytown, Great-Granny's nurse, Miss Bunt, had sat up front beside Max. Now she silently took the chair from him and wheeled it into position on the sidewalk. She held it firmly by the handles as Max ducked into the Rolls.

"Ready, Miss Hale?" he asked.

Great-Granny looked at him dourly, but she didn't move. "As ready as I'll ever be," she said in her clear, clipped voice.

Carefully he scooped her out of the car and deposited her

ever so gently into the wheelchair. Next came the lap blanket, which he tucked around her lap and legs.

Dorothy-Anne watched the ritual closely, fascinated as always by anything Elizabeth-Anne did. She idolized her great-grandmother, realizing even at her young age that the elder Hale was a very special type of woman.

Although Elizabeth-Anne's last stroke had left her paralyzed from the waist down, no one had ever heard her complain; nor did she give the impression that she was helpless. When she had walked, she had done so with erect dignity, and now that she was confined to a wheelchair, she still maintained a regal bearing. Tall and gaunt, she wore her silver hair in a thick, full permanent. Clipped to her earlobes were large jade cabochons surrounded by a fine lacework of white-gold filigree.

The bright afternoon light showed each of her eighty-one years etched clearly on her face, her skin cracked finely like the surface of an ancient painting seen through a magnifying glass. Yet the light showed more than her age. It also revealed her unique and indomitable strength. That was what was most striking about her, her unmistakable air of inner purpose. She was a woman at home in plush and polished surroundings, but also one of the world's shrewdest and wealthiest entrepreneurs, the founder of a multinational empire which included more than four hundred luxury hotels worldwide.

"Thank you, Max," Elizabeth-Anne said crisply once she was settled comfortably in her wheelchair. She focused her clear blue eyes on Dorothy-Anne and raised her eyebrows questioningly. "Shall we proceed?"

Dorothy-Anne nodded.

Elizabeth-Anne Hale lifted a hand in an imperious but graceful gesture. "Miss Bunt?"

The nurse stepped aside as the twin doormen took over. They pushed the wheelchair smoothly up the ramp, while Dorothy-Anne and Miss Bunt followed alongside on the red-carpeted stairs. The chair rounded the top of the ramp and Miss Bunt took over again, pushing Great-Granny toward the gleaming brass-and-etched-glass doors of the Hale Palace that the doormen already held open. Dorothy-Anne noticed that the doors were flanked by perfect ball-shaped topiary trees in brass tubs. She fell back as something about the tubs caught her eye. They gleamed like gold, and for the first time she noticed the engraved intertwined script H's.

HH

Hale Hotels.

Like the cherry topping a sundae, this last touch made her feel especially important. Great-Granny was a Hale. And so, she thought with a surge of pride, was she.

Elizabeth-Anne had commandeered the Tropical Court so the two of them could have lunch alone. The enormous courtyard was glassed in eighteen floors above, and Dorothy-Anne thought it was the most exciting place in the world. With the splashing fountains, thickets of exotic foliage, and towering palms, the restaurant allowed one to imagine it was in the tropics. Especially with the riotously feathered parrots and pale cockatoos with clipped wings that screamed from their perches.

The lunch was accompanied by a string quartet and served by a mustached maître d' and two unctuous waiters. The meal itself was simple but delicious: jumbo shrimp cocktails, a salad of red leaf lettuce and avocado, whole lobsters and sauteed green spinach. Elizabeth-Anne chatted warmly with Dorothy-Anne as the girl happily cleared her plates, even down to the spinach.

When the meal was over, three waiters and the maître d' brought in an exquisitely frosted birthday cake. Nine tiny candles were arranged in a circle and glowed with little halos. As it was ceremoniously set down in front of Dorothy-Anne, the quartet broke into a rendition of "Happy Birthday." Great-Granny joined the singing, her voice surprisingly clear and melodious.

The cake was served with dollops of French vanilla ice cream and a bottle of chilled Dom Perignon. Great-Granny allowed Dorothy-Anne to drink half a glass of it, undiluted. When the dessert plates were cleared away, the quartet withdrew and they were alone. The splashing of the fountains and the screams of the birds now sounded very loud. Great-Granny looked across the courtyard, and Dorothy-Anne followed her gaze. Two men carrying attaché cases were walking toward their table.

"Gentlemen," Elizabeth-Anne said, gesturing proudly, "this is my great-granddaughter, Miss Dorothy-Anne Hale."

The men looked down at her and extended their hands. Dorothy-Anne remained seated and shook hands politely. Both men seemed to have very dry, brittle skin. They were in their sixties and had gray hair and wore pin-striped suits.

"Mr. Bernstein, Mr. Morris," Elizabeth-Anne said. "Please, sit down."

As the men obeyed, putting their attaché cases down beside their chairs, Elizabeth-Anne rested her elbows on the table and folded her hands. She looked at Dorothy-Anne and came right to the point. "Mr. Bernstein and Mr. Morris are attorneys," she explained.

Dorothy-Anne looked solemn and Elizabeth-Anne laughed with amusement. "Don't look at them like that, my dear," she said briskly. "They are not here to arrest you." She smiled and took a sip of her coffee. Then she looked pointedly at Dorothy-Anne over the rim of her cup. "They are merely delivering your birthday present."

"**H**oney?"

The voice seemed to be floating in space amid swirling memories and flashes of Technicolor pictures.

"Honey . . ."

It was a warm voice, a voice Dorothy-Anne knew well and loved. She opened her eyes and snapped back to the present. She shook her head to clear it.

"Are you awake, honey? It sounded like you were talking in your sleep."

"No . . . no, I was just daydreaming. I'm okay now." She smiled at him reassuringly, but in truth she wasn't sure if she *was* all right. She had just been in Manhattan, a decade in the past; the memory had seemed so real, she wasn't sure if she was dreaming now, instead. But, no, the irrigated groves were still moving past outside the car windows. And the ache in her heart was still there.

"We're about there, honey."

She looked over at Freddie and tried to smile, then turned back to gaze out the windshield. She wondered how long she had been daydreaming. She didn't feel rested, but knew it must have been quite a while, as night had almost fallen and Freddie had already turned off the main highway, the one no one used anymore.

The sky had darkened some more, and on the horizon Dorothy-Anne saw thunderheads, low and boiling, a menacingly dark charcoal gray. But overhead they were a yellowish muddy brown, as if the sun were trying to leak through.

"Storm's brewing," Freddie said. "It looks pretty bad." He lit his cigarette with the dashboard lighter and then inhaled so that the tip glowed orange in the darkening light.

Suddenly Dorothy-Anne's attention was drawn to the old billboard up ahead. It was ancient and peeling, a Pop Art relic from long before Pop Art came into being. It was big and rectangular, with a faded coronet jutting out over the top. The little orbs atop the coronet had long since broken away, and the flakes of gold paint had gone the way of the wind and the rain. Now the crown's edge looked like jagged teeth trying to take a bite out of the sky.

She stared at the billboard as it rushed toward her, and she mouthed the faded letters which clung tenaciously to it.

HALE TOURIST COURT.

That was what it read, and it had been standing there long before Hale hotels had sprouted like mushrooms after a world-wide rainfall. Long before some clever Madison Avenue design team had come up with the elegantly intertwined HH logo. Because long before everything else, there had been the tourist court.

It was just up ahead, on the side of the road, and it wasn't worth a second glance. There were a hundred thousand motels like it across the country on roads like this one, old roads, obsolete now that newer highways had been built. The tourist court was just another row of dilapidated little cabins separated by carports, their only unique feature their roofs of corrugated metal, high, steep, and sloping. They were mansard roofs, once painted bright orange and shining with newness, now weathered dull and rusting.

But still, this particular motel was special in a way no other could ever be. It was the *Hale* Tourist Court, and it was here that Elizabeth-Anne's worldwide empire had begun.

Was it possible? Dorothy-Anne asked herself, gazing at the tourist court as Freddie slowed, pulled over, and stopped the car. The idea of it spun dizzily in her foggy, exhausted mind. Could one ignoble motel have been the springboard for an empire of international luxury hotels? Could a lone woman truly have had such vision and incredible drive as to build one of the world's largest independently controlled fortunes from these buildings?

As if the answer lay in the Buccellati urn, Dorothy-Anne weakly pulled it onto her lap, holding it close against the baby within her. Now the silver no longer seemed cold and lifeless. She could almost feel a warmth seeping through it.

Freddie helped her out of the car, but she insisted on carrying the urn herself as they walked off through the growing darkness into the roadside grove across the highway from the tourist court. She was moving as if in a daze, feeling more light-headed than ever. Once she stumbled, and Freddie took the urn from her. She felt a strange, cool sweat on her forehead, and so she let him hold it.

Her vision blurred with tears as Freddie unscrewed the cover of the urn. Wordlessly he handed the urn to her.

She did not speak. Around them, the wind had risen, and the storm clouds roiled low and angry.

Slowly she tilted the urn. The wind caught the spill of ashes, trapped them in sudden whirls of eddies, and then swiftly dispersed them in a long gray streamer. It was then that the first fat, heavy raindrops came splattering down, forcing the ashes groundward.

Now Dorothy-Anne understood why Elizabeth-Anne had requested that her remains be scattered here.

Because all things must end as they begin.

And then she doubled over as the skies broke open and the first stabbing pain seized her in its grip.

2

In the kitchen of the manager's cabin of the Hale Tourist Court, Mrs. Ramirez heard the rumble of thunder. Lifting her heavy bulk off the kitchen chair, she made her way over to the window, parted the curtains, and peered out.

The sky had become almost blue-black as night began to fall, and the flashes of lightning were coming closer. Soon the downpour would begin, flattening the crops and flooding the irrigation canals. Storms such as this were extremely rare, but she had lived here all her life and could predict the weather by the pain in her swollen ankles—which were much more accurate than those modern weather charlatans on TV. The afternoon had been the kind of damp, peculiarly stifling white-hot day that heralded a terrible storm. The Mexican laborers who had been tending the neat rows of citrus groves had left early, hurrying home before the sky burst open. She wondered whether her husband and son would stay in Mexican Town at her brother's and wait for the storm to pass.

She continued to peer out the window, then suddenly frowned. Through the gloom she could make out a big car parked on the shoulder just down the road. Then she saw the man and the woman. They were slowly coming out of the groves, the woman walking heavily with her legs spread wide. The man was supporting her and the woman was bent over as if in pain.

Just then there was a tremendous crack of lightning and the overhead light in the cabin went out. Mrs. Ramirez muttered a curse. As if the storm were not enough, now there had to be a power failure too.

She waited a moment for her eyes to adjust to the darkness, then scraped back her chair and went over to the stove where the iron pot of bubbling beans and fatback was cooking for dinner. She found the candle and box of matches, scratched a match against the wall, and lit the candle. As the room slowly brightened, she heard overhead the sudden heavy drumming of raindrops on the metal roof. By reflex she glanced up. From the sound of them, they were big raindrops, heavy and powerful, the kind that stung your face if you were caught outside.

Just then she heard the hammering at the door. Frowning, she went over and pulled it open. In the flickering candlelight she could see the tall, handsome man supporting—really half-carrying—a woman and lugging a heavy-looking silver urn in his other arm. Their faces were glistening wet, and they were both soaked through to the skin. Behind them the rain was coming down in silver sheets.

"Quickly," Mrs. Ramirez urged. "Come in before everything is soaked." Her voice was thick with a Mexican accent.

Once they were inside, Mrs. Ramirez securely shut the door, then held the candle up. There was no time to waste on unnecessary words. She looked at Freddie Cantwell. "Her time has come?"

"I don't know . . . I think so," Freddie said, the fear clear in his voice. "We were in the grove and she cried out and collapsed. She's barely conscious now."

"Follow me," Felicia Ramirez said, taking Dorothy-Anne's other arm and helping Freddie guide her through the small manager's cabin to the back bedroom. She set the candle down on the scarred dresser and Freddie gently laid his wife on the bed. He placed the urn on the dresser, then leaned over Dorothy-Anne and smoothed the hair from her forehead. Her skin felt hot. "She's feverish," he said, turning tense eyes on Mrs. Ramirez.

"How close together come her contractions?" the heavy woman asked.

"I don't know," Freddie answered hesitantly. "There was just that one, and she passed out."

"We will wait for the next, then begin to time them."

Freddie nodded, then picked up the candle and asked, "Do you have a telephone?"

"In the other room. Leave the candle here. I go get more. It is not good to leave in the darkness a woman whose time is at hand." Her voice grew quiet. "If the child enters a world of darkness, it will be forever blinded."

Startled by the woman's superstition, Freddie put the candle down and started to follow her out, but Dorothy-Anne caught his arm. He turned and looked down at her. Her eyes were wide and glazed and her voice was weak. "Freddie?" He smiled down at her, but her fingers dug into his arm with surprising strength. "Don't leave me alone, Freddie," she whispered. "Please."

"I'm going to stay right here, honey," he promised. "But first I've got to phone for a doctor."

She nodded weakly.

He pressed her hand. "Try to relax and get some rest. You'll need your strength."

She nodded again and shut her eyes. "I'll try," she said softly, giving in to the exhaustion that swept over her. She listened as his footsteps receded. Then everything seemed suddenly quiet.

The Tropical Court of the Hale Palace had been anything but quiet. Even as Mr. Bernstein took the documents out of his briefcase, the parrots and the cockatoos continued their screeching. Dorothy-Anne remembered Mr. Bernstein flipping through the stapled papers one last time and then passing them over to Mr. Morris, who also looked them over. Finally both men were satisfied that everything was indeed in order.

Mr. Bernstein turned to Elizabeth-Anne. He cupped his hand and coughed delicately. "You are certain, then, that you wish to proceed with this transaction?"

"Mr. Bernstein," she replied dryly, "as you can see, I am

over eighteen. Since I can drink and I can vote, I can certainly do with my money and holdings as I please."

"Of course, of course," he said soothingly. He looked over at Dorothy-Anne. "Miss Hale?"

With a start, Dorothy-Anne realized he was addressing her. "Yes, sir?"

"Your great-grandmother has decided to give you an . . . er . . . well, a rather generous birthday present."

Mr. Morris nodded solemnly. "Yes, a very generous gift indeed."

"In fact," Mr. Bernstein continued, "it is so valuable that although you shall own it the moment these papers are signed, you will not be able to take possession of it until your eighteenth birthday. Do you understand what I am trying to say?"

Dorothy-Anne nodded. "You mean it's being held in trust for me."

Mr. Bernstein seemed a bit surprised, but quickly recovered his composure.

Elizabeth-Anne settled back in her wheelchair and smiled proudly, but her voice was clipped. "Mr. Bernstein, let's forgo the formalities of a lecture, shall we? I may not be of sound body, but I *am* of sound mind. And my mind is made up. Now, shall we sign the papers?"

"There, there is the telephone." Felicia Ramirez turned from the candles she was lighting and pointed a thick finger to the kitchen wall.

Freddie nodded, reached for the receiver, and lifted it to his ear. There was no dial tone. Quickly he jiggled the cradle up and down with his forefinger. He turned to Felicia. "It's dead."

She waved out the match she was holding, at the same time moving toward him. "Here. Let me." Snatching the receiver from his hand, she listened, also rattling the cradle up and down. After a moment she slowly hung up. "It is the storm," she said. "The lines must be down."

"What do we do?"

"Your car?" she suggested. "You drive into town?"

27

"It's stuck," he said grimly. "I was so upset when Dorothy-Anne collapsed in the grove that I rushed her back to the car and tried to start too quickly. The wheels dug into the sand, and the harder I tried to get out, the deeper they went. It's hopeless now." He ran his fingers through his hair miserably, then asked, "Don't you have a car?"

"My husband has it," she answered quietly. "He has not returned. In a storm such as this, he is sure to stay in town. It is five miles away and it will soon be night. The trip is impossible in this weather."

Freddie's head sagged. "What do we do?" he whispered. "We never thought there would be a storm like this . . . or that Dorothy-Anne would have the baby now."

Felicia Ramirez drew herself up with calm dignity. She placed a gentle hand on his arm. "I am a woman," she said. "I have six children and I have helped deliver others. I know what to do. Go, stay with your wife. Comfort her and help her rest. I make hot water and get clean towels. It will be a long night."

When Felicia returned to the bedroom, Dorothy-Anne was awake and tossing restlessly. She tried to sit up, but after a moment let her head drop back down on the pillow. Then suddenly she grimaced and arched her back as another contraction seized her. Startled, she opened her eyes widely and gasped from the pain. Freddie grasped her hand in concern, but Mrs. Ramirez seemed reassured.

"Good," she said, checking her watch. "A long time has passed since the last. There will be time to rest before the real labor begins."

Dorothy-Anne collapsed back on the bed as the pain passed. Felicia pulled away the sheet that covered her. Gently she began to probe with her hands. She frowned to herself and then, for the first time, began to worry. She was used to her own and her cousin's wide generous hips, built to give birth. But this woman's hips were narrow and bony.

She gestured for Freddie to draw closer and lowered her voice so that the young woman would not hear what she had to say. "The passage is narrow," she murmured with concern. "She is very small."

*   *   *

Small. The whispered word drifted to Dorothy-Anne through a mist and set the swirling memories in motion. Yes, she was small. She had signed the lawyers' papers with her small schoolgirl script, then waited as they were witnessed. Then the pin-striped attorneys had congratulated her on the gift she had just received, and left. Miss Bunt had wheeled Great-Granny outside to the sidewalk, and then Great-Granny motioned for the nurse to leave them. The Fifth Avenue traffic moved downtown at a brisk pace. For a minute they did not speak.

"Dorothy-Anne," Great-Granny said finally.

Dorothy-Anne moved closer.

"Look up, Dorothy-Anne." Great-Granny's voice rose to an excited whisper. "Look up at the Hale Palace."

Obediently Dorothy-Anne leaned her head way back and stared up at the hotel. The thousands upon thousands of tons of pale limestone seemed miraculously weightless. Like a wedding cake it rose in majestic splendor, tier after tier of terraces and balconies, until the twin towers broke off and rose even higher to scrape the fast-moving clouds scuttling across the bright blue sky. After a moment she lowered her head and turned to her great-grandmother. She looked at her questioningly.

Elizabeth-Anne Hale reached out, took Dorothy-Anne's hand, and squeezed it.

"It's *yours*," Elizabeth-Anne whispered, her aquamarine eyes shining brightly. "The Hale Palace is now yours, and yours alone. Happy birthday, Dorothy-Anne."

Dorothy-Anne awoke to the sound of rain lashing the roof. Freddie was leaning over her, anxiety and fear in his face.

She turned to him weakly, her face pale and pinched. "Is the storm letting up?" she whispered.

Mrs. Ramirez seemed startled to hear her voice, but shook her head.

"My baby," Dorothy-Anne said in a tiny voice. She placed

a hand on the mound of sheet at her waist. "My baby will be all right?"

"Your baby will be fine," Mrs. Ramirez assured her gently. She joined Freddie and leaned over Dorothy-Anne, stroking aside a stray lock of the young woman's moist hair. "A woman is born to give birth, no?"

Dorothy-Anne nodded her head hesitantly. While Freddie helped her lie back down, Mrs. Ramirez said, "Now that you are awake, I examine you internally. I was about to wake you anyway." She turned to Freddie. "I will need a pan of hot water."

Freddie nodded and moved toward the kitchen, grateful to be of help. Mrs. Ramirez sat down on the edge of the bed. She reached out for Dorothy-Anne's hands and held them. The young woman's fingers felt cold and moist. "Do you feel any pain?"

Dorothy-Anne looked up into the woman's dark, liquid eyes. "Yes."

"Where?"

Dorothy-Anne leaned forward and slowly twisted around so that the sheet fell to her waist and exposed her breasts, heavy and milk-filled.

Mrs. Ramirez nodded to herself. There would at least be no problem feeding the child. She glanced questioningly at Dorothy-Anne, who reached gingerly behind her and touched the small of her back. "The pain is here."

"Your back?"

Dorothy-Anne nodded.

Mrs. Ramirez flashed her an odd look. Then she rose and pulled the rest of the sheet away from Dorothy-Anne's body. The naked young woman shivered from the sudden chill.

"It will not take long," Mrs. Ramirez said apologetically. She heard Freddie's footsteps and turned around. He was holding a pan of steaming hot water. She took it from him, set it down on the nightstand, and then, tightening her lips, dunked her hands into it. The water was scalding, but she did not utter a sound. She washed her hands carefully and shook them dry.

Wordlessly Dorothy-Anne lay back, scooted down on the

bed, and obediently parted her thighs. Mrs. Ramirez knelt before her.

Dorothy-Anne could feel the woman's fingers probing the warmth within her. She tensed, the fingers feeling rough and foreign.

"I am being gentle," Mrs. Ramirez whispered. "Please. Relax. I will not hurt you."

Dorothy-Anne smiled wanly and bit down on her lip.

As she maneuvered her fingers, Felicia Ramirez forced herself to keep from frowning. The cervix was still not wide open, though it had dilated somewhat. They still had hours to wait.

She leaned over Dorothy-Anne and placed her ear next to the magnificently swollen belly. She listened for a while and then nodded to herself with satisfaction. She could hear the fetal heartbeat, strong and separate from the mother's own. That was good.

She started to pull the sheet up around Dorothy-Anne again, when she remembered there was one more thing to check. Years ago, when she had given birth to Cesar, her second oldest, the old midwife had tested the position of the child.

Mrs. Ramirez lowered the sheet. With one hand inside the mother and the other on the swollen belly, she gently felt for the child's position. Suddenly the breath caught in her throat. Could she be doing it wrong? She quickly checked again. No, it was true. The child was not positioned right. For a third time she repeated the maneuver, just to make sure. There was no mistake.

She withdrew her hand and said, "I go wash," nodding for Freddie to follow. Once in the kitchen, she turned to him, her elbows crooked, her hands held up like a surgeon's about to be gloved.

"Well?" Freddie demanded.

"The child lays sideways," Mrs. Ramirez hissed gravely, her eyes wide with alarm. "It should come headfirst, like this . . ." She motioned with her hand as her eyes flashed like embers in the candlelight. "Your wife's baby, it lays like this . . ." She slashed her hand sideways across her belly.

Before Freddie could answer, they heard Dorothy-Anne moan weakly from the other room and quickly returned to her side.

"What is it?" Freddie asked.

"I heard you whispering," Dorothy-Anne said faintly. Her brow was still wet with sweat and her eyes glassy. "My baby . . . my baby is going to die, isn't it?"

Mrs. Ramirez looked at her sharply and crossed herself. "Do not speak of such things," she hissed.

"No. I know it's true. I know it is. I'm being punished and my baby's going to die."

Surprised by her words, but aware his young wife was almost delirious, Freddie smoothed the damp hair back from Dorothy-Anne's forehead and spoke softly. "Punished? What for? You've never done anything that deserves punishment, darling."

"Yes, I have," Dorothy-Anne moaned. She felt a wave of exhaustion, a need to escape her fear, sweep over her, and her eyes closed. But she fought sleep, determined now to speak, to get the truth out into the open. "You don't know, Freddie. Only Great-Granny understood. She protected me, but now she's gone, and I'll have to pay."

"Dorothy-Anne, you're talking nonsense."

"No, Freddie. I have to pay now," she said, her breathing shallow and labored.

"But for God's sake, what for?"

"Because . . . because I killed my mother. I killed her, and now Great-Granny's gone . . . and she was the only one . . ." Her voice trailed off.

"The only one who what?"

"Who understood," Dorothy-Anne answered, her voice the merest weary whisper.

I
Elizabeth-Anne

NEW YORK CITY

❦

August 4, 1928

1

The day Elizabeth-Anne Hale arrived in midtown Manhattan with her four children, the mercury hit ninety-six degrees and New York was a blistering furnace. The asphalt streets were baked to a soft goo and the concrete buildings seemed to writhe as they trapped the stifling air and simmered it between their canyon walls.

"Where to?" the taxi driver they hailed at Penn Station asked as Elizabeth-Anne climbed into the front seat beside him. He was worriedly watching the children clamber into the back, but when he turned to glance at Elizabeth-Anne, he was taken aback.

At thirty-three, she was not a beautiful woman, but in her excitement she was radiant. Her face was handsome and strong with its thin, straight nose and sparkling eyes, the shade of the clearest, most perfect aquamarines. Despite their jewellike radiance, her most striking feature was her waist-long wheat-gold hair, enviably fine and abundant. She wore it tightly plaited and pinned up so that it wouldn't get in the way of things. Her waist was shown off to advantage by her

35

white blouse and full-length gray calico skirt. Around her neck hung a simple pendant, a pansy encased in glass, that her husband had given her upon their engagement.

She looked at the driver, her eyes wide and sparkling, set in a well-tanned face. "Could you recommend a hotel? One that's decent but not too expensive?" she asked.

"Sure. There're hundreds of hotels in this town." He glanced into the rearview mirror at the three girls and little boy in the backseat. The trunk of the cab was half-open and tied down, loaded with luggage. "The Madison Squire's a good hotel. Not cheap, but not expensive either."

"The Madison Squire it is, then," she said, thinking they would stay there even if it were too expensive, at least for one night. The journey had been tiring and they could always change to another hotel in the morning. After that, her first order of business was to find an apartment for herself and the children.

The cabbie swung the taxi out into the traffic. "Where you from?"

"Texas." Her voice was crisp and clear.

"I'll never for the life of me understand you country people. Why come to this noisy, dirty city for a vacation when you've got all the fresh air you could possibly want at home?"

"We're not on vacation. We're moving here."

The cabbie shook his head. "Me, I can't wait till I retire and get a nice house somewhere in the country. Especially when there's a heat wave."

"We're used to heat."

"Yeah, guess it gets hot down there in Texas."

"That it does."

"What did you do there? Ranch?"

"Ranch?" She laughed lightly, chidingly. "No, Texas isn't all ranching, I'm afraid. There are other things there. Lots of other things." She smiled almost coyly, then turned to watch the city as it flashed by her window, letting her mind wander.

Elizabeth-Anne had owned and run three businesses in Quebeck, Texas: the Hale Rooming House, the Good Eats

Café, and the Hale Tourist Court she had built along the new highway. She had sold the rooming house and the café, and not for a song, either. She certainly wasn't going to advertise the fact, but in her purse was a cashier's check for nearly thirty thousand dollars. That check would nurture her dreams, it was the gateway to a new life, a new future for both herself and the children. A future that would be helped along by the income she still earned from the tourist court. It was in capable, trustworthy hands and she knew it would continue to show a comfortable profit. With that financial security, it was easier for Elizabeth-Anne to face the task of raising four children alone.

Elizabeth-Anne twisted around in her seat and smiled back at the children, but they didn't seem to notice. Their eyes were glued to the open windows, staring up at the incredibly tall buildings, and the well-dressed crowds teeming on the sidewalk.

Elizabeth-Anne looked from one child to the next, starting with Regina. She eyed her oldest daughter fondly, with deep pride. At sixteen, Regina promised to grow into a handsome woman. She reminded Elizabeth-Anne of herself, with her thick wheat-gold hair which she wore down in a fine mane that reached to her waist. Regina didn't carry a spare ounce of fat on her small able-bodied frame, thanks to her endless round of chores back in Quebeck. She was a serious girl, well on her way to womanhood, but the freckles around her nose were those of a child. In her lively, inquisitive eyes Elizabeth-Anne saw stamina and vigor. When the Mexican midwife had slapped her, she hadn't cried out in pain; she'd wailed indignantly.

Her gaze shifted. Fourteen-year-old Charlotte-Anne had been, of her three daughters, the most difficult to deliver, which Elizabeth-Anne thought ironic, as she was also the most perfectly formed physically. Charlotte-Anne's hair, too, was a rich, ripe shade of yellow, but incredibly fine and silky. She was tall for her age and very slender, with pale flawless skin, pale pink lips, and aquamarine eyes much like her own. But Charlotte-Anne's eyes were so incredibly pale, they enchanted and made one feel ill-at-ease at the same time. The pale hair, complexion, and eyes gave her a peculiar beauty Elizabeth-Anne recognized as truly remarkable.

Rebecca was the youngest of the girls, eleven, and the most sensitive of the four children. She was not startlingly beautiful like Charlotte-Anne, or blessed with the natural intelligence of Regina, but she well made up for it with a quiet determination all her own. Whereas Regina and Charlotte-Anne were both evenly blended distillations of Elizabeth-Anne and her husband, in Rebecca the mix of traits had not been balanced. She was large and gangly, and her face was her father's, strong-boned and heavy. Her eyes were a deeper blue than Elizabeth-Anne's, her brows golden like her hair. Of her three daughters, Elizabeth-Anne respected Rebecca the most. Not because she was the youngest, but because she lacked beauty, grace, and a superior intelligence, yet worked hard enough to make up for her deficiencies. Too, Rebecca's lack of self-confidence was poorly concealed, a vulnerability that kept her close to Elizabeth-Anne's heart.

And that left little Zaccheus. He had just turned four, and whenever she looked at him, the breath caught in her throat. He was the spitting image of his father, a miniature Zaccheus Hale Senior, with the very same purposeful, intelligent gleam in his blue eyes, and that wonderfully enigmatic, lopsided smile. Looking at him now, her heart again skipped a beat and she reached out and stroked the blond bangs out of his eyes. He ignored her; his blue-blue eyes were wide with wonder as he stared out at the city. Yes, she thought, he was indeed Zaccheus' son—his eyes, his lips, it was all there, an eerie reincarnation, a living reminder for her to keep close and treasure.

Elizabeth-Anne shook her head sadly. It was a fine family she had, albeit a fatherless one. She had been without Zaccheus for four years now, four years since the happy days of their marriage had ended so suddenly. Little Zaccheus had still been enwombed within her when Zaccheus had left. The love with which they had conceived their son, the love that was to have lasted a lifetime, had been shattered as easily as a thin crystal flute dropped onto a stone floor.

Zaccheus had been everything to her. After her parents,

local farmers in Quebeck, had died, she had grown up with an aunt, a kind and loving woman who had raised Elizabeth-Anne as well as she could while running her rooming house and café. Elizabeth-Anne had inherited those businesses in her late teens when her aunt died, and had continued the life of hard work and loneliness she had grown up with. It had often seemed to Elizabeth-Anne in retrospect that she had never really known happiness until she met Zaccheus. Also the child of farmers, he had come from the Midwest to Texas to seek his fortune. They had fallen in love at first sight. Brilliant and quick, he was a witty, easy talker, but also a marvelous listener. And handsome too, so handsome that he still brought an ache to her heart. They had started a family together young, but he had proven to be a decent man, a marvelous father and provider, patient and dependable, the perfect lover and friend.

Then it had all ended. Suddenly and horribly, it had ended with one freak and meaningless accident that had shattered their lives forever.

Zaccheus had been at the construction site of the tourist court, the motel he and Elizabeth-Anne were building beside the new highway. It had been Elizabeth-Anne's idea, her dream, and Zaccheus had readily agreed to it—even though the construction would take all the money they had saved— because he recognized the passion and conviction of her vision. But now, several months into the project, the work was going badly, held up again and again by mysteriously lost deliveries of supplies from the Sexton warehouse. Soon they would be out of money, but neither Elizabeth-Anne nor Zaccheus saw a solution in sight. They both knew Sexton was sabotaging the construction intentionally. He was the biggest man in the county, owning most of the land and the businesses on it, and from the start he hadn't looked favorably on competition from the Hales.

Late one night after everyone else had left, Zaccheus had gone out to the site to meet Sexton, to confront him about the lost deliveries, and the two men had argued. But Zaccheus had been nowhere near the other man when he had rushed forward in anger, tripped on the uneven ground, and fallen, splitting his head open on an edge of exposed piping.

Zaccheus had fled, knowing that no one would believe he had nothing to do with Sexton's death. He and Elizabeth-Anne had too much to gain now that the old man was gone. So he had left Elizabeth-Anne a note, explaining what had happened and apologizing, both for the stupid fate that had forced him to flee the certain death sentence a Sexton-family-controlled court would hand him, and for leaving without her. He couldn't, his note explained, ruin her and the children's lives by trying to take them with him. Instead, he had pleaded for her to remain, to raise the children, finish the motel, and nurture the dream she had started with him.

Thinking of him even now brought tears to Elizabeth-Anne's eyes, but the tragedy was four long years in the past and felt distant to her on this day of new beginnings. She had lived a long time without a word or trace of him, lived through long years of financial struggle, of personal loneliness, of need for her children. She had managed, even succeeded, but she had realized she found too little joy in her accomplishments in Quebeck. Finally she had known she too had to leave Texas, to get away from the memories of her lost marriage and to find a place where her dream would know no limit, and could be fully achieved.

Oh, Zaccheus, she thought again now unconsciously fingering the pansy chain at her neck, wherever you are, just remember that I love you. Just remain free and enjoy what you can of your new life. You're still mine, enshrined in my heart and the children's forever.

And now, as the cab pulled up to the Madison Squire Hotel at Madison Avenue and Thirty-seventh Street, the memories and hurt receded. Elizabeth-Anne took a deep breath and squared her shoulders bravely to face the hectic, strange new world, and the new life she hoped to carve for herself and the children.

"Thank you," Elizabeth-Anne told the cabbie after she paid him. "The children and I can manage the luggage ourselves."

The doorman took one look at her plain country clothes and

then ignored them, stern disapproval showing in his eyes. Even the porter, who usually sprang into action when guests arrived, hung back.

Elizabeth-Anne and the girls unloaded the trunk and then watched in silence as the cab drove off. As it did so, Elizabeth-Anne felt horribly alone. Her determined conviction that the future loomed brilliant before them dissipated like so much mist in a stern breeze and reality started to sink in. Husbandless and mother of four, she was in a strange city where she knew no one, a city of immense crowds and tall buildings the likes of which she had never seen.

She smiled bravely, so that the fear she felt would not rub off on the children. Leaning her head back, she gazed up at the forbiddingly enormous, elaborate hotel rising thirty-four stories above Madison Avenue. There was an intimidating, solid classicism about the building's ornate pilasters and carved pediments that made her feel small and insignificant, but she also thought it beautiful. Only later would she learn that only the front of the Madison Squire was so lavish; the other three sides were grimy, utilitarian brick.

She nodded briskly to the children. "Let's go inside," she said before her courage could desert her again. She hefted two of the large battered suitcases and the girls took one apiece, grimacing as they lugged them along after her, little Zaccheus bringing up the rear with the shoebox filled with his favorite toys clutched tightly to his chest.

They drew to a halt in front of the revolving doors, wondering how in the world they were going to squeeze the luggage and themselves into the small triangular glass wedges.

The problem was solved for them. Heaving an audible sigh, the doorman pushed open a disguised glass panel next to the revolving door and held it open for them.

"Thank you," Elizabeth-Anne said, favoring him with a grateful smile. His face remained studiously vacant.

As she crossed over the threshold into the lobby, Elizabeth-Anne suppressed the awe she felt, reminding herself that, as the owner of the Hale Tourist Court back in Quebeck, she too was a host to travelers and had a professional interest in her surroundings. She recognized immediately that while the Madison Squire was hardly welcoming in the homey sense, its lavish lobby certainly had a majestic, formal elegance.

Setting the suitcases down, she absently fingered the pansy encased in crystal suspended from her neck. Her sharp eyes roamed the lobby, taking in the gleaming marble walls, the veined inlaid marble floor, and the opulent brass-and-crystal chandelier glittering overhead. The Louis XVI settees and chairs dotting the room were large and formal, and Charlotte-Anne and Rebecca set down their cases and plopped themselves onto the brocade upholstery. Zaccheus Jr. let out a whoop, and making a headlong dash, leapt onto a settee of his own. Regina accompanied Elizabeth-Anne, who strode to the massive carved reception desk and fixed the clerk with a smile. It was a totally disarming smile, but it did nothing to soften the dour, haughty expression of his face.

"We need two rooms, please," Elizabeth-Anne said. "One with two beds and one with three."

The slim dark-haired man took one look at her neat but simple country clothes, sniffed disdainfully, and announced in a haughty voice, "It's seven dollars for the two rooms. I'm afraid our only vacancies are on the second floor, no view, only an air shaft. With this heat, you'll burn up. May I suggest the Algonquin or the Plaza or any of the many other fine—"

Elizabeth-Anne, who quickly estimated there were some seventy cubicles behind the reception desk, half of which had keys signifying vacancies, continued to smile radiantly. "Those rooms will suit us just fine, I'm sure."

"Well, if you insist—"

"I do."

The clerk began to say something, but the steadiness of Elizabeth-Anne's gaze caused him to think twice, and his jaw snapped shut. He fished out two sets of keys, each attached to a large brass tag with the room number engraved on it, and laid them down on the desk. "That'll be seven dollars in advance," he said.

Elizabeth-Anne counted the bills out on the desk. The clerk slid them toward him, at the same time smacking his palm on the bell to summon the bellboy, but the moment it clanged,

Elizabeth-Anne laid her fingers on it to silence it. "Just the keys, please," she said. "We can find our own way and carry our luggage ourselves."

"As you wish," the clerk said with a sigh of disapproval.

"Thank you, Mr. . . ."

"Smythe."

"Thank you, Mr. Smythe." Elizabeth-Anne picked up her two battered suitcases, and after the children had done the same, they all proceeded toward the marble staircase with its gleaming solid brass banisters.

The clerk cleared his throat noisily. Elizabeth-Anne half-turned, a questioning look on her face.

"The elevator is that way," he said, pointing in the opposite direction. "Just ring the buzzer."

Elizabeth-Anne inclined her head and changed course. "Thank you, Mr. Smythe."

He didn't reply. He didn't have to. It was written clearly in his mirthless eyes: *Country bumpkins*.

S oon after dark, the children went to sleep, exhausted from their long, exciting day.

Elizabeth-Anne crossed her arms, walked slowly over to the window, and leaned out. The desk clerk had been right, she thought. Despite the open windows, the room was stuffy and hot. But she discovered that if she leaned out and angled herself just right, she could catch a thin sliver of view—a tall, compact slice of Manhattan skyscrapers winking and glittering in the night.

She felt conflicting emotions coursing through her—a million fantastic dreams stirring within her—while at the same time she asked herself what on earth she was doing in the midst of the noisiest, strangest city in the world. It was like coming to a foreign country where she knew no one and where many different languages were spoken. After the down-home friendliness she had always known, why had she come here to subject herself to the hustle and bustle of New York, to the hordes of always rushing, unsmiling people?

An unbidden sigh slowly escaped her lips. She knew why. Because Quebeck could no longer feed her ambitions, could not match the scale of her imagination. She longed to build, to create, and the opportunities were *here*, amid the crowds and the noise, amid the energy that made the air crackle with electricity. Here, through sheer hard work, and given enough luck, she felt she could fulfill her dream. The dream she had nurtured ever since she was a child.

She smiled to herself, wondering at her ambitious cheek and gall. Other little girls she knew dreamed of meeting a handsome prince and being carried off to his castle to live happily ever after, but not her. No, her dream was far more practical, but just as romantic in its own way. For she, Elizabeth-Anne Hale, had always imagined herself as the queen of a grand hotel. She had seen one such edifice as a child, and it had been ingrained in her mind ever since. She remembered the endless games she had played alone while growing up, imagining herself not in the plain rooming house but in charge of a glittering palace filled with bejeweled guests, *her* guests. She would give them elegant meals, gentle music, sumptuous rooms, and they would line up to see her, to come stay with her in the greatest hotel in the world.

As she grew, the vision she had created as a child never changed; it simply grew clearer in her mind. Carriages became automobiles, gaslight became electric, but the quality of luxury, her personal touch, remained. And the older she became, the more she envisioned not a single grand hotel, but two, three, even a hundred—and they would all be hers. *Hers.*

The rooming house, the café, and the tourist court back in Texas had merely been the beginning. She had known that all along. They had been the first step toward realizing her dream. But in order to achieve it, she had had to leave Texas and come to New York City. Here, dreams that were too big to be contained could be forged into reality, of that she was certain. She would become a somebody. Given time, she would shine brighter than all the glittering night lights of Manhattan, more forcefully than the kaleidoscope of colors on Broadway. Because here the very air smelled of prosperity and success, and everywhere you went, you could hear the cash registers ringing. Having been born in Texas, a native-born and bred American, Elizabeth-Anne would not realize until many years later that she was, in effect, not all that different from the hordes of foreigners who had passed through Ellis Island. She did not hail from Lithuania or Greece, but she *was* an immigrant of sorts.

No, right now she knew only one thing: here she would make it. Here she would triumph.

She could sense it.

But first, she had to find a home. Then, when she and the children were settled in . . . then she would set out to conquer this city.

2

Elizabeth-Anne was not prepared for Ludmila Koshevalaevna Romaschkova, nor was the White Russian immigrant prepared for her. They had nothing in common except the town house on Gramercy Park South, and it was that which brought them together.

The elegant five-story house with its pale granite facade and tall, graceful parlor-floor windows had been left to Ludmila by a foresighted admiral in the Imperial Russian Navy who had fled the Bolsheviks with her (his mistress), four Imperial Easter Eggs by Carl Fabergé, and a numbered bank account in Switzerland filled with millions. It was a cruel twist of fate that brought a fatal cerebral stroke to the admiral, to whom Ludmila had been unofficial consort for seventeen years, on the eve of the wedding that would have finally fulfilled his promise to marry her. Only a lengthy and highly publicized court battle, during which Ludmila found herself face to face with the hatred of her departed lover's other heirs, as well as the entire exiled Russian community, had given her even a small compensation for the years she had devoted to the admiral. She received the title to the lavishly furnished town house they had shared together, but nothing else. Otherwise penniless, she subsequently converted the upper three floors into autonomous apartments and rented them out to selected tenants.

"Who there?" a raspy, thickly accented voice finally called through the door after Elizabeth-Anne had knocked on it the sixth time.

"I've seen the 'Apartment for Rent' sign outside," Elizabeth-Anne called back, trying to speak above the hysterical yapping of dogs on the other side of the door. "I would like to see it!"

"Who?"

Elizabeth-Anne spoke up louder. "I want to see the apartment!"

There was a pause. "Now, why you not say that before?" There was a series of clicks as various locks were thrown, and the door opened a crack, held there by a thick safety chain. One huge gray eye, dramatically outlined with black liner, looked her up and down. "Did *they* send you?" The voice was suspicious.

"They?"

"The Bolsheviks!"

Elizabeth-Anne suppressed a smile. "No, I'm not a Bolshevik."

"Good." The door closed abruptly, the chain rattled and clanked, and Elizabeth-Anne found herself face to face with Ludmila Koshevalaevna Romaschkova.

Elizabeth-Anne stared at the diminutive woman in fascination, feeling an immediate liking for this stranger. Madame Romaschkova might have stood little more than four feet, three inches tall in her heels, but she nevertheless projected a commanding presence. She held herself with instinctive dignity, and her carriage bespoke another, finer age. Even her thick accent, though exotic, was well-bred instead of amusing; it conjured up visions of ice palaces, tiaras studded with diamonds, and ermine-fringed gowns.

Here is a somebody, a character, someone with a past, Elizabeth-Anne thought. She didn't know how right she was.

Although by the time Elizabeth-Anne met her, the glory of

Ludmila's life in Russia was long over, you would never know it to look at her. She had retained her air of grace, beauty, and privilege simply by making time stand still, by pretending nothing was different. She was as beautifully turned out as she had been fifteen years earlier. Her figure was still excellent, with a tiny cinched waist and a well-mounted bosom, although her fine oval face had become increasingly lined, the telltale webwork of wrinkles spreading deeply into her once flawless skin. She dressed as she had in Russia, in the lavish fashions of pre-1917 St. Petersburg. Her dresses were perhaps a bit moth-eaten and tattered, but somehow that only emphasized their faded beauty. Ludmila draped herself with elaborately embroidered fringed shawls, dressed in regal, heavy brocade better suited to the cold Russian winters than the milder climate in which she now lived, and, after the admiral died, never took off the necklace he had sent her the morning after they had met—a malachite Fabergé egg encrusted with gold filigree hanging off a web of gold.

The entire effect was enough to make Elizabeth-Anne gape unabashedly.

"Well?" Ludmila Romaschkova demanded. "What are you waiting for? Come in, come in."

Elizabeth-Anne glanced down at her feet, afraid that if she moved she would step on one or more of the four white Maltese spaniels yapping at her heels.

"It is okay," Madame Romaschkova assured her. "The children, they know when you walk, they get out of the way. Quick, quick." She took Elizabeth-Anne by the arm, pulled her inside the apartment, slammed the door shut, and began locking the bolts across it.

"Are you afraid of burglars?" Elizabeth-Anne asked.

"Burglars? Burglars! Ha." Ludmila Romaschkova whirled at her, gray eyes flashing. "If only they were burglars. No, they are worse. Evil. First I have to fear the Reds, then the Whites. Burglars I could take take care of." She glowered dramatically, and then her face softened. "Come, have tea with me. First we talk. Then we look at the apartment."

Madame Romaschkova led the way into the parlor, preceded by the dogs. The dim, stuffy room was at once as

entrancing as the woman herself. It looked more like the
dusty storage room of a museum than a parlor. The furnishings were so tightly packed they had obviously once graced
all five stories of the house. As Elizabeth-Anne's eyes adjusted to the dark, she could make out two grand pianos,
three daybeds, four consoles, a marble column, a Napoleonic
candelabrum, two desks, a baroque chest, a medieval chest,
a dark carved Elizabethan table, and a gold-and-crystal Empire chandelier. Meissen parrots, lamps with fringed silk
shades, chairs with gold hooves or claws for legs, tapestries,
silver-framed photographs, icons mounted in silver, and Coptic
fragments behind glass were crammed together and on top of
each other, all in happy, riotous, clashing splendor. It was an
auctioneer's paradise, but no matter how strapped she was for
cash, Madame Romaschkova's emotions won out over her
practicality. She would never dream of disposing of a single
item.

"*This* is real tea," Ludmila announced as she poured the
strong black brew from the huge silver samovar. Elizabeth-
Anne accepted the delicate, engraved crystal cup and its silver
holder and was about to drop a cube of sugar into it.

"No, *no*," Ludmila cried. "You put the sugar in your
mouth and sip."

Elizabeth-Anne did as she was told. The tea was bitter and
thick, not at all the way she liked to drink it, but when it met
the sugar, the taste was honey-sweet.

"This is how tea is to be drunk." Ludmila sipped at hers
and sighed contentedly. She was ensconced on a green velvet
four-sided siege, a round chair with four seats built out from a
carved center post. It dated from the era of Napoleon III and
looked as though it belonged in the lobby of a Second Empire
opera house. Facing her, Elizabeth-Anne was seated on a
straight-backed Régence fauteuil upholstered with Aubusson
Royale tapestry.

Finally Ludmila leaned forward and placed her cup beside
the samovar, which sat on an octagonal folding bedouin table
inlaid with ivory. Then she sat back again and made herself
comfortable. "Now. Tell me everything about yourself," she
demanded.

"Everything? About myself?" Elizabeth-Anne looked taken aback. "Why, there's actually nothing to tell."

"There is always something to tell." Ludmila raised her chin and nodded sagely. "You are married?"

Elizabeth-Anne set down her cup. "Yes," she said carefully, "but I'm . . . alone."

"Your husband? He is not here?"

She shook her head.

"Divorced?"

"Not really."

"*Ha.* Men." Ludmila shook her head angrily. "Sometimes I wonder why we women put up with them. But do yourself favor. Next time choose nice Russian. They are the best," she finished with a decisive nod.

Elizabeth-Anne smiled. "I'll try to keep that in mind."

"You do that." Ludmila flipped open a cigarette box made of paper-thin burled wood, carefully chose a cigarette, stuck it in a long holder carved of horn, and lit it. Immediately a strong, pungent blue cloud of smoke enveloped her. She narrowed her eyes. "You have children?"

Elizabeth-Anne nodded. "Four."

"Four?"

"Why, yes. I hope you don't mind—"

"Children," Ludmila said grimly, "are noisy, dirty, and make much damage. I tell people always, you want apartment, no have children."

"Well, I really ought to be going then." Elizabeth-Anne rose to her feet and smiled apologetically. "Thank you for the tea. It was delicious."

"You barely touched!" Ludmila wagged an accusing finger at Elizabeth-Anne's cup. "Sit down, finish. Is a shame to waste."

"But I really must go," Elizabeth Anne protested. "I have to find us an apartment, and I mustn't lose any time."

"Who says you lose time? We go upstairs and I show you the apartment. Is small for five people, but very nice."

"But . . . I thought you didn't want to rent out to anyone with children."

Ludmila puffed regally on her cigarette. "Usually I don't,"

she said nonchalantly. "As soon as someone tells me children is no trouble and argues, I say, well, Ludmila, you in trouble. If someone says, well, then I must go and look at someplace else, then I know is okay." She beamed through the scrim of smoke at Elizabeth-Anne. "Now, finish your tea."

3

Elizabeth-Anne looked at Regina and smiled hopefully. "Well, what do you think?"

Regina looked around the bedroom thoughtfully. "It's nice. I think we'll like it here."

Elizabeth-Anne looked relieved. "That's why I wanted you to be the first to see it. To see what you thought." She paced the small bedroom, picking her way around the furniture. "It's smaller than what I would have liked us to have, and a lot more expensive, but the neighborhood is very good, and so are the schools. But the best thing about Gramercy Park is the park. Madame Romaschkova . . . I mean, Ludmila . . ." Elizabeth-Anne broke off with a laugh. "Somehow I still find it difficult to call her Ludmila. She just *looks* like Madame or Countess or something."

Regina laughed too. "I know what you mean."

Elizabeth-Anne continued. "Well, she told me the park is private. That only the tenants who live around it have keys, and she has had duplicates made for us. You children need fresh air and a safe place to play, and for that, this place is ideal."

Regina nodded. "But it's one bedroom short, isn't it?"

Elizabeth-Anne shrugged. "Giving up my own bedroom's a small enough sacrifice for the convenience of having park privileges. I'll be comfortable on the chaise in the parlor." She paused then and looked around fondly. "And the furniture Ludmila's lent us is so beautiful. It just isn't worth shipping everything up from Quebeck. It would cost a lot more than the things are worth."

"What's important is that *you* like it here, Mama. That *you're* comfortable."

"And I know you all will be, too." Elizabeth-Anne hugged Regina warmly, but upon releasing her, she frowned. "It's still a big change, and in a way, it frightens me."

"But you wouldn't have it any other way."

Elizabeth-Anne shook her head. "You're right, I wouldn't. Come on, let's go sit in the parlor." She led the way down the narrow hall and stopped in the doorway, studying the parlor with satisfaction. It was small but had a high ceiling and a marble fireplace. The parlor's single window looked down on Ludmila's overgrown garden in the back of the house. Standing at that window when it was very quiet, Elizabeth-Anne could imagine she was not in one of the world's largest cities, but in a peaceful country oasis instead.

But there was nothing remotely reminiscent of the country inside the apartment itself. Since she was living in Manhattan, Elizabeth-Anne had decided that her home should reflect the mood of the city; eclectic and vibrant, fashionably contemporary, yet rooted in the traditions of the past. At the same time, she meant the apartment to be a fortress in which she and the children could feel secure, a place to keep at bay the high-charged, bustling energy which greeted them whenever they stepped out the door. She had painted the parlor a rich shade of blue, though she kept the ceiling above the molding white. By using only a few large, bold pieces of Ludmila's furniture, including two huge gilt mirrors, and balancing these with the lightness of the beige carpet, she had succeeded in creating the illusion of greater space in a unique way.

One entire wall of the parlor was constructed of built-in bookshelves; the multicolored spines of the books belonging to Ludmila gave off a vibrant, pulsating spectrum of color. More important, the books covered a wide range of subjects, from the complete works of Charles Dickens to the controversial new science of psychiatry. Elizabeth-Anne knew it could only help to continue her humble education, and was fascinated by the books she now had a chance to read.

Overall, it was a simple room, easy to keep neat and clean. Thanks to the large eat-in kitchen where she preferred the family to gather, the parlor would be relatively little used, and highly respectable indeed.

"I don't know how you do it, Mama," Regina said, "but it already looks like home."

It was late afternoon on the last Saturday in September, one of those rare late-summer days when all of New York seemed to be taking advantage of the weather. Central Park was filled with families picnicking, children playing ball, and dour nannies pushing baby strollers and carriages along the paved paths, all overseen by an occasional blue-uniformed patrolman. Overhead, kites flew in the perfect puffball sky.

If it weren't for the tall sunbathed towers lining the park, Elizabeth-Anne thought, it would be easy to imagine that I'm not in the city at all, but in some pastoral countryside, like the ones in the romantic paintings we saw last weekend in the museum.

She looked around and watched the children shrieking happily and chasing each other up a grassy slope. She hesitated. They were all having such a good time. She hated to have to break it up. But after a moment she called for them to come over and gather around her. Reluctantly they approached the bench where she sat, little Zaccheus clamoring up beside her.

"But it's still early, Mama," Charlotte-Anne protested. "Do we have to go home already?"

"No, not yet," Eizabeth-Anne assured her, "but I've got something important to discuss with you. Afterward," she promised, "you can go right on playing."

The girls nodded and sat down beside her.

"I've waited a few days to tell you this," Elizabeth-Anne said, studying each of their faces. "I've found a job. I'm starting work on Monday."

Charlotte-Anne stared at her openmouthed. When she found

her voice, she spoke in a tone of incredulity. "A job? But I thought we had enough money coming in from the tourist court. And besides, you told us we've got a lot saved up in the bank."

"And so we do. But we've all got dreams to follow. All of you, and me included. Now don't look at me like that. I'm not *that* old, you know."

"Dreams?" Regina asked. "What kind of dreams?"

"Oh, you'll find out soon enough."

"Where are you going to work?" Rebecca asked.

Elizabeth-Anne turned and pointed to the elegant white building which seemed to rise up from amid the trees behind them like some fairytale castle. "At the Savoy Plaza Hotel."

"Doing what?" asked Regina.

Elizabeth-Anne sat back and folded her hands in her lap. "I'm going to be a chambermaid."

"A chambermaid!" Charlotte-Anne exclaimed in horror. "Mama, that's *dirty* work. Back in Quebeck we have *Mexicans* doing that."

"This isn't Quebeck, darling, in case you haven't noticed."

Charlotte-Anne hung her head, obviously abashed.

"Besides," Elizabeth-Anne said, "I don't intend to stay a chambermaid for long. It's only for a short while."

"But . . . *why* do you want to be one at all?" Rebecca asked.

"Because I want to see how a big hotel operates, that's why."

"Well, couldn't we just give up our apartment and stay in one for a while?" she asked.

"No, that wouldn't be the same thing." Elizabeth-Anne sat forward and her eyes gleamed with anticipation. "You see, darling, I want to see it from the *inside*, from the employees' perspective. I want to discover just how a big hotel works, and what's involved in running one."

The children all stared at her, obviously surprised.

"The thing which could conceivably be inconvenient," Elizabeth-Anne continued, "is that I've got to start by taking the night shift. It lasts from ten at night until six in the morning. But I don't really think it'll throw our lives into chaos. While you're all at school, I'll be sleeping. While you're sleeping, I'll be working. When I get home I'll make your breakfast and see you off. And I'll be up when you get back.''

"But . . . if you want to work in a hotel so badly," Charlotte-Anne persisted, "isn't there any other kind of work you can do?"

"You mean other than being a chambermaid?"

Charlotte-Anne nodded.

"I could wash pots and pans in the kitchen or become a ladies' washroom attendant, if you prefer." Elizabeth-Anne looked at her curiously. "Would you like that better?"

Charlotte-Anne narrowed her eyes. "That's not very funny."

"I didn't intend it to be. But I do intend on working in various hotels, in various capacities. For now, I'll start at the bottom."

Charlotte-Anne turned away. "Well, I just hope you won't advertise what you're going to do," she mumbled.

So that was it, Elizabeth-Anne thought. She tightened her lips and stifled a sigh, trying hard not to show her annoyance. Charlotte-Anne obviously didn't want anyone to know that her mother was a maid. In all likelihood she'd probably been telling all her school friends that her family was independently wealthy.

"There's nothing wrong with being a maid," Elizabeth-Anne pointed out. "An honest day's work never hurt anyone. There's no shame in it."

"Mama?" Rebecca said timidly.

"Yes, dear?"

"If you like, I'll help out. I'll even go to work. I think I'd like that much better than going to school."

Elizabeth-Anne gave her youngest daughter a quick hug. "I think," she said with a laugh, "that for the time being it's best you go to school."

Charlotte-Anne stared at them expressionlessly. Then she got up without speaking and walked over to the grassy slope, where she sat down in the shadows. When her sisters and Zaccheus resumed playing, she refused to join in their games.

*   *   *

Her first day of work, and she almost lost it. Circumstances had conspired and almost succeeded in making her late.

Now, *that* would have been one hell of a way to start off on the wrong foot, she thought. And to think that she had been so careful, budgeting every minute of her time. She had believed everything was under control, but there were a million things that popped up right as she was walking out the door. Zaccheus had been fast asleep, but he'd awakened when Regina and Charlotte-Anne had gotten into a violent argument. There had been that to referee, and then Zaccheus refused to go back to sleep unless she sang him a lullaby. The moment she stepped outside, it had started to rain, and she'd had to run back upstairs for her umbrella. To top it all off, the subway was delayed. And then, for no apparent reason, the train came to a stop in the tunnel, and interminable minutes crawled by before it jerked and began to roll on again.

With one minute to spare, she rushed through the employees' entrance of the Savoy Plaza. She made it to the maids' dressing room just as that night shift of chambermaids, smartly turned out in crisp black-and-white uniforms, were lining up, military fashion, to be inspected by Mrs. Winter, the housekeeper. Already, her brisk, sharp footsteps could be heard echoing down the corridor.

Elizabeth-Anne looked around the large wardrobe-lined room in panic. She started to speak, but one of the maids shook her head and motioned her to silence. She still had no uniform, but realized if she went off in search of one now she would surely be late, even docked. Worse, she might be fired on the spot.

"Pssst."

She glanced at the small maid at the far left end of the line. She was a petite black woman with merry dark eyes. She was desperately motioning for Elizabeth-Anne to fall in beside her.

The moment Elizabeth-Anne took her place, Mrs. Winter marched into the room, the glower on her face as intimidating as a drill sergeant's.

Elizabeth-Anne leaned her head forward and gazed to her

right. The maids were all standing stiffly, chests thrust out like pigeons, chins in the air, hands at their sides. She couldn't believe it! This looked more like a military parade than starting time for a group of hotel maids.

Meanwhile, Mrs. Winter continued her inspection. She strutted to the precise center of the line, spun smartly on her heel, and faced the maids in a wide-legged stance. "Good evening, ladies," she announced crisply.

"Good evening, Mrs. Winter," echoed the resounding chorus.

Elizabeth-Anne craned her head forward and stared at Mrs. Winter in fascination. She had never seen another woman quite like her. She was tiny, almost dwarflike, but had an aggressive bearing. Her black wool dress was cut severely; indeed, there was something severe about every inch of her. Once upon a time her hair had been a rich, glowing shade of honey, but now it was liberally streaked with gray. Her eyes were steely hard and her red lips perpetually pursed.

"It has come to my attention . . . ." Mrs. Winter began before breaking off in mid-sentence as her gaze fell upon Elizabeth-Anne. Her forehead creased into an irritated frown. "And what is *this*?" she asked icily.

Elizabeth-Anne stepped forward. "I was told to report—"

"*Silence.*" Mrs. Winter's voice was like a shotgun report.

Elizabeth-Anne's blood seemed to boil, sending crimson waves of embarrassment up into her face. For a moment she couldn't believe that she had heard right. She couldn't remember the last time she had been spoken to in such a sharp manner. The obvious pity of the petite maid beside her only seemed to make things worse. She had the curious feeling that all the others were holding their breath, relieved that Mrs. Winter had found a victim other than themselves, yet at the same time aware that she might at any moment turn on them. Stunned, Elizabeth-Anne found herself stepping back into line.

"Tuck your head back in and face forward," Mrs. Winter snapped. "You are, I presume, a young lady and not a turtle?"

Elizabeth-Anne's eyes flared angrily. She had bargained for many things, but not this. Still, she did as she was told.

Grab hold of your temper! she warned herself. You *need* this job. You need to see how this place operates, and you needn't take this kind of abuse for long. Just a few days, a few weeks at the most. Then you'll be moving on to someplace else.

The sharp clack of Mrs. Winter's deliberate footsteps rang out in the room, and then the diminutive woman was standing directly in front of Elizabeth-Anne.

"Your name." It was not a question; it was a command shot out from between those deceptively tiny lips.

"Elizabeth-Anne Hale."

"You may speak up. And when you speak to me, you may address me as 'ma'am.' "

Elizabeth-Anne swallowed hard. She barely knew this goading woman, but already she despised her. She hated standing there and taking this abuse, but knew for now she had little choice. In the future, she'd just have to avoid this Mrs. Winter as much as possible. Above all, she would not do battle with her. She would be above reproach. "Yes, ma'am," she said quietly.

"I presume the personnel department had you report to me?"

"Yes, ma'am. They did."

"I'm sure they did," the small woman said dryly. She paused, then looked Elizabeth-Anne straight in the eye. "We are not off to a very good start, you realize that, Mrs. Hale?"

Elizabeth-Anne raised her head.

"I'll be watching you closely. I suggest you tread very softly around me if you value your job."

And with that, Mrs. Winter turned on her heels and marched out.

4

"I'm called Dallas," the small black maid said with a Texas accent, " 'cause that's where I'm from." She lifted a towering stack of freshly laundered white towels out of the linen closet and deposited them in Elizabeth-Anne's arms. "You carry these, and I'll get another stack." She scooped up a second pile in her own arms and with a well-practiced backward kick of her foot snapped the closet door shut.

"You're from Texas?" Elizabeth-Anne asked in surprise as they walked down the plushly carpeted corridor.

"Uh-huh."

"So am I."

"Really!" Dallas looked pleased. "Then we better make sure us Texans sticks together, honey. That Miss Winter, she's just lookin' for any excuse to fire us all. Thinks it gives her power, she does."

"In that case," Elizabeth-Anne stated flatly, "we'll just have to make sure that she doesn't find any fault, won't we?"

Dallas rolled her eyes. "You're new, honey. You'll find out soon enough. No matter what you do, she'll manage to find fault. You just wait and see." She nodded emphatically. "What I can't understand is what a nice-lookin' white woman like you is doin' here. There're better jobs in this here city. Lots of them if you're white."

A half-smile came to Elizabeth-Anne's lips. "A job's a job, Dallas. There's really no difference whether you're a maid or a housekeeper like Mrs. Winter. She just gets paid more."

"Does she! Lord. I'd hate to know what she brought home last Thursday." Dallas shook her head and clucked her tongue. Then she heard the distant jingle of keys and whispered,

"Ssssh." A moment later, Elizabeth-Anne saw Mrs. Winter turning a corner and heading toward them down the corridor. Only after they had gone into an empty room to change the towels did they speak again.

"You'll help me, won't you, Dallas?" Elizabeth-Anne asked softly. "You'll show me the ropes around here?"

" 'Course I will. Miss Winter said I should, didn't she?" Dallas grinned. " 'Course, I would anyways. But first, you remember that when you hear keys jinglin' and janglin', Miss Winter's somewhere close by. And second, you get yourself some decent workin' shoes, honey. In them"—she nodded at Elizabeth-Anne's shoes—"your feet'll swell up like melons and be killin' you in no time at all."

Each night for the next week, Elizabeth-Anne pushed herself to the limit. She couldn't believe how hard the work was. She was constantly on her feet, and there was never any time to take a break. Her lower back ached painfully, and it seemed that all she ever did was stoop and carry, stoop and carry. During the very first day on the job, she earned a healthy respect for Dallas. The petite maid always seemed to be in control, and she never uttered a complaint. Somehow, her good humor was contagious. For that, Elizabeth-Anne was grateful.

The night shift, she was learning quickly, was much more grueling than the day shifts because at night the hotel ran on a skeleton staff. She was especially disappointed because she never seemed to get a chance to talk to any of the maids besides Dallas, to whom Mrs. Winter had assigned her for the entire first week. After that, she would be on her own, and she dreaded it. She was inexperienced. There were a thousand things that could potentially go wrong, and she would have to cope with it all on her own.

To prepare her, Dallas tried to remember the various situations in which she had found herself—frenzied moments, heartbreaking moments, funny moments:

". . . There I was and there he was, naked as a jaybird. Dallas got out of there fast as her little feet could carry her, that's what I did."

". . . That son of a bitch's wife claimed I stole the ring. Sure enough, next mornin' the clean-up crew found it in that carpetin'. Thick as grass it is in that suite, small wonder she couldn't find it herself. But she should of looked. Lord, I nearly lost my job that time, and never heard as much as a peep of apology from anyone."

". . . She was havin' a baby right there on the bed, and the house doctor was tied up with a man havin' a heart attack . . ."

Dallas' stories made Elizabeth-Anne aware of the multitude of situations that could go sour, and she knew Mrs. Winter was just waiting for her to make a blunder. It irked her to think that the housekeeper might end up winning their running feud—and that she might end up fired.

But what distressed her most was realizing that no matter how hard she worked as a maid, it would be a long, long time before she would really learn how the hotel functioned. People like Mrs. Winter—the various concierges, the manager, the banquet manager, the battery of desk clerks—had all been hired for their experience. There was simply no way she could hope to cram it all into several quick crash courses. But at least her experience at the Savoy Plaza had given her a basic idea of how the hotel was run, and an early appreciation of the various workers' expertise.

But she was not about to quit. Not yet, at any rate. She had decided that if she did one thing only, she would show Mrs. Winter that she wasn't about to get the best of Elizabeth-Anne Hale.

When she finally got home in the mornings, just as dawn was backdropping the skyscrapers across Fifth Avenue with pale morning light, she was ready to drop into bed and fall into a dead sleep. But that was not possible. She had to stay up for several more hours, waking the children, cooking breakfast for them, and getting them off to school. Somehow she managed to juggle her time, although even she was never clear on exactly how she did it. She only knew that she had to. Owning and running businesses in a small town, she was discovering, had been far easier than working in a huge hotel, where she was at the mercy of the whims of an enormous staff and at the beck and call of hundreds of guests. She had a fine line to tread. Every maid's territory was worked out with specifically scheduled duties, yet not one of them dared talk back to a demanding guest someone else was supposed to take care of—so there always seemed twice as much to do.

"You're lookin' real tired out," Dallas told her on her fourth day on the job. "When you get home this mornin', try to get some sleep."

Elizabeth-Anne smiled wryly. How could she explain to Dallas just how much there was to do? That she had four children and a household of her own to take care of?

Only much later did she learn that Dallas was far worse off than she. Dallas had no money saved up that she could fall back on. She depended on her meager paycheck, and there was never enough; her husband was in prison and she supported their six children by herself. She had to resort to cleaning apartments during the day in order to make ends meet.

When Elizabeth-Anne discovered this, she shuddered and felt very ashamed for daring to think that hers was an exceptional case.

Elizabeth-Anne thought it a miracle when she collected her third consecutive weekly paycheck. The two weeks she had been working on her own since her apprenticeship to Dallas had gone smoothly. The fifteen sixth-floor rooms which were her area of responsibility had been inhabited by businessmen, an aged widow, several couples, and one family with twin babies. She had been summoned at all hours of the night when the twins had "accidents," had had to clean up after the businessmen who one night got drunk and sick, had had to answer the old widow's many summonses for this or that whenever the woman couldn't sleep and wanted company, but on the whole things had gone well. Nothing tripped up Elizabeth-Anne, but whenever she ran into Mrs. Winter, the housekeeper was tight-lipped.

She's still waiting to find fault with me, Elizabeth-Anne thought to herself with satisfaction, and it's killing her that she can't.

The times she saw Dallas, always during the ten o'clock

inspections and then again at six in the morning once the shift was over, the other maid smiled at her knowingly, but never said what was on her mind. *Good for you,* the dark eyes seemed to say. But Elizabeth-Anne also recognized the unspoken warning in her friend's gaze: *Mrs. Winter always gets what she's after.*

It was Thursday night, several hours before she had to report to work. She and the children were eating supper around the big oval table in the kitchen. The girls were well-behaved, as usual, but Charlotte-Anne was being especially solicitous, even to Rebecca and little Zaccheus, whom she always liked to lord it over.

Elizabeth-Anne watched Charlotte-Anne cutting Zaccheus' meat into tiny, bite-size portions. She had never volunteered for that task before. After she had finished, Charlotte-Anne asked Rebecca sweetly, "Would you like me to pass you some more gravy?"

Rebecca shook her head. "No, thank you."

"Some more potatoes, then?"

Rebecca frowned at her. "No, thank you," she replied uneasily, wondering what was up.

Elizabeth-Anne pursed her lips, also wondering what Charlotte-Anne was after.

When they finished eating, Charlotte-Anne was the first to scrape back her chair and begin to clear the table. "It's my turn to do the dishes," she announced, taking everyone by surprise.

Elizabeth-Anne gazed at her daughter curiously, but still said nothing. She knew that it wouldn't be long before Charlotte-Anne showed her hand.

Only after the dishes were washed, dried, and put away, and Charlotte-Anne had scrubbed the deep enamel double sinks sparkling clean did she approach her mother. It was nine o'clock, and Elizabeth-Anne was in the curtained-off dressing alcove, getting ready to go to the Savoy Plaza.

Charlotte-Anne cleared her throat. "Mama?" she said in an uncharacteristically cajoling little voice.

"Yes, dear?" Elizabeth-Anne answered without turning.

Charlotte-Anne took a deep breath. "I've made lots of friends at school. And for the past three weeks I've stayed over at their houses every Saturday night."

"Yes, you have." Elizabeth-Anne strode out of the alcove to the parlor, adjusting the cuffs of her blouse. She stood in front of the mirror above the fireplace mantel and inspected herself critically. Behind her she caught sight of Charlotte-Anne's reflection. Here it comes, she thought as she watched her daughter tightening her lips.

"All the girls take turns having the others sleep over," Charlotte-Anne reminded her. "It's sort of like a pajama party, even though no one but Theresa has enough beds for us all. We pile up blankets and pillows and—"

Elizabeth-Anne turned around. "And now you think it's your turn to reciprocate the invitations?"

Charlotte-Anne nodded.

"Then by all means, we'll have a slumber party here," Elizabeth-Anne said.

"Soon, Mama? Please?"

Elizabeth-Anne raised an eyebrow. "How soon?"

Charlotte-Anne's voice grew very small. "This Saturday? Is that all right with you?"

"*This* Saturday?" Elizabeth-Anne stared at her. "But . . . that's the day after tomorrow. That doesn't give us much time."

"You'll have to be at work anyway, and I'll do everything," Charlotte-Anne promised quickly.

"But you're all young. The other parents will insist you be chaperoned."

"I've already talked to Aunt Ludmila, and she's promised to keep an eye on us. She won't mind it at all. She's lonely and likes company, you know." Charlotte-Anne looked at her mother pleadingly. "I know it isn't much notice, but it won't be a bother. Really, it won't."

Elizabeth-Anne sighed, but gave her daughter a small smile. "Very well then. It's fine with me, as long as you and your friends don't make too much noise and keep your sisters and brother awake all night."

Charlotte-Anne's face lit up and she threw her arms around

her mother's neck. "Thanks, Mama! I really appreciate it," she added with a smacking kiss.

"I'm glad." Elizabeth-Anne smiled. "I'll cook you all a nice supper before I leave for work." She looked thoughtful. "Maybe even bake a cake . . ."

"I'll do it."

"You just concentrate on having a good time, dear."

"Oh, I will! You can count on *that*."

"By the way, what time do you all usually get together?"

"Six, six-thirty." Charlotte-Anne shrugged. "Something like that."

"Good." Elizabeth-Anne smiled. "Then I'll finally be able to meet some of those friends you're always talking about. I'm looking forward to that."

"And they want to meet you too, Mama. I've told them all about you."

Elizabeth-Anne looked surprised. "You have?"

"Well, sort of." Charlotte-Anne dropped her eyes and her voice grew meek. "You won't . . . you won't tell my friends where you're going when you leave for work, will you, Mama?"

Elizabeth-Anne gazed at her daughter expressionlessly. Charlotte-Anne had never really accepted or understood the reasons her mother was working as a maid. Elizabeth-Anne wondered what her daughter told her friends about her. Well, she would find out soon enough, of that she was certain. Charlotte-Anne was a natural spinner of tales, and Elizabeth-Anne was sure she would have made the Hales sound terribly important. No matter what the occasion, she always felt compelled to impress people and to inflate her family's, and especially her own, importance. Strangely enough, it had been Charlotte-Anne who at first resisted the move to Gramercy Park because of the size of the apartment. Then, once she'd discovered just how exclusive an enclave it was, she'd changed her tune in an instant. You would have thought, Elizabeth-Anne had told herself with amusement, that it had been her idea to make the move in the first place.

A weary sigh escaped her lips. Sometimes she felt that she did not understand Charlotte-Anne at all. She was a total stranger to her in so many ways. And sometimes she feared that perhaps she never would understand her. Still, she was her daughter, and as such she loved her. And she was sure that in her own peculiar way Charlotte-Anne loved her too.

5

The excited chatter of conversation, followed by bursts of laughter, issued forth from inside the apartment as Elizabeth-Anne snapped the door shut and hurried downstairs. It was already nine-thirty, and she knew she was cutting it close. She should have left at least fifteen minutes earlier, but the girls had held her up. If she was delayed again, whether it was the subway's fault or her own, she would be late for work and have to answer to Mrs. Winter.

Miraculously enough, nothing conspired against her. The instant she stepped on the subway platform the train came blasting in and screeched to a stop. She thanked her lucky stars and arrived at the Savoy Plaza in record time. She even had a few minutes to chat with Dallas as she changed into her uniform.

"Lord," Dallas exclaimed as Elizabeth-Anne hung her best dress in the wardrobe. "You're sure all dressed up tonight." She placed her hands on her hips and eyed Elizabeth-Anne slyly. "Special occasion, huh?"

Elizabeth-Anne smiled. "Not really. One of my daughters is giving a little party for some of her friends."

"Well, you look right nice."

"Thank you, Dallas."

Their conversation came to an abrupt end when Mrs. Winter's footsteps came echoing down the hall. The maids snapped into line, and a frowning Mrs. Winter strode along in front of them as they stood in ramrod-straight formation for the nightly inspection. To date, things were going so well that Elizabeth-

Anne stood as tall, and dared to convey as much self-confidence, as the most seasoned maid.

After Mrs. Winter completed her inspection, she puffed out her chest importantly. "I have been told to give special attention to the sixth floor this evening," she announced with gravity. "That means suite six-fourteen in particular, which is within your territory, Mrs. Hale." Her eyes gleamed as she turned her attention on Elizabeth-Anne.

Elizabeth-Anne tried to hide her embarrassment. Along with several Irish women, she was one of the few white maids on the staff, and Mrs. Winter insisted on calling the Negroes by their first names and the whites by their formal surnames. It was an unfair practice, but there was nothing anyone could do about it, save suffer in silence.

"It is for that reason that I am changing our regular duty roster." Mrs. Winter motioned to one of the other maids and snapped, "Minnie, you take care of Dallas' fifth-floor territory, as well as your own. Dallas, you shall take care of all of Mrs. Hale's sixth-floor rooms. And you, Mrs. Hale, since you have so far managed to keep your nose above water, and since you look the most . . . ah . . . presentable, will be in charge of suite six-fourteen exclusively. You will, at all times, be at that particular suite's beck and call and do nothing else, no matter what. Do I make myself clear?"

Elizabeth-Anne nodded. "Yes, Mrs. Winter."

"The rest of you are dismissed." Mrs. Winter waited for the maids to file out. Then she turned to Dallas and Elizabeth-Anne once more. "Tonight we happen to have a very important guest in suite six-fourteen." She paused for emphasis. "Miss Lola Bori."

Dallas let out an exclamation of surprise, but Mrs. Winter chose to ignore it. Even Elizabeth-Anne's heart hammered with excitement. Lola Bori was a legend, the most celebrated star of the moving pictures, the person most imitated and most closely watched by all the millions of women in the nation.

"It is imperative that everything go smoothly tonight," Mrs. Winter warned, "and that every wish Miss Bori might have, no matter how outlandish or farfetched it may seem to you, is catered to. To the letter. Is that clear?"

Elizabeth-Anne nodded.

"Good." Mrs. Winter paused. "It is even more important that everyone—the public, photographers, and members of the press—be kept far from Miss Bori. She has requested extreme privacy, and the hotel management intends to deliver it. We have hired extra security guards in the lobby, but in case anyone should manage to get upstairs, it is your duty, Mrs. Hale, to guard Miss Bori. Of course, you will also not discuss her with anyone."

"Yes, ma'am."

"Very well, then." Mrs. Winter gave a wave of dismissal and they hurried out.

"I can't believe it," Dallas said in a reverential tone as they took the service elevator upstairs. "Lola Bori! I've seen her in a dozen pictures sittin' in the balcony at Loew's. And to think I might get a chance to see her in person. Lordy." She shook her head. "Wait till I tell everyone when I get home. They won't believe me, I'm sure."

"Just be careful who you tell," Elizabeth-Anne cautioned her.

"Oh, I'll be careful. Mark my words." Dallas shook her head again and clucked her tongue. "I still can't believe it. Imagine, Lola Bori right here in the hotel. A *real* celebrity if there ever was one."

In her luxurious three-room suite, Lola Bori was both drunk and depressed. The gin coursed through her, and she saw the plush pink-satin furniture of the sitting room through a slightly swirling fog. She pushed herself up from the couch, but once on her feet, she swayed unsteadily. Compressing her lips, she frowned in concentration. "Gin. Gotta get some more gin."

She wove her way toward the door and began to fumble with the lock. "Damn," she swore under her breath. Then she pressed her face against the door and began to cry softly. She didn't want any more gin. She wanted company.

After a moment she pushed herself away from the door and slowly wove back to the couch. Catching a glimpse of a face in a tall gilt-framed mirror, she stared at the reflection, then slowly approached it.

"That's not me," she mumbled. She licked her lips. "Not me at all." She shook her head defiantly at the caricature reflected in the mirror and it shook its head back at her. Her usually perfect heart-shaped lips were smeared with lipstick, and her famous pale blue eyes were puffy and swollen. For once, the much-celebrated angular cheekbones did not look worth celebrating; they were hollow and sunken. Her platinum-blond hair was matted and disheveled.

She stared at the reflection in shock, not daring to believe it was her own.

Then she let out a wrenching sob, collapsing with her head in her hands. This was *not* Lola Bori, her mind screamed. It *couldn't* be.

She was at the zenith, the pinpoint pinnacle of her career. She had intended to stay there forever, reigning from high atop her lofty gilded pedestal, far above the rest of mankind. She didn't need anyone and had meant to keep it that way. But she hadn't anticipated one thing: talking pictures.

She sank numbly down into the couch and stared blankly before her. She was through. Finished. It had happened just that afternoon, not eight hours earlier, when that bastard Josef Von Richter, her studio producer, had sat down with her, right here in this very suite, on this very couch. His devastating words still echoed in her mind.

"You cannot have the part," he had said gravely in his guttural German accent. "Not *War and Peace*."

"Of course you're joking, Josef," she said lightheartedly. But his next words, and the obvious earnestness of his tone, had shocked her.

"No, my dear," he said softly. "Your career is over. That is what I have come to tell you." He paused and looked at her, then turned away uncomfortably. "Be glad that it has lasted this long."

At first she wanted to try to laugh off his words, but they echoed hauntingly in her mind. She had known this was coming, had feared it. Now she could think of nothing, see nothing but the black cloud of doom that was descending around her, suffocating her. She struggled to speak calmly, and her words came out in a ghostly whisper. "So that's why you made me take the talkies test."

"Yes." He bowed his head in a solemn nod. "You have the face, Lola. But you do not have the voice. It is too high. Once your audience heard you speak, you would become a laughingstock."

She had leapt to her feet. "I should kill you, you filthy bastard!" she had cried, her voice filled with hate. "I should kill you!" Then she went limp, collapsing into quiet sobs.

"At the premiere of *The Woman Behind the Veil* tomorrow," he said quietly, "you and your public will see the last Lola Bori film. I am sorry, Lola. You must believe that."

She cried for a long time, then wiped her eyes with the back of one hand. "I thought . . ." She fought to retain the little composure she had left. "I thought my stardom would go on forever." She offered it almost as an apology.

His face was an expressionless mask, but she saw the sadness in his eyes. "You have lived in the pictures too long, Lola," he said. "Nothing is forever. It is that way only in the pictures."

Nothing is forever.

Now the words bombarded her again and again, echoing from the dark shadows in the corners of the room. She shook her head morosely, her eyes glittering with tears. Everything was over.

Was that possible?

She hadn't felt so lost, so completely vulnerable in years. She was helpless, achingly alone. But who was there to turn to? Who could take her bleeding heart and mend it? Who could tell her what to do, where to turn now that she had lost everything?

And then it came to her like a flash of white light: Larry.

Larry, her former husband, the investment tycoon. He had always been so strong and capable. And during their marriage he had loved her, worshiped her so. Once he had tried to buy up all the reels of a Lola Bori film he had deemed too scandalous. He had wanted her to himself. Throughout their short marriage he had loved her as no one else ever had. He

69

hadn't wanted the divorce. It had been her idea; she had insisted on it.

But did he still love her?

She clamped her lips together. If he did, she might have a chance. They hadn't spoken in years, not since she had rather abruptly walked out on him, but she knew he was in New York. And as far as she knew, he was still single. And even richer than before.

Her heart began to pump the same way it always did just before she went in front of the camera. She laughed softly to herself. Josef was wrong. There *was* one more role she could play. She could catch Larry all over again, marry him, and settle down as one of New York City's premier hostesses.

The excitement flowed through her, and fueled by anticipation and gin, she grabbed the telephone and had the hotel operator place a call to Larry's home. It had been her home once, too, and she had never forgotten the private number.

She could scarcely contain her impatience as she listened to the ringing at the other end of the line. She was almost rude to the butler who answered, announcing her name and ordering him to fetch his employer. But as soon as she heard the deep, familiar baritone voice, she broke out in a cold sweat. Larry sounded so formal and on guard.

"Lola? What can I do for you?"

She frowned, concentrating on every syllable so that she could speak without slurring her words. "I need you, Larry."

There was a pause. It was such a long moment before he spoke again that she was afraid she had been disconnected.

"There was a time I needed you too, Lola," he said without any trace of bitterness. It was a matter-of-fact statement, and somehow that seemed to make it worse.

"I know that, Larry," she said. "I was foolish. Please? Let's give it another try? For old times' sake?"

He paused for a long minute, then said softly, "I'm sorry, Lola. Some things just can't be done over. I'm not God, and neither are you. We can't bring what's dead back to life. What's happened has . . ." He sighed. "Has simply happened. Our two lives didn't mesh. Now, if you'll let me—"

But Lola's gasp cut him off. She seemed to see the room

go black before her, and she had to rid herself of the terrible vision. "Larry," she blurted out, "I've *got* to see you. I'm alone now. And I'm desperate. I . . . I can't take it anymore, Larry. If I don't speak to someone, then I'll . . . I'll *kill* myself."

"Another faked suicide attempt?" His words shocked her like cold water.

She shut her eyes and dropped her voice to a whisper. "No, Larry. This is for real. Honest." She began to cry. "It's over, Larry. Everything is over. I'm finished in the movies."

"But why?" His tone softened. "You've always loved acting. That's what you do best. Why give it up?"

"Because . . . because of the talkies. It's my *voice*. They don't like my goddamn *voice*."

"I'm sorry. I didn't know."

"Neither did I." Her eyes had a faraway look in them. "So you see, Larry, it really is all finished. All I have left is you."

"Where are you?"

"The Savoy Plaza."

"There are some people here, but I can get away soon. All right?"

She nodded through her tears. "Thanks, Larry. I'll tell them . . . the staff . . . to let you up. They're . . . screening . . . everybody."

"Just tell them 'Larry,' " he continued. "No last name. No I.D. We don't need the reporters getting word that we're seeing each other again. Not after what they put us through in the past. We don't need that kind of publicity anymore. Ever."

"No, Larry." Her voice was obedient and contrite. "I promise."

"Fine. It'll be an hour or so."

E mma Roesch had a hand with no engagement or wedding ring gracing it, a night job as a switchboard operator at the Savoy Plaza Hotel, and a boyfriend who worked as a newspaper photographer and kept promising matrimony once he could afford a wife and family.

"We can't get married just yet, honey," he told Emma over and over. "I haven't got enough money saved up. The scandal sheets don't pay that well."

"But I'll keep working," she had offered. "With your job and mine we can make it, Barney. I know we can. Lots of married couples have a lot less, and they make it."

"But I want a wife *and* a family. I want to give you a beautiful big house and lots of children. Tell you what, Em. Soon as I get a real big scoop that pays off, we'll tie the knot. But we'll wait until then. Okay?"

She had nodded doubtfully. "I'll help in any way I can."

"Hmmm," he mused thoughtfully. "Now that you've brought it up, maybe you *can* be of some help."

She had jumped at the chance. "How?"

"Well, you work at the Savoy Plaza, right? And lots of important people stay there. What if you listen in on their phone conversations every now and then? If you hear something really important, you can give me a tip and I'll come running with my camera. If it pays off, we're all set, honey."

At first she had been reluctant. "It's awfully dangerous, Barney. I . . . I could get fired."

"Not if you're careful. Look at it this way—it's an investment."

"An investment?"

"Part of our nest egg."

So she had done as he had asked, but the conversations she had listened in on had all been dull. She hadn't come up with a single item which could help him out. Until now.

As she unplugged Lola Bori's line after placing the actress's private call, she once again thought about what he had said. The conversation she had just overheard had been so engrossing that the newsworthiness of it took a moment to sink in. Then she sat up with a start.

What was more of a scoop than anything connected with Lola Bori?

Slowly she glanced around to make sure she would not be overheard. At night the hotel switchboard had half the operators on duty that it had during the day, so there was no one nearby.

She reached out with her plug and plunged it into the switchboard. Her head throbbed with heady excitement. It was finally happening! At long last Barney would get his long-awaited scoop, his salary would be raised, and she would be dressed in her bridal gown. She almost jumped when he answered his phone.

"Barney?" She spoke in an uncharacteristically low voice. "Remember what you told me to watch out for?"

When the bell for six-fourteen rang in the maids' station, Elizabeth-Anne hurried down the hall to Lola Bori's suite. She was by no means star-struck; from an early age she had had to face things in a practical way, and that left little room in her mind for daydreaming about film stars. Still, she *had* seen several Lola Bori movies, so neither was she entirely immune to the glamour of a star. But the moment she saw Lola Bori in the flesh, any illusions she might have had vanished.

This can't be the same woman, Elizabeth-Anne thought with shock. This harridan with her unruly white-blond hair and puffy eyes, this lurching drunk in the powder-blue satin robe slipping off her shoulders—this could not be the same exquisitely glamorous star she had seen on the silver screen.

Lola Bori placed one hand on her hip and eyed Elizabeth-Anne up and down.

"I'm going to have a visitor." Lola held her head high, stretching her swanlike neck. "I want you to inform the desk, and show the gentleman in the moment he arrives."

Elizabeth-Anne inclined her head. "Yes, ma'am."

"The visitor's name is Larry. He is to be asked for his first name only. No I.D. He'll be by himself. No one else is to be let up." She swayed unsteadily on her feet, then delicately leaned against the doorjamb. "Is that clear?"

"Perfectly," Elizabeth-Anne promised her.

Elizabeth-Anne was waiting by the elevator. The night clerk had called to inform her the man named Larry was on his way up. When the car doors opened, she raised her eyebrows in surprise as a short man holding a package draped with a cloth stepped out of the elevator. He was dressed in somewhat shoddy clothing, hardly the class of visitor Elizabeth-Anne would expect Lola Bori to have. But then, Lola Bori hadn't been what she expected either. "I'm Larry," the man said, stepping out of the elevator.

"This way, please," she said politely. "Miss Bori is expecting you."

Elizabeth-Anne led him down the hall, then knocked on the white door of suite six-fourteen.

"Come in," the muffled voice called from inside.

Elizabeth-Anne opened the unlocked door. She stepped aside to let the man enter, then quickly shut the door again.

Lola Bori was in front of the mirror combing her hair with drunken fascination. "You're early, Larry," she chided. "You said it would be an hour. I haven't even had a chance to fix myself up . . ." She turned to face him, and the color drained from her face. "Who are you? What are you doing here?" she gasped.

Barney flung aside the cloth that had hidden his camera and the shutter clicked, the flash burst, and sparks rained down on the carpet, capturing, for all posterity, the tragic devastation of a fallen star.

6

In all the years she had worked at the Savoy Plaza, first as a maid, then an assistant housekeeper, and finally head night housekeeper, no one had ever seen Mrs. Winter in such a state of agitation. Her face was splotched with purple spots of rage as she paced up and down in front of Elizabeth-Anne and John Holmes, the night clerk.

Behind her, in the shadows, stood a tall stranger. His hair was shiny black, except for the temples, where it was lightly streaked with silver. Even elegantly dressed in an evening suit and an open, formal cape, his wide shoulders and slim hips were plainly evident. His face was handsome but craggy, with a strong nose and wide, sensual lips. His right eye was deep blue, but his left was covered with a black eyepatch. He had lost the eye in a hunting accident, and the patch gave him the air of a dashing but distinguished pirate. He stood erect, unblinkingly surveying Holmes and Elizabeth-Anne. Due to the eyepatch, Elizabeth-Anne couldn't read his expression.

"This," Mrs. Winter said between tight lips, "is the gentleman Miss Bori *was* expecting. How you mistook the lout you admitted for this gentleman, I will never understand."

Holmes hung his head, but Elizabeth-Anne kept her chin raised, her eyes steely. Only the faint coloring of pink on her cheeks gave away her emotions, which were misread by Mrs. Winter. Elizabeth-Anne was not filled with shame or fear. Stung by the older woman's words, especially in front of a stranger, she was seething with anger.

"Miss Bori," Mrs. Winter went on, "had to be given a sedative by the doctor." She frowned at the floor, crossed her arms, and tapped them with her fingers. "I don't know how we are going to explain this." She paused and glared up at Holmes. "How could you have been so *stupid*? How could you let a photographer upstairs?" Then she twisted her head in Elizabeth-Anne's direction. "And you! Actually letting him into Miss Bori's room. This is scandalous. *Scandalous*." She shook her head in disgust. "Nothing like this has ever occurred in all my years here."

"I didn't know he was a photographer," Holmes said miserably, his face ashen. "He introduced himself as Larry."

"Miss Bori herself told me to show a 'Larry' to her room as soon as he arrived," Elizabeth-Anne added quietly. "How could anyone else have known to use that name?"

Mrs. Winter clenched her hands at her sides, ignoring Elizabeth-Anne's pointed question. "The point is that neither of you suspected that anything was wrong. I find that extremely hard to believe."

"There was no reason to suspect the press knew Miss Bori was admitting a guest," Elizabeth-Anne retorted. "And anyway, Miss Bori is known to be . . . well, somewhat eccentric. Why should we have expected an impostor?"

Just then two uniformed security guards entered and Mrs. Winter turned around to face them.

"We've finished searching the hotel," one of them said with obvious discomfiture. "The photographer is nowhere to be found. Someone thinks they saw him slip out by the Fifty-ninth Street entrance."

"Thank you," the housekeeper said icily. "You were both on duty in the lobby at the time of his arrival and failed to intercept him. Therefore you may come in and join us. What I have to say pertains to you also."

Hesitantly the guards lined up beside Elizabeth-Anne and Holmes.

Mrs. Winter narrowed her eyes. "As of this very moment" —she checked her watch—"all four of you are dismissed. And if I have *my* way, management will not—I repeat *not*— reinstate you." She smiled grimly. "Please do not expect any references."

"But it's not our fault," Holmes cried. "I need this job. I have a wife with a child on the way."

"Then I should think you would have been more careful."

"Madame." The voice was soft, but there was no mistaking the tone of authority in it. It was the first time the handsome stranger had spoken, and as he did so, he stepped forward out of the shadows.

Mrs. Winter gazed at him questioningly.

"This incident was most unfortunate," he said, "but considering that someone has dared to assume *my* identity, and further, that Miss Bori and I—and not the hotel—were the actual victims, I believe I might now have the right to say something?"

"By all means." Mrs. Winter managed to keep her face expressionless, but she failed to hide the irritation in her voice.

The man went on, unperturbed. "You may have gathered that Miss Bori is not quite herself at the moment. She has suffered a . . . a severely painful personal loss. The fault here lies with me, for instructing that I be announced by my first name only.''

Mrs. Winter bristled. ''You are very kind, sir, but still, you are not to—''

''Blame?'' He held up a hand to silence her. ''Madam, it is obvious that these particular four employees are blameless. I would think that someone who might have overheard the telephone conversation between Miss Bori and myself, and alerted the press, is the real culprit in this case.''

Mrs. Winter's white face turned scarlet. For a moment Elizabeth-Anne thought the older woman would actually faint.

''I think,'' the stranger continued, ''that, everything considered, everyone has suffered enough for one evening. I happen to be a personal friend of the owner of this hotel, and I'm sure that a good word to him about all of you, as well as an assurance that Miss Bori and I would like to let this matter die as quick a death as possible, will settle the matter satisfactorily. It would be far more constructive than any punishment meted out hastily.'' He bowed his head in Mrs. Winter's direction.

For once, Mrs. Winter was hesitant. She was torn between conflicting emotions: fury, that her authority was being questioned; fear, that he was obviously going to go over her head and speak with the hotel's owner; and relief, that he and Lola Bori would not hold her responsible for what had transpired. ''Well . . . if you insist, sir . . .'' she stammered.

He smiled, showing even white teeth. ''I do.''

''Very well, then.'' Mrs. Winter clapped her hands together. ''Back to your stations, all of you. But let me warn you''—she wagged a stern finger at the four employees—''if something like this should ever happen again, and so little initiative is shown in the future . . .'' She let the threat dangle heavily in the air. ''Return to your posts.''

The three male employees, relief written all over their faces, hurried out of the room.

''Well?'' Mrs. Winter eyed Elizabeth-Anne coldly. ''What are you waiting for?''

Elizabeth-Anne faced the housekeeper squarely. Her eyes

were cold, but she kept her voice even. "With all due respect, I think you owe us an apology."

Mrs. Winter stared at her. "Indeed."

"And furthermore, as of this moment I am handing in my resignation. Working conditions under your supervision are intolerable. Were I the owner of this hotel, I would never allow my employees to be treated in such a fashion. Perhaps the others need their jobs badly enough to put up with you, but I, thank God, am not that desperate."

"You . . . you wicked young woman." Mrs. Winter's voice grew shrill. "How dare you turn your back on my benevolence."

"It is you, Mrs. Winter, who is wicked. And as far as your benevolence is concerned, you certainly weren't left with much choice, were you?" She took a deep breath. "Good night."

"Good riddance is what I say," the housekeeper snapped at her. "I knew you were trouble from the first time I set eyes on you. Get your things out of the wardrobe immediately and don't ever set foot in this hotel again. Don't even bother changing out of your uniform. Get your things and leave this *instant*."

"Gladly, ma'am."

Aware of the one-eyed stranger's amused expression, Elizabeth-Anne marched shakily into the adjoining wardrobe room. When she came back out, she wore her coat over her maid's uniform and had her clothes piled in her arms. Both Mrs. Winter and the stranger were gone.

Once she was on Fifty-eighth Street, hurrying east toward the Lexington Avenue subway, a car pulled up and followed alongside her at her walking pace. She gave the stately yellow-and-black chauffeur-driven Rolls-Royce one glance and ignored it.

"Miss!"

She glanced over at the car with irritation. It was the one-eyed stranger.

"I have nothing to say to you," she said grimly. "Haven't you and your precious Miss Bori done enough for one day?" She tossed her head and continued walking.

"Could I give you a lift home?"

"I'll take the subway, thank you." She began walking faster, casting occasional sideways glares at him.

"You're quite independent, aren't you?" There was a peculiar note of challenge in his voice.

She fixed her eyes straight ahead. "I like to think so."

Without warning, she crossed Madison Avenue and pretended to continue marching across Fifty-eighth Street. She knew the Rolls had no choice but either to drive straight ahead, or to make a right turn down Madison or a left turn and head uptown. As soon as the car continued to follow her along Fifty-eighth Street, she pivoted on her heel, retraced her steps back to Madison, and disappeared around the corner. She waited a moment before peering from behind the building.

When the red taillights of the stately car joined the traffic on Park Avenue, she let out a deep breath, leaned against the building, and buried her chin in the pile of clothes she carried. For a moment her eyes stung with tears of frustration. She was furious at the unfairness of it all, not so much for herself as for the others who needed their jobs desperately. Nor was her anger directed exclusively at Mrs. Winter. The stranger, Larry, his drunken film-star friend, and their subterfuge deserved it equally. The hotel staff, she realized suddenly, were the pawns of the guests. If Larry hadn't been enough of a gentleman to speak up for them, they would all have been walking the streets and no one would have cared.

How awful of him, she thought with uncharacteristic bitterness as she continued walking. If it hadn't been for him, none of them would have been placed in that awkward situation in the first place. The Larrys and Lolas of this world, she decided, were a breed she could easily live without. And as she descended the steps to the subway platform, she hoped she would be able to wipe the unpleasant incident—and any memory of Lola and Larry—right out of her mind. Just as she was certain at that very moment Larry had already forgotten about her.

*   *   *

S
he was wrong.

When the yellow-and-black Rolls-Royce pulled up outside the double-width limestone town house on the north side of Seventy-fourth Street, the man in the backseat tapped his fingers on the armrest.

By God, but that woman has spirit, he thought. That and something else . . . something about her shows class. An indefinable air of . . . independence. Arrogance. Self-assurance. Of not really being a maid at all.

Who, then, was she?

He wanted to find out more about her, and made a mental note to have her checked out.

But fate did not allow it. The next morning Lola Bori was found dead in her suite at the Savoy Plaza from an overdose of sleeping pills, and he found himself busy exorcising the ghost of his former wife.

The maid from the Savoy Plaza became only a tantalizing memory.

For her part, however, Elizabeth-Anne found she was unable to forget the man she knew only as Larry. Having seen him for mere minutes, she could nonetheless at will conjure up his image perfectly: the solitary midnight-blue eye she'd barely glimpsed, the tall, trim physique, the carriage of self-assurance. Unbidden, at any hour of the day or night, she would think of the handsome one-eyed stranger, and a full vision of him would magically appear in front of her.

Not so with Zaccheus. There were those times, and they were increasingly common these days, when she was hard put to conjure up her husband exactly the way he had looked. After the years they had spent together, she suddenly found it difficult to remember him clearly. Some indefinable quality was always wrong, and yet she could never put her finger on just what was missing.

It made her feel angry. And guilty. Zaccheus hadn't been gone much more than four years. He was still her husband—legally and morally—as well as the father of her children. She had no right to sweep him into the recesses of her memory and let a stranger take that honored place of lust and longing.

Yet too many things conspired to make the handsome one-eyed stranger gain preeminence in her waking dreams.

For one thing, there was the eyepatch which he wore with such flaunting self-assurance, such *pride*; it spoke of a defiant, independent spirit she felt was akin to her own.

For another, there was his honesty, even if she didn't care to acknowledge it. He *had* spoken up in defense of the hotel staff in front of Mrs. Winter, and she knew, deep down inside, that that had taken courage.

There had been, too, the way he had spoken to her from the rear window of the Rolls-Royce, with those sensual lips bared into that—was she imagining it now?—damning devil's grin.

But most of all, it was the trio of events which had piled up, one on top of the other during that fateful twenty-four-hour span, which had etched him dramatically and indelibly on the fabric of her life. First there had been the incidents with the photographer and Mrs. Winter. That had been followed by a terrible fight with Charlotte-Anne once she had gotten home. And, as if to make certain that that night could never, ever be forgotten, the next morning the newspapers had been filled with the news of Lola Bori's tragic suicide. And the photograph—that very same damned photograph that had caused all the trouble to begin with—had accompanied the articles.

Together the events made for the ingredients of one mighty unforgettable nightmare. And Larry seemed to be at the center of it all.

She hadn't expected things to turn out the way they had. She had only taken the job in order to acquaint herself with the hotel business. She had quit it because of Mrs. Winter, because of her frustrations, because, too, she had learned all she could as a maid.

During the subway ride home, all she had been looking forward to was a peaceful, quiet few hours to herself, and then a sleep from which she would awaken refreshed and rejuvenated.

That was hardly what ensued once she reached the apartment a little past midnight. Her footsteps were heavy as she trudged up the stairs with her bundle of clothes. For a moment she paused on the landing to catch her breath, more exhausted than during any of the previous weeks when she had worked the entire night through. The incidents with the photographer and Mrs. Winter had drained her both emotionally and physically.

The lights were on in the apartment and Charlotte-Anne's party sounded like it was still in full swing. She could hear the excited chatter of voices and see the crack of bright light under the front door.

She shifted the clothes in her arms, dug in her purse for her keys, and unlocked the door. At first no one heard her come in. When she walked into the parlor, she saw Ludmila on the chaise, fast asleep. Her head was tilted sideways against one shoulder, her hands folded in her lap and her eyes shut. Her mouth was open, and she was snoring heavily. Charlotte-Anne and her friends sat on a mound of blankets and pillows on the floor, busy giggling over some joke. They listened to Ludmila's snores, whispered something, and burst out into more laughter.

"Dees. Dees ees zee vay I snore," one of the girls mimicked. She twisted her mouth in a parody of Ludmila's and emitted a nasal snort.

The others burst into giggles. The moment they became aware of Elizabeth-Anne, however, the laughter subsided.

"Mama!" Charlotte-Anne looked up in surprise. Then she jumped to her feet. "I didn't know you'd be back so soon."

"Neither did I." Elizabeth-Anne smiled wearily.

"I thought you were invited to stay overnight." Charlotte-Anne paused and emphasized: "In *Southampton*."

Elizabeth-Anne stared at her daughter. This was the first time Charlotte-Anne had actually dragged her into one of her lies. She wanted to put an end to it right then and there, but she stifled the urge, realizing this was neither the time nor the place to lecture her daughter. She would wait until the next day, when the other girls were gone.

Charlotte-Anne turned to her friends. "Mama gets constant invitations to spend weekends at someone's country house," she said. Then she drew closer to her mother and lowered her voice. "Why did you come back so soon? Is something the matter?"

"Nothing that can't keep until tomorrow." Elizabeth-Anne glanced down the hall at the closed bedroom door. "Your sisters and Zaccheus are asleep?"

Charlotte-Anne nodded. It was then that she noticed the bundle in her mother's arms. Her eyes went dark as she recognized the clothes Elizabeth-Anne had worn earlier that evening. Quickly she snatched them out of her grasp, turned around to shield them from her friends, and made a pretense of studying them. "Why, Mama," she said over her shoulder. "These are the things you left in Southampton last summer. It was so nice of Mrs. Belmont to have kept them, wasn't it?" She forced light laughter. "But she really should have lent you a suitcase." With the speed one might dispatch a poisonous snake before it struck, she shoved the clothes behind the curtained dressing alcove. Behind her back, the other girls exchanged curious glances among themselves.

Meanwhile, without thinking, Elizabeth-Anne slowly unbuttoned her coat, exposing the long-sleeved black maid's uniform with its white collar, cuffs, and starched apron. She sank wearily down into an armchair, her head back and eyes closed. Despite Charlotte-Anne's transparent charade, it felt good to be home. At last she could feel herself calming down.

Suddenly she became aware of the girls' animated whispers.

She opened her eyes. Charlotte-Anne's friends were holding a huddled conversation among themselves, glancing at her out of the corners of their eyes. Charlotte-Anne was standing near the door, trembling and white-faced.

Elizabeth-Anne looked at her daughter, surprised by the deathly expression in her eyes. "Charlotte-Anne? What is it?" she said cautiously, wondering what on earth had happened to affect her daughter so.

Charlotte-Anne looked away. "N-nothing," she mumbled miserably.

Elizabeth-Anne glanced around the room in confusion. The sudden tension seemed almost palpable. She couldn't understand what was going on, but was shocked to realize Charlotte-

Anne had, without a word, been ostracized from her circle of friends. And in her own home.

The obvious ringleader of the girls had an arresting face, with a pointed chin and hazel eyes. She got to her feet, signaling that the powwow was over.

"It's late, Mrs. Hale," she said haltingly, refusing to meet Elizabeth-Anne's eye. "I know we were planning to stay the night . . ." She glanced at the other girls for confirmation. They all nodded solemnly. "We'd . . . we'd really like to leave now, Mrs. Hale."

Elizabeth-Anne looked startled. She sat forward, her hands grasping the arms of the chair. "Whatever for?" She gazed from one to the other, but they refused to make eye contact with her. "I thought you were all having such a good time."

"We're . . . I mean, *I'm* . . . not feeling very well. We'll get our things together and find a taxi. We can go to my house."

Elizabeth-Anne glanced quickly at Charlotte-Anne. Her daughter was trembling as though with ague.

As the girls prepared to leave, Ludmila awoke with a start and looked around owlishly. "What time is it? Is it morning already?" she asked sleepily, rolling her R's.

As soon as the girls left, their footsteps trudging noisily down the stairs, Charlotte-Anne exploded. "I think I'm going to die," she wailed. "Oh God, I'll never be able to face them again. I can't even go back to school."

Elizabeth-Anne stared at her. "What *is* it?"

"You mean you don't know?"

"No, I'm afraid I don't," Elizabeth-Anne said evenly.

Charlotte-Anne turned on her mother, her eyes burning with a fierce hatred. The tears were streaking down her hot cheeks and her heart-shaped lips were contorted in pain. "Just look at yourself, Mama," she hissed. "You came in here and had to flaunt your uniform, didn't you? Your *maid's* uniform."

Dazedly Elizabeth-Anne looked down at herself. She was still clad in her working uniform. After everything that had happened earlier, she'd forgotten all about it. And now Charlotte-Anne was convinced she had exposed it on purpose.

"Don't you see?" Charlotte-Anne cried. "Now they *know* you're a common maid. That's why the party broke up and they don't want anything more to do with me." And she looked at her mother with the most intense loathing Elizabeth-Anne had ever seen.

"Darling, I didn't mean to spoil the party. You've got to believe me. I've had a terrible evening and I simply—"

"*You've* had a terrible evening!" The cords in Charlotte-Anne's neck were standing out in bold relief. "I *hate* you!"

"Don't you think," Elizabeth-Anne said calmly, "that if you had told them the truth instead of making up all those lies, they wouldn't have minded?"

"Oh, you have an answer for everything, don't you, Mama? Well, I have an answer for you too." She stamped her foot. "I *hate* you, Mama! *I hate you!*"

Elizabeth-Anne stood white-faced and quiet, unable to believe what she was hearing. Perhaps she *had* been inconsiderate in her exhaustion, but Charlotte-Anne's reaction seemed so out of proportion. "Darling, please calm down. I'm sure we can talk this over and—"

"I never want to speak to you again," Charlotte-Anne sobbed. "Not for as long as I live." Then she covered her face with her hands, ran to the bathroom, and slammed the door with such force that the walls shook.

Elizabeth-Anne stared after her, her head spinning.

Ludmila waited a moment, then pushed herself to her feet. "I think," she announced slowly, her accent still thick with sleep, "that we go down to my apartment and give her a little time to compose herself." Her eyes sparkled mischievously. "It may be Prohibition, but I have saved a few cases of very fine 1909 Bordeaux. Come." She patted Elizabeth-Anne's arm. "I think we could both of us use a drink, no?"

E lizabeth-Anne looked down into her wine and swirled it around again. It glowed hypnotically rich ruby red inside the baronially proportioned cut-crystal goblet.

"Well? You drink wine, not watch it grow old," Ludmila growled. "It does that in bottle."

Elizabeth-Anne smiled apologetically and took a sip. The

wine was smooth and fragrant, curiously heady. She could feel it relaxing her tense muscles.

"That is better." Ludmila nodded. "So, now. Let me see. The girls, they quickly desert Charlotte-Anne. And she is angry with you. And you have lost job." She pursed her lips and shook her head. "Is not very good day."

"You can say that again. And now what do I do?" Elizabeth-Anne's voice was weary. Even Ludmila's dogs seemed to sense the women's moroseness and kept quiet. "The only reason I took that job in the first place was to see how a hotel is run. From the inside." She screwed up her face painfully. "Well, that's over now."

Ludmila stared at her accusingly. "Why not tell me this before?" she demanded sharply. "I could have told you. You will never see how a hotel works, not as maid. What you need, if you want to start hotel, is money. That is all. You simply buy hotel and hire help. Is that easy." She lit one of her pungent cigarettes and veiled herself inside a noxious cloud of smoke.

"Money!" Elizabeth-Anne gave a low, deprecating laugh. "That's the only thing there never is enough of."

"But you say you have money saved up." Ludmila squinted at Elizabeth-Anne through the smoke. "Is much?"

"Much?" Elizabeth-Anne's voice was unchanged. "It depends on what you mean. It's a lot for some people, little for others. But for a hotel?" She laughed bitterly.

"That does not matter. If you want something bad enough, then you will get it."

"It isn't that easy, and you know it. You're always complaining bitterly that you don't have enough money."

Ludmila made an irritated gesture with her cigarette. "Enough! What is enough? Me, I am too old to gamble. If I were younger . . ." Her gray eyes took on a faraway look and she smiled faintly. "When I was younger, I gamble all the time. I become a mistress. That was a gamble. I go to court in this country for my lover's money, that was more gamble. But if I had a little money and I was your age . . ."

Elizabeth-Anne stared at her. "Yes?" she prodded, afraid to show her quickening interest.

"You told me you get money every week from the . . . the . .

Elizabeth-Anne nodded. "Yes, from the tourist court."

"Good. And it is enough to live on, to pay the bills?"

Elizabeth-Anne nodded again.

"So what you have in the bank is, how you say, mad money?"

"No," Elizabeth-Anne corrected her. "It's what we can fall back on in case something should happen."

"How much do you have in bank? Not that I am curious, you understand. Just to see if it is enough."

Elizabeth-Anne hesitated. What she had on deposit in her savings account was sacrosanct; it was something you did not advertise, not even to your friends.

"Please, I only want to *help*," Ludmila pleaded with soft urgency. She leaned forward on the siege, took Elizabeth-Anne's hands in her own, and smiled reassuringly. "If it is hundred dollars or hundred thousand dollars, the amount does not matter to me. It is only what it can do. Do you understand?"

"Yes, I think so." She took her hands from Ludmila's and sipped her wine thoughtfully. "There really isn't any reason why I should keep it a secret from you." She paused. "It comes to thirty thousand dollars."

"Thirty thousand! My God, then why you worry?" Ludmila's aging, faded-rose features beamed with pleasure. "Is plenty."

"For a hotel?" Elizabeth-Anne shook her head. "For that I need hundreds of thousands."

Ludmila wagged an admonishing finger at her. "Not," she said pointedly, "if you are willing to take little chance."

"I'm not so sure I like the way you said that," Elizabeth-Anne said slowly. "I never like to take chances, not with my money. I'm not a gambler."

"You said you start this tourist court, no?"

Elizabeth-Anne nodded.

"And if you start hotel, that is gamble too, no?" Ludmila eyed her shrewdly.

"Well, I *suppose* you could call it that."

"Good." Ludmila sat back with satisfaction and exhaled a

plume of smoke. "First, you must change bank. There is man of East Manhattan Savings Bank who will help us. His name is Vladimir Nikolsky. I know him from long ago, in Russia. He is only White Russian I still see socially. He will know who you can see about good chances instead of bad chances. There are specialists for this. But even before that . . ." For a long moment she regarded Elizabeth-Anne thoughtfully, one cracked-lacquer fingernail poised on her lips as her expressive gray eyes swept over her friend from head to toe. "Hmmmm," she said to herself. "Yes . . . I suppose . . ."

Elizabeth-Anne returned her stare quizzically. "Why are you looking at me like that?"

"Because," Ludmila explained patiently, as if to a child, "it is most important to create an impression. You must look success before you can be success. So first, we do you over. That is all."

"Do me over?"

Ludmila gave a quick nod and stubbed her cigarette out in the Imari bowl she used as an ashtray. She narrowed her eyes. "Yes, we do you over," she stated in such an emphatic voice that Elizabeth-Anne knew it was senseless to argue. Ludmila's mind had been made up.

7

Lester Lottoman, the assistant manager of the East Manhattan Savings Bank, pursed his lips thoughtfully as his eyes swept the rows of figures covering the most minute fluctuations in the bank's assets. After a moment he took off his silver-mounted spectacles, rubbed his weary eyes, and pushed the ledger aside. There were times when the endless numbers in need of balancing, checking, and rechecking repaid him for his vast patience with the heady thrill of accomplishment. That was when he caught an error everyone else had overlooked because he had the patience of a hunter. But there were other times, such as this, when the numbers all merged into senseless hieroglyphics and bored him no end.

"Mr. Lottoman."

The sharp voice startled Lester and he jumped, then looked up at the approaching manager of the East Manhattan Savings Bank, Mr. Nikolsky.

"Mr. Lottoman, this is Mrs. Elizabeth-Anne Hale," Vladimir Nikolsky said, indicating the woman at his side. "I trust you will see to it that she receives all the necessary banking attention she needs?"

Lester Lottoman nodded, looked at Elizabeth-Anne, and half-rose to his feet. "Please have a seat," he said, gesturing to the chair beside his desk.

Elizabeth-Anne sat with a minimum of fuss.

"I shall be in my office with Madame Romaschkova," Nikolsky told Elizabeth-Anne with a slight bow. "When you are finished, please join us."

"Thank you."

As Lottoman sat back down, he found himself taking an instant liking to this Elizabeth-Anne Hale. She was dressed elegantly, but looked sensible, and carried herself well. "And what can I do for you, Mrs. Hale?"

Elizabeth-Anne raised her chin. "I have thirty thousand dollars on deposit in this bank, Mr. Lottoman, as well as a respectable monthly income from a motel I own in Texas."

He nodded encouragingly.

"What I would like is to go into the hotel business. Here in New York."

"You would like to *buy* a hotel?"

She nodded. "And it has come to my attention that there are ways I could increase my funds, perhaps enough in order to buy a hotel."

"You mean . . . by investing?"

"I do." Elizabeth-Anne took a deep breath. "Mr. Nikolsky was kind enough to refer me to you because you are related to a highly respected investment banker."

"Lawrence Hochstetter of Hochstetter-Stremmel. Yes, he is my brother-in-law."

"Then I should like to meet him. You see, Mr. Lottoman, I'm serious about investing my money. As long as the risk is reasonable."

He stared at her thoughtfully, seeing an attractive, obviously intelligent woman who clearly meant business. His brother-in-law could only appreciate making her acquaintance, and Mr. Nikolsky would approve of any help Lester could give his friend.

"It just so happens that Mr. Hochstetter is giving a party at his town house this very evening, Mrs. Hale. I think we should attend."

"If you're certain it's not too much trouble," Elizabeth-Anne said hesitantly. "I wouldn't want to impose."

"And you won't, I assure you." He smiled suddenly. "I'll pick you up at eight o'clock."

She gave him her address and then they shook hands. As she left, he regarded her with a strangely wistful expression. There was something about her quiet dignity that appealed to him. Lester Lottoman was, perhaps, one of the first to fall under her spell.

But he wouldn't be the last.

"Regina? Charlotte-Anne? Anybody home?" Elizabeth-Anne listened for a moment, then shrugged as she pulled the key out of the lock. She picked up her shopping bags, carried them into the tiny foyer, and returned to make certain the door locked automatically when she closed it.

She listened to the quiet of the apartment. It had that peculiar empty-house stillness about it. She suspected that Regina had taken her sisters and brother across the street to the park. She missed the greetings of the children, and their excited accounts of their day. But she was also grateful for the silence.

After she and Ludmila had left the bank, Ludmila had headed home and she had gone to do some shopping. Now she was exhausted. She'd had to buy an evening gown to

90

wear that night, even though she knew she couldn't hope to compete with the other guests at the Hochstetter town house.

Elizabeth-Anne dropped her keys into the porcelain bowl on the hallway table, took off her hat, and shrugged herself out of her coat. As she hung it on the coat rack she caught a fleeting glimpse of a stranger in the mirror. At first she was startled; then she realized it was her own reflection. She laughed softly to herself. She still hadn't gotten used to the "new" her, the woman who had emerged from Ludmila's "doing-over."

She faced the mirror squarely, studying her reflection. Had she really changed that much, or was it only the new clothes and hairstyle, the dim foyer and its tricky shadows?

She leaned closer into the mirror. No, she really *had* changed in the three months since she and the children had moved here. She was now beautifully dressed and groomed, thanks to Ludmila. Her friend had been right, Elizabeth-Anne realized. Good clothes and style made life easier. Whether in a store, restaurant, or bank, her appearance ensured that everyone worked hard to please her.

But the change, she realized with a start, went much deeper than just her surface appearance. Her features had gained a maturity they had never had before. She exuded a confidence which, combined with her innate sensuality, had caused her bearing to become almost regal.

For starters, Ludmila had changed Elizabeth-Anne's hairstyle. She had insisted they splurge on an expensive, fashionable coiffeur once, explaining they could then keep up the style themselves. Not for her the faddish bobbed hair of the twenties or the utilitarian style she had favored in Quebeck. She now wore her hair combed down from a central part, though this could not be seen with the velvet helmetlike cloches she wore out-of-doors. Her ears were hidden by two short braids on either side of her face, which were coiled into small, delicate twin knots, lustrous flaxen jewels the color of Kansas wheat, which made earrings obsolete. Her pale eyebrows were no longer light; plucked into fine pencil-line arches, they were tinted a darker shade so that they were more expressive. Her eyes were deepened with the faintest aquamarine eye shadow possible, and other than a muted shade of lipstick, this was the only makeup she wore.

If part of her newly acquired confidence came from enhancing her physical attributes, then the rest was due to her new clothes, which she found herself far more comfortable in than the plainer outfits she had worn in Texas. Not for Manhattan the long severely cut skirts and the pale blouses she had always worn. New York was, after all, a cosmopolitan city which demanded chic. She could not hope to afford the clothes she would have liked to buy, but she had managed by emphasizing quality and style, choosing the cut and the colors which suited her best. In short, she dressed elegantly but within her budget, thanks to Ludmila.

Her friend had taken her to the thrift shops of the Lower East Side, which were rife with secondhand bargains. "Many poor Jewish immigrants have rich uptown relatives," Ludmila had told her. "They help poor relations by giving their old clothes."

So it was on Orchard Street, among the hubbub and haggling, the pushcart peddlers and sidewalk vendors, that Elizabeth-Anne found Seligman's Secondhand Store and the outfit she now wore. Perhaps it was secondhand. But the fine quality and aura of sophistication it lent her were first-class.

"Only two buttons are missing," Marty Seligman, the proprietor of the store, had pointed out when Elizabeth-Anne had inspected the blouse with its collarless neckline and puffed sheer sleeves that gathered snugly at the wrists. It was otherwise in perfect condition, but she'd hesitated. The buttons were unusual, and she knew she couldn't hope to find replacements.

"For you I throw in these for nothing," Seligman said shrewdly, showing her and Ludmila a box of tiny seed-pearl buttons.

Ludmila had insisted upon clinching the deal. Elizabeth-Anne discovered, to her great delight, that when she and Ludmila replaced all the buttons with the pearls, the blouse was even more beautiful. The shimmer of pearls against the café-au-lait net was the perfect foil, and made wearing jewelry unnecessary. Instantly the blouse became her favorite.

Both the front and back panels were embroidered with café-au-lait braid, and the hip-length hem was finished with a border of tiny pearllike fringe of crocheted balls, which, coupled with the pearl buttons, gave her an air of refined gentility.

Any other person might have chosen to wear the blouse with a skirt of matching color, but not Ludmila, and Elizabeth-Anne quickly saw her point. Together they chose an off-white pleated wool skirt of just over knee length, an original from the House of Worth in Paris. Before Elizabeth-Anne it had graced an ample dowager from Carnegie Hill, but some judicious tucks had made it a perfect fit. For a jacket, Ludmila had once more insisted on contrast and chosen a cerise wool, so cherry bright that it could have been picked off a tree.

Gone forever were Elizabeth-Anne's sturdy country boots with their myriad eyelets and long laces. She and the girls wore shoes of soft, supple leather now, with modest heels and straps across the ankles. She was, Elizabeth-Anne decided, as well-dressed as many a society matron, and for a fraction of the cost.

Her inspection of herself over, she picked up the shopping bags and went into the parlor. She set the bags down on the chaise longue upon which she slept, the foot of which was draped with a beige mohair blanket.

From out in the foyer came the sound of a key turning in the lock.

"Mama? You home?"

The voice burst forth cheerfully, the way Rebecca always sounded when she came home. As the youngest of the three girls, she was not yet caught up in the shifting moods of her older sisters, who were beset with the magnified worries of adolescence. In character, Rebecca was also the closest to Elizabeth-Anne. She was the most artless of the children, the least prone to tantrums, the most unlikely to talk back, and, above all, the most sensitive. Sometimes the nagging thought crept into Elizabeth-Anne's mind that Rebecca was her favorite, and whenever it did, she would force herself to squelch it.

I've loved each one of them more than the others at one time or another, she reminded herself firmly. But in truth I love them all equally.

But these thoughts lasted only an instant and she quickly turned to greet Rebecca with an enveloping hug. "How are you, darling?"

Rebecca grinned up at her. "I'm fine," she said breathlessly, winded from racing up the stairs. And then the excited sentences tumbled out of her in a rush. "Regina had us walk all the way to Grand Central Station but Zaccheus got tired and we had to take turns carrying him most of the way and Charlotte-Anne's complaining that she's got blisters on her toes . . ." She took a deep gulp of air. "They're on their way up." She giggled then. "Regina and Charlotte-Anne and *Zaccheus* are on their way up," she corrected herself, "not the toes. Well, those too."

Elizabeth-Anne laughed and tousled her daughter's hair. "It sounds like you've had quite an afternoon."

"Oh, we did! And we were careful, we really were. Regina saw to that. We didn't talk to any strangers. And we saw the most marvelous clothes in a shop window. A sweater Charlotte-Anne said she'd die for! But it's so expensive." She sighed dramatically. "But it would look so good on her, Mama, really it would," she finished with a knowing glint in her eye that made Elizabeth-Anne smile inwardly.

"Well, maybe you can point it out to me soon," Elizabeth-Anne suggested, thinking that if Charlotte-Anne wanted it so badly, perhaps she would buy it for her and hide it away until Christmas. The holiday season was only a little more than a month away.

Elizabeth-Anne turned as she heard the others come trooping in. Regina was carrying Zaccheus, who was fast asleep. "Hi, Mama," she called out softly for fear of waking him.

"Hello, darling."

Charlotte-Anne walked by glumly, her head held low. "Hi," she mumbled under her breath, making a beeline for the bedroom.

Elizabeth-Anne gazed after her in silence. Days had passed since their argument, but Charlotte-Anne still behaved as though it had occurred only hours ago. She had been morose ever since, never saying more than a few perfunctory words.

Well, a few more days would heal their rift, of that Elizabeth-

Anne was certain. But even that thought gave her little comfort. She despised dragged-out fights; they took altogether too much out of you. And she hated Charlotte-Anne's silent treatment even more.

They're only growing pains, she told herself, not for the first time, that's all that's the matter with Charlotte-Anne.

Rebecca spied the shopping bags on the chaise. "Oh, Mama," she cried excitedly. "You've been shopping."

"Yes, I have to go to a dinner party tonight."

Rebecca seized the bags and rummaged through them. She let out an awe-struck whistle as she held up the gown Elizabeth-Anne had bought at Seligman's. It was made of beige crepe roma and had a deep jabot which fell in a V from the shoulders to the hem. The sleeves were long, with flaring cuffs, and at the ankles the double skirt ended in an inverted pleat. The gown was feather-light and classical in its very simplicity, and fell in beautiful, luxuriantly loose folds. Best yet, it needed no time-consuming alterations. She would be able to wear it that night. Only a spot near the neckline, which could easily be hidden with a brooch, gave away the fact that it was secondhand.

"It's beautiful," Rebecca whispered in awe. Then her voice grew pensive. "What party are you going to, Mama?"

"It's really for business," Elizabeth-Anne explained. "A gentleman from the bank is going to take me to meet an investment banker. That's why I'm going. I'm not deserting you all to just have fun," she finished teasingly.

Rebecca let the gown drop on the chaise. "This gentleman . . . is he handsome?"

Elizabeth-Anne gazed at her with a startled expression. "Why do you ask that?"

Rebecca shrugged. "Is he?"

"I don't know. I haven't even thought about it."

"Mama?"

"Yes, dear?"

"It's been years since we've seen Daddy."

"I know that, darling," Elizabeth-Anne replied softly.

"Are we . . . are we *ever* going to see him again?"

"I hope so," Elizabeth-Anne replied quietly, feeling tears spring to her eyes.

"I hope so too." Rebecca paused. "You know what's the worst thing of all?" she whispered.

Elizabeth-Anne shook her head.

"I . . . I can't even remember what he looks like." Rebecca turned her tear-streaked face up at Elizabeth-Anne. "You remember, don't you, Mama?"

Elizabeth-Anne forced a smile, but she felt a trembling inside herself. "Of course I do, darling," she said. "Of course I do."

But as she held her daughter tightly against her and closed her eyes, no matter how hard she tried, Elizabeth-Anne could not conjure up a clear vision of Zaccheus Hale.

As Ludmila walked slow circles around Elizabeth-Anne, her sharp, piercing gray eyes were lost in thought. "The gown is fine," she said at long last. "But be careful with the safety pins or you will stick yourself," she cautioned with an admonishing wag of her finger.

"I'll be careful," Elizabeth-Anne promised her, grateful for her friend's advice. Trust Ludmila, she thought, to notice just where the soft, smooth fabric bunched just ever so slightly, or where it did not fall quite the way it should. She knew the slight alteration was invisible to a less critical eye.

"The shoes, they are so-so. But they will do," Ludmila said slowly to herself. "But the jewelry . . ." Her face wore an expression of disgust as she flapped one hand back and forth in the air. "That brooch will not do at all."

Elizabeth-Anne gazed down with dismay at the brooch she had pinned over the spot near the neckline. She had inherited the cameo from her aunt and always treasured it, but she knew that Ludmila was right. "It's the only brooch I own," she said slowly. "I have to hide this spot somehow."

"Do not worry. I will lend you one." Ludmila nodded to herself. "Now, what coat you wear?"

Elizabeth-Anne motioned over to the chair.

"That?" Ludmila looked horrified. "No. No, *no, no.* Never."

"But it's all I have for this weather," Elizabeth-Anne protested. "I have to wear it."

"I lend you one."

"Surely it won't fit."

"Why? Because of my size?" Ludmila looked hurt. "The coat I give you, it is made for Russian winters. It is long, on me to the ground. Even the sleeves are too long. It will fit. Now, what time is it?"

Elizabeth-Anne glanced up at the clock ticking on the mantel. "He'll pick me up in less than fifteen minutes."

"Fifteen!" Ludmila cried. "Then we have not a moment to lose. I be right back."

Elizabeth-Anne shook her head as the diminutive older woman rushed out. She wondered in all earnestness what she would do without her Russian friend.

A few minutes later a breathless Ludmila came charging back up the stairs. She carried two large burled-wood jewelry cases in her arms, and towed an enormous coat of pure white Russian lynx bellies across the floor.

"Ludmila!" Elizabeth-Anne was aghast when she saw the coat. "I couldn't possibly!"

"You must."

"Not that coat. It must be worth—"

"Much money, I know." Impatiently Ludmila shrugged aside Elizabeth-Anne's protest. "You just keep quiet."

"But . . . what if I should lose it?"

"Lose it?" Ludmila narrowed her eyes. "No woman *I* ever know lose her fur. Now . . ." She deposited the boxes on the table. "Now," Ludmila said, "we choose the jewels." She bent over the boxes, lifted the lids, and began rummaging through them. Elizabeth-Anne let out an exclamation of surprise. Ludmila was always complaining about not having enough money, and if a tenant couldn't come up with the rent on the precise day it was due, she threatened to suffer heart attacks. Yet these boxes held what must surely be a king's ransom! Diamond tiaras, belts of rubies, pearls of all sizes and shapes, rings, earrings, bracelets, and brooches—all gifts from the admiral. It was all stuffed so haphazardly into the boxes that the ropes of pearls were knotted, and no single earring was with its match.

"*Yes*," Ludmila cried suddenly. "This—this is the piece!" She held up a brooch. "Is beautiful, no?" she asked, not bothering to mask her own pleasure. "It was created in St. Petersburg by Edward Wilhelm Schramm, who worked for Fabergé. Is a masterpiece, no?"

Elizabeth-Anne could only nod speechlessly.

"Well? Hold it! Do not be afraid to touch it." She thrust it into Elizabeth-Anne's hand.

Slowly Elizabeth-Anne lifted the brooch. It measured three inches in length and two inches in width, an enamel ellipse set with rubies and diamonds and crisscrossed by a ruby-and-diamond Byzantine-style cross. "Words cannot describe it," she said.

"So? Put it on. No, here, let me." Ludmila unpinned the cameo and attached the Russian brooch precisely so that it hung gracefully where the cameo had been. Then she stood back and clapped her hands together. "Is marvelous," she pronounced. "Now. Into the coat." She lifted it and waited for Elizabeth-Anne to duck down and slip it on.

Ludmila was right, Elizabeth-Anne noticed. The coat, which was oversize on her diminutive friend, fell neatly just below her knees, while the lynx hairs at the edge of the sleeves just brushed the backs of her hands.

"My God." Ludmilla let out a deep breath. "You are stunning."

Elizabeth-Anne turned to the mirror and couldn't believe the vision of elegance that greeted her eyes. "I can't thank you enough," she told Ludmila warmly. "You're my . . . my fairy godmother."

"We all need godmothers sometimes." Ludmila glanced behind her at the door as the bells chimed. "Now, off with you before your troika turns back into a pumpkin!"

Elizabeth-Anne bent down and hugged Ludmila warmly. The tiny Russian exile got up on tiptoe and returned the embrace Russian fashion, kissing both cheeks and then depositing one last kiss directly on her lips.

8

Lester Lottoman smiled at Elizabeth-Anne. "Here we are," he said as the taxi rolled to a stop, double-parking beside a row of gleaming limousines whose chauffeurs were gathered in little groups on the sidewalk.

Elizabeth-Anne peered out the window at the Hochstetter town house and felt any last vestiges of confidence seep out of her. This was no town house, at least not in the ordinary sense that described the row houses lining Gramercy Park or the streets of the Village. She held the lynx lapels of her coat close to her throat, newly grateful for Ludmila's generosity. This house was one of the last of a dying breed, a stately miniature palace of the type which once lined Fifth Avenue.

As Lottoman helped Elizabeth-Anne out of the car, she continued to stare at the building in awe. It was surrounded by a high wrought-iron fence and stood three proud stories tall. The first floor was raised, with carved double doors and coach lights. The high mullioned windows were gracefully arched in the French style and were ablaze with light. Elizabeth-Anne could hear the muted strains of music drifting out to the street and wondered at her nerve, coming here to meet Lawrence Hochstetter. How could she ask such a man to help her invest her money, money which, she realized now, was to him surely no more than loose change.

Lester Lottoman laughed nervously. "Well, we can't just stand out here, or we'll freeze. Let's go in, shall we?"

Shyly he hooked an arm through Elizabeth-Anne's and led her to the gate and up the wide, sweeping steps to the front door. The butler recognized him on sight. "Good evening, Mr. Lottoman," he said in a low, British-accented voice, his face carefully devoid of expression.

" 'Evening, Bevin."

"The other guests are in the salon, sir. I believe Mr. Hochstetter is expecting you." He bowed his head in Elizabeth-Anne's direction. "May I help you with your coat, madam?"

Elizabeth-Anne tightened her grip on the lynx lapels. She didn't want to let Ludmila's prized coat out of her sight, but with a laugh reminded herself she could hardly wear it indoors. "Thank you, yes," she said, recovering her composure.

Bevin took her coat as she gazed around in the foyer, where everything was of the finest marble, from the busts perched in their niches to the sweeping staircase that curved up three stories to a huge glassed-in rotunda.

"This way, Mrs. Hale," Lottoman said, touching her hand and keeping his fingers poised on it.

He guided her down the length of the hall, where a liveried footman opened two towering doors. At the sight of the salon, Elizabeth-Anne sucked in her breath. The room was covered in murals, skillful portrayals of Rome before it fell into ruin, with distant temples and statuaries, urns and strutting peacocks, columns, cornices, delicate pink clouds and rosy sunsets. The murals covered every surface—the walls, ceiling, even the doors—and gave the room an open, palatial feeling. But it was not museumlike or sterile; the overstuffed chairs and couches of green and gold kept the room cozy. Behind an enormous concert grand piano sat a black pianist in a tuxedo playing Cole Porter and singing softly, and everywhere she looked, there were formal floral arrangements. All this on a sea of beige wall-to-wall wool carpeting which matched her crepe gown.

But even more startling were the guests. She counted to twenty and then stopped, realizing that it was pointless to continue. Never before had she seen so many beautifully turned-out couples, elegantly tailored tuxedos and lavishly styled evening gowns. Or so many waiters circulating with silver trays of champagne—and at the height of Prohibition.

This must be, she decided, a make-believe Hollywood world. She almost pinched herself in order to prove it was all real, that she had not entered some fantastically concocted dream. She felt she had stepped over the threshold into another dimension, into the world behind one of the exclusive doors of the socially prominent, the politically powerful, the beautiful, the wealthy, and the accomplished.

"Lester Lottoman, you *rake*!"

The woman swept toward them, wrapped in a form-fitting silver sheath that was missing only its mermaid's tail. She wore a necklace with matching earrings of tourmalines and diamonds, and a predatory shark's smile.

"H-hello, Marisol," Lottoman stammered in such obvious anguish that Elizabeth-Anne glanced at him sharply out of the corner of her eyes. "I . . . I didn't know you would be here."

"My, my, I *bet* you didn't." The woman's eyes swept over Elizabeth-Anne. Then she turned back to Lottoman. "This doesn't look at *all* like Edith, I'm afraid," she said with a pout. "No, not at *all*."

"Well, no." Lottoman's Adam's apple was working nervously. "Edith's at h-her cousin's. M-Mrs. Hale here is interested in investing at Hochstetter-Stremmel, so I . . . I naturally thought the best way for her to meet—"

"When the cat's away, the mice will play, eh?" Marisol's icy eyes sparkled mischievously. "How *delicious*. And you of all people, Lester! To think we all thought you were a dreary little wallflower. Well, trust *me* to keep a secret. My lips are *zipped*. If you're good, that is. You see, I've met this most marvelous young German in Newport, and Heinzy followed me all the way here, would you believe?" She lowered her voice confidentially, at the same time making certain Elizabeth-Anne would not miss a word. "He's hung like a *horse*, I swear. Anyway, I'm so terrified he'll find greener pastures, and since there's nothing like a little competition to spice up one's love life, you simply must meet him and help make him jealous." She jiggled her shoulders, flashed a wide-open-mouthed smile and took Lottoman by the arm, propelling him forward through a throng of guests. "He won't be but a minute, dear," she sang sweetly over her shoulder to Elizabeth-Anne, as she threw her a lewd kiss.

Lottoman twisted around and gazed helplessly back at Elizabeth-Anne. She smiled and shrugged. For a moment she stood there awkwardly, watching the throng swallow him up.

She felt curiously empty-handed and lifted a flute of champagne off a waiter's tray, but it didn't dull the sensation.

She could feel several guests flick her curious glances while others studied her with longer, openly appraising looks. She turned away, her face prickling with heat. She felt marooned, alone in the sparkling dream world where she knew no one, where she did not fit.

Slowly she crossed the room and stood near the piano, sipping her champagne. Minute after minute crawled by, and Lottoman still did not return. Occasionally she caught glimpses of him across the room. He was craning his neck constantly, his eyes searching for her, but the woman named Marisol was not ready to relinquish him.

"Damn," Elizabeth-Anne whispered under her breath, tightening her lips in annoyance. She knew she shouldn't have come, but that hardly helped now. She was here to meet Lawrence Hochstetter, one of the country's foremost financial wizards, who was, by varying accounts, either a brilliant business tactician or a pirate. The only person who could introduce her had been snatched away. Her doubts were mushrooming, but just as she was about to leave, a deep, familiar baritone voice beside her said, "Excuse me, haven't we met somewhere before?"

Startled, she turned to face the speaker and nearly spilled her champagne. *It's him,* she thought with a sinking feeling. Oh dear God. *Him.*

Standing inches away was the attractive stranger she had met at the Savoy Plaza, Lola Bori's friend, the one who had caused so much trouble. The man, a little voice inside her admonished her, who had averted just as much trouble as he might have inadvertently caused to begin with. The man she could not, try as she might, forget.

But she ignored that little voice. She was unable to speak, unable to move. All she could do was to stare stupidly at him. The unbidden thought occurred to her that he looked even more attractive now than he had when she first saw him. His blue-black hair was swept over his lean skull, the gray at his temples gleaming like polished sterling. He held himself casually, yet peculiarly erect, like a panther ready to pounce. His craggy features, while attractive, were decidedly predatory, and his sensual lips were cocked in a slight smile. He wore tiny diamond studs in his shirt, which twinkled mockingly at her. She noticed that this time his black eyepatch was not cloth, but leather, which somehow only served to enhance his devil-may-care appearance.

And here she was, lost in a crowd of strangers, her escort gone, and the only person she'd ever seen before had met her while she had been a maid. She felt like a cheap impostor. She had no right to be here, and now she would be exposed.

"Seems the last time I saw you, you were dressed somewhat differently," he said, his one eye bold and deep blue. Or was it filled with contempt? "Do you usually make a habit of crashing society parties?"

She bristled, feeling for all the world like a porcupine raising its armor. "If you'll be so good as to excuse me . . ." She turned to leave, but he caught her arm, his fingers feeling strangely warm through the thin material of her dress.

"Not so fast."

She stared down at his hand. "I think you had better let me go," she whispered.

He laughed, his even white teeth flashing. "I let you go once, remember? I don't know if I should do that again. I'm not used to having to chase after a maid."

Her face flushed. How dare he hurl such an insult at her! Rallying her forces of self-control, she glanced around the room in hope of finding Lester Lottoman to rescue her from this forward stranger, but he was nowhere in sight. "I have no intention of suffering insults from you," she replied coldly.

"Is that so?" he asked, relinquishing his hold on her.

"It is." She turned and stared at him, and their eyes met. For a long moment, neither could look away, and Elizabeth-Anne felt a wave of something she thought must be revulsion sweep through her at the same time her knees turned weak.

Why does he have this effect on me? she wondered angrily. Why does he look even more handsome than the last time I saw him? And why can't I stand him?

She tore her eyes away from his and craned her neck again,

desperately searching the room for Lester Lottoman, who now seemed to have vanished completely.

"Looking for someone?" the stranger asked. "Your escort, I presume?"

"You presume correctly," she snapped in reply. She dared not look at him again. Her feelings concerning him were altogether too strong, too strange and overwhelming. How could a stranger fill her so completely with hate and . . . yearning? She drew in her breath and tightened her lips in irritation. She mustn't think of him at all. Yes, she would simply pretend he wasn't there. Then perhaps he would ignore her and go away.

"Perhaps your escort deserted you?"

But that was too much to ignore. "He did not. I'm certain of it."

"Then may I get you some champagne while you wait?"

She glanced down at her empty hand. In her confused state, she hadn't even realized that she had set her glass down on the piano, and a passing waiter had already scooped it away.

"I . . ." she began hesitantly, then changed her mind and sniffed. "No, thank you."

"I can't argue with that," he said, "especially not during Prohibition. It's a crime, how liquor flows here, isn't it? However, you still haven't told me what you are doing here, and maybe that's a crime, too."

She thrust her chin out indignantly. "I needn't tell you anything. But if you must know, I've come to see someone."

"Oh? And who might that be?"

She glanced sideways at him and gave a triumphant little smile. "Mr. Lawrence Hochstetter."

He raised his eyebrows. "I see. You seem to move in exalted circles. Do you know Mr. Hochstetter personally?"

She could feel her temper rising to the bait. "Would I be here if I didn't?"

He glanced around. "Well, it doesn't look like you really know many people here."

"Looks," she retorted tartly, "can be deceiving."

"I see." He suppressed his maddening smile. "Then perhaps you'll do me the honor of introducing me to some of your friends. I'd be delighted, for instance, if I could make the acquaintance of that lady over there."

Elizabeth-Anne's guard went up. "Wh-which one?"

He pointed. "The one in the white and green."

Elizabeth-Anne looked over at the woman, noting she seemed the most elegant of all the guests. She stood tall, her angular cheekbones and regal nose hinting at champion bloodlines. Her moon-licked black hair was swept back into a chignon, and she wore an exquisite three-tiered bracelet of diamonds on her right wrist. A necklace of two strands of huge black pearls hung from her swanlike throat and her white chiffon gown was diaphanous, embroidered with delicate pale green leaves.

"You do know her, don't you? I mean, you just got through telling me—"

"Oh!" Elizabeth-Anne clenched her fists at her sides. She was at once angry and afraid. She had talked herself into an impossible situation with this insufferable stranger, and although she was never prone to lying and had little practice at the art, she now found it the only possible course to take. "Of course I know her," she snapped irritably.

He nodded. "She looks familiar to me, too. I know I've met her before, but I can't seem to recall her name."

Elizabeth-Anne took a deep breath. In for a penny, in for a pound. "It's Gloria," she said quickly.

Before she knew what was happening, he was propelling her toward the woman.

"What are you doing?" she hissed helplessly.

"You and I are going to chat with Gloria." They reached the group where the woman was holding court. "Gloria . . ." he began with a rakish smile.

The woman turned to him in amazement. "Lawrence Hochstetter, you mean to tell me that after all these years you still can't remember my name?"

He grinned sheepishly at Elizabeth-Anne, who wanted nothing more than to have the floor open up and swallow her whole.

"I'm sorry, Robyn," he told the woman. "It's just a little

joke played in very bad taste. Blame it on too much champagne. This young woman here . . ." He glanced at Elizabeth-Anne. "Why, she looks pale. Perhaps she's ill. Be a dear, Robyn, and show her to the powder room, will you?"

"You are *awful*," Elizabeth-Anne whispered to him. "You set me up deliberately—"

But he ignored her, whispering in Robyn's ear, "And whatever you do, don't let her out of your sight. I don't want her to leave, not under any circumstances. Oh, and tell Bevin to change the seating arrangements. I want her to sit on my right during dinner."

Robyn narrowed her eyes.

"Well, make that the left. You, dear Robyn, will sit on my right."

With a satisfied nod, Robyn hurried after Elizabeth-Anne, who was weaving her way through the salon with slow, trembling dignity, like a somnambulist.

After speaking with Bevin, Robyn rushed to the powder room, where she found Elizabeth-Anne. She pushed her gently down onto one of the chintz-upholstered settees. "Just relax for a few minutes. If you need anything, let me know. I'll be right here."

Elizabeth-Anne nodded, but she sat numbly, waiting for her blood pressure to lower. She had never felt so humiliated, so insulted, so *angry* in her entire life.

Closing her eyes, she leaned her head back and took a series of deep, slow breaths. She had to calm herself and try to think. It was a fine fix she had gotten herself into, but there was no problem she couldn't solve, either, if she thought it out rationally. Or was there?

"Are you feeling any better?" Robyn asked.

Elizabeth-Anne glanced at her and nodded.

"Good. Some of your color is returning." Robyn smiled, produced a shagreen Cartier compact, snapped it open, and leaned into the gilt-framed mirror. She began dusting her cheeks with powder. "I wouldn't worry about Larry too much," she advised offhandedly.

"Why do you say that?" Elizabeth-Anne's voice still quivered slightly.

"Because he has the worst mean streak of anyone I know." Robyn eyed herself critically and then powdered herself some more. "He loves to play practical jokes on people. I take it you were the victim this time."

Elizabeth-Anne smiled wryly. "I left myself open for it."

"Hmph. That's beside the point, if you ask me. But I will say one thing for him."

"What's that?"

"He treats everyone equally, man, woman, or child. He doesn't make any exceptions for the supposedly 'weaker' sex." Her voice grew wistful. "Still, sometimes it would be nice if he treated a lady like a lady." Her powdering finished, Robyn snapped her compact shut. Then she turned around to face Elizabeth-Anne and leaned her hips back against the top of the vanity, smiling faintly. "I still don't know how you did it. Of course, you're very attractive, but, pardon my saying it, beauty is cheap. This city is filled with thousands of women more attractive than either one of us."

Elizabeth-Anne looked perplexed. "I don't think I understand what you mean."

"Come, now. You're the first woman in a long, long time that Larry's been smitten with."

Elizabeth-Anne felt the hot blood rush to her cheeks. She dropped her eyes to study her lap. "I'm sure you're mistaken," she murmured softly.

"Me? Mistaken?" Robyn laughed good-naturedly. "Not on your life. Listen to me," she said, approaching the settee, the chiffon train of her gown billowing behind her. She sat down beside Elizabeth-Anne and took her hand. "There was a time I wanted Larry very badly. But he married someone else instead."

"Is he still married?"

Robyn shook her head. "No. But he chose her over me, and then he and his wife had a rather ugly divorce, which was played up in all the papers. Meanwhile, I married my husband, so when Larry was free again, I wasn't. Now we're simply friends, like brother and sister. But we like each other much more now than we ever did before.''

"But . . . why *didn't* he marry you?" Despite herself, Elizabeth-Anne was fascinated. "Why did he marry that other woman?"

"Because she offered him what I couldn't. I suppose you have the same quality that he thought she had. Only he was wrong about her. He overestimated her by a long shot. You see, Larry loves nothing more than a mystery. He's always intrigued when he discovers someone who he thinks has a lot more than meets the eye. That way he's got something to unravel. But his wife tricked him. She put on a good front in the beginning, but he found out soon enough how shallow she was.''

"And that's why he divorced her? Just because she was no longer a mystery to him?" Elizabeth-Anne was shocked.

"Well, that was part of their problem. The main reason, though, was a film she'd made. He thought it was too lewd, so he tried to buy up every reel in existence. It made her terribly angry. She accused him of sabotaging her career and God only knows what else. As a result, it was *she* who wanted the divorce.''

"So she was an actress."

"Oh, yes. A fine one, I'll grant her that much. You've probably heard of her. She committed suicide only recently.''

A chill swept through Elizabeth-Anne. She fidgeted with her hands and her voice dropped to a whisper. "It wasn't . . .'' She groaned despairingly. "It couldn't have been—''

"Lola Bori. The one and only." Robyn shook her head and smiled sadly. Then she clapped her hands together and brightened. "Well, I think that's enough maudlin gossip for now. It's time we got going. Knowing this house as well as I do, I think dinner's about to be served. Without us, if we don't hurry.''

"You go on ahead," Elizabeth-Anne said quickly. "And . . . thank you.''

Robyn looked surprised. "Whatever for?''

"Telling me what you did.''

"Oh, pooh, that's nothing. If we're to become friends, we

shouldn't keep *too* many secrets from each other, should we? I mean, a few always add a little spice, but too many . . ." Robyn shook her head and rose from the settee. She held out her hand. "Let's go eat."

"I can't," Elizabeth-Anne begged off. "I . . . I have to be going."

"Nonsense. I won't hear of it. You're staying."

"Don't you see? I can't face him. Not now."

"Why? Because you're still embarrassed by his childish prank?"

Elizabeth-Anne was silent. How could she explain that her humiliation paled in comparison to what she'd just learned? The fact that Larry Hochstetter had been Lola Bori's husband— the same Lola Bori for whose suicide she herself couldn't help but feel some responsibility—had changed everything. Now she knew she would never be able to face him again, not for as long as she lived. Small wonder he took such obvious delight in putting her down. How he must hate her!

Robyn misread her reluctance. "Don't hold his jokes against him," she advised lightly. "As I told you, he's the same with everyone. He didn't single you out. Besides, sooner or later he'll come around and apologize, and you won't want to miss that. And I'm not supposed to tell you this," she continued, "but the reason Larry sent me in here after you is that he doesn't want you to leave."

"I can believe that," Elizabeth-Anne said bitterly. "This way he can torture me some more. And I must say, I deserve it."

"On the contrary, you little fool," Robyn said with a bright laugh. "He's *smitten* with you, Now, out we go." She pulled Elizabeth-Anne to her feet and smiled. "A little food never hurt anyone. Nor did a little conversation. You'll learn soon enough. Neither Larry Hochstetter nor Robyn Morgan ever takes no for an answer."

Elizabeth-Anne gazed into Robyn's eyes. "Please, can't you just leave me be?"

"I'm afraid not." Robyn propelled her toward the door. "Oh, and there's one more thing."

Elizabeth-Anne raised her eyebrows wearily.

"If we're to become friends, which I'm sure we will, you'll have to start trusting me, all right?"

Elizabeth-Anne gave a little nod.

She wouldn't have believed it, but it was the beginning of a friendship that was to last a lifetime.

The rest of the guests were already seated in the dining salon when she and Robyn came in. Elizabeth-Anne glanced around with a none-too-sanguine confidence. She felt even more embarrassed than she had before. Dinner had obviously been delayed for her and Robyn Morgan.

Robyn turned to her and smiled reassuringly. "Take heart," she whispered gleefully. "We *must* be important. Had it been anyone else, they would have started already. And for God's sake, slow *down*. This is our grand entrance." She held Elizabeth-Anne back, forcing her to walk more slowly, while turning her regal whippet's face toward the guests, with a flashing smile that wasn't in the least apologetic.

As they approached the table, Elizabeth-Anne saw there were only two empty places to the left and right of the host. She wasn't going to be let off that easily, she thought with a sinking feeling. Lawrence Hochstetter had made certain she'd be rubbing elbows with him, a sitting target for the butt of his jokes.

Reaching the head of the table seemed to take forever. The formal dining salon easily sat thirty-four for a formal sit-down dinner. In a pinch, such as tonight, the dining table accommodated fifty diners, rubbing elbows but eating comfortably. As in the salon, the ceiling soared to a height of twenty feet, but here the dado was painted to resemble carved stone. It reached to waist height, and above it the walls were covered with murals of shepherds and shepherdesses, classical gnarled olive trees, and a cloudy pink sky with plump cherubs cavorting in midair. The rug underfoot was a richly patterned, palace-size Aubusson, and hanging from the ceiling above the sixteenth-century table were four fragile Venetian glass chandeliers bristling with lit beeswax tapers. The fifty matched chairs were genuine Louis XIV. The china was antique, floral

Meissen rimmed in gold, the crystal was Waterford, and the cutlery was heavy Georgian sterling.

Elizabeth-Anne couldn't help but show her surprise when she noticed Lester Lottoman seated beside Marisol in the least important seats near the foot of the table. He was staring at her in disbelief, but Marisol's face was far more expressive. The beautiful features registered pure envy.

"Ladies," Larry Hochstetter said loudly enough for the entire company to hear, "I trust we didn't rush you?"

"You needn't worry, Larry dear," Robyn assured him lightly. She leaned down, kissed his cheek, and took the seat on his right. "I'm dreadfully vain, I know. But then, so is Elizabeth-Anne." She glanced around the table. "At least *our* noses don't shine."

"Indeed they do not," he replied, "though ours smell food. Still, I can't imagine you worrying about anything cosmetic, Robyn. The lily needn't always be gilded."

"As far as I'm concerned, it can never take enough gilding," she retorted, and they all laughed politely.

Elizabeth-Anne found herself relaxing. So there would be no mention of her earlier hurried departure from the salon. Even her and Robyn's late arrival for dinner was excusable.

Larry Hochstetter signaled the majordomo, and then an army of waiters filed in with overloaded trays of food. Dinner began in earnest.

What followed was the longest dinner Elizabeth-Anne had ever sat through. It was also the most elegant and the most fascinating. Larry Hochstetter was in top form, a solicitous host and a marvelous raconteur, full of charm and humor. Robyn was the perfect foil for his wit, and the two of them got along famously.

But on and off, Elizabeth-Anne found herself feeling sorry for her new friend. Robyn was obviously in love with Larry, but just as clearly he did not love her, at least not in the intimate sense. Still, they seemed the best of friends, and both of them made an effort to draw Elizabeth-Anne into their conversation. Soon she was glad that she had stayed. She was quickly changing her opinion of her handsome host.

"Larry imported his chefs from Paris," Robyn confided as

the first course arrived, a cold lobster mousseline, served in small porcelain cups decorated with truffles. "No one in this country can hold a candle to them. Just wait until dessert."

"Why dessert?"

Robyn smiled secretively. "You'll see soon enough."

Elizabeth-Anne found the food not only superb in taste, but beautifully served and garnished. The main course consisted of roast rib of veal. On each tray was a string-bound rib roast for six, sitting in a lake of its own juices, each rib end sprouting a white paper ruffle. To either side of the roast was a border of scallop of mashed potatoes, executed with a pastry bag and then browned in the oven. These borders kept the veal juices from soaking into the vegetables all around; the inside of each scallop held peas, asparagus tips, and carrots.

But Robyn had been right; the dessert proved to be the pièce de résistance.

"Larry sent his dessert chef to Murano to learn the art of glass blowing," she said from across the table as the perfect spun-sugar apples, filled with apricot mousse, were set in front of each guest. Elizabeth-Anne stared at hers in amazement. The life-size apple had been blown so artfully it looked as though it were made not of sugar, but of delicate glass, and the apricot mousse inside it glowed richly. She hesitated to eat it, it looked so beautiful. But as soon as she had taken her first bite, her taste buds burst to vibrant, glorious life.

The two of them were seated in front of the fire in the upstairs study. The guests had long since departed, and the servants were cleaning up downstairs. Robyn had been the last one to leave. Now Elizabeth-Anne and Larry Hochstetter were alone.

"I must say you've chosen the most convoluted method of meeting me," he said. "Why didn't you just make an appointment and come by the office?"

"Because I wasn't sure about the minimum amount of investment capital your company would require. And besides . . ." Elizabeth-Anne permitted herself a smile. "I'm not interested in your office handling my affairs.'' Her aquamarine eyes went steely. "I want you to do it personally."

He took a sip of his cognac. "You've thought it all out carefully, haven't you?"

"Not really. I'm still very new at this. I just try to be cautious, that's all."

"And if I decide not to handle your affairs personally? Then what?"

She smoothed her gown over her knees. "I don't know," she said after a moment. She looked over at him. "There are others, I'm sure."

"There are." He nodded. "Investment bankers are a dime a dozen in this town. But they're not Hochstetter-Stremmel."

She inclined her head. "And I know that for a company like Hochstetter-Stremmel, thirty thousand dollars isn't a lot of money." Elizabeth-Anne paused. "But to me it is."

He grinned. "Don't let anyone try to tell you otherwise. It's a lot of money any way you look at it."

She glanced at him in surprise. He wasn't as conceited about business as he could be in his personal life. "Spoken like a true banker."

"Which I'm not," he pointed out. "I simply invest money for people. Based on educated guesses, economic forecasts, past performances of companies, and gut instinct."

"Do you think . . ." she began slowly. Then she laughed chidingly at herself. "I know it's an unfair question, but do you think I would be able to multiply my money enough eventually to buy a hotel?"

"Given the right investments and a good economic climate, I don't see why you couldn't. Once you've gotten a hundred thousand dollars together, we can start playing little games that can help speed up the process."

"Games?" She paused and frowned. "What kind of games?"

"Taking bigger risks. Buying on margin. Buying a hotel by getting a mortgage. That sort of thing. But what we have to do first is invest your money simply and cautiously. Money makes money. The first hundred thousand is always the hardest. The same goes for your first million."

"And it's relatively . . . safe?"

113

"Safe enough. But everything in life is risky. There is no such thing as a hundred-percent surefire bet. I'd be lying if I didn't tell you that."

"And if you were in my shoes? What would *you* do?"

He grinned. "Exactly what you're doing. That is, if I had the good sense to seek out someone like myself."

"Fair enough." She nodded. "I'll bring a cashier's check for thirty thousand to your office tomorrow."

"I'll go one better than that," he said, raising his glass. "I'll have my car pick you up and we'll have lunch. You can hand over the check and we'll celebrate."

She smiled. "You do have your own way of doing things, Mr. Hochstetter."

"Larry," he said with soft intensity. "If we're to enjoy a profitable business relationship, then you must call me Larry."

"Larry, then." She got to her feet. "Until tomorrow," she said, holding out her hand in a businesslike manner.

He shook it. "Until tomorrow. Bevin will see to it that Max drives you home." It was a long moment before he let go of her hand.

She went downstairs, humming to herself.

He went into the master bedroom suite, whistling softly.

Neither of them could know that in only three hundred and sixty-two days, on October 29, 1929, the worst stock-market crash in history would bring the world to its knees.

9

Elizabeth-Anne's gaze wandered past Larry Hochstetter to the windows and out onto the conical roofs and needle-spired tops of the buildings beyond.

Until she and Larry had begun having their biweekly luncheons here in the private dining room of Hochstetter-Stremmel, thirty-eight floors atop 70 Pine Street in the heart of the financial district, she had often enough glanced wonderingly at the banking temples of lower Manhattan. She had tried on countless occasions to imagine what it would be like to look out at the world from so high a vantage point, but imagination had failed her. Now she experienced the soaring elevation firsthand, and often, but it still had lost none of its magic. She felt she could reach out and touch the tops of the surrounding buildings with her fingertips, and she had learned to appreciate just why the crowns of these stone monoliths were so ornate. Not for the people on the ground, who couldn't see them anyway; no, they were meant to be appreciated from atop similar buildings. This lofty world was truly more than physically distant from the street far below and ordinary men. From up here, ships entering or leaving the harbor were tiny and insignificant, people were ants, and their problems were nonexistent. Only her own business interests were of importance.

For over ten months these luncheon meetings had been a tradition. They had missed only two or three in all that time.

She drew her gaze back to Larry and smiled across the table at him. If anyone had told her the night of the dinner at the Hochstetter mansion that her interests would mushroom the way they had in such a short period of time, she would have laughed aloud. But it was no laughing matter.

Larry pushed away his dessert plate and slid the report across the white tablecloth. With her hand she pulled it closer and turned it around to face her. It consisted of four pages. The first was the title page, and it was neatly typed and centered:

CONFIDENTIAL
Breakdown of Securities
and Investments
of
Elizabeth-Anne Hale
as of Oct. 28, 1929

She smiled to herself in anticipation as she turned to the first page. Then the smile froze on her face. For an instant she wasn't sure if she were seeing a typographical error. She glanced sharply across the table at Larry.

His expression was inscrutable.

She consulted the page again. The same figure seemed to jump off it. In less than a year her thirty-thousand-dollar investment had been parlayed into . . . was it possible? She didn't dare think so.

She gazed down at the figure numbly.

"One hundred and sixty-seven thousand, three hundred and forty-three dollars, and ninety-two cents," she murmured slowly.

No, she decided, there had to be a mistake.

She flipped the pages and ran her index finger along the rows of numbers breaking down the individual investments, dividends and, in one case, a stock that had split. There was also a new mining-company stock, Horseshoe Investments of North Dakota, which had struck a minor vein of ore a week previously.

Finally she let out a deep breath and closed the report. For a moment she couldn't trust herself to speak.

"I'm impressed," she said in a soft voice. "It's almost . . . *frightening*."

"If it seems to have grown a little faster than we anticipated," Larry explained, "it's only because you gave me carte blanche to do as I saw fit. Once in a while a little bird whispers a hot tip in my ear. Not that it happens often, mind you, but if it sounds good, and not too good to be true, then I follow my intuition. Still, it was ultimately your decision to stay out of everything and let me handle it the way I saw fit that made it possible."

She chuckled. "Well, I'm certainly glad I did."

"So am I."

"Larry . . ." she began tentatively. She glanced up and waited as Berty, the Hochstetter-Stremmel cook-butler, cleared away their plates. He was a pale ghost of a man, but he cooked like an angel. "It was delicious," she told him with a smile.

He bowed his head gravely. "Thank you, madam. Coffee?"

"Please."

He poured it from a silver pot on the sideboard and brought

the cups over to the table. The coffee was black and steaming, served in translucent English bone china.

Once Berty was gone, Elizabeth-Anne toyed with her cup. Her face was expressionless. "I feel a little guilty, Larry."

"Guilty?" He grinned suddenly. "Why on earth should you feel guilty? Because you've come by a little honest money?"

"You know better than that." She frowned again. "It's you, Larry."

"Your ever-faithful servant, ma'am." He bowed his head gallantly.

She was not amused. "It isn't fair," she argued. "The only reason my money has increased this much is that you've been giving my account your undivided attention. Far more than it warrants."

"Guilty, ma'am."

She steepled her fingers and rested them thoughtfully against her lips. Over the past ten months, she and Larry had grown very close. From the beginning there had been that intense physical attraction between them, but she had suppressed it, confused by her memories of Zaccheus. So, in his own fashion, Larry had doted upon her. Oh, the sparks hadn't stopped flying, but they had had to grow beyond that. They had gained a healthy respect for one another, until one day they realized the friendship they had built had blossomed into something more: he loved her, and she him.

It had been slow in coming, especially on her part, but once the realization dawned, it had hit her squarely, knocking her senseless. He had begun asking her up to the house for dinner, or out to restaurants and the theater. And for the first time since Zaccheus had left, she had invited a man into her own home, wondering how the girls would take to him. They all did, although they were uneasy at first. In fact, it had been Charlotte-Anne whose reaction had surprised her the most. On the one hand, Charlotte-Anne was delighted to make the acquaintance of a true society celebrity, rumored to be one of the five richest men in New York. On the other hand, when Larry left to go back home, she had turned to Elizabeth-Anne and snapped, "He's nice enough, Mama. I like him. But nobody can take Daddy's place. Not *ever*."

Elizabeth-Anne had looked at her in surprise. "Whoever said I wanted him to?"

Charlotte-Anne looked at her curiously. "It's plain to see, Mama. Whenever he's around, you flush and your whole face lights up. When you know you're going to see him, you sing to yourself all day. It's not that I mind your seeing him. I *like* him. But Daddy's still out there somewhere, I *know* he is. I don't think you should share yourself with anyone, at least not until we know for sure what's happened to Daddy."

"Darling, I'm not sharing anything with Larry. Like you said, he's a very nice man, clever and attractive. But you needn't worry." She smiled faintly. "I'd never do anything that might compromise the way I feel toward your father."

"Yes, Mama."

The evening after that, Larry took her to the theater, and then he and Elizabeth-Anne ate a late supper at the town house. The meal was light, the champagne was heady, and they both wanted to make love. For a long moment Elizabeth-Anne felt horribly torn. Then she'd pushed herself away from him and said huskily, "No, Larry. It isn't right. Not yet, at least. Not while Zaccheus is still alive somewhere."

He had acquiesced, and she'd left soon after. The tension between them became unbearable. They didn't see each other again until their next weekly lunch. At first they had both felt the strain, but then he'd asked her out again, and things had returned to normal. They never discussed their physical intimacy again. They never so much as kissed one another. Yet somehow their love for each other kept growing steadily, fueled, perhaps, by their frustrated physical desires.

She stared across the table at him now. He was gazing back at her in his usual quiet manner.

For a moment she felt very bad. She loved him, of that she was certain. And he loved her. Since he couldn't show her physically how he felt about her, he showed it to her in the next best way he knew how, obviously going out of his way tending to her investments. And all for . . . what? she asked herself. Not even a kiss?

Here she was, an adult in New York City, a woman of substantial means, with the rare opportunity to love a second time, and she was afraid to make love to the man she . . . loved? Desired?

No, she wasn't *afraid*, she corrected herself. Nor was it simply lust. She felt *guilty* about loving another man, that was all. Guilty because somewhere inside her she still loved Zaccheus, still loved all that he represented, even if she could no longer visualize him clearly. And guilty because she loved the children she had had with Zaccheus, the tangible, living product of the love they had shared. Whenever she felt doubts, she had only to look at the children.

But Zaccheus was gone, she reminded herself, and she couldn't let the children rule her life. It wasn't fair. Not to Larry and not to herself.

Now she took a deep breath and her voice trembled. "Larry . . ." she said softly. "Tonight . . ." She gazed across the table into that fathomless single midnight-blue eye of his, and it was like being sucked into an ever-deepening vortex. "Tonight . . . let's see each other tonight? I've waited so long. I don't know if . . ."

He regarded her sadly. He loved and respected her too much to force himself upon her. "Are you sure?" he asked softly. "Absolutely sure?"

She nodded. "I'm sure."

There was a sudden knock on the door, and a middle-aged, severely dressed woman stuck her head into the room. "Mr. Hochstetter," she said apologetically, "there's a call from a Mr. Wharton. He says it's extremely urgent. I can transfer the call in here."

"Please." He pushed back his chair, smiled at Elizabeth-Anne, and crossed the room. He picked up the extension phone and listened for a while. After speaking briefly, he slowly put the phone down, his lips puckered thoughtfully. Then he hurried back to the table, seized Elizabeth-Anne's financial report, and punched the intercom button.

"Miss Gordon, bring me the file of my own investments. Quick."

"What's happened?" Elizabeth-Anne asked. "Is something wrong?"

"Wrong? No, not at all. Someone's feeding us a red herring, and I can smell it. It stinks. That was my contact at Horseshoe Investments. The stock's starting to drop like crazy."

"But . . . why?" She stared at him. "I thought they just hit a new vein."

"Which petered out." He smiled grimly. "So they say."

"So we're going to sell?" she guessed.

"Yes and no. We're going to sell everything *except* Horseshoe, which we're going to buy up." He compressed his lips and nodded to himself, thinking aloud. "Something's up. Old Man Carruthers would never leak the word if a vein petered out, not unless he sold his shares quietly first. No, he's buying up even more stock. They must have struck the mother lode. My guess is Carruthers is trying to bring the stock prices down and then buy it all up cheap."

"And we're buying too?"

"We're going to try like hell to buy up every share before he gets his greedy little paws on them. We're liquidating everything in order to raise cash."

"And . . ." Elizabeth-Anne's voice trembled. "And if you're wrong?"

"Then, my dear Elizabeth-Anne," he said lightly, "we're up what's proverbially known as Shit's Creek." He grinned then, his face flushed with excitement. She had never seen him like this. Now she understood the pantherlike image he brought to mind.

"Now, off you go," he instructed her. "I'll see you tonight. Meanwhile, I've got a lot of trading to do. For you and for me. By five o'clock I want us both to own the majority interest in Horseshoe Investments."

At six o'clock that evening Larry called Elizabeth-Anne at home. She snatched up the phone.

"*Fait accompli*," he said. "Congratulations, Mrs. Hale. We are now both, for better or for worse, the majority stockholders in Horseshoe Investments."

"Should I be pleased, or is it too early to tell?" she asked cautiously.

"It's still a little early, but certain rumors I've heard sound good. Carruthers was waiting for the stock to go down to four dollars a share from eight-fifty. I beat him to it. I snatched up all the shares for four-fifty. I hear he's livid. Especially since he started the run with his own shares, and was waiting for everyone else to dump theirs."

"So he's out of the picture completely?"

"No, he's got a few shares left. Not many, just enough to become an irritant."

"So it looks good." It was a statement, not a question.

"I daresay it looks very good."

"And if . . ." She stopped herself just in time.

She heard his laughter echoing across the wire. "And if I turn out to be right, how much are you worth? That's what you wanted to know, isn't it?"

"Well, I mean, I couldn't help wondering, but . . ."

"If, and I repeat, *if* I am right, then you can count your blessings. You'll be worth . . ."

She held her breath.

Abruptly he changed the subject. "Get dressed up real nice and pretty. We're going to celebrate tonight."

She tightened her grip on the telephone. "Larry! That isn't fair. You started to say—now, out with it."

"No, it's not fair." He chuckled.

"That's better. Now tell me."

"All right. Just remember that it's a gamble. We won't really know for sure for a week or so."

"I . . . I'll keep that in mind," she promised in a shaky voice.

"Well, as of an hour ago, you *could* be worth over a million."

She sucked in her breath and stared at the telephone. "A . . . million," she gasped.

"Or more. Or nothing."

"I think," she said slowly, dazed by the prospect of losing or winning that kind of stake, "I think I feel like I'm going to faint."

"No you're not, darling. You're going to get all gussied up. Just for me."

"Yes, Larry."

As she hung up, she sighed softly to herself, her eyes sparkling. The prospect of being a millionairess no longer seemed important.

He had called her darling.

Pulled by a single white horse, the landau rolled slowly past the dark, whispering trees of Central Park. The hack in his top hat was perched on the raised driver's seat, and Larry and Elizabeth-Anne sat in the back, just forward of the furled black canvas canopy. All around, Manhattan had decked itself out in its most glittering, beguiling jewelry. The city surrounded them, a three-sided jewel box sparkling with a million lights. Overhead, the sky was a sea of dark velvet, the perfect backdrop for the thousands of diamond stars. They seemed so close that Elizabeth-Anne felt she could reach up and pluck a handful.

She snuggled further beneath the coarse lap blanket. "Would you believe I haven't been in a buggy since I left Texas? There we longed for cars. And here it's the reverse. It's a *treat* to ride in a buggy." She laughed softly.

He turned to her, his arm around her shoulders.

Her face became serious. "Thank you, Larry," she said softly.

"What? What did I do?"

"For understanding how difficult this is for me to . . . well, to do what we're going to do." She laughed nervously.

He placed a hand on her chin and turned her to face him. "Say it," he said softly. "There's nothing to be ashamed of. Love is beautiful. Put it into words."

She took a deep breath. "To make love, then." She smiled timidly. "Was that better?"

"Much." He hugged her close, and she could feel the warm strength of his arm, smell the faint pleasant manliness of him. She leaned her head back on his shoulder as she gazed up in wonder at the night sky. "What I really meant was, thank you for making it so easy for me. So romantic. First the candlelight dinner. Now the ride."

He tightened his grip and leaned down to kiss her. For a long moment he looked deeply into her moonlit eyes. The aquamarine irises were dilated in anticipation, a deeper, richer, more fathomless shade of clear blue than he had ever seen them. "My God, but you're beautiful," he marveled in a whisper, his lips brushing against hers, his breath warm and full of longing.

A surge of expectation rippled through her, bolts of electricity dancing from her head to her toes. He lowered his face and covered her mouth with his so that their lips were united, and their tongues tasted of each other's softness and warmth. She shut her eyes and reached up, pulling him down even closer. If anything could last forever, she prayed silently, let this be it.

"I think," he suggested quietly, whispering against the soft skin of her cheek, "it's time we headed home."

She opened her eyes then, and gazed up at him with such trusting tenderness that it was the only answer he needed.

His bedroom was on the second floor of the house, and the drapes were pulled tightly across the windows. The room was a haven, a serene private world of its own. As was the case downstairs, the walls had been painted by a master artist from Italy, and the muted trompe l'oeil architectural features—paneling, pilasters, and ceiling moldings—seemed real enough to touch. The bed was huge, replete with a rich green silk canopy and a headboard trimmed in elaborate gold appliqué which completed the heightened, sensuous feeling of *grand luxe*.

But Elizabeth-Anne was oblivious of her surroundings as Larry held her close.

"You have beautiful hair, my darling," he whispered softly, unpinning the braided coils at her ears. The freed hair fell loosely and he stroked it almost reverentially, letting it flow between his fingers like soft molten gold. "Beautiful," he murmured over and over.

She shook her head, loosening her hair completely. Then she felt him fingering the minuscule buttons at the back of her dress. "You have perfect shoulders, too," he whispered as he pulled the dress down around her breasts and planted a light kiss on each shoulder blade. "You don't know how I've dreamed of touching you like this."

Then he kissed her deeply on the lips, and she felt light-headed and lost. He moved behind her, suddenly as naked as she was, his powerful legs pushing against hers, his stiff, erect penis brushing the small of her back. He kissed the nape of her neck reverently, then turned her so he could cup her breasts in his hands, ever so gently kneading them while he kissed her deeply, as if trying to discover the wellspring of her femininity. She moaned, letting her head fall backward, her hair cascading free all around her, marveling in the exquisite sensations he brought her. "Love me," she murmured. "Love me now, Larry, now."

He showered little kisses on her ears, mere whispers of breath, then drove her to mad, excruciating ecstasy with the faintest circular whorls of his tongue. His lips moved downward, brushing against her breasts, flicking against her hard nipples, tempting her, teasing her, giving her but the faintest taste of what was to come. His tongue caressed her navel and then traced its way across the tauntly stretched sleek flesh of her abdomen. When at last he licked tentatively at her firm blond mound, she moaned aloud and gripped him fiercely by his muscular shoulders as she exploded, lost again and again in waves of shuddering pleasure. She felt so extravagantly exquisite, so sublimely rewarded, so clearly driven out of her mind that she wasn't altogether certain the world wasn't coming to an end.

Without warning he scooped her effortlessly into the air, one hand under her spine, the other supporting her bent knees, and carried her like a sacrificial offering to his huge canopied bed.

And then he lowered her gently into that sea of green and gold, so very gently that at first she wasn't even aware of his putting her down. For a moment he could only stare at her lying there, her golden hair fanning out in all directions.

When he climbed carefully on top of her, she was transfixed by the sight of his well-proportioned body, each contour heightened in definition by the shadows cast by the dim lamps. He knelt silently over her, his head bowed. She felt his moist thumbs stroking her nipples, and she arched her back in an instinctual feline motion, her sinuously curved torso lifting clear off the bed, her long white throat exposed, her lips half-open, the rows of teeth perfect and smooth. Flesh touched flesh, and his tongue wrought a trail of sweet anguish from her navel up to the cleft of her bosom, around her ear and neck. He burrowed, moaning, into the smooth pit of her arm, and then moved his lips again to her mound, cleverly playing among the spirals of her hair. She clutched him urgently, but he forced her arms to her sides. "Later," he whispered. "Just lie still now."

She nodded and swallowed. It was a torturous game. After a few minutes she could no longer stand it, and she grasped him fiercely, her mouth emitting gasps and eloquent little screams of pleasure. He fell forward in a lunge, grabbed her up, and kissed her deeply. She could feel his penis growing ever more erect, and for a moment she panicked, suddenly fearful of completing the act.

He seemed to sense her hesitation and pressed himself to her, entering her in one sure, powerful stroke. She closed her eyes, raising her pelvis instinctively to meet him as the pure warm thought filled her mind: *Yes, this is right. This is perfect.*

They lay utterly still for a long time, savoring the fullness of the moment they had waited so long for. And then he thrust again slowly, a long, sure caress that he repeated again and again until each stroke seemed to pull out of her a deeper well of ecstasy and he was plunging into her over and over with raw passion. She cried out, gripping him tightly with her thighs and arms, clinging to every surging, bucking movement he made, and then suddenly he moaned deeply and was filling her and she felt her own body tremble and explode. He shuddered and collapsed, burying his face in the soft ambrosial comfort of her breasts.

His breath was coming in gasps, each lungful of air he exhaled a cool whisper against her burning flesh. She couldn't speak for a long time, and they lay still, not needing more than each other's body.

Finally he asked, "Can you stay the night?" His voice was muffled.

"I wish I could." She traced her finger along the ridge of his backbone. "But I can't. You know that. The girls . . . I *am* supposed to set a good example for them, and a good mother doesn't stay out all night."

He laughed, then shifted around to face her, his head leaning on his elbow. "In that case," he said soberly, "it's time for round two."

She gazed at his phallus. Remarkably, it was erect again. She grinned. "Insatiable bastard."

When she got home it was already past two o'clock in the morning. She slipped quietly up the stairs and managed to let herself in without making a sound. She locked the front door, then tiptoed into the living room. There, she stopped in her tracks. The girls were seated on the chaise, wide-awake but avoiding her gaze. Their faces were red. Clearly they had been crying.

A dark shadow of shame and self-revulsion swept through Elizabeth-Anne. She was overcome with guilt as she stared slowly from one to the other. Then she dropped her gaze. The pain of seeing them so hurt tugged excruciatingly at her heart.

So they have somehow guessed what I've been up to, she thought. They know that I've cheated on my husband, on their father. I should have known better. I should have, but the temptation was too strong. I've failed them as a mother.

God forgive me, she prayed silently.

"Girls . . ." she whispered hoarsely.

Charlotte-Anne and Regina pushed their sister to her feet. As always, it was Rebecca who was made to speak up for the others.

With trembling hands Rebecca held out two sheets of paper. It was a letter. "I . . . I think you'd better sit down, Mama," she said, handing it to her and bursting into tears.

Elizabeth-Anne stared down at the two sheets of paper, at her husband's small, familiar script. She couldn't believe that suddenly, after so long with no word, she now held a letter in her hand. And tonight of all nights. But then, before her guilt could blossom further, she began to read—and the pain of the words seared her very heart and soul.

My dearest wife and beloved children,

I know this letter coming out of the blue will be a shock. After so long without word, it grieves me more than I can say that this is all I have to send you. Because by the time you receive this, it will all, thank God, be over. It's best this way. You must trust me and believe that with all your heart.

I'm writing from Texas, but I have not returned here as a free man. I am writing from my prison cell. The past has finally caught up with me, and I'm through running at long last. Please understand when I say I'm relieved, almost grateful, that the running is over. It gave me nothing, because it kept me from you.

I have been sentenced to death. I know those words will be hard to read, but please understand how *grateful* I am. I'll be free of the past at long, long last. The warden is a good man, and he promised to keep this letter and not mail it until the sentence is carried out. I asked him to hold onto it because I'm afraid that otherwise you would come here, and if there is one last request I have, it is to shelter you from that painful good-bye. That is my last wish, and probably one of the only things I can do anything about anymore. Please forgive me for my long silence. This letter is not intended to distress you. Please receive it in the spirit in which it is written. I love you, my dear wife. All these years of hiding and running— I've loved you throughout them. That love was what kept me going, and that love is what makes this ignoble end for me somehow noble. You and our children—that is all that matters. That is all that has ever mattered.

Darling, you are young and beautiful, and the young, they say, are resilient. Be so, for my sake. Don't let it all have been in vain. Now that you know my fate, look at it through *my* eyes if you can. At least now we'll both be free. The past is behind us. I can stop running and hiding, and you can build a new life for yourself. A new and *better* life. Don't shut yourself away. You have so much love and happiness and laughter to give, and my one hope is that you can rebuild your life with a man more deserving of your love than I. Whatever you do, don't mourn for me. Don't shed tears. I know you've done all that these past few years. If my conscience would permit it, I would not write this letter at all, to save you from more grief, but you *must* know what is happening so that you can at last be free. Free to choose your life and loves. Free to start over. Do that, darling, for me. Otherwise my death will have been for nothing, and I can't bear to think of it that way.

Remember one thing, and one thing alone. I am not sad. How could a man be sad when he leaves the one thing behind which matters most—a wonderful family? That is my legacy, and that is what gives me peace and the courage to face these last hours.

What more could a man ask for?

My love always,
Your husband and father,
Z.

Elizabeth-Anne's face was like ash.

Her life, everything she had ever lived for and loved, seemed to melt to ruins before her eyes.

Zaccheus—her husband. Her falsely accused husband, the father of her children. Zaccheus—dead.

Could it be possible? Could a man be executed for a crime he hadn't committed? Was his life really over? The last time she had seen him, he had been so alive, so full of vibrant warmth. Was this cold paper really the last she would ever have of him?

The room seemed to reel around her, the children's tear-streaked faces revolving faster and faster, until everything was a featureless blur, until everything was black. Blessedly, she passed out.

It was past midnight, the morning of Friday, October 29,

1929. In just a few hours the stock market would crash and the Great Depression would begin.

All America would grieve, but it was a reality Elizabeth-Anne would be unaware of for a very long time. Because her own grief was too all-consuming. Losing money was one thing. Losing a loved one in the flash of a sudden bolt of lightning was another thing entirely.

10

The world had turned mad. Her life had exploded, and everything was suddenly crazily off kilter.

Like a mortally wounded animal, Elizabeth-Anne crawled into her nest and ceased to function. She lay dazed on her chaise longue, half-dressed, and covered with a cashmere blanket, refusing to get up except to drag herself to the bathroom. It was as though she were sick. And she was. She was sicker than she had ever been in her life, only it was not a malady for which a doctor could prescribe medication. It was an illness of the spirit. Zaccheus had died, and something within her had died along with him. From the moment she had read the letter, the world stopped spinning and ground to a halt. Seconds, minutes, even hours and days were no more.

She withdrew completely, not even able to communicate with the children. They locked themselves in their room, as miserable and mournful as she. But they at least could still shed tears. In her, the pain festered and rankled her soul. The pain manifested itself physically, and was so all-pervasive that even little Zaccheus, who was too young to comprehend what had happened, realized instinctively that something was terribly wrong and that Mama wasn't herself at all. He became just as quiet and withdrawn as Elizabeth-Anne, but with one pitiable difference. He was frightened.

Two days and a night passed. The pain which consumed

the girls had not decreased, but at least they managed to function in a zombielike state which could pass as the first step, however trifling, of the many which they would have to go through in order to fully cope with, and accept, the tragedy that had engulfed them.

Elizabeth-Anne, however, was catatonic, not in the true medical sense of the word, but she was in so deep a state of shock that she no longer cared about anything. She could come to no decisions, nor feel any lessening of the brutal pain which stabbed her so deeply. She was aware of what was going on around her, but it was all unfolding as if in a dream. She knew that the children needed her now more than ever in their lives, but for the first time she was incapable of coping. Her own pain was too unbearable. All she had been able to do was erect an invisible wall between herself and the world that no one seemed able to penetrate. The past days had eaten up her entire resources of strength. There were simply no more reserves she could fall back upon.

When another three days had passed, the resilience of the young began to manifest itself more visibly. The girls were still brokenhearted and given to periodic outbursts of tears, but at least they had begun to function a little less by rote. Regina cooked for them, and all the girls took turns attempting to force food on their mother. But Elizabeth-Anne would only stare at it blankly. She didn't touch a bite.

The sisters gazed at one another in worry.

Five days, and their mother was wasting away.

Ludmila was alarmed.

She couldn't recall a day going by without her and Elizabeth-Anne paying each other a visit, and for days she hadn't seen hide or hair of the Hales. She knew that they were at home because she had heard them moving about in their apartment. She had been tempted to go upstairs on countless occasions, but something had held her back. Intuitively she sensed that Elizabeth-Anne and the children wanted to be left alone. Whatever the reason for their sudden need to shut themselves away, she was certain that it was a private matter, but it hurt her feelings that they did not share their heartaches with her. Still, she respected their need for privacy.

But when day after day passed and she still did not hear from Elizabeth-Anne, and the stairs did not tremble with the sound of the girls traipsing off to school in the mornings, her soft old face went tight with worry. Anxiously she began pacing her cluttered apartment.

This was totally unlike the Hales, she told herself. So out of character. Whatever could have happened?

Then a terrible thought flashed through her mind. Today was Saturday, the second of the month, and Elizabeth-Anne's rent was due. Elizabeth-Anne had never been late in paying it. What if . . . what if she had lost all her money in that horrible stock-market crash? Slowly Ludmila sank down onto the siege, lost deep in thought. Hadn't she, Ludmila Romaschkova, been instrumental in suggesting to Elizabeth-Anne that money could be invested? Hadn't she paved the way for her to seek out an investments counselor in the first place? And what if her well-intentioned but ill-timed advice had caused her friend's entire nest egg to be wiped out?

Ludmila's head spun dizzily and she shut her eyes. Who could have foreseen the future? Who could have guessed that such a disaster might descend upon the country and wipe out so many fortunes in one fell swoop? If her worst fears were confirmed and Elizabeth-Anne now found herself penniless, then Ludmila felt she was at least partially to blame. She would have to make it up to her friend somehow.

She nodded to herself. Elizabeth-Anne was proud. Perhaps the reason she was holed up was that she could not pay the rent on time.

She might even have lost every penny she had.

Or perhaps she was so shattered by the loss that she could not bear to face it—or the woman who had suggested she invest her money.

Or worse, she could be contemplating suicide.

Every day the papers were full of reports that dozens of people who had lost their fortunes or life savings had leapt to their deaths, had shot themselves, gassed themselves, slit their wrists.

The thought of it filled Ludmila with icy terror. She sprang to her feet, no longer able to just sit and wait. She knew something was terribly wrong upstairs. Elizabeth-Anne, the girls, and little Zaccheus were more to her than mere tenants; they had all become fast friends. They were *family*.

She was going to go upstairs at once to find out what had happened.

A t first she had rapped softly on the door. She had heard movement inside the apartment, and the muffled voice of one of the girls. Rebecca, she guessed, though it was hard to tell. When no one came to the door, she had knocked harder. And then harder. Finally she pounded on the door with her shoe.

Pausing to take a deep breath, she heard a creaking of the floorboards. She could see a shadow darkening the crack of dim light under the door and sensed rather than saw someone peering out at her through the tiny peephole.

"It's me, Ludmila," she called in what she hoped sounded like a cheerful voice.

The floorboards creaked some more, and she heard whispers. Finally the door opened as far as the safety chain allowed. Rebecca's huge eyes peered out at her.

"Rebecca, thank God you are all right . . ." Ludmila's voice trailed off and her face creased with a frown. Rebecca usually projected a lively, radiant quality. Now her eyes were dull and lifeless.

" 'Lo, Aunt Luddie," she murmured quietly.

"Hello, Rebecca," Ludmila said, cocking a curious eyebrow. "How nice to see you. May I come in? I want to talk with your mother."

"She doesn't want to see anyone." Rebecca started to shut the door.

"Wait." Swiftly Ludmila wedged her foot between the door and the doorframe. Drawing herself up as imperiously as her four feet, three inches would allow, she used her most commanding tone of voice. "I demand you open door immediately."

Rebecca hesitated. Her sisters might not have listened, but

she was just young enough to obey an adult's command. She nodded morosely, waited for Ludmila to remove her foot, and closed the door. Then she unhooked the chain and let Ludmila in. The tiny Russian dashed over the threshold calling, "Elizabeth-Anne! Elizabeth-Anne!"

As she hurried into the dim gloom of the living room, Ludmila felt something give under her feet. There was a splintering crack and she looked down at the floor, then wrinkled her nose in disgust. She had stepped on a dinner plate crusty with leftovers. She frowned to herself and gazed around the usually perfect room in disbelief. The curtains were drawn and the air was stale. Clothes were strewn all over the floor. Dirty dishes and smudged glasses were piled up on the tables. This was very unlike Elizabeth-Anne, to whom cleanliness was next to godliness.

Then she spied her friend lying in the deathlike silence on the chaise. She drew in her breath sharply. Elizabeth-Anne was staring right at her, but Ludmila realized that the aquamarine eyes were unfocused. They seemed to gaze right through her. With a shock she noticed how haggard Elizabeth-Anne looked.

She approached the chaise and took a seat on its edge. "Are you sick?" she asked softly. When Elizabeth-Anne did not reply, she placed a hand on her forehead. "No, there is no fever." Slowly she withdrew her hand and stared down at her friend.

Elizabeth-Anne let her head loll sideways, staring vacantly away from her.

Ludmila leaned closer to her. "I be right back," she said softly, patting Elizabeth-Anne's shoulder. "Do not worry. I call doctor."

For the first time Elizabeth-Anne seemed to show signs of life. "No," she whispered hoarsely. "Don't call a doctor."

Ludmila glanced up as Rebecca scuffed slowly toward her. The sight of the child tugged at her heart. She shook Elizabeth-Anne gently. "What is it?" she cried urgently. "Is it because of money? Did you lose money because the banks have failed, the stock market crashed?"

Elizabeth-Anne's eyes dropped shut. "Please," she begged in a whisper. "Leave me alone. That's all I ask."

"*No*. We are friends. Or do you forget?" Ludmila reminded her. "If something is wrong, then I have right to help."

"No one can help," Elizabeth-Anne sighed. "Not even God. Not anymore."

Ludmila glanced sharply at Rebecca. The girl nodded her head solemnly.

"In God's name," she demanded, "what happened here?"

Rebecca shrugged wordlessly and drifted away, joining Regina and Charlotte-Anne, who were standing in the bedroom doorway. They all gazed at Ludmila with much the same empty expression that was still on Elizabeth-Anne's face. What on earth and in heaven could have happened to bring on such moroseness? Ludmila wondered.

Suddenly little Zaccheus pushed his sisters aside and came running out of the bedroom. He threw himself at Ludmila and buried his face in her lap. He began sobbing noisily.

Ludmila stroked his head with one hand, and with the other she sought Elizabeth-Anne's hands. Touching them, she sucked in her breath. They were cold as ice, lifeless. She realized she might never discover why Elizabeth-Anne and the children were all so miserably dejected. Well, in the end, it was none of her business. If Elizabeth-Anne ever decided to tell her, then fine. If not, then that was fine, too. Meanwhile, there were more important matters at hand. Somehow she had to pull Elizabeth-Anne and the children out of their despondency. She had to get their minds off what was bothering them.

Ludmila was no stranger to crises. She had gone through enough of them herself to know just how to deal with them. In this case, action was called for.

She rose abruptly to her feet, marched over to the window, and yanked aside the curtains. Glorious sunlight came streaming in. She pushed the window as far open as it would go. The sudden gust of air felt deliciously refreshing.

Ludmila turned to the girls and clapped her hands. "Now," she proclaimed in a voice which discouraged any talking back, "we will all clean house. It is disgusting mess. You,

Regina, get broom. Charlotte-Anne, you get mop. Rebecca, help me tidy.''

The girls stared at one another, and a signal seemed to pass among them. Slowly, albeit reluctantly, they obeyed.

Ludmila hurried downstairs, dug through her dresser for her oldest, most worn Hermès scarf, and tied it around her head. For several hours she worked alongside the girls, scrubbing, polishing, and dusting. It was good therapy; the girls even began talking to each other in low voices. Their conversation was far from cheerful, but it was a beginning.

''I'm hungry,'' Zaccheus finally complained.

Ludmila stopped washing a window and frowned. She had been too preoccupied to realize that she was hungry too. Now that she thought about it, her stomach began rumbling.

''I go cook,'' she declared. She put down her rag, went downstairs, and came back with an alarmingly small amount of groceries. While the girls continued to clean, she set to work in the kitchen. Just before she was ready to serve the food, there were a series of urgent knocks on the door.

''Answer it, somebody,'' she called over her shoulder. ''I'm in kitchen, cooking.'' She dipped a spoon into the hot oatmeal, lifted it to her nose, and sniffed it critically. To her, it smelled wonderful. It wasn't simply run-of-the-mill oatmeal; it was an expensive Irish oatmeal, much coarser than the regular kind, and she considered it a rare treat. She neither noticed the girls' faces nor heard their groans when they had come in to see what she was preparing.

There were more knocks on the door, this time louder, more insistent.

With a dark face, Ludmila marched out into the hall and flung open the door. ''Oh, is you,'' she growled.

Larry Hochstetter looked down at her in surprise. He couldn't contain his laughter. Ludmila looked thoroughly ridiculous in her ancient brocade dress, the fringed shawl draped around her shoulders, the malachite Fabergé egg hanging around her neck, and the old scarf knotted around her head. She looked for all the world like a cross between a miniature empress and the most lowly scullery maid.

''Well?'' she hissed. ''You think something is funny?''

He tried to wipe the smile off his face. "No, not at all." He swallowed with difficulty.

"And don't just stand there like idiot. Come in."

"Greetings and salutations, madam," he said with a flourish of his hat and a wink. "There's nothing like a warm welcome, especially from a beautiful woman."

She waved the spoon threateningly. "You better watch your tongue, young man." She squinted dangerously up at him. "It took you long enough to come and visit."

"I called a hundred times, but no one would answer the telephone. I took it to mean no one was at home." He frowned, sniffed the air, and wrinkled his nose. "What on earth is that ghastly smell?"

Ludmila drew herself up to her full height. "That smell, *monsieur*," she said acidly, "is my cooking. You don't like it, you don't eat it."

"I stand corrected. It is my mistake. In fact, it must be that smell emanating from downstairs that I thought I smelled here. But *this* smell." He made a production of sniffing. "This smell is delicious. Truly." He grinned at her.

Her face softened. "What took you so long?" she whispered conspiratorially. "It has been five hours since I called you."

"The meeting took forever," he explained. "I didn't get out of the bank until fifteen minutes ago."

"I only hope you can do something. No one will tell me what happened, but they act as if the end of the world has come."

He handed her his coat and hat and took a thick envelope out of his breast pocket. Waving it excitedly, he said, "This, if anything, will get her up. You'll see."

Ludmila regarded him dubiously. "I hope so. She just lies there and says nothing."

She watched him go into the parlor. The moment he caught sight of Elizabeth-Anne lying on the chaise, he froze. But Ludmila smiled encouragingly and gestured him to go closer. She noticed that his face had undergone a rapid transformation. Gone was the teasing good humor, replaced by extreme concern.

"Elizabeth-Anne," he said, his voice thick with concern as he approached the chaise. "Darling, what *is* it?"

She stared up at him. No, she wasn't staring *at* him, he realized with a pang. She was staring *through* him.

"What's the matter, my love?" he asked softly. He brushed his fingers across her cheek. "What is it? Are you ill?"

Her lips moved faintly, and he had to lean close to catch the words she mumbled. "At least you aren't dead too. At least you're alive," she whispered through cracked, parched lips. Then she shut her eyes in relief.

He placed an index finger on her lips and felt them. They were dry and split. "Jesus, you're dehydrated." He turned around. "Get me some water, somebody," he called out. "And stir plenty of sugar into it."

"Not thirsty," Elizabeth-Anne mumbled thickly.

"Yes, you are. You'll drink what I give you."

"Leave me alone," she pleaded. "Nobody wants to leave me alone."

"First you'll drink, then I'll leave you alone. Is that a deal?"

She nodded wearily. Charlotte-Anne brought over a cup of water. He took it from her, placed a hand behind Elizabeth-Anne's head, and made her sit forward. He put the rim of the cup against her lips. "Drink."

Like a child, a very sick child with no fight left, she obeyed. After she'd drained the cup, he gently lowered her head. Then he got up and gestured for the girls to follow him into the kitchen.

"Something's got to have happened," he whispered angrily. "I've never seen anyone in such . . ." His eye caught the murky, bubbling oatmeal. "You're going to eat *this*?" he asked incredulously.

"And what," demanded Ludmila from the doorway, "is that supposed to mean?"

"You all stay here. I want to talk to you, but I've got a call to make first." He marched back into the living room and called his town house.

Bevin, the imperturbable butler, answered the phone on the

second ring. Larry told him to connect him with the kitchen. A moment later the head chef came on the line.

"Marcel? Mr. Hochstetter here. How fast can you prepare a feast? An hour? No, it's got to be a lot quicker than that. I'll give you twenty minutes. Make sure it's hot and meaty. Plenty of fruit and vegetables. And something sweet. Pack it in picnic hampers. I'll send Max up with the car to fetch it. Have someone drive back down with him."

Ludmila folded her arms and watched Larry from the kitchen. Her gray eyes held an expression of quiet respect. Ah, she thought dreamily, this was like the old days in Russia. This was like something her Fedor, God rest his soul, would have done.

Larry went downstairs to speak to his chauffeur. When he came back upstairs, he joined Ludmila and the girls in the kitchen. "Well?" he demanded. "Anyone care to tell me what happened to throw your mother into such a depression?"

The girls avoided his gaze.

"I'm waiting."

Rebecca swallowed. "We . . . we can't tell you," she said in a shaky voice. "It was too awful! Too awful!" Suddenly she burst into tears and ran to Ludmila, who coiled her arms around her.

He sighed. "As you wish. Just remember, if you want to talk to somebody, I'm available at any time. All right?"

Regina and Charlotte-Anne nodded wordlessly.

He went back into the living room and sat on the edge of the chaise. "Elizabeth-Anne?"

"You promised you'd leave me alone," she mumbled.

"I need your signature on something."

She nodded. "Okay."

He slid the papers out of the envelope, unfolded them, and handed her a pen. "Here." He pointed. "You have to sign here."

She didn't protest or even ask what the document was. She signed her name sloppily and held out the pen. "Here. Now, please . . ." she begged. "You've gotten what you've come for."

He flipped through the pages. "You have to initial each page, too."

She listlessly did as she was told.

"And once more here, where it's been changed."

He folded the papers and laid them down beside her. "You haven't even asked about the investments."

"No."

"In fact, if memory serves me right, I haven't talked to you at all since before the crash. Don't you want to know where you stand financially?"

She shook her head morosely. She didn't care.

His voice grew excited. "Elizabeth-Anne, listen to me. Our gamble paid off. The mine's struck a mother lode. Much more than I ever dared hope for! By sheer coincidence, we sold all our portfolios a few days before they were worthless. But the mine's going strong, crash or no. You're probably worth millions. *Millions.*" He frowned at her. "Did you hear what I said?"

"Millions." She turned her head sideways on the pillow and stared out into space.

He shook her gently but firmly. "Did a word of what I just said sink in?"

"Something about millions. You lost millions."

He rolled his eye in exasperation and shook her more roughly, as though he were trying to shake some sense into her. "Would you listen to me, goddammit? *Neither* of us lost a *dime*. We're worth more than ever."

She frowned. "I don't understand."

"Horseshoe Investments. Does that ring a bell?"

She shrugged. "So it's gone. It doesn't matter anyway."

"But it's *not* gone." He laughed. "You're a genuine twenty-four-karat millionairess."

"What good is having money if the banks have shut their doors?"

He laughed again. "Banks! Who cares about banks? It's *gold* we're talking about. Beautiful, yellow, rich-as-Croesus gold! At first I was afraid that vein was just a stringer. You know, a few inches thick and not too long? But it isn't. We're yielding forty-eight ounces of pure gold a ton."

"What?" Her forehead creased with a new expression. Realization was slow in coming, but it was dawning nevertheless.

"Hold out your hands, darling. I've something to give you."

She did so and he said, "Look here." He reached into his pocket, took out a handful of what looked like rough pebbles, and dropped them into her hands like so much loose change. "There's a lot more where these came from."

She clenched her fingers and brought her fists up to her face. Slowly she unclenched them, then sucked in her breath. Glittering in the palms of her hands was gold, rough, beautiful, glittering gold nuggets. She stared at them, mesmerized by the sight of that rich yellow as mankind has been mesmerized by it for thousands of years.

"You mean . . ." Her voice faltered. It was almost more than she could comprehend. "We really haven't lost everything?"

"Lost it? Hell, no! We're probably the only two people in the entire country who're way ahead of the game."

"But . . . how could that be?"

"You trusted me and I gambled. And we won."

Her face suddenly seemed to lose its drawn slackness, as thoughts spun crazily in her head. Zaccheus was gone forever; he had been cruelly snatched from this earth and there was nothing she or anyone else could do about it.

But Larry was alive. Not only alive, but with her, here and now. And thanks to him, her fortune wasn't lost. If he was right, she was rich. Rich enough to fulfill her dreams. Could that be? Could the fates have decided that tearing Zaccheus away from her and the children was enough cruelty for the moment?

"Now, look at the papers you signed, darling," Larry said softly, a mysterious smile hovering on his lips. "Look what you just bought yourself for a thousand dollars down." His one eye sparkled with excitement.

"But . . . if money is so scarce, why spend it? Shouldn't I hang onto it?"

"No, you shouldn't, because all over the city and clear across the country, property is going begging. It's a buyer's market. People are wiped out financially. They can't meet their mortgage payments. The banks are repossessing left and right, and they're trying to cut their losses. Of course, you'll have to pay off the remaining twenty-three-thousand-dollar mortgage, but you got yourself a bargain, young lady.''

"Twenty-three thousand dollars! But . . .'' Her mouth hung wide.

"You can afford it, believe me. For you it's a drop in the bucket. What we'll do is this. Every two weeks, you'll buy another piece of property.''

She shook her head in disbelief. This couldn't be happening. It was all too much, too fast. She was dreaming. Perhaps Zaccheus' execution had been a nightmare, and her mind was forcing a more pleasant dream to take its place.

"What did I buy for twenty-four thousand dollars?'' she asked softly.

"Well, read it.'' He thrust the documents she had just signed under her nose, rattling them. "*Read* it, for God's sake.'' He dropped them into her lap.

She stared down at the pages. Slowly she began to read. As recognition dawned, she read faster and faster until she was tearing breathlessly through the pages. Finally she sat back and stared at him with a stunned expression. Her breathing was coming in rapid gasps, and her rib cage was pounding uncontrollably. "The . . . the *Madison Squire Hotel*?''

He nodded.

"It's mine? It's true?''

"As the children say, 'Cross my heart, hope to die, stick a—''

"No, we won't! Enough has been stuck in one of your eyes to last you a lifetime.''

He smiled faintly. "I'll concede it was a poor choice of a ditty.''

"But . . . *Larry*.'' She sat up straight, half in excitement, half in newfound anguish. "But we *can't*. We can't just walk in and . . . and take advantage of people's misery. It's *stealing*.''

"No, it's not. What you're actually doing is bailing people out of bad trouble. If they can't meet their payments and the banks repossess, they're bankrupt. They lose it all anyway, but legally they still owe the rest of the mortgage. Don't you see? You're *helping* people. And at the same time, you're helping yourself."

She was unable to speak.

"And this is just the beginning," he cried exultantly. "You'll see. You wanted a hotel, right?"

She nodded.

"Well, you've got it. But you're going to get a lot more. This is just the beginning. Apartment houses, hotels . . . you'll buy a string of them. All for pennies on the dollar. Never in my life have I known a riper time to buy property. The economy will change, you'll see. And you'll own a *chain* of hotels stretching clear from coast to coast."

"It's frightening," she said in a tiny voice.

"Is it? Or is being poor even more frightening?"

She nodded.

His eye gleamed. "And with the gold coming in steadily every day—just think of it, darling. You'll clean up. Your dream has come true. Not once, but a thousand times over."

But she couldn't think of it in those heady terms. Not yet. At the moment, she could think of only one hotel at a time. Even that was difficult.

She stared down at the legal documents. "It's mine?" she whispered in disbelief. "The Madison Squire is really mine?"

"All yours. Lock, stock, and barrel. One hundred percent yours."

"Oh, Larry." And, finally, she began to cry. She lunged forward and flung her arms around him. "I . . . I don't know what to say. Just when my whole world was collapsing all around me . . ." She looked up, startled. "Who could that be?"

"That," said Ludmila, hurrying across the room, "is door." She went to open it. Elizabeth-Anne craned her neck. One of Larry's uniformed servants was standing with two huge wicker hampers shaped like large suitcases. She stared at the servant, then turned speechlessly to Larry.

"That happens to be food," he said. "You'll need your strength, darling. You don't look like you've eaten in days."

Tears were rolling down her cheeks.

The servant looked around, quickly moved some chairs out of the way, and spread a blanket out on the living-room floor. When he opened the hampers, Elizabeth-Anne couldn't believe her eyes. They had been custom-made and compactly held fine bone china, heavy sterling cutlery, hand-cut stemware, and artfully folded white linen napkins. In amazed silence Elizabeth-Anne and the girls watched the man deftly arranging the place settings. He opened bottles of champagne, and then out came the food: paper-thin slices of smoked salmon with rows of lemon slices and parsley, ice-cold dishes of Beluga Mollasol caviar, toast and water wafers and pumpernickel, deviled eggs and steak tartare, tiny cornichons, several cold roast chickens, piles of rare pink roast beef, pickled vegetables, velvety peaches and ripe bananas, and wonderfully glazed petits fours and a creamy Sacher torte.

Elizabeth-Anne realized she was ravenous.

"Once we finish our little picnic," Larry said, "we'll head uptown to inspect the hotel. Tell you what: as owner's prerogative, why don't you and the children move into the royal suite and live there? I was there once for a party for a European duchess, and if memory serves me right, it's an enormous penthouse duplex. It even has a kitchen, although I think you'll be too busy to cook. You'll probably use room service or the dining room mostly. But best of all, it's got a wraparound terrace, planted with trees and shrubs."

"The royal suite? Us?" She stared at him. "Could we? I mean . . . *really*?"

He laughed. "Can't you get it through that thick skull of yours? It's *yours*, darling. You own it."

"B-but I can't be seen . . ." She sputtered as vanity took hold of her. She grabbed handfuls of her hair and pulled her fingers through it. "I need to wash my hair, bathe, and get ready. I can't go anywhere like this. Charlotte-Anne, run a bath for me. Regina, sweet, fetch my beige shoes—"

"Whoa! Not so fast," Larry laughed. "There's time for all that. Let's eat something first, shall we?"

She laughed suddenly. "I think I'm going to cry."

He stroked the tears from her cheeks with his fingers. "You *are* crying, darling."

"Oh, Larry, I'm so happy. You've saved my life."

"Well, I wouldn't put it quite like that."

"I would." She nodded solemnly. "You did."

"Then you owe me a favor. I want to come along and see the hotel. Is it a deal?"

"See it?" She jumped up. "You'll see it, all right, Larry Hochstetter! You'll see it till you're sick of it, if I've got anything to say about it."

The excitement was infectious. Suddenly, miraculously, the girls and even little Zaccheus joined in, all of them talking animatedly and laughing and crying. Magically enough, in the midst of their greatest tragedy, they had all come to life.

And so had Hale Hotels.

11

This time when they pulled up outside the Madison Squire, they were received quite differently. The Rolls-Royce worked wonders. The moment the huge car approached, the doorman and porter came running. They fell all over themselves to be helpful, even before the seven passengers had piled out of the car.

"Good afternoon, madam. Good afternoon, sir," they chorused solemnly.

Larry ignored them, Ludmila sniffed, and Elizabeth-Anne smiled graciously. The four children stared up at the huge building with wide, excited eyes.

"The luggage, please," the porter said to Max.

The big chauffeur stood with crossed arms and shook his head wordlessly. The porter retreated hastily, and the doorman made a beeline for the giant brass-and-glass doors. He unlocked a side door and held it wide for them, his eyes focused straight ahead.

Inside the lobby, the same self-important Mr. Smythe stood

sentinel behind the reception desk. This time, there was nothing disdainful about his attitude; he clearly did not recognize them.

"Good afternoon, mesdames," he greeted them. "Good afternoon, sir." He favored Ludmila, Elizabeth-Anne, and Larry with a tight, nervous smile, and didn't as much as blink a disapproving eyelash as little Zaccheus let out a whoop and tore across the lobby. He raised his eyebrows inquiringly. "Do you have reservations?"

Elizabeth-Anne smiled faintly. "No, Mr. Smythe, we do not."

For a moment he looked faintly surprised that she knew his name. Then he smiled self-importantly and adjusted his tie with the lacquered fingertips of one hand. "Of course, reservations are not really necessary," he conceded.

"I didn't think so," she said pleasantly. "You'll have someone show us up to the royal suite?"

She couldn't help but feel a faint triumph at how that *really* threw him. "Of . . . of course, madam," he stammered. "R-right away." He clapped the bell on the desk with the flat of his palm and opened up the reservations ledger. He pushed it around to face her. "If you'll be so kind as to register?"

Larry stepped forward and flipped the ledger shut. "I don't think this is necessary, do you?" he asked softly.

Mr. Smythe's throat made a warbling sound as he cleared it. "Well, sir, the hotel regulations require that—"

"Mr. Smythe, is it?" There was no misinterpreting Larry's tone.

"Yes, sir." Mr. Smythe was bewildered and looking painfully uncomfortable.

"You might not know it yet, my good man, but from this moment on it is Mrs. Hale who makes the rules round here. You see, she intends to take up permanent residence in this hotel."

"Yes, sir, but—"

"Also, I think you should know that she is now the proud owner of this establishment."

Mr. Smythe blushed crimson. "Oh, I . . . I . . . of course," he stammered, now at more of a loss than ever. "In . . . in

145

that case, I'll show you up to the royal suite personally." He raised a hand and snapped his fingers once. A gaunt, well-groomed middle-aged woman hurried out from the office behind the desk. "Mrs. Carleton," Mr. Smythe said without turning around to look at her, "take over for me, please."

"Yes, Mr. Smythe."

"I'll be up in the royal suite if you need me." He came around from behind the desk and turned to Larry and Elizabeth-Anne. "If you'll be so kind as to follow me, please," he said with a slight bow. He crossed the marble lobby to the bank of elevators, his leather heels clacking noisily.

Elizabeth-Anne, Ludmila, Larry, and the children followed, but they took their time. Elizabeth-Anne was taking the opportunity to study the splendid lobby. She breathed deeply as she gazed around, unable to believe that this small, glittering, palacelike hotel was now truly hers. It seemed impossible, like something out of a dream.

Mr. Smythe was waiting for them outside the elevator, and the uniformed elevator operator was holding the door open. By the way the man was acting, Smythe had clearly let him know just who Elizabeth-Anne was.

Once they were all inside, the operator shoved the door shut and pressed down on the brass handle. As they rose smoothly skyward, Mr. Smythe cleared his throat and said apologetically, "The royal suite takes up the entire top two floors of the hotel. I'm afraid the elevator goes only as far as the first of those floors. There are two staircases, however, connecting both floors of the duplex. One is quite grand, and the other is for the staff and emergency use."

"That is quite all right, Mr. Smythe," Elizabeth-Anne assured him.

He nodded, then stood silently, his fingers ticking nervously against the sides of his trousers. Elizabeth-Anne gazed up at the sweeping hand of the floor indicator above the door. As they approached the eighth floor, a bell chimed and a yellow light went on, indicating a stop call, but they rode on without stopping.

"Just a moment, please," Elizabeth-Anne said.

Both the elevator operator and Smythe turned to face her. The elevator bobbed to an abrupt halt between floors.

"Someone is summoning the elevator on the eighth floor, I take it?"

"Yes, Mrs. Hale," the operator said timidly.

"From now on, unless there is an emergency, I want every elevator to stop whenever and wherever it is summoned. It doesn't matter who is on it. I intend for the guests to be king around here, not me and my family. The guests pay good money to stay here, and we will pamper them and keep them coming back to stay here time and again. Is that clear? No inconvenience for the staff, or my family, is too great when it comes to satisfying my paying guests. They're going to get more services for their dollar here than anywhere else."

"Yes, ma'am," the operator said in a tiny voice.

Elizabeth-Anne nodded. "Fine. Also, I would like to point out that there are smudges on the paneling on this elevator. And the brass needs a good shining."

"Yes, ma'am."

"I'm going to inspect every elevator in this building at noon tomorrow. I want them all to gleam like new."

"Yes, ma'am."

She smiled. "Just so we understand each other and don't get off on the wrong foot. Now, let's backtrack down a floor and pick up whoever summoned this thing."

As she looked away, she caught Larry's approving gaze, and she shrugged. As long as she could have her way—and with Hale Hotels she *would* have her way—one motto would ring out loud and clear: nothing under the sun would be too much when it came to her guests. She would have them coming back. Again and again.

And that, she knew, was what would make her hotel shine above all others.

By the time they reached the royal suite several minutes later, the word was obviously out. The moment the elevator door slid open, a maid greeted them. She was a short Irish woman in her late thirties, and her black-and-white uniform was crisply starched. "Good afternoon, Mrs. Hale," she said in a thick brogue. "Welcome to the Madison Squire. My name is Moira, and I'm permanently assigned to this suite. Anything you want, you just call me.''

"Thank you, Moira.'' Elizabeth-Anne smiled warmly at her and turned to Smythe. "I believe that Moira can show us around just fine. I appreciate your taking the time to show us up here."

Smythe tried his best to hide the fact that he was perturbed. He didn't like to be summarily dismissed. "As you wish," he said, bowing stiffly.

"Meanwhile, Mr. Smythe," Elizabeth-Anne said slowly, "could you tell me when the day shift finishes?"

"At five o'clock."

Elizabeth-Anne consulted her watch. "Very well. That gives us half an hour. Please see to it that everyone from the day shift is assembled in the dining room at that time. I wish to have a talk with them."

"Yes, Mrs. Hale."

"And I want you to do the same thing for the night shift. And the morning shift. Assemble them after their shift is over so that I can speak with them."

"But . . . the shifts are eight hours apart. Wouldn't you care to rest and—"

"Mr. Smythe," Elizabeth-Anne said patiently, "rest is for the guests, not the staff. From this moment on, I am not only the owner of the Madison Squire, but a member of the staff as well."

"Yes, Mrs. Hale." Rebuked, he backed into the elevator. Only once the door closed did he allow himself to wipe the beads of perspiration off his glistening forehead.

N o one had to tell Elizabeth-Anne what it was like to meet the boss for the first time. She remembered only too well the day she had met Mrs. Winter.

"Nervous?" Larry had asked her as she'd prepared herself for her first meeting with the staff.

She'd nodded and shut her eyes.

"If you like, I'll be there with you," he'd offered.

She'd opened her eyes then and smiled painfully. "Sorry,

no," she'd told him softly. "This is something I have to do alone, Larry. Otherwise I'll never gain their respect."

His look told her that he understood perfectly.

She could feel the day shift's tension and anxiety crackling like electricity in the air of the dining room the moment she came in. It was a big room, and everyone was seated around the white-draped tables, which had already been laid out for dinner. As soon as she made her appearance, Mr. Smythe approached her, and the staff quickly rose to their feet. Maintenance men, maids, bookkeepers, telephone operators, kitchen help, reception clerks, porters, bellboys, waiters, chefs, and the doorman—the entire lifeblood of one eight-hour shift at the Madison Squire was assembled before her. And lifeblood of the hotel they were, she well knew, for without the essential human services the staff provided, the Madison Squire would be but an empty shell.

Slowly she made the rounds of the room, her keen aquamarine eyes appraising everyone as Mr. Smythe introduced her. She shook hands with everyone and tried to remember the faces and names as best she could. There was such a large staff. But in time, she was certain, she would learn to call them all by their names and learn a little about them.

Finally, the personal introductions over, Elizabeth-Anne stood alone in the front of the room. "Please be seated." Her voice sounded suddenly weak, and she cleared her throat.

There were the sounds of chairs scraping and starched uniforms rustling, but otherwise the tense silence could have been cut with a knife.

Elizabeth-Anne took a deep breath. She felt as nervous as everyone else, but she knew that she must not show it. She had to appear in total control. This was her staff, and in order to get them to do her bidding, she must gain not only their respect but also their affection.

Swiftly she counted heads. There were ninety-seven employees sitting before her, and they were now her responsibility. The weight of it made her feel overwhelmingly alone. She took a deep breath to steady her nerves. Then she clasped her hands in front of her.

"Ladies and gentlemen," she began softly, "I know you've all had a rough day and that you're tired and anxious to get home. So I'll try to make this relatively brief." She paused and smiled reassuringly. "You do not know me, and I do not know you. That, at least, puts us on an even footing. However, within a few days we'll all be better acquainted with one another. Some of you have been here for a long time, others not so long. It is especially traumatic for long-term employees to find out that the business they have worked for is undergoing a change in ownership, because that usually means a change in management as well. Usually, but not always.

"I understand the way you feel perfectly. New bosses can be tough, and you'll have to prove yourselves all over again. Some of you will not like me. And I will probably not like some of you either."

She allowed herself a chuckle. At least the ice was broken, she noticed. The staff looked a little less worried already.

"However," she continued, "that is all beside the point. The only persons with whom you must be popular are the guests. I intend to make the Madison Squire the shining star of all the hotels in this city, indeed the *country*, and in order to do that, I need the help of each and every one of you."

She paused, her eyes sweeping the faces before her. They were all sitting at attention, digesting every word.

"You will find out that I am a fanatic when it comes to cleanliness and services. We're going to glow and sparkle, all of us. And since I live upstairs, I'll have an easy time keeping my eyes on each and every one of you. Which doesn't mean I intend to frighten you. Not at all. It's only to keep you all on your toes."

She paused again, watching them exchange wary glances.

"Starting tomorrow, I want the person in charge of each section of this hotel to give me a guided tour. That includes bus stations in the dining room, linen closets in the halls, and even the boiler and heating equipment in the basement. This is all necessary, because I wish to know this hotel inside and out, and no one knows it better than all of you. I also wish to get to know each of you personally, because we are a team. I may happen to own this hotel, but I'm as much a member of the staff as any of you.

"Now, to some rather unpleasant business. When you arrive for work in the morning, I want every one of you to drop by the personnel office. You are all to hand in letters of resignation."

A sudden murmur rose from the employees.

Elizabeth-Anne raised a hand to silence them. "This is not to say that any of you will be let go. You will be instantly rehired, but on new terms. Each of you will again go through a probation period. This will give us a chance to see how well we work together. If we discover we don't get on, you will not be fired summarily. You will receive severance pay and references. I know this is not easy to live with, but I believe it will give all of you an opportunity to prove your worth."

She inclined her head.

"By Friday of next week, I also expect the head of each department to prepare a report describing how things can be improved." She dropped her voice so everyone would have to strain to catch what she was saying. "You will discover that although I am demanding, I tend to reward hard work. Those of you who deserve it will get raises. Naturally, I won't be giving any of this away for nothing. It will be up to each of you to prove you deserve it."

She stopped and smiled brightly. "Meanwhile, let me reiterate that I welcome the opportunity of working with you. And don't forget, we are all a team. I'm counting on you to make the rest of us look good. I want this hotel to be filled to capacity at all times, and to do that, our reputation must spread. That is all in your hands. And to give you some incentive right away, despite the resignation letters I expect from all of you, I am hereby raising all salaries by ten percent."

There was utter confusion mixed with the wariness now.

She continued to smile. "Now, let's hope you all earn it. Good night." She turned and left the room. In the silence that followed her out, one could have heard a pin drop. Only after she closed the dining-room doors did pandemonium break out.

* * *

Larry was waiting outside the dining room for her. "I caught your speech," he said with a chuckle.

"Eavesdropping, eh?"

"No. I was just on my way out, and I happened to overhear it. You're good. Very good."

She smiled nervously. Now that the meeting was over, she allowed her misgivings to show.

"In fact," Larry added admiringly, "you were brilliant. You not only hung a killing sword over their heads to make sure they work their damnedest, but at the same time you gave them across-the-board raises to let them know just how much they stand to lose." He grinned hugely. "It seems I've underestimated you. You're quite a businesswoman. Much more of one than I realized."

"More than I realized too," she admitted in a weak voice.

"Well, now that you've proved it, what do you say we ride up to the house? I still have plenty of champagne in the cellar."

She shook her head. "Thanks, but no. Not that I couldn't use a drink, but it's been one helluva day."

"You can say that again." He leaned forward and kissed her on the lips. "I'll drop by tomorrow, how's that? Then I'll bring the champagne. A whole case as a housewarming present."

Her smile was dazzling. "I'd like that. And, Larry?"

He raised his eyebrows.

"Thanks."

"What for?"

"You know what for, Larry. Everything. Everything."

The star-spangled night was cool and velvety as Elizabeth-Anne stepped out through the French doors and stood on the terrace. All around her, Manhattan glittered and shimmered, a vertical fairyland of crystalline towers and gleaming lights. She had tried to sleep, but it was impossible; too much had happened too suddenly.

She was filled with a soaring sense of anticipation and wondrous excitement. Not all that long ago, she and the children had been in this hotel under very different circumstances. It seemed yesterday she had leaned out of a window in this very building, determined to take the city by storm and forge a brilliant future for herself and the children. Now it was starting to happen, and this terrace, this entire building, a whole square block on Madison Avenue, was hers, and hers alone.

She breathed deeply of the sweet night air and her own heady success, a gleam of sparkling resolution shining in her eyes. Yes, she had come far in a short period of time. But not far enough, she thought. There was still so much to be done. So much more to be achieved and built and forged out of nothing. By God, she would conquer this city, she would tame this cacophonous teeming giant and call it her own, and after she was through with that, she would conquer the country, and then the world.

Hale Hotels.

She savored the sound of those two short words on her tongue, tasting them, letting their power and strength course through her. From up here, high atop the city, it was easy to take strength from the present, to see into the future, to feel the pulse of the entire world. It wasn't difficult to imagine an empire of hotels spanning the earth.

For a long time she stood alone on the terrace of the Madison Squire, a solitary woman gazing out at a sleeping world, planning and dreaming, determined to make everything she ever wanted come true.

She did not hear him, but she felt his presence as he came out onto the terrace and stood behind her. She turned slowly to face him. "I thought you had left," she said softly, gazing at his moonlit face. "I thought I wouldn't see you until tomorrow."

"I did leave," Larry answered. "But tomorrow seemed too far away. I had to come back and see you. I knew you'd be standing out here. Surveying your world."

She laughed. "Guilty."

"It's beautiful, isn't it?"

She nodded, the tears shining in her eyes. "Larry," she

whispered quietly, "oh, Larry. You've made me the happiest woman in the world."

He drew her close to him, wrapping his arms around her. She sighed contentedly as he held her against the rugged warmth of his body.

"I want you to be happy," he whispered, nuzzling the nape of her neck with his lips. "I want you always to be happy. You and I, we're special, Elizabeth-Anne. That's why we're standing here right now, instead of down there. We dare to dream, both of us. We dare to take chances and lock horns with fate to make our dreams our reality."

"I love you, Larry." Her voice was the barest whisper in the night.

"And I love you." He kissed her, tasting her vital urgency, feeling her powerfully trembling body. They kissed a long time, the lights twinkling all around them, and then he took her by the hand and led her inside, up the sweeping stairs to the second floor of the duplex, to the huge master bedroom, where they celebrated success and dreams, achievements and each other, by making fierce, urgent love until the sun rose brightly in the east.

II
Charlotte-Anne

NEW YORK CITY

❧

March 20, 1931

1

At precisely seven A.M. on this Friday, as on every other weekday morning of the year, three sharp businesslike raps on the bedroom door awoke Charlotte-Anne.

"Go 'way," she mumbled, which was exactly what she mumbled every weekday morning. As usual, her words were ignored. The door opened and Dallas, Elizabeth-Anne's friend from the Savoy Plaza, whom she had lured away to be her family's housekeeper, at far better pay, came bustling in full of good cheer. For once she wasn't loaded down with the huge breakfast tray room service normally sent up. Elizabeth-Anne had left strict instructions that the family would breakfast together that morning.

" 'Morning," Dallas sang out. She crossed over to the French doors and yanked aside the thick butter-yellow drapes.

"Go '*way*, Dallas," Charlotte-Anne moaned irritably. She scowled as she buried her face under the pillow.

"Now, now, Miss Charlotte-Anne, your Mama said you got to be up at the stroke of seven, and I aim to get you out of bed just when she said. Breakfast's at the table this mornin'.

Your mama, she wants to discuss something important with you all.''

Dallas grasped a corner of the off-white satin comforter and pulled. She and Charlotte-Anne had suffered through this daily ritual hundreds of times, and Charlotte-Anne, knowing full well what was coming, grabbed hold of her end of the comforter. A fierce tug of war followed. Dallas won out; she always did. For one thing, she was wide-awake, which Charlotte-Anne wasn't; for another, the satin was slick and liked to slip out from between Charlotte-Anne's fingers.

Once Charlotte-Anne gave way to Dallas' swift, forceful yanks, the comforter slid to the foot of the bed like a rumpled soft-sculpture accordion. Charlotte-Anne shivered, but knew she would get no sympathy from Dallas, who was not one to coddle children and considered Charlotte-Anne, at seventeen, very much an adult in any case.

Elizabeth-Anne Hale had given Dallas carte blanche to run the apartment and the children as she saw fit. Dallas knew their mother trusted her implicitly, and she took seriously her responsibility to see that the children became nicely behaved and dutiful adults. Mrs. Hale had become an extremely busy woman, and she didn't always have much time on her hands to see to the children herself. She had had to delegate a lot of authority, and Dallas wasn't about to let her down.

Charlotte-Anne lay there in her ecru lace nightgown, still huddled against the chill with her head buried under the pillow.

"Come on, Sleeping Beauty," Dallas growled softly, giving the fluffy down-filled pillow gentle but firm smacks with the palms of her hands. "It's a lovely day out. Still a little on the dark side, mind you, but it's gonna be beautiful. Can't you just smell it?" She lifted her head, sniffed appreciatively, and smiled. "Spring is finally in the air.''

As Charlotte-Anne continued to refuse to respond, Dallas shook her head, gazing about her and wondering for what must have been the hundredth time why such a beautiful room was wasted on such a lazy girl. Of all the rooms Dallas had seen in all the years she had spent working in luxury hotels, this particular room was her favorite. The entire decor spoke of femininity and grace. The walls were covered in richly carved French Provincial paneling, but all the other furniture—the chairs, the curvaceous headboard, the bombé chests with their pregnant wooden bellies, the lady's dresser with mirror and settee, the sheer gauze curtains and heavier drapes—it was all done in soft, creamy ivory with just a hint of butter yellow for accent. On the dresser, chests, and nightstands stood papery yellow potted daffodils. There was something intensely ladylike and yet sunny about the room; even on the dreariest of rainy days it seemed to Dallas that the sun was shining here.

It was a room fit for a princess, which was how Dallas looked upon Charlotte-Anne and her sisters. And little Zaccheus was a prince. Crown prince and princesses of an empire which already comprised seven hotels, three right here in New York City, along with one each in Baltimore, Philadelphia, Boston, and Washington, D.C. And that wasn't counting the Hale Tourist Court in Texas. Not to mention, Dallas reminded herself, something about shares in a very lucrative gold mine. And from what Dallas' small but alert ears had picked up, Elizabeth-Anne Hale would be off to buy another tourist court today, somewhere on Route One.

Elizabeth-Anne's success didn't fill Dallas with envy. It had just the opposite effect: it gave her hope for all womankind. Sometimes she still had trouble believing that the woman she had first met as a fellow maid was now the mistress of the growing Hale empire.

I'm glad she has what she does, Dallas thought to herself with a satisfied chuckle. She deserves it, and so do I. I'm paid handsomely now, and the working conditions are sure a lot better than any I've ever known elsewhere. She nodded to herself. No longer was there need for her to work two jobs, and she didn't have to spend a dime on food, either. Leftovers from the hotel kitchen were hers to lug home. Unbelievable as it seemed, she was even starting to tuck a little money away each week for her own children's future.

"C'mon, now, honey child," Dallas warned Charlotte-Anne, grabbing hold of the creamy ivory pillow and tugging on that too.

"All right, all right," Charlotte-Anne mumbled grumpily, her voice muffled by the pillow. She flung it aside angrily, then sat up, yawning. She rubbed the sleep out of her eyes with her knuckles. Even disheveled, her beauty was startling.

Since the Hales had moved to the Madison Squire almost a year and a half before, Charlotte-Anne had matured considerably and now looked much older than her seventeen years. All of her youthfulness had been shed. Her gangliness was gone, and her body was tall and slender. Her handspan waist, coupled with the rich, solid swell of her breasts, provided a voluptuous figure that was in tantalizing contrast to her pale complexion, which lent her a flawless, haunting porcelain beauty. Her hair was her mother's, the same rich ripe shade of ready-to-harvest wheat, but her eyes, with their peculiar, unsettling shade of pale aquamarine, were the slightly tilted, slanting eyes of a predatory cat. At the same time, small and defiant as her face was, she could appear deceptively frail and sweet-looking, thanks to her tiny, pale pink lips and perfect, pearly small teeth. She gave off an air of flawless and enchanting doll-like beauty, but that was on the surface. Beneath the demureness she affected was a poorly concealed toughness, a stubborn will of iron, and a feisty tiger's mind of her own. No one knew this better than Dallas, who was the first person to set eyes on her each morning, before she could settle into the image of sweetness she tried so hard to project.

"Best you hurry," Dallas warned her. "You've got half an hour. Breakfast at seven-thirty sharp. Your mama's expecting you to be on time."

"I hear you, I hear you," Charlotte-Anne answered testily.

Dallas eyed her suspiciously and then left, closing the door softly behind her.

Charlotte-Anne waited until the door closed, then stuck out her tongue. Without further ado, she swung her legs out over the bed, her feet doing a tiptoe dance as she felt for her slippers. Finally finding them and wiggling them on, she stood up and stretched lazily. Then she pulled on her rose silk robe, tied the pink sash around her minuscule waist, and walked over to the French windows. She looked out for a long moment. It was indeed a perfect early spring day. As she watched, the city grew lighter and came into sharp, stony focus.

On an impulse, she opened the terrace doors wide and stepped outside. Briskly she massaged her forearms against the sudden chill and did a quick little dance. The terra-cotta tiles were cold, and the chill soaked right through her thin slippers. But for the moment, any discomfort was forgotten. She leaned forward on the brick parapet and stared dreamily out over the city. Thirty-three stories below, the traffic on Madison Avenue was still light, waiting for the morning rush hour.

She shook her head. Considering all the traffic and bustling people, and the low vacancy rate of this hotel, she'd never have known that the country was plunged into the depths of a depression. From up here, she couldn't see the pitiful look of hopelessness worn by so many walking on the street below her. The suites in the Madison Squire were filled, and so were most of the expensive rooms. It was the inexpensive rooms that went begging. Which only showed, she thought in bewilderment, who was really hurting.

She pushed herself away from the wall and turned to go back inside, when something pinkish caught her eye. Could it be?

She stooped down in front of the redwood planter to investigate.

It was! The first of the season's crocuses was braving the weather, its tightly cocooned winglike petals peering out from beneath the dark soil. It was an omen, she decided.

Humming softly to herself, she went back inside. Today was special, and so far, everything was working out perfectly, much better than she'd hoped.

She danced through her bedroom, arms extended, and swooped toward the bathroom door.

Yes, everything was going *much* better than she'd anticipated. She could sense that. The fact that her mother was going to be gone all day proved it; the fact that she wouldn't be back until tomorrow reinforced it further.

Her hum turned into a song as she filled the ceramic washbasin with ice-cold water. She slipped out of the robe and nightgown and splashed handfuls of frigid water into her face. As she dabbed herself dry with a huge soft white bath towel, she eyed herself critically in the mirror. She was pleased with what she saw.

She ran the big tortoiseshell comb through her hair. Suddenly she froze, the corners of her lips drooping into a distressed frown. Maybe everything wasn't as perfect as she thought. Perhaps her mother *had* gotten wind of her plans. Why else would she have insisted on them all having breakfast together this of all mornings?

Charlotte-Anne ran down the gracefully curving carpeted stairs of the duplex, her fingers nervously tying her hair back with a navy-blue silk ribbon. She could hear muted voices in the living room.

Damn, she thought to herself, her lips tightening in frustration. She was late again, and they were probably waiting for her to start eating.

She knew that with each passing day she was taking longer to dress, but it was all because of her despised school uniform. Each morning, she was determined to somehow make it look more stylish and she would experiment in front of the mirror. It wasn't her fault, it was the Brearley School's. The elegant building on East Eighty-third Street might house one of the finest girls' schools in the country, but she hated going there. Even more, she hated dressing sedately in plain white blouses and dark blue skirts like some child. She considered herself much too sophisticated for the schoolgirl look, with the short white gloves and her hair tied back with a ribbon. Worse yet, the school was for girls only. How she yearned to throw off the shackles of that school! She would have liked nothing more than to burn her uniform and have her hair styled nicely for a change.

Well, she would do that soon now, she promised herself. Very, very soon. *If* everything went well. And if it didn't, she would make sure another opportunity presented itself.

She stopped running before she reached the living-room doors, and entered the room with a slow, gracious walk.

The rest of the family was already seated around the table

at the far end of the room, just as she had feared, waiting for her. Elizabeth-Anne, Regina, Rebecca, Zaccheus, and Larry Hochstetter turned to gaze at her.

Seeing Larry startled her. She hadn't expected him. Family breakfasts were rare enough, because of her mother's grueling schedule, but breakfasts with guests were rarer still. She wondered what had prompted this unusual turn of events.

" 'Morning," she said in what she hoped was a light, cheerful voice. Her mother held up her cheek and she kissed it. Charlotte-Anne favored Larry with the best smile she could muster, ignored her sisters and brother, and slipped into her seat.

"Now that we're all here," Elizabeth-Anne began, without so much as a disapproving glance at her errant daughter, "we can have our little discussion. As you all know, I've never made a serious decision that might affect you without consulting all of you first." There was a radiant smile on her face and her cheeks were tinged with a pinkish color that made her look much younger than her thirty-six years. But from her fidgeting hands Charlotte-Anne saw that her mother was unusually nervous.

Charlotte-Anne instantly felt the heavy load slipping off her shoulders. She had been fretting for nothing. This breakfast discussion had nothing to do with what she had feared. Gratefully she tried to concentrate on what her mother was saying.

"As you all know, it's been nearly a year and a half since your father . . . died." Elizabeth-Anne had carefully planned her speech, but her voice trembled nevertheless.

The children nodded, their faces suddenly solemn. Elizabeth-Anne glanced quickly at Larry, who sat beside her and held her hand in silent encouragement, his face carefully expressionless.

"There comes a time," Elizabeth-Anne said slowly, "when all of us must take a good, hard look at our lives. We must look behind us, to the past, to promises made. We must consider the present, in which we live now. And we must look forward to the future, to what it might hold for us. As you all know, I loved your father very much, as did all of you. And I *still* love him. However, the fact remains that he is gone. We've all mourned him for a long time. We were alone for years before he died. But now, while we will always hold him dear to our hearts, we must look toward the future. This was his last request." She paused, letting her words sink in. Then she smiled and looked hopefully around the table. "I think you all like Larry?"

Her children nodded.

"As you all know, Larry and I are leaving for New Jersey this morning to buy a new property. But we have other, more important plans in addition. As soon as the papers are signed, we're planning to go on to Elkton, Maryland. It isn't much further, and civil marriages are performed there with a minimum of fuss and delay." She paused and added softly, "Larry and I decided we'd like to get married."

The mention of marriage was totally unexpected, a shocking bolt of lightning out of the blue. Regina's hand slipped, and she knocked over her glass of orange juice, which spread across the white linen tablecloth. Charlotte-Anne sat still as a statue, her slice of toast in one hand, her butter knife in the other. Only her pale eyes moved, and they swept around the table at the silent tableau.

Her mother and Larry were facing each other, exchanging encouraging, hopeful smiles.

Regina's mouth was hanging open as she stared in horror at the yellow juice stain.

Rebecca still held a cup of hot chocolate poised at her lips.

The silence was broken by seven-year-old Zaccheus. "Are you going to be our new daddy?" he asked Larry in his clear voice.

The spell was broken and everyone began to move at once. Rebecca lowered her cup, while Regina righted the glass and dabbed at the stain with her napkin.

"I like to think so," Larry told Zaccheus. He glanced around. "It all depends on you and your sisters."

"I told Larry long ago," Elizabeth-Anne said hesitantly, "that we always discuss an important decision which affects us all. We'd like to hear all your opinions."

"Yes!" Zaccheus cried excitedly. "I think yes!"

"Regina?"

Regina stopped dabbing the stain and looked across the table at her mother. Now eighteen, she spent her days, and a good portion of her nights, at Columbia University, where she was immersed in her studies. She hoped eventually to become a pediatrician. Regina realized only too well that with each passing day her own life was just unfolding, and her mother's, which until now had been an intrinsic part of it, no longer revolved around her. Both mother and daughter needed separate lives, and she understood this. Eventually, all birds flew off to make their own nests, and she was certain she would soon too. She had been hoping for a long time that her mother would have a second, luckier chance at love, and the news of her impending marriage had startled her because it seemed too good to be true. It was everything she had prayed would happen.

Regina nodded solemnly, her brow wrinkling as she sought the correct words. "You both have my blessings," she said huskily. Then she jumped up, hugged her mother, and kissed Larry.

The tears sparkled in Elizabeth-Anne's eyes as she said, "Thank you, dear. Both Larry and I appreciate it." She switched her gaze. " 'Becca?"

"I miss Daddy, of course," fourteen-year-old Rebecca said slowly, biting down on her underlip. "But I know nothing will ever bring him back." She stared down into her hot chocolate as though the answer lay somewhere in her murky cup. "And you're right, Mama. Life goes on." She nodded and looked up, meeting her mother's gaze. "It's okay by me."

Elizabeth-Anne let out a breath of relief and smiled warmly at her youngest daughter. Then she leaned farther across the table and asked, "Charlotte-Anne?"

Hearing her name, Charlotte-Anne jerked her chin up. Throughout the conversation, her mind had been swirling with the unexpected news as she quickly tried to evaluate how it might affect her own plans for her brilliantly plotted future. Like Regina, she was just realizing that her own life was beginning; unlike her sister, she saw ahead of her a life which

Judith Gould

was far removed from what she considered the pedestrian orbit of her mother's world. As long as the marriage didn't interfere with what she wanted, and she knew it wouldn't, then it was fine with her. In fact, on second thought it was one of the best things that could have happened. Her mother led an extremely busy life and had little enough time left over for the family as it was. Now, with a husband, she'd be more occupied than ever, and that, Charlotte-Anne observed with a twinge of hope, meant that her plans would come to fruition even faster. She'd have to account for even less of her time.

She nodded and gave a brief hint of an assenting smile.

"That's settled, then." Elizabeth-Anne sat back with obvious relief while Larry quickly got to his feet, leaned down, and kissed her happily.

"Watch it," she said with a good-humored laugh. "You'll muss my hair." Elizabeth-Anne then watched joyfully as Larry rushed from chair to chair, kissing and hugging the entire family.

"Mama could do a lot worse," Regina told him. "A *lot* worse."

He laughed, pleased. And then everyone began talking at once—everyone except for Charlotte-Anne, and nobody noticed her thoughtful silence. When Larry sat back down, he tapped his coffee cup with a teaspoon.

They all fell silent and looked at him expectantly.

"First of all, on behalf of your mother and myself, thank you. Second, I want you to know that I'm not going to try to take your father's place. No one can do that. You won't have to call me 'Dad' or anything like that, unless you want to. 'Larry' will do just fine. And third, your mother and I would be honored if you would all come along to Elkton with us and attend our wedding. I should warn you, though, we won't be back for a week. From Elkton we're going on a working honeymoon of sorts, to see what the staffs of the Calvert Hale in Baltimore, and L'Enfant Hale in Washington, and the Penn Hale in Philadelphia have been up to. If that interferes with your schoolwork or other plans, you could always head straight back here from Elkton. If you even want to come that far, that is. We'll leave it all up to you."

Zaccheus clapped his hands, and Rebecca cried out, "Oh, I'd love to come!" She giggled. "Especially if I get to miss school."

Regina frowned thoughtfully. "Speaking of school, I've got an exam today, but . . ."

"Then you stay, dear," Elizabeth-Anne said quickly, reaching across the table and patting her hand. "Larry and I understand perfectly. I know you've been studying like crazy for this exam. It would kill us if it were all wasted now." She smiled. "Charlotte-Anne?"

Charlotte-Anne looked up quickly. Her pale eyes were curiously veiled. "I . . . I'd love to come, but I've got . . . I've got exams today too," she lied.

Elizabeth-Anne glanced at Larry. "Perhaps we should wait a while longer," she suggested. "Then we can plan the wedding to coincide with everyone's schedules. It doesn't have to be so hurried."

"Absolutely, definitely, certainly *not*. I won't hear of it," Charlotte-Anne cried quickly, turning to them with an expression of utter disappointment. Her pulse was racing. The success—or failure—of her plan depended on her being left to her own devices. The marriage played into her hands, and their being gone an entire week was manna straight from heaven. It *had* to take place.

"You two go ahead and tie the knot," she said forcefully. "I won't hear of the marriage being put off on account of any of us. Not, that is, if you want *my* blessings." She eyed them shrewdly and added, "If you're willing to wait, then you can't be absolutely sure you really want to marry each other, can you?"

"Oh, but we are," Elizabeth-Anne assured her.

"Then prove it."

"Well, if you insist," Elizabeth-Anne said doubtfully.

"I do. And I'm sure everyone else feels the same way." Charlotte-Anne looked down at her plate, lowering her eyes lest anyone catch the triumphant gleam in them. She felt a surge of anticipation coursing through her. On her way to school this morning, she would stop by the hotel office on the second floor under the pretext of typing up an article for the school newspaper. She'd done that on fifteen or twenty occasions already this past year. Except that there had never actually been any articles. Instead, she had been typing notes on Hale Hotels' letterhead. Just like all the others, the note she typed this morning would beg that she be excused from the second half of the schoolday for a doctor's appointment. Then she would forge her mother's signature. Much practice had made it near-perfect.

She smiled, thinking what fools her teachers were. And how they worried about her fragile health! She constantly had to fight to keep from laughing out loud, they were so solicitous of her. The truth was, she hadn't been near a doctor's office in close to a year. She was the very picture of perfect health.

What was it Mickey Hoyt had told her that last afternoon they spent together?

"No sacrifice is too much."

That was it. *No sacrifice is too much.*

Not for what she wanted.

2

The perfect morning turned into a rotten afternoon.

By one o'clock the Manhattan sky was awash with boiling gray clouds. Charlotte-Anne glanced up at the sky and cursed herself for not listening to the weather report, not arranging to be excused from school at noon sharp instead of twelve-thirty, and refusing to take an umbrella. She should have listened to Dallas, who'd warned her that it would rain. But she was sick of having to listen to Dallas. If you weren't careful, she would mother you to death. And if you didn't obey, she'd rat on you in no time.

Well, today she wouldn't. The happy couple was off to get married, far from any worries about what Charlotte-Anne was up to. And who, she asked herself, had the time to worry about something as mundane as the weather when the rest of her life was at stake?

She hurried down the crowded sidewalk, pushing and shoving as the first fat cold raindrop splattered on her shoulder. Scowling and holding her book over her head with one hand, and hanging tightly onto her bulging briefcase with the other, she began to run, ducking to avoid the masses of umbrellas which, with the first drops of rain, sprouted up everywhere like a forest of giant black mushrooms. She reached Madison Avenue, had to wait for the light to change, and then hurried across the street, heading east on Forty-second Street at a run. One more block and she'd be inside Grand Central Station.

The cloud burst soon became a deluge and her tan camel's hair coat was soaked by the time she got inside the dry, cavernous warmth of the station. Now she was sure she'd catch hell from Dallas later. She stopped to shake off the excess rain and catch her breath. She was drenched through and through, and her teeth were chattering.

Well, right now *that* was the least of her worries. She was here to change in the ladies' room anyway. Whenever she had a rendezvous with Mickey Hoyt, she carried a change of clothes instead of books inside her ample briefcase. After all, she couldn't show up to meet him looking like a frumpy schoolgirl, not after all the stories she'd made up about herself.

She'd told him she was twenty and unhappily married to a very jealous man, which was why she had to meet him so furtively. She'd even bought a cheap wedding band, which she always slipped on her finger before she met him. No detail was too minute, as long as it added credibility to her ruse. She had the strong suspicion that if he should ever find out the truth—that she was actually seventeen and living at home with her family—she'd be in a real pickle. He was too well known in this city, too famous to walk away from it untarnished. His career, which meant everything to him, could suffer only so many scandals. If his reputation were threatened he'd drop her like a hot potato. And if that happened, then all her glorious, glamorous hopes would be dashed.

Well, it wouldn't happen. She simply wouldn't let it.

She rushed into the ladies' room, to any observer a frantic schoolgirl but emerged fifteen minutes later an entirely different person. Walking with stately grace, she was a radiant, breathtaking beauty, a stylish, modern young lady from the top of her head to the tips of her shoes.

Striding through the shopping concourse on her way to the baggage lockers, she caught sight of her reflection in a darkened store window. She felt the first real thrill of pleasure since it had started to rain. Soaked or not, she looked terrific.

She had dried her hair as best she could, then pinned it up so she looked even taller and more mature. She topped it with a tiny forest-green flannel hat, rather like a bellboy's, with a long scarf attached that she tied at the back of her head. The matching jersey blouse was the same green, too lightweight for this cold, atrocious weather, but it had been the only thing she could find to match the skirt, which was a circular cut, of heavyweight flannel. Her tan accessories—a foulard neckerchief, a belt of calfskin, and lisle stockings—contrasted wonderfully with all that green. The gloves she wore were soft, supple suede, just a shade of green lighter than the blouse and the skirt.

The clothes belonged to her mother, who, thank God, was nearly the same size she was, and she'd had to sneak them out of the apartment. They didn't quite go with her sedate schoolgirl coat, but she had no choice but to wear it. Trying to sneak one of her mother's bulky coats past Dallas' eagle eyes was more than she could manage. She just thanked her lucky stars that she'd been able to sneak out as many clothes as she had on so many occasions thus far. But she'd been careful. After she wore them, she sent them down to the hotel dry cleaners, and then intercepted them on the way back and hung them up.

When she reached the baggage lockers, she found an empty one and locked her satchel and sopping-wet school uniform inside it. She dropped the key into her minuscule pale tan calfskin handbag. All physical evidence of the schoolgirl was gone. Even her mannerisms had changed. Her walk was charged with a disturbing sensuousness, at once fresh and arresting, and she gave the impression of being curiously remote, yet fully secure in the effect she projected. Her pale eyes glittered with brilliant lust, her creamy smooth skin bloomed with an anticipatory flush, and every gesture she made was swift and fluid.

This was the adult in her which struggled constantly to break through the schoolgirl mold, but at home, around family and friends, she kept this grown-up part of herself locked away. She was afraid of ridicule, of being teased and condescended to. But now she felt deliciously free and unburdened. Men turned to stare appreciatively, and women appraised her with envious glances. She pretended not to notice, and to be aloof from it all, but she savored every moment of it.

As soon as she got back outside, she shivered. It was raining even harder than before. If she waited around for it to let up, she would be late, and Mickey wouldn't like that. Like her, he was stealing these precious hours, and every minute counted.

She turned up the collar of her coat. She hated getting drenched again, but she saw little choice. She mustn't do anything to irritate Mickey, especially not after the promise he had made her the last time they had been together.

She began to dash west across Forty-second Street. The Algonquin wasn't that far, and with any luck, the rain would taper off.

Which, of course, it didn't.

While she rushed through the storm, her mind was not on the rain, but on her career and Mickey Hoyt —in that order.

As far as she was concerned, her fate had been sealed the moment the curtain had risen on her first Broadway show nearly a year earlier. Sitting in the audience, thrilling to the excitement of what was unfolding onstage, she knew then and there where she wanted to be. Not in the audience, but on the stage. She hungered to become a star, like the ones who were captivating her. She wanted to become a great lady of the American theater, an actress who reveled in applause. But even more important, *she* would become that rarest of the rare, a truly *great* actress. With her own emotions, she would milk her audiences of theirs. She would manipulate them to laughter and tears, to love and hate. It didn't seem all that farfetched. She had the talent. Everyone said so.

In school the previous year, she had joined the Dramatic Society and had tried out for a play. The role she had won had been a minor one, but she had applied herself so diligently that she'd managed to stand out and steal the show. She had been so good that this year, there had been no contest. She had been cast in the starring role of a short, brilliant drawing-room comedy by James M. Barrie.

She had let her studies slide as she threw herself into her part with such abandon that her teachers felt compelled to send a caustic note to her mother.

"If Charlotte-Anne would only apply herself as diligently to all her schoolwork as she does to her acting . . ." the note had begun. She had seethed with fury. Couldn't they see, the fools? Were they blind? It was *acting* she had to learn about, not economics or endocrine glands.

But the night of the play, at the final curtain call, she knew that all the aggravation, and her failing grade in geometry, had been worth it. She was inundated with so much intoxicating applause that she'd had to take deep breaths to keep from getting dizzy.

She had played the role so perfectly that the incredible had happened. As the play progressed, she had actually *become* the character. The rounds of applause she had earned catapulted her to the loftiest heights she had ever known.

Everyone in the school suddenly admired her. She was told time and again that nobody had ever noticed how beautiful she was. Even classmates who had once snubbed her or who had never spoken to her before, and even boys who had ignored her up until now, finally clustered around her. She was asked out for dates, her advice was sought. She had never been so popular in her life, and she'd never realized just how powerful that could make her feel.

Her fate, which had revealed itself so clearly to her when she'd sat through that first Broadway show, was now truly sealed. She would become an actress. She was determined to see her name in lights.

Even her mother and sisters had congratulated her profusely on her performance, although none of them took her acting ambitions very seriously. "Someday," she promised them softly as they drove home after the play, "I'm going to be an actress."

"That's lovely, dear," her mother had said. "You were really very good. For a while I actually forgot it was you up there on the stage."

They were flattering words, the very compliment any actress was dying to hear. Yet she could sense that no one, especially her mother, greeted her announcement with the seriousness due it. No one seemed to understand that beside acting, everything else paled in significance.

Her name in lights.

She didn't need to study history and mathematics. She needed to study dramatics, *theater*.

She even went so far as to try to discuss this with her mother one night. Elizabeth-Anne had smiled at her. "But, darling, everyone needs to learn the fundamentals. After you've conquered the basics, of course you can go to college and study theater. No one is trying to stop you."

"But . . . you've often told me that *you* didn't get much formal schooling," Charlotte-Anne pointed out, hoping to somehow wheedle her way out of attending Brearley and into acting lessons from a coach instead. "It hasn't hurt you any."

"That's true," Elizabeth-Anne had replied. "But believe me, there are many times when I wish I'd been able to learn a lot more." She sighed. "But in Texas, things were different. There, school wasn't nearly as necessary as it is here."

Charlotte-Anne had nodded silently. Somehow, she just couldn't get her point across. Oh, her mother understood about her wanting to do something, but what she couldn't seem to understand was how important it was for Charlotte-Anne to stop wasting time on useless learning and to concentrate wholeheartedly on the career she had chosen. She had gone to bed with a leaden heart. She couldn't even close her eyes. She thought all night about acting, and it consumed her.

Then suddenly, in the wee hours of the morning, just before dawn, the idea had occurred to her. Why hadn't she thought of it before? She was right here in Manhattan, for God's sake! Why didn't she just go to auditions? Then, if she got a part, nobody would dare stop her. Not if she proved herself.

Of course, she did have school to contend with.

If necessity was the mother of invention, then ambition was the father of deceit. The idea didn't so much germinate as explode in her mind.

There *was* something she could do about school! She would simply play hooky. There was no reason she shouldn't be able to get away with it. She was an actress, wasn't she? And if she was caught, then too bad. It was worth the risk for the chance to see her name in lights.

And so it began—the conniving, the typing of her "mother's" notes excusing her from school, the "suffering" from a multitude of ailments for which she had to "consult the doctor," the painstaking practice and forging of her mother's signature, the changing clothes in the ladies' room at Grand Central. She called herself Carla Hall, since she hadn't dared to use her real name. The Hales were becoming too well known in the city. And every actress needed a stage name, she rationalized. Carla Hall was an easy name to remember; she was going to make sure no one would ever forget it.

She scoured the papers. Each time she saw an ad for an open audition somewhere, she resurrected one of her ailments and spent the afternoon trying out for whatever show it was. All the auditions seemed to be held in dingy lofts or dirty, rickety rehearsal halls on the West Side.

It had been a rude awakening. She had expected something very different, but there was nothing remotely glamorous about auditioning for a show. Most of the time she didn't even get a chance to see the script before it was handed to her to read aloud. It was simply sink or swim. She was made to feel like an insignificant steer in a huge herd of cattle.

She didn't exactly know how, but she persevered, although

there were countless times when she thought she might as well give up and go back to school. The competition was stiffer than she had ever imagined. She had never guessed that there were so many beautiful girls in this city, all far more talented than she. And they all seemed to have one thing in common: they all wanted to become actresses.

It wasn't long before she could recognize her fellow aspiring "theater trash," as they called themselves. They all looked hungry, starved for food as much as for success. Without fail, they tended to downplay their beauty, as though trying to prove they were mere putty, malleable for any role. Their clothes were rather seedy and very casual. They didn't seem to care at all how they dressed. All that mattered was the greasepaint they were certain flowed in their veins. At each audition, Charlotte-Anne was only too painfully aware that she was too finely dressed and glowing with good health.

If the auditions were grueling, then the reactions she provoked from the other aspiring actresses were even more torturous. She could feel the waves of open hostility rolling toward her. One girl would poke another in the ribs and gesture at her; yet another would mimic a lady, haughty chin in the air, hands adjusting the flounces of an imaginary gown. She caught whispers of the nickname they had dubbed her with. "Miss Rich Bitch."

Their icy expressions were all the same, and she could read them with no difficulty: What's *she* doing here? Who does *she* think she is? Does she really think wearing a hundred dollars on her back will get her a part?

She felt so alone, and there was no one she could turn to for encouragement. Only two things kept her going; hope that an opportunity to showcase her talents would arise, and the belief that she was special. That *she* was one of the chosen few. But whenever she looked at the others, her heart would sink.

If they only knew! she cried to herself. She didn't want to look different. She would have given anything to blend in with the crowd. It was ridiculous, but the crux of the problem was that she didn't have anything suitable to wear. Her school uniform was definitely out of the question. Nor could she wear her own clothes, which made her look too young, too girlish. She had had but one option—trying to look older than her mere seventeen years. As she saw it, she had no choice but to sneak out with her mother's clothes. The only trouble was, all her mother's outfits were now expensive, extremely well cut, and very ladylike.

It's just another necessary sacrifice, and a damn strange one, she told herself over and over. Let them all laugh behind my back. Let them call me "Miss Rich Bitch." I don't care. I'll show them. *I'll* make it.

Audition followed audition, and she always heard the same words repeated over and over. They might as well have been a recording. "Thank you. If we decide to use you, you'll hear from us. Next!"

For weeks she didn't dare audition for a musical or any show that required dancing. She knew she could neither carry a tune nor perform the simplest dance step. But finally, out of desperation, she decided to try it. It couldn't hurt, she told herself. What could they do other than turn her down?

The show was a long-running smash musical revue called *Reach for the Stars*, for which a new cast was being assembled. The rehearsal hall where the auditions took place, like the others, was in the West Forties. If anything, it was an even more dilapidated building than all the others she had been in so far. She was the twenty-eighth girl in a lineup of about fifty, and she recognized a lot of the actresses from previous auditions. It seemed that nobody ever got a part. Yet there was a peculiar air of brave camaraderie about the girls. Most of them knew each other and tried to put one another at ease.

With trepidation Charlotte-Anne sat quietly on one of the rickety benches awaiting her turn. With each passing minute she was filled with a mounting sense of dread.

One by one the other girls before her went into the rehearsal room. She heard them all sing, accompanied by an out-of-tune piano. They were all so good. Even through the closed door she could tell that much.

Oh God, she prayed silently. I can't carry a tune or read music. I can't even dance. I'll just make a fool of myself.

Just as she made up her mind to leave, she heard a name being called out.

"Carla Hall!"

She froze. They called her again, and somehow she managed to get up, her legs weak, her body shaking. She armed herself in the only way she knew how, by squaring her shoulders and assuming an aloof, steely, ladylike veneer.

The big audition room was bare and dim. An upright piano had been placed in one corner, so that the player faced out. Four men and a woman sat in the shadows at the far end. A young man in baggy trousers thrust a sheet of music at her. She stared at it stupidly and turned to the piano player. He looked grizzly and unkempt, half-hidden behind a veil of cigar smoke. Then the out-of-tune piano began to pound. She stared down at the undecipherable notes she held in her hand. She took a deep breath. Perhaps she could fake it. She had heard enough renditions of the same song for the last two hours.

She opened her mouth to sing, but no sound came out. The piano player stopped after playing the first few bars. Horror-stricken, she looked at the five people at the other end of the room, but they didn't seem to be paying any attention to her. Slowly she turned to face the piano player, who was rolling his eyes. He started over.

Again nothing happened.

The young man in baggy trousers marched toward her and snatched the music out of her hand. He flung open the door. "Next! Ethel Broward!"

In dismay Charlotte-Anne stared at the four men and the woman. She had been dismissed, this time without even an "if-we-want-you-we'll-give-you-a-call."

She hadn't even rated that.

As though in a dream, she saw the next girl come in, a confident, smiling brunette in her mid-twenties. Charlotte-Anne knew she had to leave, but she couldn't move. Her feet seemed to be nailed down to the floor.

"Well?" the young man demanded. "You waitin' for a miracle?"

That snapped her out of it. She turned around, and clapping

a hand over her mouth, ran from the room. Her eyes were burning as she burst out into the waiting room, where the others were staring at her. She hurried down the flight of steep stairs. She thought she was going to be sick before she ever got outside.

She leaned against the grimy brick wall, taking deep lungfuls of fresh air. The queasiness slowly left her, but she was sobbing loudly, the tears spilling down her cheeks. She had never felt so humiliated in her entire life.

She heard footsteps behind her and turned away, hiding her face.

"Hey, there's always another time, kid," a man's tenor voice said gently. "Not everybody was cut out for song and dance. You just came to the wrong audition is all. Mistakes like that happen all the time."

She wiped away her tears and sniffled. "I'm not a kid," she said thickly. "I'm twenty years old."

It was her first lie to him, the first of many. But at the time, it didn't seem to matter.

"So you are."

She turned around slowly. He seemed to tower above her, handsome, rugged, yet somehow slick and polished. His eyes were agate and hypnotic, and a half-smile hovered on his lips. He was one of the four men who had been sitting at the far end of the room, but now he looked curiously familiar. She had the feeling she should know who he was, but she couldn't place him.

He grinned apologetically. "Sorry. I didn't mean to call you a kid. It's just an expression."

She smiled and nodded. Then suddenly her heart seemed to shrink. Now she knew why he looked so familiar! She had seen his picture in newspapers and magazines on countless occasions. She had even caught one of his shows the year before. He was Mickey Hoyt, one of the most brilliant stars of the New York stage.

His eyes shimmered with a marble gloss. "Come on, I'll buy you a cup of coffee."

For the first time in her life she felt an instinctive physical longing well up inside her. It was as though something deep within her, which had always lain sleeping, was suddenly awakened. She found herself nodding. She was spellbound.

He placed a hand under her elbow and guided her toward Times Square. "Been having a tough time of it?" he asked as they walked.

She nodded, trying to keep up with his long strides.

"I know what it's like. I've been there too."

"You?"

"Sure. You don't think I was born onstage, do you?"

She shrugged. "No. It just comes as a surprise, that's all." She frowned. "Sometimes it seems like I've cornered the market on rejections."

"I wouldn't worry too much if I were you. You're beautiful, possibly one of the most beautiful women I've ever seen, and believe me, I've seen a lot. But you've got them all beat. You project a certain quality, something the other girls don't have. There's something of the reserved New England lady about you."

"I'm from Texas originally."

"I know that. Your speech says so. But your attitude is strictly Bostonian."

Her brow furrowed. "Maybe I should try to get rid of my accent?"

He shook his head. "I wouldn't worry about that. What you need are good roles. There's plenty of those which call for your kind of accent."

"And they're impossible to get."

"Not really."

She looked at him with quickening interest. "Do you know something I don't know?"

"No, but I've got something you don't have—connections. Lots of people in this town owe me favors. This business is strictly 'you scratch my back, I'll scratch yours.' All I have to do is call in some old debts to see about getting you some decent scripts. Some you can study and try out for without going through those humiliating cattle calls."

She couldn't believe her ears. "You could really do that?" Her voice was a whisper.

"Why not?" He grinned easily. "I'm Mickey Hoyt, aren't I?"

She nodded solemnly.

"It'll take time, though. The most important thing is to find you the right script. But I warn you, it won't be a big part. Just a decent one. The rest is up to you. Think you can handle that?"

"Can I!"

He stopped walking. "Here we are."

She stared up at the lovely building. "This isn't a coffee shop," she said softly.

"No, it isn't. It's the Algonquin. But room service does send up a decent pot of coffee."

She looked hesitant.

"And I confess, I did lure you here." He smiled disarmingly. "Under the most dishonorable pretext."

A faint flush crept through her skin, and she looked away.

"You don't have to come up. But I'd like it," he said softly. "We can always sit downstairs in the lobby and just talk."

"No, that's okay." She glanced up at him. His eyes seemed to reach out and become part of her. As he held her gaze, she had the sensation that the earth had stopped moving, that they were the only two people alive.

As though she was under hypnosis, she followed him into the hotel and up to the nineteenth floor. When they reached room nineteen-nineteen, he closed the door and locked it.

He turned around and smiled at her. "Don't worry, I won't get you pregnant. There are other ways to make love, you know."

She watched him unzipping his trousers. She stared down at him with fascination. His phallus was already semierect, large and reddish purple. So this was "the plumbing" all the girls in school whispered about. When her brother had been a baby, she had seen his tiny genitals, but this was the first time she had ever seen a grown man's penis. She had had no idea that it could be swollen so large, or look so angry. For a moment, panic seized her.

She felt his hands on her head, pushing her down to her

knees. The carpet was thick and soft. She stared up at him. His eyes were glowing intently, like burning embers.

"Come on, baby," he said, his voice soft and husky. "Eat me. Eat me good."

It wasn't making love, she realized; but it didn't matter. She did as he asked, and when he let out a growl, she instinctively removed her mouth and turned her face away. Semen spurted thickly through the air. Then he held her, and the only thing she could tell herself was that it was worth it.

No sacrifice was too much.

When she arrived at the Algonquin, she was as wet and lovely as a drenched swan. No one stopped her as she hurried through the lobby. Despite her soggy state, she looked like she belonged. She had the nonchalant bearing of one accustomed to luxury.

She headed straight for the elevators and went directly upstairs. He was always waiting for her, always in the same room, and always on Friday afternoons. Now, after all these weeks, room nineteen-nineteen had become her home away from home.

And perhaps today . . . Dared she hope that today, at long last, he would finally have found the perfect script for her to read?

When she stood in front of the door, she brushed some of the rain off her coat, took off her hat, and shook it dry. She patted her hair and took a deep breath. Then she knocked softly three times.

She could hear footsteps on the other side of the door. In a moment it would open, and he would stand there, tall and handsome, melting her with his dazzling smile and the promise in his eyes.

A key turned in the lock, but when the door swung open Charlotte-Anne let out a strangled cry. It wasn't Mickey Hoyt standing before her; it was Elizabeth-Anne.

"I think," her mother said in a quivering voice, "that it's time you and I had a serious talk."

3

When Charlotte-Anne came out of the examination room, her face was pinched and she avoided looking at her mother. She didn't think she could ever face anyone again, but especially not her mother.

Dr. Rogers, a large lugubrious man with watery gray eyes, caught Elizabeth-Anne's gaze. He shook his head discreetly and went back into his office.

Elizabeth-Anne allowed herself a deep sigh of relief. Then she sank back in the waiting-room chair and closed her eyes.

During the ride home, Charlotte-Anne stared morosely out of the car window. Neither she nor her mother said a word. Elizabeth-Anne seemed both disappointed and embarrassed and when they got home, she silently followed Charlotte-Anne into her room and shut the door.

"You're still a virgin," she said softly, sinking down on the edge of the bed. "Thank God." She looked directly at Charlotte-Anne.

Charlotte-Anne's face blazed scarlet. She sat down on the chair at her dressing table and hung her head in shame.

"I won't pretend that this hasn't come as a shock," her mother said. "Just before Larry and I were set to leave, the telephone rang. It was one of your teachers. She was very worried about your health and wanted me to reassure her that you were all right."

Charlotte-Anne groaned inwardly.

"Do you realize," Elizabeth-Anne asked softly, leaning forward, "that you've missed twenty-seven afternoons of school this year? *Twenty-seven*?"

Charlotte-Anne closed her eyes. She'd been "ill" a lot of days, but even she hadn't realized they added up to that many. "I . . . I can explain," she whispered falteringly.

"I wish you would." Elizabeth-Anne looked at her daughter curiously. "This day has been no end of unpleasant surprises. After the call from school, Dallas was in here making your bed when your phone rang. Naturally, she answered it."

Charlotte-Anne felt her stomach turn sour. She should never have given Mickey Hoyt her number. She'd done it only because he'd insisted.

"It was someone named Mickey," her mother continued, "and he asked for Carla Hall. Of course Dallas was too surprised to correct him. He left a message for you. He said he couldn't meet you today, but that he'd be at the Algonquin next Friday, as usual."

"And he just came out and told Dallas that?" Charlotte-Anne asked in bitter disbelief. "Just to try to end everything between us?"

"I can't speak for him," her mother said. "Perhaps he wanted to do that, perhaps he didn't. But for us it was a simple matter of deduction. Larry went to see the desk clerk at the Algonquin, who, of course, was very discreet and claimed to know nothing. Under the circumstances, that was to be expected. But when Larry took him aside and told him you were underage, that he was prepared to go to the police and file charges, and that this could possibly result in a case of statutory rape, he recalled everything. It seems," she added dryly, "that room nineteen-nineteen was becoming quite well known for your Friday afternoons."

Charlotte-Anne shook her head miserably.

"Of course, Mr. Hoyt should have known better. He's too well known in this town to think he could get away with something like this. However, I'm sure it's not entirely his fault, though I might like to think so." Her mother looked pained. "I won't pretend I'm not disappointed in you, Charlotte-Anne. I am. However, we are all human. We all make mistakes. Especially when we're young."

"I'm not a child anymore," Charlotte-Anne said softly. "I'm a woman, Mama."

Her mother looked at her and nodded. "It seems impossible that you've grown up so fast. I still sometimes think of you as a child. Now I realize that was my mistake."

"It wasn't your fault, Mama."

Her mother sighed wearily. "Perhaps it was, and perhaps it wasn't. I don't think we'll ever know the answer." She rose to her feet. "I have some serious soul-searching to do. I suggest we wait until tomorrow to decide how to handle this." She crossed the room to the door.

Charlotte-Anne lifted her head and looked at her. "You hate me, don't you, Mama?" she asked thickly.

Her mother turned and looked at her with surprise. For the first time, Charlotte-Anne was truly aware of her mother's strength. "No, I don't hate you, Charlotte-Anne. There are things you do that I might not like or approve of, but you are my daughter." Elizabeth-Anne's voice grew gentler. "I could never hate you, no matter what you did. I love you. Someday, when you have children of your own, you'll understand."

For a moment Charlotte-Anne looked at her in amazement. Then her vision blurred with tears. "Mama?"

"Yes, dear?"

"I love you, too," Charlotte-Anne whispered.

Elizabeth-Anne smiled. "I know that."

"I'm really sorry, Mama," she cried despairingly. "For all of this. All I've been thinking about was my . . . Oh, damn! I've ruined your plans and Larry's. I've been so selfish."

A soft expression veiled Elizabeth-Anne's eyes. She was, Charlotte-Anne realized, handling this highly unpleasant matter with the utmost fairness. Somehow, Elizabeth-Anne Hale was managing to keep her own emotions under tight rein.

"The property is still available," Elizabeth-Anne said, "and I'll sign the papers for it in a few days. And Larry won't run off, that much I know. Nothing was postponed that couldn't have waited a few days anyway. The only thing that matters to me is that you don't get hurt."

Charlotte-Anne gave a little nod. A lump was blocking her throat and she could not trust herself to speak.

Elizabeth-Anne opened the door. "I'll see you later, dear."

"Yes, Mama." Charlotte-Anne watched her mother leave.

Only after the door closed did she fling herself onto the bed and burst into tears.

She was desolate with humiliation and remorse, and terribly angry with Mickey. God, how she *hated* him. He had not only been indiscreet, but his behavior had been downright despicable. She should never have trusted him. She had told him that she was married and that no one must find out about their Friday afternoons. It didn't matter that she had lied to him. She had had a reason, and a good one. But he had gone out of his way to disgrace himself and her, the bastard!

She could only deduce that he'd deliberately tried to end their relationship, in the ugliest way possible. And that meant one other thing as well, which was what hurt her the most. He had never meant to help further her career. It had all been idle talk. Just a way for him to control her.

She felt dirty, tricked, and used.

"I have come to a decision," Elizabeth-Anne told her the next day as they sat in the living room. "Painful though it may be, I think that in the long run it will work out for the best."

They were sitting alone, facing one another on the matching apricot couches. Charlotte-Anne had been awake half the night and had finally come to terms with the truth about Mickey Hoyt. She had not loved him; she saw that clearly now. She had been merely dazzled by who he was and what he had promised to do for her. And he had liked her for those needs of his which she could fulfill. It hadn't been easy to look at it in those bare-boned, brutal terms, but it had been a necessary exercise. Coming to grips with what she and Mickey shared—or, more important, what they hadn't shared—had left her with a new kind of maturity, and for the first time she was seeing her mother not from a youthful vantage, but as a fellow adult.

She felt she was appreciating her mother for the first time. Elizabeth-Anne Hale was an attractive and well-groomed woman, very much the lady in her exquisitely tailored Jane Regny suit with its jacket flaring slightly at the hips and its skirt reaching to mid-calf. No one would ever guess that she came from a small town in Texas. Looking back at the past few years, Charlotte-Anne realized that she had never known anyone quite as adaptable as her mother, who could accomplish so much and do it with such style.

Up until now, Charlotte-Anne had been listening attentively and speaking only when called upon to do so. She had decided, for once, that no matter what decree her mother meted out, she would not put up an argument.

"As we both know," her mother was saying, "your grades at Brearley this past year have been . . . well, shall we say, unsatisfactory?"

Charlotte-Anne smiled wryly. "They've been atrocious."

Elizabeth-Anne laughed. "Whatever you say, but there's no need for us to hurl insults. I realize now what I, and I suppose every mother in the world, did not want to have to face." She sighed sadly. "That a child she loves dearly has grown up right in front of her eyes. You are now an adult, Charlotte-Anne, and I think it's time I treated you as one.

"At any rate, I believe your unsatisfactory grades in school have been due in large part to the energies you have lavished on your theatrical ambitions instead of your studies. Therefore, I think it would be nice now if you expended at least half as much attention on your studies as you have on the theater. However, you are nearly grown up, and some things cannot be forced. Whether more schooling serves you or not is yet to be seen. But as a young adult, I think there is no harm if you acquire a little polish. I'm sure even the actress in you will agree with that."

Charlotte-Anne nodded.

"I want you to know that I don't blame you for what has happened," Elizabeth-Anne continued. Her voice was soft and wistful. "I have been lax also. I've been paying altogether too much attention to the business, and neglecting my family in the process. I should have seen what was happening with you, but I never took the time. However, that's all water under the bridge now. We should look back on the past only in order to learn from it. Otherwise the past is useless."

Elizabeth-Anne paused for a moment. It was important that

Charlotte-Anne realize that what was coming was what she believed was best for her, not a punishment. She had thought about it all night long, and this morning she had made some telephone calls. Still, good intentions all too often pave the road to misery. It seemed so difficult to try to set things right.

"I surmise," Elizabeth-Anne said gently, "that you have been hurt by this . . . this involvement with Mr. Hoyt?"

Charlotte-Anne looked thoughtful. "Yesterday I thought I was, but I'm not so sure about it today. He used me, I see that now. But I tried to use him, too. Only I wasn't as good at it."

Elizabeth-Anne nodded. "That's a very mature outlook, and I'm pleased. I know it hurts to have to put things in such brutal terms. Nevertheless, I think it would be a lot easier for you to get him totally out of your system if you were further removed from his orbit. Residual feelings always linger awhile, especially with a well-known person. Each time you see his picture in a magazine or his name on a billboard, you are bound to feel a little pain."

Charlotte-Anne frowned thoughtfully. "I don't think that will pose much of a problem now. I can handle it, I think."

Elizabeth-Anne held up a hand. "Nevertheless. The school to which I've decided to transfer you is a boarding school."

"Mama!" Charlotte-Anne cried, truly surprised.

"Please hear me out, dear. You must understand that this is not a punishment of any sort. It's a fine school where they can teach you a lot. And not just about mathematics and history, though they teach that too. L'Ecole Catroux is basically a finishing school. They turn girls into young ladies and prepare them to face society. Besides, I don't think a little bit of international exposure will hurt you."

"Interna . . ."

"A young lady needs to travel, Charlotte-Anne, and I hear Switzerland is quite lovely. At the risk of repeating myself, a little grace and polish never hurt anyone. L'Ecole Catroux is in Geneva, and it comes highly recommended. A lot of American girls go there, as well as English girls and others from all over the world, all from the finest families. You will make new friends that you would otherwise never have an opportunity to meet. Neither will it hurt you to pick up another language.''

Elizabeth-Anne paused, her face set with pain. ''It hurts me to see you go. You *must* believe that. I still find it difficult to face the fact that you're grown up now. If it were up to me, I'd like nothing more than to keep you with me always, and smother you. But that's selfish, and I refuse to ruin your life. You must learn to be independent. I know that now. That's what made you try so hard to become an actress, and drove you straight into Mr. Hoyt's arms. He was not so much to blame as I.

''It is my sincerest wish that you will remain at Catroux until the end of next year. However, if you wish to come home or quit on your eighteenth birthday, which is only six months from now, I leave the choice entirely up to you. You will be of age and legally, at least, capable of making your own decisions.

''If, at that time, you still want to pursue an acting career, I will help you in any way I can.''

Charlotte-Anne looked at her mother. ''Switzerland sounds so . . . so far away. I've never been gone from home.''

Elizabeth-Anne leaned forward and reached out, placing her hands over Charlotte-Anne's. Her voice was as gentle as her touch. ''There comes a time, Charlotte-Anne, when each of us must take the first step toward independence. That is what you will do now. Try to look at it this way: as a result, you'll be better prepared to face the world than most.''

''About your offer to help me pursue acting when I return. It stands even if I come back in six months?''

''Yes.''

''I mean . . . you'll really help me?'' Charlotte-Anne stared at her mother.

Elizabeth-Anne faced her squarely. ''I think you know by now that I never make promises I don't keep.''

Charlotte-Anne nodded.

''If you're serious, yes, I'll do what I can. I'll support you financially so you can concentrate fully on acting and *nothing* else. I'll pay for acting classes, or coaches, or whatever it is you need. And you can live away from home if you like. I'll even try—if it's within my power, that is—to open whatever doors I can." She smiled mysteriously. "I hear that investors in shows can sometimes pull enough strings to get someone a part. God knows, I have enough money. I'm sure some producer wouldn't mind parting me from some of it."

"Oh, Mama!" Charlotte-Anne looked ready to burst into tears. She was at once relieved and elated. She had expected her mother to lecture and punish her. Instead, she was being offered everything she wanted. On an impulse, she jumped up from the couch, slid over to her mother's, and squeezed her tightly.

"I hope," Elizabeth-Anne said, "that you'll promise to learn as much as you can at Catroux, and give the teachers as few problems as possible. And as for the trip across the Atlantic, you won't be alone. Robyn Morgan is sailing for Europe next week on the *Ile de France*, and I've arranged for you to take the same crossing. She said she'd be delighted to have you accompany her."

Charlotte-Anne was overjoyed. They'd known Robyn for years now and Charlotte-Anne not only liked her, but also admired her. Robyn Morgan wove that indefinable spell around herself which Charlotte-Anne hankered for. And while six months spent at a strange school in a foreign country frightened her, it wasn't really *that* long. She'd waited in vain for at least three months for Mickey Hoyt to pop up with a script.

"And now," Elizabeth-Anne said, getting to her feet, "I think it wouldn't hurt if we did some shopping. You'll need some new clothes. We can't have a Hale arriving in Switzerland in rags, can we?" Her eyes twinkled with amusement. "Or in her mother's clothes?"

Charlotte-Anne looked contrite. "I'm sorry, Mama."

Elizabeth-Anne laughed. "I will say one thing," she said, putting an arm around Charlotte-Anne's shoulder. "You do my clothes justice."

"Mama?"

Charlotte-Anne's tone was so serious that Elizabeth-Anne looked at her daughter worriedly. "Yes, dear?"

"Larry . . . you're going to marry him, aren't you?"

"Of course! We've got it all set up. In fact, he's running

around town making the arrangements right now. We'll be married here in a civil ceremony downtown, followed by a very small wedding at the Little Church Around the Corner. Just for family and a few assorted friends like Robyn and Ludmila.''

"I hate to have to miss it.''

"And I wouldn't have you to, not for the world.'' Elizabeth-Anne laughed. "I told you Robyn was coming, didn't I? Well, she can't be in two places at once. And neither can you. The wedding will be held in the afternoon a few hours before you sail.''

Charlotte-Anne felt the warmth of the hand between herself and her mother. Suddenly she realized how much they loved each other, although they'd never said it. She took her mother's hand and lifted it to her lips. "I'm glad, Mama,'' she said. "I wouldn't want to leave with any hard feelings between us.''

"And I wouldn't want that either.''

"It's funny, you know?'' Charlotte-Anne looked at her. "I never knew we could talk like this.''

"Just remember, anytime you want to discuss something with me, feel free to do so.''

Charlotte-Anne nodded. "You know what?'' Her eyes began to well with tears. "I . . . I feel that we're closer than we've ever been before. Like we're not just mother and daughter. I feel like we're . . .''

Elizabeth-Anne smiled into her daughter's eyes. "Friends?'' she asked.

4

Spring burst upon New York in its glorious splendor just in time for the wedding. It was one of those rare sparkling days, a balmy surprise tucked between two late-winter cold spells. It took little imagination to fancy Elizabeth-Anne as a June bride.

The little church on East Twenty-ninth Street was filled with white lilies, roses, carnations, tulips, and peonies. Charlotte-Anne gasped as her mother was led to the altar, a tiny white bouquet of lilies of the valley in her hands. Elizabeth-Anne had never looked more lovely. She wore a dove-gray lace dress, gray satin picture hat, and gray satin pumps. Around her neck was the three-strand pearl necklace Larry had given her that morning. And he looked splendid beside her in his custom-tailored dark suit with a white carnation in his lapel and a dark velvet patch over his eye. It was hardly the society wedding of the year, although if they had so chosen, it could easily have become that. It was simply a lovely wedding for family and a few close friends, which was just the way they wanted it. Ludmila cried and blew her nose noisily throughout the ceremony.

Then, a few hours later, it was time for Charlotte-Anne to leave. Larry's stately yellow-and-black Rolls-Royce, which Elizabeth-Anne was to keep in perfect running condition for the rest of her life, and which was still festooned with garlands of white flowers for the wedding procession, was loaded with new Vuitton luggage, a going-away gift to Charlotte-Anne from Larry. They drove over to the West Side, where the *Ile de France* was berthed.

Elizabeth-Anne and Larry had secured her a large first-class stateroom next to Robyn's, but they hardly had a chance to glance at it. Shortly after they boarded, a deep blast of the liner's horns carried mournfully across the water.

"It's time we left," Larry said.

Charlotte-Anne nodded. It was with both excitement and a heavy heart that she bid her family farewell. For the first time since she could remember, she felt truly close to them all. Now she realized with a pang just how sorely she would miss them.

"Well, Mrs. Hochstetter," Charlotte-Anne said to her mother. "How does it feel to be married?"

"Truthfully, quite the same as before," her mother said with a smile. "I've loved Larry for a long time. But the hotels will still be *Hale* hotels; I'll keep my own 'stage' name, so to speak. In public I'll still be Elizabeth-Anne Hale.

But in private life I'm Mrs. Lawrence Hochstetter." She smiled at Larry, then looked intently at Charlotte-Anne. Her voice broke. "I'll miss you, dear."

"And I'll miss you, Mama. Too bad I won't be around for the move."

"Move?" Elizabeth-Anne looked puzzled. "What move?"

"To the Hochstetter mansion, of course!"

"Oh, dear me, no. It's the other way around. Larry is moving into the penthouse with us. We decided quite some time ago that we'll be comfortable enough there. Besides, I'd feel strange rattling around that mansion. And then, there's the economic side of it. Why pay for a huge staff of servants when we have the entire hotel staff at our disposal? Dallas and a chauffeur are all we need. The hotels will simply absorb Larry's servants. This way they won't be out of work, and at the same time, we cut our costs."

"Always the businesswoman." Charlotte-Anne smiled. "You'll never change, Mama."

Elizabeth-Anne pretended to look shocked. "I surely hope not." The tears shone in her eyes as she hugged her daughter. They exchanged kisses and she pressed a small box into Charlotte-Anne's hand.

"What's this?" Charlotte-Anne asked curiously.

"That's your father's necklace. The pansy charm. I want you to have it to remember us by."

A sob escaped Charlotte-Anne's lips and she hugged her mother again.

Larry enveloped her in his arms and she stood on tiptoe to kiss him. "Thank God stepfathers are never wicked."

"I'll miss you, big girl. Just make sure you don't stay over there too long."

"Oh, I wouldn't."

"Don't be so sure. Europe has its magic. Some people love it and stay forever."

Then Zaccheus shook her hand and gave her a reluctant peck on the cheek. "Gee, you sure I can't come along, sis? This boat sure is neat."

Charlotte-Anne smiled at him. "I'm sure," she said, smiling down at him sadly. She turned to Rebecca, and they embraced.

"I know we didn't always see eye to eye," Charlotte-Anne told her thickly, "but I'll miss you. I love you, and always will."

"Me too." Rebecca kissed both her cheeks.

Charlotte-Anne nodded and threw her arms around Regina, who burst into tears. "This is the first time we've ever been apart."

"Don't worry," Charlotte-Anne assured her older sister. They exchanged quick kisses. "I'll be back soon. And I'll be the actress while you'll be the doctor. Bet you'll even deliver my kids, huh?" Her voice grew husky. Her bravado was deserting her. "We'll see each other in no time."

Regina nodded and smiled through her tears.

Neither of them could know that they would never see each other alive again.

Charlotte-Anne watched as her family got off the ship. She stood outside on the deck, gripping the varnished railing as though trying to draw strength from the wood. She leaned over the railing and looked for them in the crowd at dockside. Finally she spied their familiar faces, and she waved excitedly. There was another deep, mournful blast of the horn.

"Why, you're crying!" a voice said from beside her.

Charlotte-Anne turned and saw Robyn, looking stunning in a small hat with a short veil shading the top half of her face. She was smoking, and her cigarette was stuck in a long ivory holder.

"*I* only cry at weddings and funerals," Robyn declared. "*Never* at sailings." She took a puff on her cigarette and exhaled. "I did cry a little this afternoon at your mother's wedding, you know. Weddings always have that effect on me." She paused. "Larry's found himself a fine lady."

Charlotte-Anne nodded. "I know."

"Well, I suppose I'll go inside and make certain the maid is unpacking my things. If clothes are kept in suitcases for too long, they take forever to hang out. I'll leave my side of the connecting door unlocked in case you need anything. Feel free to visit anytime. After all, we're neighbors now.''

"Thank you, Mrs. Morgan.''

"Miss *Morgan*?'' Robyn tilted her head back and laughed. "You dear sweet child. Don't make me feel so terribly old. You and I have a long week ahead of us, and we'll be running into each other every time either of us turns around. We might as well call each other by our Christian names.'' She inhaled on her cigarette, exhaled a plume of smoke, and cocked her head. "On trains and ships it *is* the thing to do. You must call me Robyn.''

"Robyn,'' Charlotte-Anne repeated tentatively.

"That's better.'' Robyn flashed her a smile, gave a tiny wave with her fingertips, and went back inside. The horn blasted again, this time with more urgency. Charlotte-Anne waved down to her family as the lines were cast off and the heavy ship began to move away from the pier, nudged by the tugboats that surrounded it like a gaggle of ugly ducklings clustered around a beautiful mother swan. Charlotte-Anne kept waving long after the individual faces receded from sight. Soon the ship was backed out into midstream and the tugs poked at it until the bow faced downriver,

Charlotte-Anne blinked back her salt tears and lifted her head. Dusk was coming rapidly, and the purple sky overhead was streaked with reds and oranges. On the shore, the massive concrete monoliths already glittered with a million lights. Only now did she realize that in the years since she'd come to New York, she had never noticed how truly beautiful and impressive the city was. She had gotten too used to it. When she'd walked on the sidewalks or crossed the streets, she had never taken the time to look *up*. That was how you had to see this city, with your head tilted back. She thought of so many things she'd never done, so many little, seemingly inconsequential things. They all seemed so important right now.

"Damn,'' she swore in a tight little voice. "I don't want to leave. I don't want to go to school in Switzerland. I only want to go home.''

For a long time she stayed out on the deck. Darkness came swiftly as the ship sailed down the island and off through the harbor. Charlotte-Anne walked back along the promenade deck, watching the Statue of Liberty slipping by. Then the ship headed out into the Narrows and the lights of the city receded, growing dimmer and dimmer in the distance. She had the impression that New York was Atlantis sinking slowly into the sea. Then it was swallowed up completely by the blackness of the ocean and the sky.

They were at sea. A brisk, chill wind tugged at her clothes, fluttering and snapping her skirt. The other passengers had long since gone inside. She was alone on the deck.

"Charlotte-Anne! Goodness, what are you still doing out here? I've been searching the entire ship for you. I've even had you paged. Why didn't you answer? For a while I was sure you'd gone overboard."

Charlotte-Anne turned around. Robyn stood resplendent in a floor-length gown of cascading ruby taffeta with a matching stole that she clutched around her creamy bare shoulders. Her ears, neck, and hands sparkled with rubies and diamonds.

"You look beautiful." Charlotte-Anne's pale eyes swept Robyn from head to toe. "Is there a party?"

"Party! We've both been invited to sit at the captain's table, and you're not even changed yet." Robyn shook her head in despair and murmured, "Is there a party!"

Charlotte-Anne turned away and stared sorrowfully out at the dark expanse of sea. The long, receding wake glowed with phosphorescence. Somewhere far behind it was home, where she longed to be now. She needed some time to herself, alone, to sort out her feelings and adjust to the temporary shipboard world, and, even more important, to prepare herself emotionally for life in a foreign country.

"I really don't think I feel up to it tonight, Robyn," she begged off.

Robyn's eyes flashed. "Nonsense. An invitation to sit at the captain's table is practically a royal summons. And besides, you're not going to rob me of the pleasure of arousing everyone's envy as we descend the staircase of the Grande Salle à Manger together. We're clearly the two most beautiful women on board, and I intend to break some hearts. There's the most marvelous Italian prince in a suite right down the corridor from us. He's been invited to the captain's table too. Luigi di Fontanesi." A little sigh escaped Robyn's lips.

"I met him once or twice. He's so dashing, and *filthy* rich. And a bachelor yet! Women throw themselves at him left and right, but so far he's managed to keep himself from getting involved with any of them. There was even a rumor going around a couple of years back that some girl in Deauville had tried to commit suicide over him." Robyn looked temporarily deflated. "Too bad I won't have it said that I rob the cradle. He's just a wee bit too young for me. He's older than you, though, but not that old. Somewhere in his late twenties. Now, get inside, or do I have to drag you in and dress you myself? I took the liberty of going through your things, and I picked out what you're going to wear. The maid's already steamed it and laid it out."

Charlotte-Anne was somewhat overwhelmed by Robyn's barrage of chatter, but she managed to plead, "Not tonight. Please."

"Yes, tonight!" Robyn's tone left no room for further argument. "I promised your mother I'd take care of you. And to Robyn Morgan that means two things. First and foremost, protecting you from all things evil. And Luigi di Fontanesi is *deliciously* evil. And second, exposing you socially. I refuse to take no for an answer."

"By the time you've finished dressing," Robyn growled impatiently, lighting a cigarette and pacing the stateroom, "dinner will long be over."

Charlotte-Anne glanced at Robyn's moving reflection in the tilted mirror. "I'm *hurrying*," she mumbled, her mouth full of bobby pins. She was sitting in her slip in front of the built-in dressing table, deftly pinning up her hair. "There, finished," she said finally. She removed the remaining pins from between her lips, pivoted on the stool, and faced Robyn. "How does it look?"

Robyn stopped pacing and nodded with approval. She had never seen Charlotte-Anne with her hair up, and she approved of how it furthered the impression of slender height. "Wait a minute. Hold this." She handed Charlotte-Anne her cigarette holder, leaned down, and pulled loose a few carefully chosen tendrils of Charlotte-Anne's hair. "It shouldn't be *too* perfect," she explained. "You've got a young innocence about you, and we should emphasize it." Her fingers worked deftly, arranging several "vagrant" tendrils of hair to frame Charlotte-Anne's face. "There. Perfect. Now, turn around and look."

Charlotte-Anne pivoted again and studied herself in the mirror. Robyn was right. The new arrangement heightened her heart-shaped face and emphasized the widow's peak she was hardly aware she had.

"Now, into your dress."

"Just a moment." Charlotte-Anne pulled open a drawer and took out the slim box her mother had pressed into her hand just before sailing. She lifted out the pansy charm. For a moment she held it suspended between both hands and looked at it closely. She had never really studied it before, and now she admired its fine filigreed silver and the deep purplish-blue hue of the pansy captured in the crystal, the richness heightened by the flower's center of rich yellow.

She was glad her mother had given it to her. It was something familiar, a link to the past, and she realized at once that it would mean as much to her as it had meant to Elizabeth-Anne.

"Here, let me." Robyn took the necklace from her and secured it around her neck. Charlotte-Anne touched the charm. It felt cool and smooth, and filled her with confidence.

She rose from the stool, crossed over to the bed, and picked up the sleeveless evening gown her mother had bought for her. Made of layers of pure white diaphanous chiffon, it was Grecian in its simplicity. She lifted it over her head and let it float down smoothly over her.

"You look," Robyn said, stepping back in disbelief, "like nothing I've ever seen before." She sounded delighted. "Believe *me*, next to you everyone else will look garishly overdressed."

"Oh." Charlotte-Anne's face settled into a frown. "It isn't enough? Perhaps a bracelet or some makeup or—"

"No, no," Robyn laughed. "I meant it as a compliment." She removed the cigarette from the holder, stubbed it out in an ashtray, and dropped the holder into her clutch purse. She took Charlotte-Anne by the arm and led her to the door, then opened it and switched off the lights. "Let's go knock 'em dead."

5

The Grande Salle à Manger towered three decks high, and the murmur of conversation and the strains of elegant music wafted up to the top landing of the grand staircase. Charlotte-Anne clutched the banister on the top floor and gazed down. All her confidence seeped out of her. Even from this height, the dining room was a sea of elegantly turned-out men and exquisitely gowned women. She wished she had inherited her mother's easy confidence and adaptability.

She looked pleadingly at Robyn.

"You look exquisite," Robyn assured her with a smile. "Your mother chose well for you. The gown is just right for your age and figure, and I never knew anyone could project such clashing worldliness and formal innocence with pinned-up hair. You're simply ravishing. Now, down we go."

Charlotte-Anne took a deep breath. Below, the first course was just being served by an army of white-jacketed waiters. She saw heads leaning back as diners looked up at her and Robyn. Even from three floors below, she could feel the eyes appraising them. The grand staircase had been designed for sweeping entrances, and it terrified her because she realized that just as it could show off elegance and grace, it would magnify the slightest humiliating flaw.

She clutched the banister more tightly, the glances from below making her knees go weak. Oh, if only they hadn't arrived late! If only she hadn't spent all that time out on deck, they would have been just two more in a crowd descending the staircase. Now, making a grand entrance by themselves, she was certain something terrible was going to happen. She would trip on her hem or stumble on the carpet and go falling down an entire flight of steps.

"Chin *up*," Robyn sang softly under her breath, her lips

composed in a careful smile as she led the way. Charlotte-Anne couldn't help but marvel at the older woman's poise, at the swanlike neck with its regal chin, and the elegant definition of the slanting patrician cheekbones. Robyn was lithe and polished, and seemingly unaffected. As she stepped forward, beginning the long descent, her ruby taffeta gown billowed out from her tiny waist and the snug fit of the low-cut bodice.

Here goes, Charlotte-Anne told herself, following Robyn as she admonished herself. Just go steady. Put one satin slipper in front of the other, and repeat that process until you reach the landing. After that, there's only one more deck to go, and then you're on the bottom.

Once more she glanced down at the sea of upturned faces. This was like . . . She caught her breath. Yes, just like being onstage. Somehow that thought gave her confidence and she squared her shoulders and moved on, more relaxed. She was still unaware of the sensation she was creating. She was so young and unaffected, so like a young gazelle in her freshness and grace, that she was breathtaking. The white chiffon accentuated her every move, and with each step she took, her confidence grew a little more.

Only when she reached the middle landing, where Robyn turned and waited for her, did she realize the effect she was having on the diners below. Her audience was captivated; she could feel it. It was like the electricity coursing between an actor and the audience. Together she and Robyn swept down the last flight, two elegant swans, one red and one white, and all eyes in the Grande Salle à Manger were upon them.

She wondered if it was her imagination, or if the orchestra really did switch to an elegant waltz to accentuate their entrance. Her face blushed pinkly, and the rosy glow only served to heighten her beauty. Robyn turned to her, a half-smile on her lips, her eyes sparkling.

The instant they reached the foot of the staircase, the maître d' appeared as though by magic. "Madame. Mademoiselle." He bowed gracefully to each one of them in turn. "This way, if you please."

He led the way through the sumptuous mirrored room. They swept through the sea of tables, white-draped and gleaming with silver and crystal, past millions of dollars' worth of jewelry on dazzlingly clad women. The *Ile de France* was a flagship of oceangoing luxury, and once again Charlotte-Anne marveled that despite the misery of the Depression, there was still so much wealth in evidence.

When they reached the table of honor, the captain was already on his feet. He stood with his shoulders squared and his resplendent black uniform seemingly gilded with ormolu. His face was distinguished, his hair silver, and his eyes dark.

"Bonsoir, Madame Morgan." He bent over Robyn's proffered hand and kissed it with a flourish. "It is an honor to have you aboard once again."

"You flatter me, Captain Louvard, that you even remember me."

"No, it is I who am flattered, to have you sail with us so often, madame."

Robyn turned to Charlotte-Anne. "May I introduce my traveling companion, Miss Charlotte-Anne Hale."

"A pleasure, indeed." The captain bent over Charlotte-Anne's hand. "Mademoiselle."

The captain made the introductions with the gentlemen, all in ties and tails, standing and the ladies remaining seated.

"May I present Mrs. Reichenbach," Captain Louvard said, beginning on his right.

"Mrs. Morgan and I are old friends," the buxom woman with thinning red curls and several chins elucidated. "I'm pleased that we're making the same crossing, my dear. It's nice to run into familiar faces."

"Especially those who aim to win back their poker losses?" Robyn teased.

Mrs. Reichenbach laughed heartily, her bosom heaving. Then she eyed Charlotte-Anne and sighed softly. "You look so lovely, my dear. Though it's devastating to be reminded of one's own lost youth."

Charlotte-Anne smiled gratefully. This was an accolade indeed. Mrs. Reichenbach was well known as one of New York's premier hostesses, and the wife of the country's richest and most powerful newspaper publisher. More powerful, it was rumored, than even William Randolph Hearst.

Captain Louvard gestured across the table. "His Eminence, Giovanni, Cardinal Corsini, special envoy to His Holiness, the Pope."

His Eminence smiled politely, but with little warmth. His face was that of a medieval prince of the church, thin and hollow. He inclined his head. "Ladies."

"His Grace, the Duke of Fairfax, and Her Grace, the Duchess of Fairfax."

The duke, standing, bowed; seated beside him, his wife nodded and smiled graciously. The duke was thin and white-haired, the duchess much younger, and very beautiful with her rosy English complexion.

"His Excellency, Ambassador and Señora Pérez de Cabral," the captain said next, and added gallantly, "Ambassador and Señora Pérez are Argentina's latest diplomatic gift to France."

The ambassador was an elderly man with the face of an aesthete. Señora Pérez was a pale-skinned Buenos Aires beauty with coal-black eyes, sensuous lips, and jet-black hair pulled back in a chignon. She wore a gown of gold brocade, and around her neck hung the largest emerald Charlotte-Anne had ever seen.

"It seems, captain," the ambassador said with a smile, "that your country lost a fine diplomat when you decided to devote your life to the sea."

The captain smiled and his gaze shifted. "The Honorable Chief Justice Alexander Goode of the United States Supreme Court, and his wife, Mrs. Goode."

Charlotte-Anne shifted her gaze. The justice was a portly, imposing man with a leonine mane of white hair. He looked uncomfortable in formal dress. His wife was tiny and projected good humor. "How do you do?" they both chorused, then laughed. "It seems," Mrs. Goode said, "that we're always saying the same thing at the same time. Rest assured, it's not rehearsed."

Charlotte-Anne laughed politely.

Captain Louvard turned to the next guest. "General Erich von Kersten, from Munich."

General Kersten was red-faced, meaty, and Teutonically correct. He took a few steps back, walked around the table, and clicked his heels together smartly. He bowed low over their hands and smiled broadly. "One charming lady is a gift, but two charming ladies are heaven-sent."

Charlotte-Anne could almost feel the effort it took Robyn to keep from cringing. Even she was glad when the general went back to his seat.

"And last, but certainly not least," the captain said softly, "His Highness, Prince Luigi di Fontanesi."

Charlotte-Anne turned to her immediate left, by reflex now proffering her hand. He was standing directly beside her, and took her hand gently in his. It was then that she met his eyes. Their gaze held, and for an instant she felt paralyzed.

He was by far the most handsome man she had ever encountered. His bold, tawny yellow cat's eyes seemed to burn through her, and his white teeth gleamed predaceous. He seemed to tower over everyone, and even though he was formally dressed she could sense the sheer power of his physique, the wide animal shoulders of the athlete tapering down to a small waist and narrow, tight hips. She could almost taste the unabashedly lusty appetite in his sensuous lips and feel the cynical indolence of his bearing.

He bowed low over her hand and his breath lingered a moment too long. She felt a chill, mixed with a blast of heat coursing through her.

"You are very beautiful," he said so softly that she strained to hear the words.

Startled by his highly charged, brazenly lengthy touch, she felt her cheeks blaze crimson. She snatched her hand back and dropped her eyes. For some reason she felt curiously violated. She had never known a man who could simply look at her, and with an ever-so-light touch reach deep down to the depths of her soul. She was glad that everyone else had resumed the meal. It took her several moments to collect her composure. At least, she thought, her reaction to him hadn't been noticed by anyone.

But then Robyn caught her gaze and smiled knowingly.

Charlotte-Anne flushed again. Were her feelings *that* transparent?

"Mademoiselle?"

Charlotte-Anne turned to Captain Louvard and smiled awk-wardly as he held her chair for her. She took a seat at his left, and then he helped Robyn into hers at his right. At first she was relieved not to be sitting beside Robyn. She didn't want to have to put up with her knowing looks. What was it she had said up on deck? The prince was "deliciously evil." And, Charlotte-Anne amended, dangerous. Why else would that woman in Deauville have tried to commit suicide over him?

Yet, while she was glad to be spared her friend's scrutiny, she felt uneasy in this crowd of strangers. Everyone was so much older than she and so much more accomplished. What could she possibly have in common with ambassadors and cardinals and princes? She found herself yearning to sit unno-ticed at one of the other of the dozen tables in the room.

She gazed hesitantly around and then suffered her second shock. Only now was she aware of who was sitting on her left—Prince Luigi di Fontanesi.

She slid her napkin off the serving plate and unfolded it slowly in her lap. Then she raised her head, having decided she would avoid looking at him or speaking with him. Every-thing about him frightened her—his indolent self-assurance, his striking good looks, the physical power radiating from him, his unsettling ability to look deep into her soul.

She was grateful when a waiter placed the first course in front of her. Looking down into her shallow soup plate, she saw four poached quail eggs in mushroom caps floating in a rich golden sauce sprinkled with red caviar. Ordinarly such a treat would have delighted her, but now all she saw was bountiful satisfaction for an appetite that had deserted her. Still, eating was something to do. She seized her spoon, intending to concentrate fully on the food before her. Her efforts were in vain.

From her left, she couldn't help but sense his amused searing gaze burning through her with such intensity that her hands began to shake. It infuriated her, because she knew good and well that he strove exactly for the effect he was achieving. And she knew he must be silently laughing at her.

She tightened her lips, disgusted with herself for allowing

him to cause such a violent reaction to rage within her. But "allowing" had little to do with it. She felt totally helpless.

She couldn't wait for this dinner to be over with.

She concentrated more closely on her plate, absently pushing the food around with her spoon. Around her, the conversations became more heated, and snatches of phrases seeped into her consciousness becoming a collage in her distracted mind.

"Are you entering the Monte Carlo Grand Prix this year, Prince Luigi? . . ."

"The social reforms begun in Argentina in the last decade . . ."

"Economic chaos . . ."

"Since 1924, Duke Fairfax, when the labor government first . . ."

"Really, Cardinal Corsini, the Treaty of Conciliation between Cardinal Gasparri and Premier Mussolini . . ."

"Isn't Paris in the spring *just* like Buenos Aires in the winter . . ."

"The effects of the Hawley-Smoot Tariff on world trade . . ."

"No, the Weimar Republic and President Hindenburg . . ."

"Prince Luigi, as an aviator . . ."

"But despite the Depression, the Empire State Building *is* nearly completed, isn't it . . ."

"My dear, dear Mrs. Reichenbach, if you only . . ."

"Germany will not permit herself to be shackled . . ."

The various statements rippled and rose in intensity around the table, punctuated by the clinking of crystal and china and the scraping of silverware. Charlotte-Anne felt out of her league, possibly because she wasn't paying attention. She was too busy concentrating on one thing, and one thing only—trying to avoid Prince Luigi di Fontanesi's attention.

"And what do you think, Mademoiselle Hale?"

Charlotte-Anne started and turned to her right. The voice belonged to the captain. She'd totally missed his question. And somehow, during it all, the plates had been switched. She hadn't even noticed the whole spiny lobster, red shell stuffed with crabmeat, that was now sitting before her.

"I'm sorry, Captain," she said apologetically. "I wasn't

paying attention to anything but the food. It looks so . . . so *extravagant*."

"And a smart young lady you are," General Kersten boomed from across the table. "In my country, work and politics are for the men, and the kitchen and the bedroom are for women. More women should feel the way you do."

Charlotte-Anne was too shocked to speak before Mrs. Reichenbach said, "Indeed. I'll have you know, General, that many women are as accomplished as men, and some even more so. History will bear me out. Every year, more and more women are making gains, both politically and professionally."

"With all due respect, Mrs. Reichenbach," the general said, laughing, "you disagree that giving birth to and caring for children are not a woman's commitment?"

"I said nothing of the sort," Mrs. Reichenbach retorted. "All I'm saying is that one must have an open mind. One should strive not to nurture preconceived notions about men and women's roles."

"I think Mrs. Reichenbach has a point," Robyn put in. She placed her elbow on the table, leaned forward, and gestured to Charlotte-Anne. "Miss Hale's mother is a businesswoman. She started by building one tourist court in Texas, and she now owns a chain of tourist courts and hotels. She is doing extremely well, and continuing to expand. And, I might add, she has four children she has been raising herself, without the benefit of a husband. As a widow—"

"Ach," the general said irritably, cutting her off and waving away Elizabeth-Anne's accomplishments with a flick of his hands. "An individual! Life is not for the individual."

"And who, pray tell, *is* life for?" Mrs. Reichenbach asked indignantly.

"The masses, of course. One cannot judge all women by one remarkable woman, especially a successful one. Name me other women who can match men point for point."

"Amelia Earhart." The soft voice belonged to Luigi di Fontanesi.

Surprised, Charlotte-Anne turned to him without thinking.

For once, he was not gazing at her, but had locked eyes with General Kersten.

"Ach, Fräulein Earhart!" The general laughed. "So the intrepid Fräulein Earhart and two other fliers flew from . . . well, across the Atlantic, at any rate."

"Newfoundland to Wales in 1928," Prince Luigi said quietly.

"See?" the general intoned. He smiled tolerantly at Robyn and Mrs. Reichenbach. "But did not your Charles Lindbergh fly from New York to Paris in . . . in . . ." He looked at Luigi.

"Nineteen-twenty-seven," the prince said softly.

"You see! His transatlantic flight took place one entire year earlier than Fraülein Earhart's," General Kersten said with smug triumph. "And *he* flew without a crew. Fräulein Earhart would do well to stay at home and have children."

"General," Luigi said easily, "I myself have on two different occasions tried to fly the Atlantic. Once solo, and once with a crew of two, just like Miss Earhart. Twice I was forced to turn back. If I could not accomplish something that a woman could, does this speak ill of me as a man, or well of her as an aviator?"

"Surely, my dear prince, accidents of fate occur every now and then. I would not let Fräulein Earhart get the better of me simply because she managed a flight when you could not. There are always extenuating circumstances."

"But you agree, then, that Mr. Lindbergh, and not I, is the better pilot?"

"Well, perhaps," the general said uncomfortably.

"And if Mr. Lindbergh is the better flier, because he accomplished what I could not, then do you think that Miss Earhart might be also? For exactly the same reason?"

"As I said before," the general answered heatedly, "accidents of fate occur. I stand by what I have said before. Men are born leaders. The American, Herr Lindbergh, has proven that. But in the coming years, even the Americans will be outdone. By the *Germans*. My government will see to that. On land, in the air, and on the sea. All you have to do is look at what is happening around the world. India, once the backbone of the British Empire, is boycotting British goods and rejecting the idea of taxes without representation. England is weakening by the day. America has slipped back into the lull of isolationism licking her wounds. One by one, the major powers are getting weaker. But one day soon, Germany will prove herself more powerful than ever before. We will be a nation to be reckoned with.''

"I see," Chief Justice Goode said dryly. "Then you are privy to more information than any of us. It was my opinion that Germany is weak. The Weimar Republic has difficulty keeping up with its reparation payments. How do you suggest that Germany will increase in strength when multitudes of her people cannot even buy bread?''

"And whose fault is that?" The general's face grew even more red. "Germany is being sucked dry by her enemies," he hissed, leaning across the table with fiery eyes. "But we Germans will not stand for it much longer. The French," he said, smiling at Captain Louvard, "and with all due respect, the British also," he added, nodding apologetically at the duke and duchess, "everyone in Europe and America has ganged up on the Fatherland. But time will tell." He clenched his hand into a fist. "I know one thing. Germany will not always be weak.''

"Perhaps you know that, General," Ambassador Pérez said, "but I happen to know that the evening is young, the dinner marvelous, the wines excellent, and the ladies exceptionally beautiful. I propose—''

But once started, the general was not about to give up graciously in midstream. "The Fatherland is like the proverbial phoenix," he cut in forcefully. "Germany will rise out of the ashes stronger than ever, her peoples united as one. It will not be long now. President Hindenburg's days are numbered. A new man named Adolf Hitler has growing support—''

Mrs. Reichenbach laughed lightly. "I've heard of your Adolf Hitler, and his Beer Hall Putsch—''

"Herr Hitler was premature, that was the problem. When the phoenix that is Germany finally rises again, things will change." General Kersten nodded ominously. "You shall see. And the stranglehold the Jews have on us—''

There was a sudden clatter as Mrs. Reichenbach's fork dropped onto her plate. "Begging your pardon, General Kersten. I, for one, am Jewish. And let me assure you—"

"As I have said before," Ambassador Pérez broke in, "the evening is too young and beautiful for us to talk politics."

"The ambassador is quite right," Captain Louvard added quickly.

"And you," a voice said softly from Charlotte-Anne's left, "have not yet eaten a bite of your two courses. Perhaps that is what makes you the most beautiful woman aboard?"

Charlotte-Anne colored as she met Luigi di Fontanesi's predatory gaze.

"I would be honored," he said, "if after dinner you would accompany me to the ballroom."

"I'm . . . sorry." Charlotte-Anne tore her eyes away from his and stared at her lobster. "But I'm otherwise engaged," she murmured. "I have made plans."

"Then change them."

"But they're very important." She was still frightened of him, yet fascinated by the way he had stood up for women and Amelia Earhart. She couldn't shake the feeling that he had sparred with General Kersten only for her benefit. Or was that merely her ego?

Robyn leaned forward and smiled. "Oh, but, my dear," she said cunningly. "Of course I won't mind if you change our plans. I wouldn't dream of holding you to them. Besides, there's something else I am simply *dying* to do. Like winning back my past poker losses from Mrs. Reichenbach. You and the prince go ahead and dance."

Charlotte-Anne felt her stomach shriveling into a tight, nervous chestnut. She cursed Robyn's fine-tuned hearing. Did nothing escape her? And what did she think she was trying to do, anyway? Play matchmaker between her and the one person who frightened her more than anyone else she had ever met?

Charlotte-Anne didn't want to dance. Not with anyone, and especially not with the prince. Besides, she didn't know how.

She did not dare look at Luigi. "I'm afraid my dancing is

awful, your Grace," she murmured more to her lobster than to him.

He laughed suddenly. "I can tell that you Americans are truly democratic. However, the duke and duchess are 'your Grace.' I am simply 'your Highness.' "

She blushed again, aware that every eye at the table was on her.

"However," he continued, "I would be honored if you exercised your democratic prerogative and called me 'Luigi.' "

She turned slowly to him.

"And as for your dancing, which you are afraid is not very good, believe me when I say that mine is excellent. No one can dance terribly when she dances with me. I know how to lead."

"In that case," Robyn said lightly, "I'm sure that Miss Hale would not only be honored, but she, too, would like to extend to you the courtesy of being called by her first name. Wouldn't you, dear?"

Whether Robyn's statement was a comment or a rebuke, Charlotte-Anne did not know. In either case, it left her with no choice but to go dance with Luigi di Fontanesi. She lifted her chin and stared straight into Luigi's dark smoked-glass eyes. "In that case," she said in a trembling voice, "I suppose I must thank you, and accept."

Even as she said these reluctant words, her heart gave an excited leap. Which, when she considered it, was not at all unpleasant.

He escorted her by the arm to the Grand Salon, where the etched-glass windows soared to a height of more than seven yards. Already the ballroom was a sea of floating couples. Above the elegant strains of the waltz in progress she could hear other, more muted sounds: the swishes of silks, the rustles of satins and taffetas, the whisper of velvets. Couples danced across the shiny parquet floor like graceful miniature music-box dancers captured inside the massive jewel box of the ballroom.

He led her to the edge of the dance floor, conscious of her nervousness. She smiled stiffly, but the effort was fading fast, and her heart was sinking rapidly. Luigi had promised to lead her, had assured her that she would dance beautifully. But now, faced with the effortlessly graceful dancers surrounding her, she wasn't quite so sure it would be possible. All the women present were letting their gentlemen guide them, but they were also *dancing*. She felt miserable and foolish. She was certain that she would make a spectacle of herself.

She found herself yearning for L'Ecole Catroux. Why couldn't she have already attended the school and have gained the polish so necessary to a young lady? Why had she been thrust into the midst of all this luxury while she was still so unprepared for it?

She looked at Luigi, and the breath caught in her throat. He was gazing out at the dance floor, his eyes searching for an opening, his face in glorious profile. It was a classic Roman face carved from alabaster, the nose perfect and strong, exactly like Michelangelo's *David*'s, the chin determined, the lips curved and jutting sensuously, the black hair gleaming and combed slickly back. He was a Roman marble come to life, sinuous and powerful, his face and body a reminder of his heritage. He was the perfect image of the languid playboy, but any vapidity about him was dispelled by the high cheekbones and the two strong, almost cruel lines running from his nose down to the corners of his mouth.

He turned to her, his face coming into full view, and again she caught her breath. He bowed slightly, a mere forward motion of his head, and then she felt his hands slip onto the small of her back, sending ripples up and down her spine. He touched her other hand, enfolded her gently, like a most precious flower, and then began to move, sweeping her onto the dance floor. She gazed down at someone else's feet and tried to imitate the steps. She stumbled and he caught her, drawing her closer.

"No, no," he said, his breath a whisper. He began twirling her slowly, gracefully. "Do not look down. Do not try to do anything. Only move along with me. Like this. See . . . It is not so difficult. Do not concentrate on it. . . . Now you are doing fine."

She nodded, her mind reeling as she felt the heat of his

lithe body, the crackling electricity of his touch. She looked up into his face and let herself go. Before she even realized what was happening, he was sweeping her around the dance floor, his every move perfect, leading her so exquisitely that it appeared that she was as proficient a dancer as he. The strains of the waltz were a soft, muted pulse, seemingly tailored to their every move.

He gazed down at her, his lips curved into a smile. "You dance beautifully," he said softly.

"Do I now?" She smiled crookedly and cocked her head. "I thought you told me it would be because you lead so well."

"Ah, but I am, am I not?"

"Are you always this sure of yourself?"

"Almost always. I have a way with beautiful women." His eyes flashed mischievously. "Or so they tell me."

"I see. And what if I told you that I have a way with handsome men?"

He grinned at her. "Then I might believe you. After all, you attracted me, did you not?"

"Did I?"

"What do you think?"

"I think you're very cunning," she said. "It was you who watched me throughout dinner, trying to make me uncomfortable."

"Now *you* are the one who is being cunning."

She simultaneously blushed and glared at him, but they continued waltzing without missing a step.

"And you look even more beautiful when you are angry." He smiled. "When your eyes flash brilliantly."

She looked away from him. The massive salon moved around them like a merry-go-round, and the other couples swished and laughed softly . . . exchanged secrets. Women gazed at Luigi longingly, and eyed her enviously. She caught sight of Robyn dancing in the arms of Ambassador Pérez, smiling that knowing little smile of hers. So Robyn wasn't playing poker with Mrs. Reichenbach, she thought. It had been a trick to get her and Luigi together. But she couldn't think about it for long. The waltz stopped with a flourish, the figures on the dance floor stood frozen for an instant, with only the ladies' gowns still swaying. Then everyone clapped politely.

Another waltz began. Before she knew it, Luigi was spiriting her around even more effortlessly than before.

"Ah, so the fire has finally died in your eyes," He said at long last. "Then you are no longer angry with me."

She was silent.

"Are you going to stay in Europe long?" he asked.

Despite herself, she had to gaze back up at him. There was something magnetic about him which drew her. "I don't know. Six months at least. Longer perhaps."

"I wish it were for a very long time."

She didn't speak.

"Perhaps forever?"

"Don't," she begged in a whisper. "Don't talk like that."

"You are uncomfortable?"

She nodded.

"Then I will change the subject." He paused. "This is your first trip to Europe?"

She nodded again.

"You are on what the Americans call 'The Grand Tour'?"

"No. I'm going to Switzerland. To finishing school."

"Then you are very young."

Startled, she gazed at him. His voice had been one of surprise.

He frowned. "How old are you?"

She sighed. "Does it matter?"

"Sometimes it does. I do not wish to rob the cradle."

She laughed, remembering how earlier that evening Robyn had said the very same thing about him.

"Is something funny?" He looked hurt.

"No. I'm sorry. It was just your choice of expression."

"Then my vernacular? It is wrong? If so, you must tell me."

"No, it's correct." She struggled to look more serious. "But I'm not exactly still in the cradle."

"That much I am very aware of." His gaze burned deep into her, flooding her body with shocking warmth. He pressed her closer to him, and she felt the tightening of his hands, the heat of his legs through her diaphanous chiffon, and the hard strength of his manhood. "I think," he said in a whisper, "that I am in love with you."

Now her step faltered, but he caught her, swirled her on.

"Do you say that to all the women you meet?" she asked with a tinge of bitterness.

"No."

"Then why to me?"

"Because you are young and beautiful. There is a fresh innocence about you which is lacking in most women."

"Is that what you think?" She looked up at him in a childlike way, her hands light, as though she were about to extricate herself.

"Aren't you innocent?" he prodded gently. "Or am I wrong?"

"You . . . frighten me."

"Why?" he asked. "Because you have heard something about me? Because I have a . . . a rather tarnished reputation?"

She met his eyes. "Don't you?"

His face was devoid of expression. "I am afraid I do."

She nodded. "That is part of what frightens me. The rest is . . . well, your title. Your self-assurance. And you are probably the most handsome man—" Damn! She bit down on her lip. Why had she let something foolish like that slip out? Now she felt like a schoolgirl.

"Physical attractiveness can be a millstone around anyone's neck," he said. "You should know that. You yourself are extraordinarily beautiful. Surely you have noticed that beauty hampers?"

She was silent.

"Am I the first man who you were ever attracted to?"

She thought briefly of Mickey Hoyt. She had been attracted to him, yes. But she'd been more attracted by who Mickey was than by anything else. She shook her head. "No. I've never really been attracted to a man. But I've . . . I've been hurt. And I don't want to be hurt again."

He stopped dancing abruptly, and they stood in the middle of the floor facing each other. His hands were still holding her. The waltz strains and swirling couples swirled around them. "And you think," he asked softly, "that I have not been hurt also?"

Her voice was husky. "I . . . I don't know." Then, before she knew what she was saying she blurted out, "At Deauville—the woman who tried to commit suicide over you . . ."

"That much-publicized case." He laughed shortly. "She wanted to marry me. What else is new?"

"And you didn't want to marry her?"

His gaze was level. "No. Not her."

"But she died, or nearly died. Over you."

His smile was grim. "Nearly died? She took pills, yes, but not enough to kill herself. She tried to trap me into marriage. Nothing was too much, as long as she got what she wanted. Which she did not."

Charlotte-Anne turned away.

"You don't believe me?" he asked gently.

"That a man like you can be trapped?"

"Am I so different from other men?"

"Yes. No." She was confused. "I don't know."

"That woman in Deauville. She was a baroness. I warned her before we ever saw each other seriously that it was to be a brief affair. Somehow she thought that it wouldn't matter. That she would gain a hold over me nevertheless. She tried. It was not until several weeks after we met that I realized she would do anything to marry me. She thought that by making love to me . . ." His voice trailed off in mid-sentence.

"That you would marry her?"

He nodded. "She waited long enough until she could tell me she believed she was pregnant."

Charlotte-Anne looked startled. "Was she?"

"I do not know." He shook his head. "I suppose now I will never know."

They began to dance again, this time more solemnly.

"But . . . did you try to find out if she had a child?"

"She never showed pregnancy, if that is what you mean. If she was carrying a child, she could have lost it when she tried suicide, or had an abortion. Or else it was just another ruse."

Charlotte-Anne stared into his eyes. "I feel sorry for you," she said slowly.

He smiled then. "I have gotten over it. But it is nice to know that somebody believes the truth. Most people don't. I have been made out to be a womanizing ogre. Nobody wants to believe otherwise."

"I do."

"Why? Because somebody wanted you also? Or you him?"

"Because *I* wanted him," she said, sighing. "Because, like the baroness, I would have done anything. Only . . ." She tightened her lips.

"Only what?" he prodded gently.

"It wasn't him I wanted. It was what he could *do* for me. Now, looking back on it, I'm very ashamed of myself."

"You are young and inexperienced. Perhaps you did not know better."

"But I did. And you?" She raised her chin. "You are experienced."

"Yes, I suppose you could call me that. But I was no match for a much older and even more experienced woman." He grinned. "I'm afraid I am very weak when it comes to temptations. It seems I can never say no. Not even to you now."

"But I'm not trying to tempt you."

He held her closer. "I know that. Which makes you all the more tempting."

Her eyes fell and they danced on in silence. The waltz ended, and another began.

"I'd like to share the night with you," he whispered.

She pulled herself away. "I'm sorry." She shook her head. "I'm not ready for that. I've got to go. It seems we've danced forever, and I'm tired and out of breath."

They stopped and he led her off the floor. "Perhaps you would like some fresh air?" he suggested. "We could take a walk on deck."

She shook her head. "No, I think I need time to myself."

"Because I frighten you?"

Her features contracted in a little frown, and she shook her head again. She didn't know what was happening to her, only

215

that she ached deeply for him, longed for his touch. How could she explain to him that her own feelings frightened her far more than anything he could do to her?

He held both her hands in his. "Then I will escort you to your stateroom."

"No, I'd rather you didn't."

He looked deeply disappointed. "If that is what you wish," he said.

"I do. And thank you." She gave a little smile. "It was a most memorable evening."

"I will see you again?" he asked hopefully. "Tomorrow?"

"Perhaps tomorrow." Then she turned and quickly left, leaving him standing alone, his face brooding.

Robyn came up to him from behind. "And to think that you never once asked me to dance," she said chidingly.

Scowling, Luigi turned to her. "I'm sorry. I do not feel like another dance. Perhaps some other time." Then he turned away again and stared across the massive room.

Robyn said nothing, but her sharp eyes followed his gaze. Charlotte-Anne had just reached the door, a slender figure in white.

It was the first time in years that a woman Luigi had danced with had not ended up in his bed.

6

"You," Robyn said pointedly as she took a seat in the narrow green-leather armchair, "disappeared awfully fast last night." She was wearing a pale pale Empire-style peignoir with a high bodice and a matching gossamer robe, and she held a cup and saucer in her hands.

Charlotte-Anne sat up in bed and shrugged. "I was tired," she mumbled evasively.

"Were you now?" Robyn cocked her head and eyed her curiously. "Or were you running away?"

"Running away? From what?" Charlotte-Anne stood up and stretched.

"Not from *what*," Robyn corrected. "From *whom*."

Charlotte-Anne flipped hair out of her eyes. "What time is it?"

"Nine-thirty. In other words, time to have breakfast and get some fresh air. We can't have you sleeping your life away. You're far too young to do that. And besides . . ." Robyn took another sip of her black coffee. "I gather that someone is waiting up for you."

Charlotte-Anne went into the small bathroom and looked at herself in the mirror above the sink. She was pleased with her reflection. She couldn't ever remember looking as well rested or having slept so soundly. "What time's breakfast?" she called over her shoulder.

"Any time you want it," Robyn called back. "I took the liberty of ordering it on a tray. If I hadn't, by the time you'd get to the dining room they would be serving lunch. Your breakfast's on the dressing table in my stateroom. Help yourself."

"I don't mind if I do." Charlotte-Anne came back out of the bathroom. "I'm ravenous."

"It's the sea air." Robyn smiled. "I'm the same way."

Charlotte-Anne went through the connecting door to Robyn's stateroom. After a moment she came back. "That's *all* there is to eat?" she asked in disbelief.

"A lady," Robyn said, "does not need anything more in the morning than a cup of black coffee and a single croissant. That's all I had, and that's all you'll have."

"*Robyn*." Charlotte-Anne scowled at her in disgust. "I'm used to having eggs and toast and sausages. There's not even any sugar."

"And you don't need any. You'll get used to black coffee soon enough."

"But . . . it's so bitter."

"It's an acquired taste, and I think it's high time you acquired it."

217

"And I hardly ate a bite at dinner last night," Charlotte-Anne protested. "Besides, I'm not fat. I don't need to go on a diet."

"No, you don't," Robyn agreed. "Not yet, at least, because you are young. But when you're my age, you'll thank me. As to dinner, I know you ate next to nothing. That's not my fault, it's yours, so don't complain. Now, have your coffee and croissant, and then get bathed and dressed. I've made a date for shuffleboard at ten. You'll like it. It's a lot of fun."

"And what if I don't want to play?"

Robyn made a gesture of impatience. "Don't always be so argumentative. If you don't want to play, you won't have to. It's that simple. But eat your breakfast and get ready, for God's sake. I'll run you a bath."

"I might be a while," Charlotte-Anne murmured, a frown drawing her brows together. "Why don't you go on up ahead? I'll join you later."

"Oh, no, you don't. I'm staying right here; otherwise you'll never get out of this cabin."

Charlotte-Anne sighed and went to get the breakfast tray. She carried it into the bathroom with her and ate while soaking in a tub of fragrant bubbles.

She was surprised to discover she was humming softly to herself.

But Robyn, pressing her ear against the bathroom door and listening, wasn't in the least bit surprised. Not by the humming, nor by how much care Charlotte-Anne later took getting dressed.

The sun shone brightly and the salt air was tangy and fresh. The winds of the North Atlantic were cool, whipping the pennants and fluttering the French tricolor which hung from the stern. Overhead, the wind tugged the dark plumes of smoke out of the massive funnels and pulled them backward toward the horizon. All around, the ocean looked endless and bluish gray, each triangular wave topped with foamy little crests.

Robyn looked very stylish dressed in a pair of loose-fitting gray twill trousers, a white sweater, and a string of marble-sized pearls. It was considered a rather daring if casual morning outfit, but as long as she didn't wear it past noon, it was acceptable shipboard attire.

Charlotte-Anne, standing off to one side and watching the game of shuffleboard, was dressed in an oyster-colored cashmere-and-silk sweater, a modest off-white pleated wool skirt, and oyster leather shoes. She had brushed her hair and tied it back with a silk ribbon, and it made her look much younger and more vulnerable than she had the night before. The moment Luigi caught sight of her from a distance, he hurried toward her. At that moment he knew she was truly the most beautiful young woman in the world, at least for him. He was used to armies of cool, sophisticated society beauties, but Charlotte-Anne's fresh radiance was something entirely new to him, and made any woman he had ever known pale by comparison.

"Good morning. You are a sight for sore eyes," he marveled, smiling at her. "I trust you slept well?"

She smiled at him and nodded. He looked even more handsome in daylight than he had in the Grande Salle à Manger or on the dance floor. His complexion looked more marblelike, and the dark blue blazer, white slacks, and paisley ascot suited him perfectly.

"Now that you're well rested," he said, taking her by the arm and leading her away from the shuffleboard game, "I insist on one thing."

"Oh?" She turned her back to a lifeboat and raised her eyebrows at him. The wind whipped at her skirt. "And what is that?"

"That you devote the entire day to me."

"Oh! But I couldn't." She made a little gesture. "I mean, I'd bore you in no time at all." She glanced at a ripe-bodied brunette who paraded past, eyeing him openly.

He looked at the woman, then back at Charlotte-Anne with a grin. "As you can see, there is no contest. I would much rather be with you." He took her hands, held them, and gazed deep into her eyes. "I want *only* to be with you," he emphasized softly. "Is that too much to ask?"

She didn't reply.

"Do I have your permission to share your company, or must I get it from someone else?"

Charlotte-Anne laughed, and suddenly all her nervousness seemed to drain away. In the bright daylight, he seemed far less threatening than he had the evening before. "If that's what you want," she replied, "who am I to ruin your day? But you must promise me one thing."

"And what is that?"

"That you won't let me starve. Robyn thinks that every woman needs to watch her weight, and I'm *famished*."

"In that case, I will not let you starve. The Café-Grill should already be open. If not, I am certain a steward can bring us something. Myself, I have feasted on shad roe for breakfast, but there is nothing we Italians like so much as a woman with an appetite."

"Prince Fontanesi, you have yourself a deal." She stuck out her hand and they shook on it.

The rest of that first day at sea flew past in a magical blur. They swam in the long swimming pool; he tried to teach her to play tennis up on the sun deck; they watched *The Champ* with Wallace Beery in the theater; they shopped in the arcade, where he insisted upon buying her a blown-glass unicorn she admired; and then they dined once again at the captain's table. And somehow, during it all, they found time to talk about themselves. That night, after dinner, they went up on the sun deck and stood under the canopy of stars. It was late, and they were alone. The moon was a crescent riding high in the heavens. The waves slapped against the hull many decks below, and from somewhere forward drifted the muted strains of a waltz. Common sense told her that the *Ile de France* was a floating city filled with hundreds of passengers and crew members, yet somehow she felt as though she and Luigi were two people standing alone atop a bluff that rose up out of the middle of the Atlantic Ocean.

She had never felt so tormented, so torn in two.

As the lightheartedness of the day had worn on and evening had approached, she once again found herself reverting to the opinion she'd formed of Luigi yesterday—that everything about him was quite frightening. Yet at the same time, she envisioned his arms intertwined with her body, imagined running the palms of her hands down his broad naked back, which she knew would be smoothly muscled and warm. She trembled, at once fearing yet hungering for his touch. But most of all, she was tormented by the thought that his touch might never come.

He was so unpredictable, as though he was of some other species. He was unlike any of the American men she had met. None of them had that sensuous, dangerous sense of purpose lurking beneath a thin veneer of alabaster skin. One part of her insisted she resist him when the time came; another whispered that she plunge headlong into any offered passion, no matter how short-lived or ill-timed, no matter how much she could get hurt in the process.

She had never before felt so many conflicting emotions, and was desperately confused. She wished she could seek advice from somebody, but realized instinctively that even Robyn could not help her; she was on her own. She had to choose either to follow or to abandon the dictates of her heart.

It was with a shock that she suddenly realized she barely knew him. It didn't seem to matter.

Already she was deeply in love with him. But he was Luigi di Fontanesi, one of the most sought-after and eligible bachelors in the world, and she knew that could mean only one thing. Her love for him, whether she gave in to it or not, was a doomed thing, because surely it was one-sided.

How was she to know that Prince Luigi di Fontanesi, heir to one of the oldest titles in all Italy, the only child of one of his country's richest and most-respected families, was thinking exactly the same thoughts about her?

She glanced at him out of the corner of her eyes. He stood with his back to her, leaning against the railing with his hands tucked in his pockets as he stared out at the sea. The pale moonlight and the muted deck lights cast his shadow along the teak planks underfoot. His face was cast in a frown of indecision, his lips tightly compressed in thought. His eyes seemed faraway, but that was only an illusion. His thoughts were focused on something very nearby. On Charlotte-Anne.

Slowly he turned to face her. She stood tall and slender,

sheathed in wraithlike white. The wind swirled and tugged at her gown. Her pale eyes caught his gaze and glowed iridescently, like a cat's in the night.

He, too, had never been so at odds with himself. And suddenly he knew why; he had never really been in love before.

For once, he was taken completely by surprise. Could it be love? God only knew, he'd had more than his fair share of women, especially considering he was only twenty-nine years old. But always, whether the woman was aristocrat or peasant, blond, brunette, or redhead, single or married, of creamy ivory skin or rosy English complexion, he found that the moment they first made love the relationship began to die its sometimes slow, sometimes quick, but always inevitable death. Because all those women had one thing in common; they had all believed that his bed was a direct line to his wedding band. They never stopped to consider that he would recognize the true nature of their desire, that their lust was for his principality and not for him.

But Charlotte-Anne had not thrown herself at him. Indeed, she had at first fought him off. He knew she was special. There was a natural aura, an innocence blended with regal poise, that made her the perfect candidate for his *principessa*. She looked born to the part. But far more important, he thought she was the most desirable woman he had ever seen. Until now, love and sex had been separate entities in his mind. Now these two desires—one a physical longing he had never had any problem sating, the other a mystery which had always eluded him—had merged neatly, creating one strong, throbbing emotion which pulsed so powerfully through him that he was confused. He found himself yearning for the simple, familiar relationships of his past, for the advantage of never becoming involved. But there was a disadvantage too, and he only realized now what he had been missing. He had never before felt quite as incredibly alive, or exhilarated, as when Charlotte-Anne was with him.

Here was a woman who seemed to embody everything he had ever sought. For once, he was frankly terrified. He wondered how to proceed. He did not want to do anything that might frighten her off. If love was this rare and this enchanted, then he wished to nurture it forever.

She would make the perfect Principessa di Fontanesi.

He wanted to marry her.

He stood there for what seemed an eternity. He devoured her with his eyes. His body craved her, but he realized that his heart craved her just as much, if not more. And she just stood silently gazing back at him, her head held high, her hair gleaming like molten silver in the moonlight.

"Charlotte-Anne?" His voice was soft as he reached out and gently pulled her close. She looked up into the sculptured planes of his face. It was at once so strong and firmly molded, yet so aristocratic and delicate. His black hair gleamed sleekly, and his lashes were dark and thick around his glowing eyes.

Her jawline tightened, and her eyes glittered up at him as his strong arms enveloped her.

"I love you," he said simply.

She sighed then, and looked away.

"I want to marry you," he whispered into the shell of her ear.

Her head jerked and she stared at him with a startled expression. "What did you say?"

"I want to marry you," he repeated.

Her pulse raced. "But . . . but you don't know anything about me," she protested in an unsteady voice.

"I know enough." His voice was sure as he pressed his lips to hers. It was a velvet kiss, not short, not long, somehow almost chaste. He smiled down at her. "You have not given me a reply. Or perhaps you have, with your kiss?"

"No . . . I mean . . . I don't know anything about you," she went on helplessly.

"What is there that you need to know?" He tightened his arms even more firmly around her. "Only that you love me."

"Other things," she said weakly. "Little things."

He met her gaze then, and seeing her earnestness, chuckled softly. "Let me see. I am twenty-nine years of age and I have no brothers and no sisters. My parents live in Italy, and they constantly chastise me because they think I am wasting my life flying airplanes and racing cars. I have spent the last few months traveling across America, and now I am returning to Italy. Premier Mussolini has summoned me, and when Il Duce calls, people respond. Even di Fontanesis. It seems he has plans for me.''

"Plans?"

He nodded. "He wants me to take a commission in our armed forces, which probably means I will have very little time to fly and race, both of which I love with a passion." He smiled good-humoredly. "Is there anything I have left out?"

She looked up at him for a long moment, her face serious. "You're teasing me," she said.

"Perhaps. But it is all true."

She took a deep breath, her body trembling. Her mind was swirling in a vortex. It was all doubtless the truth, but those few threadbare facts were a fraction of the fabric which composed his whole self. Love required compatibility, and that was composed as much of strong bonds as of thousands of idiosyncrasies. What was he like when he was angry? What were his favorite movies? Where had he been to school? What was his favorite color? Was he ambitious? How could she love someone when all these and so many other things about him were a total mystery to her? After all, what *did* she know about Luigi di Fontanesi?

Next to nothing.

Yes, she knew only one thing. And it was the only thing that mattered.

She wanted him.

She yearned to share all his secrets, craved to discover all the little things about him. Wasn't that love—that endless journey of discovering a person over a period of many years?

She sighed, her mind a swirl of confusion. Her deep-rooted physical fear of him, as well as that paradoxical physical yearning which consumed her—the way he seemed able to arouse her passion with a single burning glance, the electrical charges that tore into her whenever he touched her—was that love? Or was it merely an overpowering chemical reaction rooted in physical attraction?

No, it must be love, she decided. Why else, when he was

near, did she have no control over her emotions? Why else did she let him guide her heart? Her very soul?

"You are so silent," he said. He grinned down at her warmly, and she drew a deep breath of fear mixed with anticipation.

"Luigi—" she began, but he swooped down and his lips sought hers with a hunger she had never known. For a moment she struggled, gripping his hard, muscled arms with her fingers, and then she went limp and shut her eyes, losing herself in the heat of his kiss. His hands caressed her, his arms trapped her. She felt her breasts pressed flat against his solid chest as he kissed her even more deeply. His thighs rubbed against hers and she felt the warmth radiating from him, felt too the firm, urgent outline of his penis straining against the fabric of his trousers. And then she let herself go completely. Warm currents of lust lapped at her around the edges, receded, and then came curling in on a tidal wave which swept violently over her. She felt she was drowning helplessly, and she couldn't remember a time when she had ever felt anything sweeter.

He raised his head, and her eyes opened slowly. His gaze and hers lingered and merged, and with one hand he let go of her to stroke the creamy skin of her cheeks, the graceful curve of her neck, raking his fingers through her hair, running his hand softly down the youthful hardness of her breasts.

"I think," he said between urgent little sucks on her lips, "that it is time to consummate our love."

Her eyes flared and she stiffened, but words deserted her.

"I never take no for an answer," he whispered, "not when we both need it so much." He knew how he felt about her, and knew there was no longer any need to wait.

He gripped her more fiercely and kissed her again. His lips moved slowly, taking soft little nibbles out of hers, and then he kissed her deeply, until she was dizzy and lost in his desire, in her own. As though in a dream, she found herself being led off to the plush luxury of the Trianon Suite.

When they reached his suite, he took her by the hand and led her to the bedroom door. She hesitated for a moment, and he raised her hand to his lips and held it there without speaking; words were not necessary. Then he stepped aside, so that she could enter first. For a long moment she looked into the dark bedroom, where only twin pools of light glowed at each side of the bed. Then she gazed at him. His head was tilted, his eyes glowing softly. She took a deep breath and entered the room.

Champagne was already uncorked on the nightstand, the gold-sheathed neck of the bottle sticking out of the silver ice bucket at a jaunty angle. The music of gentle violins wafted from the speakers built into the paneled headboard. The quilted satin coverlet on the big double bed shone with the rich softness of burnished gold.

Her heart skipped a beat, and anger swelled up within her. So he had expected her to spend the night and make love. Why else the music and champagne? He had planned this, connived at it. He had known she would come.

He saw her sudden stiffness and said, "I always listen to music and drink champagne at bedtime. Other people want a whiskey or a cognac. I prefer champagne. I find it helps me to sleep."

She nodded and bowed her head. The anger seeped back out of her as quickly as it had risen. A clock ticked softly. The air smelled salty, and faintly of cologne.

She sensed that he was right behind her. The moment he closed the bedroom door, she felt his hands at her waist. Almost without applying any pressure, he turned her around to face him. She gazed up into his eyes, and the secret of all the little things she yearned to know about him began to be revealed to her. She noticed the slight indentation in the very middle of his underlip. He gazed at her half-open lips, at the slight, charming overbite, the pearly smooth whiteness of her perfect teeth.

She lifted her arms, gently draping them around his neck. And so the night began. They made love with great care.

He is a sorcerer, she thought, and I am under his spell.

His hands were a silken glide along the smooth velvet of her bare arms. She no longer feared what might happen. This was a rite which women have passed through since time immemorial, and her primordial instincts guided her.

She watched in rapt fascination as he removed his clothes, enthralled by his economic movements as he slipped out of his shirt and trousers and folded everything neatly on a chair. His tightly packed muscles rippled and shifted with his every move. His buttocks were small and firm, his hips almost nonexistent. She hadn't realized how slender and lean his body was, or how long it stretched gracefully from waist to shoulders.

He turned to her again, his face alive with a strange animation, his sex strong and erect.

He led her to the bed, then leaned over and snapped down the burnished gold coverlet. As he straightened, she laid her hands on his shoulders, then parted her lips, and he opened his mouth to receive her kiss. Her body trembled as the last vestiges of her youth fell away, shed by this night. He held her away from him and gently raised her white gown over her head. The silken fabric felt like cool, clinging fingertips lightly massaging her flesh. When she was naked, she stood silently with her hands at her sides, as though waiting for his appraisal. He slid the pins out of her hair one by one. When she shook her head, the blond curls bounced lightly down around her face. He seemed pleased, smiling as his fingers flowed through her soft curls and she let her head loll backward. He pulled her to him then almost roughly, pressing her full breasts against his chest and his rigid penis against her soft belly. She moaned and he lowered her backward onto the bed. She felt the satin coverlet shifting gently under her as his smooth flesh slid atop her own. Moist lips brushed moist lips, and darting tongues playfully sought each other, caught up in a sensuous dance.

He closed his lips on her strawberry nipples and rolled them gently between his teeth. Then he kissed her everywhere, awakening every inch of her body with his tongue, gently teasing her shoulders, elbows, the soft inside of her knees. Her body trembled with pleasure and, no longer able to lie still, she returned his caresses, raking her nails ever so lightly across his buttocks, then taking his small, hard nipples between her own fingers. His lips returned to her breasts and as he bit her gently she felt her nipples swelling and becoming erect. Closing her eyes, she let herself float among the exquisite bursts of pain and pleasure, returning each sensation to him as he electrified her.

Slowly he let go of her nipples and kissed her deeply, then turned her on her side, kneading and kissing the smooth velvety skin of her buttocks. He ran his tongue up and down the ridges of her spine so that she cried out and tensed, and then his mouth nuzzled the nape of her neck. She had never felt sensations quite so delicious or so entirely consuming. Every nerve of her body seemed tuned to him as he turned her again and trailed a line of burning kisses down from her neck, between her breasts and over her flat belly. Then slowly, tantalizingly, he bowed his face between her thighs. Without needing to be guided, she rolled her hips up to meet him. His tongue caressed the taut mound, then sought out the very core of her ecstasy, his tongue playing at the velvety flesh until she felt herself mad with desire and arched her entire body in fine agony.

As he rose and prepared to mount her, she swallowed hard and wet her lips. Suddenly she was afraid. She felt his legs rubbing against hers, and then she felt his organ probing between her legs. His penis nestled there, poised, and then as he kissed her deeply she felt a searing pain. She moaned, and he froze, then began to pull out of her.

"No," she whispered, her eyes glazed over with a loving determination. She shook her head. "It's all right, Luigi. Don't stop."

"You are sure?"

She nodded, and then he kissed her again, at the same time slowly but surely thrusting into her. She grabbed a corner of the pillow and bit down as something within her tore and gave. She could feel a dampness seep down her thighs as he continued gently to slip in and out of her flesh. His pace, at first slow, built steadily until her pain was forgotten and she found herself pressing her hips against him to match his rhythm. He reached under her to clasp her buttocks and press her closer, and then she felt they were truly one, welded together as he reached again and again more deeply into her. Tension filled her body and her breath was coming in short little gasps when she suddenly felt herself leap free of a precipice and fall into a world of thick, exploding pleasure. Wave after wave enveloped her as he buried himself within her and froze, crying out, his whole body taut as the ecstasy throbbed between them.

Then he collapsed on top of her, his breathing raspy, his skin slick with perspiration, their bodies still joined.

When, after a long moment, he lifted himself off her and lay down beside her, she looked away, afraid to meet his eyes.

She felt his firm hand on her chin as he turned her to face him. "I love you, Charlotte-Anne," he whispered solemnly, kissing the tip of her nose. "I must marry you. You must be mine."

His eyes melted her fears, and her heart began to beat again.

"And you?" he asked softly. "Do you wish to marry me?"

She smiled tremulously. Her eyes glowed, but her heart was weary. Oh, if it were only so easy! But for another six months, she was still underage. She had promised her mother to attend L'Ecole Catroux for at least half a year. What if he didn't want to wait that long?

Still, she found herself nodding, and a warm contentment rushed through her. She stared up at the ceiling as he raised the coverlet over them both. The room went dark as he turned out the lights.

His body felt warm against hers. He draped an arm over her and nuzzled close to her. She felt so safe, so relaxed, that sleep wasn't long in coming.

Her last conscious thought was that now she knew, she no longer felt torn. She loved him.

And suddenly an acting career no longer seemed important at all.

7

The suspense was killing her.

Elizabeth-Anne had never felt so nervous in her
entire life. Her ears were ringing with tension and her
mouth was dry. Outwardly, though, she appeared calm, if a
little sleepy with indifference. She glanced at Larry, sitting
across from her at the white-draped table. He too looked the
very essence of languid ease, although she knew that his
insides were just as knotted as hers.

She and Larry were closing in for the kill, and neither of
them had any way of knowing whether or not the quarry was
going to escape.

"It's a game," Larry had told her forcefully in the yellow-
and-black Rolls-Royce on the way to this meeting. "Just
don't forget that. It's just a poker game, and though the
stakes are high, forget they're even there. Remember, you
win some and you lose some. The only trick is to win more
often than you lose."

But that, she thought now, was easier said than done.

This particular "poker game" was not taking place in a
casino or the smoky back room of a seedy bar. They were
seated at a long dining table in the lavish banquet room of the
Shelburne Hotel on Fifth Avenue and Sixty-second Street.
Besides the two of them, the other "players" were four
lawyers, two representing Elizabeth-Anne and two representing Milton Shelburne, an accountant for each of them, as
well as a representative from each of their respective banks.

Elizabeth-Anne glanced at Milton Shelburne. He was their
quarry, and a formidable one. He was tall, with a paunchy
stomach that kept him a foot back from the table. His black-
olive eyes were shrewd, his thinning dark hair combed back,
and his mustache was well-trimmed. He wore a custom-made

suit, and heavy gold cufflinks shone from under his pin-striped cuffs. He looked every inch a wealthy and powerful man, and the pungent Havana cigar he was smoking only reinforced that image. Although Elizabeth-Anne realized that he was in all likelihood even more nervous than she or Larry, he did not show it either. In fact, despite the stakes, everyone at the table looked sedate enough for a church social.

Elizabeth-Anne was dying to check the time, but she didn't glance at her wristwatch. She reiterated over and over to herself just how important it was to give the impression that she and Larry believed time was of no consequence. They had to lull Milton Shelburne into a false sense of security, as though there were no pressure to finish the negotiation quickly. If they didn't, Shelburne might get wise and manage to wiggle out of their trap by somehow working out a better last-minute deal with one of the other bidders who had earlier dropped out.

As things stood, it was the most peculiar negotiation Elizabeth-Anne had ever taken part in. To begin with, it had come as a totally unexpected eleventh-hour sale, although she was not supposed to know that. She and Larry had been in New Jersey, finally buying the tourist court whose purchase she had delayed, along with her wedding, after she'd discovered Charlotte-Anne's affair with Mickey Hoyt. Charlotte-Anne had departed for Europe a week before, and Elizabeth-Anne had finally felt ready again for business. As soon as she had gotten the message that the Shelburne had unexpectedly come on the market, she had insisted they change their plans. Instead of going on to Baltimore, Washington, and Philadelphia to check on her hotels there, they had hurriedly returned to New York. After an all-night session with her lawyers and accountant, a bleary-eyed Elizabeth-Anne had met with her bankers at nine that morning, then gotten busy and called around town.

And had hit paydirt.

One of her many contacts had the lowdown on Milton Shelburne, and had given it to her. It was supposed to be a well-kept secret, but the word was that Shelburne was in a very bad state. True, it was the word of only one source, but

Elizabeth-Anne had trusted her contact implicitly in the past and it had paid off. So now she felt confident that no matter what impression Shelburne projected, there was no way he could hold out. He had until five o'clock of that very afternoon to come up with a buyer, or else all would be lost.

At a few minutes to five, he would take whatever they offered.

Elizabeth-Anne knew that she had to have the Shelburne Hotel. It was the kind of opportunity that arose only once in a lifetime. The Shelburne was located two blocks north of the Hotel Pierre, and it took up an entire city block. The imposing structure had been designed in 1887 by Henry Janeway Hardenbergh, the same man who had given New York the Dakota Apartments and the Plaza Hotel. But nowhere was Mr. Hardenbergh's genius as readily evident as at the Shelburne Hotel. The sprawling lobby could have come straight from a Renaissance palace, with its gracefully arched ceilings and triforium walkways. But it was the huge central courtyard that made the structure so distinctive. Elizabeth-Anne could already picture the fantasy jungle she would create under that soaring ceiling of skylights at the Shelburne, rich with lush palms, splashing fountains, and masses of potted orchids. But what she and almost every New Yorker agreed was the building's *tour de force* were its majestic twin spires that rose high above the street to scrape the clouds.

She knew that if she did not get the Shelburne today, in all probability it would forever elude her.

The time to buy property and buildings had never been better. All over the country, the real-estate market was as depressed as it had ever been. Without an end to the Depression in sight, buildings went begging. Even so, the Shelburne was one of those unique buildings that, unless you were blessed with exceptional luck, was forever out of reach.

But luck was smiling on Elizabeth-Anne. She could *feel* it. In order to make buying the Shelburne an affordable reality, all she and Larry had to do was drag out the negotiations until a few minutes before five.

She felt a cramping stab of pain in her intestines. How much longer did she have to wait until five o'clock? She felt she had been sitting at the table forever. At ten o'clock that morning, three other parties had converged on the Shelburne along with her in order to bid on the hotel. Negotiations had dragged on all morning, and Milton Shelburne had been playing it close to the chest, never budging from his asking price. Elizabeth-Anne, who knew of his financial predicament, couldn't help but admire him for his bravado, but the three other bidders eventually got annoyed. One by one, they had left, two of them withdrawing their initial offers and the third hotelier telling Shelburne that his offer still stood, should he be interested.

Elizabeth-Anne's hopes had soared. What the hotelier hadn't realized was that Shelburne had only until five o'clock to conclude the deal. What remained now was in the hands of fate. If Shelburne reached that hotelier in time, then the Shelburne Hotel would elude her. On the other hand, if he couldn't reach him . . .

She exhaled slowly, silently. It occurred to her that it was poetic justice that both she and Milton Shelburne should wear the exact same armor—seemingly infinite patience and a look of nonchalant ease.

So far, she, Larry, and their two lawyers had not so much as submitted a single monetary bid. They had merely sat back quietly and let the others haggle. She had planned to wait until the very last minute, as if she would then top the highest offer Shelburne had received. She had felt, correctly, that any bargaining on their part would only serve to push the price up. Their silence had not gone unnoticed by the others, and especially not by Milton Shelburne. Their presence only seemed to weaken the others' positions and strengthen Shelburne's, who believed he would be rewarded for holding out. It never occurred to him that Elizabeth-Anne had discovered his Achilles' heel.

In prosperous times Shelburne's fortune had accumulated to a staggering sum, but very little of it constituted real money. He had owned large parcels of commercial real estate throughout Manhattan and Brooklyn, and had watched the crash, the Depression, and the banks gobble up his properties one by one. His credit had always been good, and he had originally amassed his wealth by overextending at the banks; he was well-known for buying marginally and for making swift thrust-and-parry deals. By keeping every building and property he owned totally separate from the others, each run by a differently incorporated company, he had set things up so that should the worst ever happen and any number of his companies topple, the rest would remain staunch and strong. But even he had not been able to predict a calamity on the scale of the Depression. His empire did not, perhaps, topple all at once, but it fell ignobly in bits and pieces. The Shelburne Hotel was his last holding, as well as the single most valuable piece of real estate he had ever owned. As the others had been, it was mortgaged to the hilt. Ever since his empire had begun crumbling, he had quietly sought a buyer for the Shelburne, but one thing or another had always come up. Either his asking price had been too high or his potential buyers bowed out at the last moment. When he had finally found someone serious, a cruel twist of fate had ruined that opportunity as well. The day the papers were to be signed, his buyer had found himself bankrupt overnight. It was one of the harsh realities of the Depression, but the fact that those occurrences were commonplace hadn't made it any easier a pill to swallow. It seemed to him that his financial future was doomed.

Until now.

His decision to auction off the hotel had created sufficient interest for four potential buyers to show up and bid on it. The fact that two of them had backed off and walked out didn't worry him. After all, one offer still stood. And from what he had heard about Elizabeth-Anne, she was grabbing up property all over the place as if there were no tomorrow. Her presence could indicate only one thing; she was serious. She meant to end up with the Shelburne Hotel.

His fatal mistake was that he didn't know just how serious she was.

He glanced casually to his left, trying to read her thoughts. Just as she had all day, she appeared calm, quiet. She sat tall and straight, her dark suit, pale blouse, and rope of pearls conveying an air of sedate financial solidity. Her aquamarine eyes were veiled with a faraway look and the slight dark circles caused by the past two grueling days were artfully hidden by carefully applied powder. She looked for all the world like a spectator watching a stage play with only the mildest amusement.

Aware that Shelburne's gaze had shifted to her, Elizabeth-Anne kept herself composed. When she felt his eyes wandering away from her, she glanced at Larry. Then she frowned at some papers and shuffled them in front of her. It was a subtle way to check her wristwatch without appearing to do so. She pursed her lips thoughtfully before finally speaking.

"Of course," Elizabeth-Anne said slowly, "we would all like to get this matter settled as quickly as possible." She frowned at the papers in front of her. "What worries me, and I know it worries Mr. Hochstetter also, is that the patronage of the Shelburne has declined markedly over the past year. And from glancing through the books, I see that the operating expenses are very high. The Shelburne requires an extraordinarily large working capital."

"The Shelburne is a first-class hotel," Milton Shelburne put in smoothly. "The staff could always be trimmed." He inclined his head in Elizabeth-Anne's direction and permitted himself a faint smile. "From what I have heard about you, Mrs. Hale, you're very proficient at trimming costs without visibly sacrificing any services."

"Be that as it may, the Shelburne is an entirely different ball game from my hotels." Elizabeth-Anne rattled the papers in her hand. "My hotels are more modest and easily manageable. The Shelburne, as you know, is one of this city's largest hotels, with over seven hundred suites and rooms, many of which require extensive remodeling and renovation. The public areas have become rather seedy as well, and require a considerable investment. Frankly, I'm worried that I may have a difficult time operating the hotel as well as paying a heavy price for it."

"But you haven't even mentioned a price yet," the senior partner of Shelburne's two lawyers pointed out.

"No, I haven't." Elizabeth-Anne picked up a pencil and scribbled a few doodles in the margin of one of her papers.

Then she pulled back her suit sleeve and looked pointedly at her wristwatch. "Gentlemen, I'm afraid it is getting late. I suggest we break off for today and continue again in the morning." She made as though to rise.

"Wait." The blood drained from Shelburne's face. "I'm sure we can come to some sort of satisfactory agreement." Shocked at Elizabeth-Anne's suggestion, he was for the first time feeling the noose of panic tightening around him.

Elizabeth-Anne held her breath and watched Larry closely. The trap was about to be sprung, but Larry's face was completely devoid of expression. Even now that the time to pull off the coup was at hand, no matter how much excitement they felt, they would keep it subdued and continue about business in a totally unemotional and impassive manner. Business, Elizabeth-Anne and Larry both knew, allowed no room for emotions.

"In that case, Mr. Shelburne," Elizabeth-Anne said quietly, "Let me make you our offer." She glanced at Shelburne's banker and his lawyers. "Gentlemen, I am offering to assume the mortgage on the Shelburne as it stands now. I also offer to pay you, Mr. Shelburne, the amount of sixty-five thousand dollars in cash."

Shelburne looked as though he had been struck. Then he gave a hollow, mirthless little laugh. "You're joking, of course."

Elizabeth-Anne shook her head. "No, Mr. Shelburne. I never joke about business matters. I am dead serious."

"But . . . but that is preposterous," Shelburne sputtered.

"Is it?" Elizabeth-Anne folded her hands in front of her and leaned across the table toward Shelburne, her eyes gleaming with a hardness Larry had never before seen and which he now found extremely interesting. It emphasized to him just how much she really had learned and grown since they had met.

"Mr. Shelburne," Elizabeth-Anne said patiently, "the outstanding unpaid mortgage on this hotel is still a quarter of a million dollars. When you purchased it, you paid a hundred fifty thousand dollars down, and over the past ten years you have paid off another quarter of a million of the principal. I needn't remind you that money is in short supply at the moment, or that the market for real estate has plunged. And much as I hate to have to bring it up, I have checked around, Mr. Shelburne. You are in no position to bargain, nor to turn down the offered sum. You are, in fact, dirt poor. If you do not accept my offer, which will at least pay you sixty-five thousand dollars, not only will you lose this hotel in . . ." Elizabeth-Anne pointedly consulted her watch, then looked back up and met Shelburne's eyes ". . . in twelve minutes, but you will not even have the satisfaction of having sold it. You will see it repossessed, and who knows? I might even get a better bargain if I wait a few more minutes." She paused, and her voice grew softer, almost pitying. "Look at it this way, Mr. Shelburne. You have one of two choices open to you: make sixty-five thousand dollars, or lose everything."

Shelburne was trapped, and he knew it. "Who told you about five o'clock?" he whispered hoarsely, his face pale. "Did you?" His head snapped accusingly toward his banker, a gaunt, brittle man with a high, sloping forehead. At the moment, he projected not so much the image of a banker as that of an undertaker.

"No," the man answered, shaking his head and clearly miffed by the suggestion. "The First Mutual Bank of Manhattan, as you well know, is the very soul of discretion."

"Well, somebody must have leaked the word," Shelburne snapped. He was suddenly sweating profusely, beads of perspiration popping out all over his forehead. He tugged his handkerchief out of his breast pocket and unceremoniously mopped his face. Then he got unsteadily to his feet and turned to Elizabeth-Anne. "I'm afraid that I must refuse your offer," he told her with weak dignity. He smiled stiffly at her, then at his banker. "I think you are both forgetting that I've had another offer for four times that amount earlier this very afternoon." He allowed the faintest smile of relief to hover at the corners of his lips. "And that offer still stands. You all heard it being made."

"We heard it, yes, and you stand to make four times what I offer *if* you accept before five o'clock," Elizabeth-Anne reminded him. "Don't forget, after five the bank will repossess the Shelburne, and it will belong to them. Not to you."

Milton Shelburne stared at her, realization dawning. "You tricked me," he hissed. "You dragged things out all afternoon just to trap me."

Elizabeth-Anne looked at him with a stony expression. "Call it whatever you wish," she said easily, "but remember, our offer still stands. Until five o'clock on the dot, that is. You have ten minutes, Mr. Shelburne, in which to conclude your deal with the other party. Whether or not you decide to deal with us is entirely up to you. However, at precisely five o'clock, if you have not accepted our offer, it will be withdrawn."

Shelburne turned to his lawyers. "She can do this? And get away with it?"

They nodded wordlessly, avoiding his eyes.

"This . . . this is sheer *lunacy*." Shelburne's voice rose with indignation.

With deliberate slowness Elizabeth-Anne pushed back her chair, got to her feet, walked to the foot of the table, and picked up the telephone. Whipping the cord around, she brought the telephone to Milton Shelburne and set it on the table in front of him. "You are welcome to call the other party and accept his offer immediately." She looked at Shelburne challengingly. "However, should that deal fall through for any reason, you are still free to accept our offer, as long as it is before five o'clock. Either way, you can't lose." She amended that statement gravely: "Well, at least not everything."

Shelburne licked his lips and stared down at the telephone.

"Call," Shelburne's banker urged. "For God's sake, Mr. Shelburne, place the call."

With trembling fingers Shelburne reached for the telephone and dialed.

For a moment Elizabeth-Anne had to shut her eyes. It was almost more than she could bear. This was not business. This was a jungle with no rules and no laws. She felt heavy with guilt; at the same time, she knew her actions were necessary, *fair*. Hadn't it been Shelburne himself who had refused the other offer to begin with because he had been so certain she would top it? His greed and lack of acumen were causing his downfall, not her.

"Get me through to Mr. Spencer." Shelburne's voice was high-pitched with tension. "Tell him it's urgent."

Everyone looked away from him, unable to witness his growing misery.

"What do you mean he hasn't come back this afternoon? He left here hours ago! You've *got* to know where I can reach him." His voice cracked. "Well, if he gets in before five o'clock, have him call me."

Elizabeth-Anne let out a weary sigh. There was no sweetness in this victory. Her intestines were as knotted as they had been all day.

Shelburne let the receiver drop from his hand. It landed on the table with a clatter as he sank back down into his chair.

The minutes seemed to crawl by. No one spoke. Everyone kept glancing at the time and staring at the telephone.

The telephone did not ring. By 4:49 Mr. Spencer still had not called.

At precisely five o'clock Milton Shelburne buried his face in his hands. "All right, Mrs. Hale," he whispered hoarsely, his voice muffled by his fingers. "I accept your offer."

J ust before nine o'clock Elizabeth-Anne finally laid down her pen and pushed the last of the papers away from her. "There," she said softly.

She didn't show it, but she couldn't remember a time when she'd been as relieved to get something over with. The two days she had now been awake, and the tension of the Shelburne negotiations, topped by Milton Shelburne's heart-wrenching defeat, had taken their toll on her. Nothing sounded more pleasant than to go home, crawl into bed, and sleep as long as she pleased.

But she wasn't only tired. She felt frightened too. Sixty-five thousand dollars in cash, as well as assuming a mortgage of a quarter of a million dollars, might have been a bargain, but the amount of money she had just spent staggered her. She knew too that refurbishing the hotel to its former grandeur—which she felt *must* be done—would require another staggering sum. Nor had any of her other properties been bought outright. All except the tourist court in Quebeck were partially financed. Larry's motto had always been to use OPM—other people's money—whenever possible. OPM had its definite advantages, to be sure. It could also, however, lead to disaster. A deeply-rooted fear kept gnawing at her: should the rich vein at the gold mine peter out, and Horseshoe Investments collapse, she would find herself in the exact same straits as Milton Shelburne.

"Gentlemen," she said in weary but sure voice, "I think it's time we called it a day, don't you?" She smiled thinly at them.

They nodded. Shelburne himself had left hours before, signing the necessary papers and leaving the rest to his lawyers. Now they, as well as the rest of his and Elizabeth-Anne's negotiating teams, placed their copies of the contracts in their briefcases, snapped them shut, and rose to their feet. Each man perfunctorily shook her hand and murmured congratulations before filing out of the room.

As soon as Elizabeth-Anne and Larry were alone, the big room seemed empty and oppressive. Elizabeth-Anne allowed herself to show just how drained and exhausted she was. She took a deep, noisy breath and sank down into the maroon leather chair she had occupied all day. Her eyes were burning in their sockets and she rubbed them with her knuckles.

"You're tired," Larry said.

She nodded, tilted her head back, and shut her eyes.

Larry came over and stood behind her chair. He placed his hands on her shoulders. "Let's go home," he said. "You've had a tough day."

"I'll be all right," she said. "Just give me another minute."

"We're in no hurry." He began massaging her back, rubbing her knotted muscles with firm circular motions of his fingers. "You don't look very happy," he said, "but that doesn't surprise me. It's like postpartum depression. I can't remember a time when I haven't felt depressed after pulling off a deal like this. Still, I must congratulate you. Together we've managed one of the biggest business coups of the Depression. You bought this hotel for a fraction of its real market value.''

"I know that. And it bothers me." She let out a strangled sigh as he continued massaging her back. "Business is business, and I'll not forget that. It's Darwinism, pure and simple. The survival of the fittest. But I don't have to like it."

"No, you don't." He paused, his fingers suddenly still on her back. "But do you think for an instant," he asked her, "that if the shoe were on the other foot, Shelburne would have hesitated to take *you* to the cleaners?"

"No, I don't doubt that either." She reached up, covered his hands with hers, and held them on her shoulders. "I'm frightened, Larry."

He chuckled. "Why?"

"For one reason, the survival of the fittest. Today I was the fittest." She twisted around to look up at him. "But what about tomorrow? Where will I be then?"

He knew she didn't expect an answer. "And the other reasons?" he asked.

"I suppose it's because the numbers all add up to so much. And because paying off what I owe is all tied in to Horseshoe Investments. Larry, what if the gold mine should dry up? What then?"

"Then we're both sunk," he said grimly. "But I don't think that will happen, not for a long time. Bear in mind that in business you've got to run ahead of the tide, and that's exactly what you're doing. There are times to be conservative, and times to be daring. The trick is to know which way to lean. Today was one of the times to be daring, and it paid off." He leaned down and kissed the nape of her neck. "It's healthy never to grow overconfident, but you can only worry so much before you worry yourself sick."

She nodded. "I'll try to keep that in mind." She smiled wanly.

"Anything else bothering you?"

"Many things. For one, I own a good chunk of real estate which is worthless should the bottom of this country's economy drop out any further."

241

"The economy will pick back up, trust me." He paused. "Do you have any idea just how many depressions and recessions we've gone through in this country?"

She shook her head. "No."

"Well, listen to this, and then I'm sure you'll feel better," he said. "In 1869 we had what the financial community likes to call 'Black Friday.' It resulted from investors trying to corner the gold market."

She gave a low, mirthless laugh. That was hitting just a little too close to home.

"In 1893," he continued, "we had another similar financial panic which resulted in a four-year depression. Then the same thing happened all over again in 1907. We've recovered each time, darling. Rest assured, the United States will pick itself up by its bootstraps and pull itself out of this depression just like it has from all the others, or my name isn't Lawrence Hochstetter."

"All right, you've convinced me. As long as there's enough money around for our guests to afford to stay at our hotels, I'll try not to worry too much."

"That's the spirit."

"Now, what about running all these hotels and tourist courts? Larry, they're scattered all over! I'm running myself ragged trying to keep up, and now we have the Shelburne, too. It's time we set up an umbrella company. As I've found out, I can't keep managing a growing empire this size all by myself. I'm spreading myself much too thin."

"This umbrella company, whatever you choose to call it—" Larry interjected.

"Hale Hotels," she said promptly.

He laughed. "We've been married seven days, and you still insist upon using 'Hale' instead of 'Hochstetter.' They warned me about independent women."

"It's only because Zaccheus and I had the vision to start the tourist court, which began all this. I owe it to his memory, Larry. And the children are Hales. This will give them something to grow up into. A chance to *be* somebody."

"I know that," he said gently, "and I'm secure enough to accept it."

Then Elizabeth-Anne's voice grew more businesslike. "I can head up Hale Hotels. Directly under me, I'll have to have two or three good executives—vice-presidents, I suppose—that I can trust. Each will be responsible for running a certain number of the hotels and tourist courts, and they'll be answerable only to me. The individual managers of the hostelries, in turn, are answerable directly to the executives, unless, of course, I give a specific order and thereby supersede theirs. The rest of the staff of each individual hotel or tourist court is answerable to the managers. But any executive order, and especially any order from me, can supersede the manager's. You get the general idea?"

Larry nodded his assent. Tired though she was, the gears of Elizabeth-Anne's mind were clicking everything into place. "In other words," she concluded, "we set up a chain of command, with me sitting at the top of the pyramid."

He grinned. "Just like Cleopatra, my sweet."

She smiled. "Now, don't sweet-talk me!" She poised a finger against her lips. "I suppose it would be a good idea if we gave each executive a specific territory," she said. "He'll handle everything within that particular territory, and nothing else. Say, one gets New York, another has Pennsylvania and New Jersey, the other has Baltimore and Washington. That'll cut down on a lot of running back and forth. Maybe he should even be based in his area instead of here in New York."

"That's a good idea," he said admiringly. "You catch on fast."

Elizabeth-Anne's face grew pinched. "But how do I know I can trust anyone else to wield so much power?"

"If you intend to keep expanding, you'll have to delegate authority and hope you can trust the people you hire. In fact, you'll have to even if you don't expand any further and just decide to keep managing the hotels and tourist courts you own now."

She nodded. "And I don't think I'll have to worry about finding good executives. Not if I offer a decent salary and a good bonus to whoever drums up the most business. Nobody thrives on keen competition like an executive. And in these times, it's an employer's market. There are thousands of terrific executives out there, some of them out of work, and others looking for better jobs. That's what we'll do,'' Elizabeth-Anne said with finality. ''But we have to make sure the executives we hire are *very* good. I only want the cream of the crop.'' She paused. ''How long do you think it will be before we can set up the Hale Hotels umbrella corporation?''

''No more than a few days. A week at the most.''

She smiled. She was already beginning to feel a little less nervous, and her doubts were under control. But her physical weariness wasn't. As she and Larry continued to talk, her eyelids started to droop. She had almost fallen asleep sitting up when a knock came on the closed door. Her eyes flew open. ''Come in,'' she called out. She turned to Larry. ''Who can *that* be?''

He stubbed out his cigarette and got to his feet just as the door opened. Two girls, one blond and one brunette, stood in the doorway. From their dress Elizabeth-Anne saw they were obviously prostitutes.

She stared at them in disbelief. What had come of this hotel, she wondered, to let girls wander in off the streets? And why hadn't the hotel detectives intercepted them? The next thing you knew, they would be working the lounges or sitting in the lobby drumming up business. This was one thing she would have to put a stop to.

But before she could open her mouth, Larry was striding across the room toward them. She watched in amazement as he took out his wallet and counted out five crisp one-hundred-dollar bills for each of them. They smiled at him, tucked the money into their bosoms, and blew him a kiss before turning and leaving.

''What was all that about?'' Elizabeth-Anne asked. Then suddenly it dawned on her. For the first time since they had met, she felt she could murder Larry. ''You didn't,'' she hissed at him in a shocked whisper.

He looked at her, his face cool and expressionless. ''I did,'' he admitted, lighting another cigarette. ''You didn't really expect me to leave anything to chance, did you?''

''Oh, Larry! It makes everything so . . . so cheap.''

''Why? Because when Spencer walked out, the girls had

been arranged for? Perhaps it was ruthless, but sometimes the end justifies the means. It was a gamble, but it paid off, didn't it? While Shelburne was trying to get hold of Spencer so desperately, he never even suspected that he was right upstairs.'' He grinned.

"I'm so *ashamed*," Elizabeth-Anne whispered. Despite the warmth of the room, she hugged herself with her arms and shivered. "You lured him into a sexual trap just so Shelburne couldn't find him." She shook her head miserably. "And I thought he simply couldn't reach Spencer."

"Elizabeth-Anne, it worked. You must remember that. Because of this, a lot of people turned out happy. Spencer had a wonderful opportunity to release his tension without his wife ever finding out about it. The girls got paid twice, once by him and once by me. And you got the hotel for a song."

Elizabeth-Anne shut her eyes. She couldn't believe what she was hearing. Her victory had been sour enough before finding out this. Now it had curdled completely.

Wearily she pushed herself to her feet. They might as well go home now. Just remaining in the hotel left the taste of bile in her mouth.

It had been a day of surprises. Thank God the surprises were over.

But when they got back to the Madison Squire, the desk clerk handed her a cable. She tore it open, then realized that the surprises had just begun.

She stared down at the message and had to read it and reread it several times before it sank in:

MAMA PLEASE DO NOT BE ANGRY STOP HAVE MARRIED AND AM VERY HAPPY AND VERY MUCH IN LOVE STOP I AM NOW THE PRINCIPESSA DI FONTANESI STOP I WILL WRITE IN DETAIL SOON STOP PLEASE DO NOT BLAME ROBYN STOP I LOVE YOU VERY MUCH AND HOPE YOU GIVE US YOUR BLESSINGS STOP MUCH LOVE CHARLOTTE-ANNE AND LUIGI DI FONTANESI

8

Three thousand, five hundred miles across the Atlantic in the dark, mountainous Alps, the train's iron wheels protested with a long ear-splitting screech as if braked to a halt. The express was one carriage longer than usual; coupled to its rear was the luxurious royal-blue private coach emblazoned with the coat of arms of the di Fontanesis. The carriage's interior was like a compact, luxurious house, with a parlor, bedroom, small kitchenette, bath, and quarters for the private steward.

In the small bedroom paneled in rich Carpathian burled elm, Charlotte-Anne was awakened more by the sudden stillness than by the drawn-out screech itself. She opened her eyes. She could hear voices barking sharply outside on the platform. She sat up. Then, careful not to awaken Luigi, she got out of bed and slipped into the rose-colored robe Luigi had bought her in Paris. She tied the sash around her waist and went over to the window, parted the heavily fringed thick brocade curtains, and looked out.

She had to shield her eyes. The platform, the cluster of buildings, and the train were bathed by blinding floodlights which gave everything a startling, surreal quality.

The train had stopped at the Italian border.

She slid down the window and leaned out. The mountain air felt thin and chilly. Everywhere she looked she could see uniformed officials and border guards wearing glossy high riding boots, peaked, visored caps, and flared breeches. The uniforms looked very official, and somehow very intimidating.

She heard the soft bang of a door. Then she saw Aldo, the white-jacketed private steward of the di Fontanesis' coach, hop down to the platform. He stopped to talk to some officials directly under her window and she repeatedly caught the words "Principe di Fontanesi, Principessa di Fontanesi" amid his rapid-fire bursts of Italian. She saw him offering them his, Luigi's, and her own passports, but the officials shook their heads and didn't even bother to check them. Then one of them happened to look up. The moment he saw her, he touched his visor with his fingertips, murmured "*Scusi,*" and moved on to the next car.

She frowned thoughtfully to herself. When the *Ile de France* had docked in Le Havre, her and Luigi's faces had been carefully scrutinized and compared with their passport photos. And again, when the train crossed the Swiss border, they had been required to go through rigorous border formalities. The ever-efficient Swiss had even given the private carriage a thorough search. What they intended to find, she had no idea. The fact that the coach belonged to the di Fontanesis, or that Luigi was a prince, hadn't seemed to matter in the least.

But to the Italians it obviously mattered a great deal. They didn't bother to glance at the passports. No officials walked through the coach. It was as though she and Luigi enjoyed diplomatic immunity. It was the first time she was made truly aware of the awesome power the di Fontanesis wielded in their own country. She was not yet used to the courtesies accorded to the nobility, and she found the present situation peculiarly unsettling.

She was about to push up the window when a commotion farther down the platform caught her attention. A young man had jumped off one of the carriages in the front of the train and had broken into a run. The border guards did not bother to chase him. It was unnecessary as other guards all around the platform easily encircled him. He sensed that he was trapped, stopped running, and raised his arms above his head.

With a shock, Charlotte-Anne watched as one of the guards slipped the revolver out of his gleaming holster. The guard stretched out his arm, aimed, and fired a single shot.

The crack of the gunshot reverberated like thunder. The young man jerked as the bullet slammed into his back, and the force of the shot threw him forward. She winced as he fell heavily to the concrete. He landed on his face and lay without moving.

Two guards ambled over to him. One of them had his hands on his hips, the other was replacing the revolver in his holster. Without warning, they gave the man a sharp kick and flipped him over on his back. The young man slowly raised his head. His face was screwed up in pain. The guard raised his boot, and with all the force he could muster, slammed it down on the prone man's face.

Charlotte-Anne heard the agonized scream. She could almost feel the crunching of her own facial bones, and felt the gore rise in her throat.

She ducked her head back inside and slammed the window shut. For a moment she leaned back against it and took a series of deep breaths. After a moment the nausea began to subside.

She heard a movement in the passage outside the bedroom. Crossing over to the door, she opened it and saw Aldo, the steward, returning to his quarters.

Aldo gave a little bow. "Yes, Principessa?"

She glanced behind her. Incredibly, Luigi had slept through the gunshot and the screams. She closed the door so the sound of their voices wouldn't awaken him. "Aldo," she whispered in a trembling voice, "they just shot a man . . ."

Aldo nodded, his features carefully composed. For a moment she imagined a flash of hatred in his dark eyes, but when she looked closely, it was gone. Or it had never been there in the first place. "I saw, Principessa," Aldo said in his heavily accented English. "It was probably an *anarchisco*."

"But . . . but there was no need to shoot him. He had surrendered."

The steward shrugged. "The leader of every country has many enemies. Il Duce has his fair share also."

"But . . . couldn't they have just arrested him? Did they have to shoot him in the back?"

Aldo looked down at the floor. "This is Italy, Principessa. The laws are different here from America."

"But—"

"Try to forget it, Principessa," he advised softly. "Pretend that it never happened."

She stared at him. "But it *did*. I can't just stand by—"

"If there is nothing else . . ." Aldo gave another little bow and went on to his quarters. She watched him leave, then slowly returned to the bedroom. She glanced at Luigi, who was sleeping soundly on his side.

She slipped out of her robe and crawled back into bed. The mattress shifted and Luigi stirred and turned over on his other side, facing her. His eyes opened and he squinted sleepily at her. "You are awake."

"Yes." She nodded. "We're at the border." She took a deep breath. "Luigi . . ."

He yawned. "Hmmmm?"

"They just shot a man."

"Who did?"

"The border guards."

"Do not worry about it," he said with a yawn. "No one would dare to shoot you."

She looked at him with shock. "That's not what worries me. They shot him in the *back*. An unarmed man. It was terrible—"

His voice was a soft murmur. "Do not concern yourself with such things. It was official business. Do not involve yourself." He coiled an arm around her. "Tomorrow is a long day. Try to get some sleep. You will need it."

She stared at him, but his eyes were already closed. Then she heard his soft snores. He was fast asleep again.

Even long after the train had begun to speed into the darkness again, sleep eluded her. Finally she slipped out of bed, put her robe back on, and walked to the plush parlor at the front of the carriage. For a long time she sat on a tufted velvet armchair by the window. The Italian Alps were majestic and deceptively peaceful in the morning light. The sky seemed clear. The landscape was somehow sharper, more dappled with light than any she had ever seen before.

Italy.

She was in Italy now, yet another country where she had never set foot. The country which was her home.

She shuddered as the real significance of her marriage hit her for the first time. She was not just any woman anymore. She was a princess, a member of one of the most powerful families in all Italy. She was an important part of a culture which was entirely new to her. This was now her home, a land ruled by fascism. She had read about Mussolini in the papers back in New York, but he hadn't made much of an impression on her. Italy had always seemed so far away. She had never thought Il Duce or fascism would ever really affect her. But now it did, and she realized it was a situation that disturbed her deeply. She had witnessed a man being killed, or at least seriously wounded, treated sadistically. This was a horror of fascism she hadn't known about. Yet for a di Fontanesi, life was coddled. Something as routine as a passport check had been waived.

What was it Aldo had said?

"This is Italy. The laws are different here."

She wondered if she could adjust to this new climate. What kind of laws condoned outright cruelty and murder? What kind of country would be her new home, anyway? She knew fascism well enough now for it to be repugnant to her. Could she live under its iron fist?

Many dark shadows and doubts flitted batlike through her mind. She was filled with dread. She couldn't help wondering how her mother had taken the news of her marriage. Surely she'd long since received the cable, sent two days earlier from Le Havre.

She smiled to herself grimly. Elizabeth-Anne would probably be furious, but there was nothing she could do. Charlotte-Anne was, after all, the Principessa di Fontanesi, and her mother would simply have to adjust to that fact. She might have been born a Hale, but she was a Hale no longer.

But much as her mother's reaction concerned her, and the scene at the border horrified her, neither was truly the cause of her anxiety now. Rather, she was thinking of the night before.

Aldo had turned down the lace-edged sheets, which Luigi informed her had been embroidered by the nuns of the order of Our Lady of Peace. After she and Luigi had had a nightcap of champagne, they had made love. She had felt strange, making love on sheets embroidered by nuns who had taken vows of silence.

Then, just before they'd gone to sleep, Luigi had told her the thing that now filled her with such dread. She shuddered again even now her heart jumping with icy fear.

Luigi had not informed his parents of their shipboard wedding.

He was brinigng home a bride no one expected.

9

The nearer the winding country road brought them to the ancestral home of the di Fontanesis, the more Charlotte-Anne sensed her husband coming to life. An undercurrent of excitement emanated from him, his eyes shining with an intense pride. It only served to make Charlotte-Anne feel very much the outsider and to deepen her doubts.

For him there were memories around every turn. Proudly he pointed out the sights to her. Here he had once been thrown from a horse; there his family's properties started, continuing for twenty kilometers as far as the eye could see; blanketing the hills, there were their olive groves; those shorter, well-tended green furrows were vineyards; that entire village had paid annual rent to the di Fontanesis for the past four hundred years. Of course, he explained, the rent was still being collected only because of its long, time-honored tradition. It was the family's varied other business interests—notably banking and industry—upon which its real fortune was based.

In Rome, their private railroad car had been disconnected from the train, and they had spent the night at the di Fontanesi villa bordering the Borghese Gardens. Then they had driven the remaining seventy-five miles southeast to the country estate of the di Fontanesis in the shiny new red Bugatti which had been waiting for Luigi in Rome. After Larry's stately yellow-and-black Rolls-Royce, riding in the smaller, sporty Bugatti convertible was, Charlotte-Anne thought to herself, like taking a ride on a roller coaster. Especially with Luigi at the wheel. He was an expert driver, but a fast one. Along with aviation, racing was his great love, and although she constantly begged him to slow down, he only laughed.

The closer they got to his home, the faster he seemed to go, which increased Charlotte-Anne's discomfort because she was not nearly as eager to reach the palazzo as he was. She was increasingly nervous and worried, convinced that he should have let his parents know about their wedding. She should have insisted upon it. What kind of reception could a mystery bride expect? In her mind she conjured up a vision of his parents, grim and aristocratic: his father, the Prince Antonio, a thin aesthete with a threatening, almost ecclesiastic demeanor; his mother, the Princess Marcella, a Medici descendant with a cunning, cold nature. The di Fontanesis could trace their lineage back to the twelfth century; one of their ancestors' fifteenth-century offspring had even been pope.

Despite her fearful anticipation, she couldn't help admiring the beauty of the landscape they passed through. Between the villages, they drove along humpbacked hills, their sunny sides clad with the green vineyards reclaimed from the reluctant, rocky soil and cultivated over many centuries, their shadier sides grayish-green with olive groves. Here and there rose the occasional piercing spires of the stately cypress trees. Tiny rambling villages precariously crowned the hilltops or nestled deep in the valleys. Everywhere along the twisting road, local farmers tended their fields with the same implements their ancestors had used. As they drove past, the farmers would lay down their tools and stare at the bright, fast car with expressions of wonder.

Each time they entered a village, Luigi slowed down impatiently, though Charlotte-Anne was grateful for it. Chickens strutted the narrow, dusty streets, pecking the ground for food, until the red car sent them fluttering and squawking. Charlotte-Anne leaned her head back and stared up at the buildings. The stucco was peeling, exposing the thick stone walls beneath. In every village, tall stone church steeples towered over the rooftops, which were speckled with different-colored tiles. It was a land where time seemed to have stopped centuries before. The border incident Charlotte-Anne had witnessed began to seem further and further away.

"I didn't think it would be so beautiful here," she said.

Luigi glanced sideways at her. They had just left a village behind them and were speeding along an open stretch of road. "What?" he called over the rush of the wind and the roar of the engine.

She cupped her hands and shouted, "I said it's beautiful!"

He grinned then, and once again she was struck by just how handsome he was, how he could simply look at her and make her melt.

Abruptly he slowed down and pulled the car over. As he engaged the hand brake, she looked at him in surprise. "Is something wrong?" she asked.

He shook his head. "We are almost there now. It is only a few minutes farther."

She nodded.

He reached for her hand and held it. "You are nervous?"

She grimaced, then nodded again.

"There is nothing to worry about," he assured her. "My parents do not generally eat young ladies for dinner." And with that, he threw the car back into gear and they hurtled around one last curve, where he abruptly braked, turned right with a protesting screech of the tires, and swung off the road onto an even narrower drive that was smooth and well paved.

"This is it," he exclaimed as the car burst past two enormous stone pillars guarding the entry to the property. Charlotte-Anne twisted around in the red leather seat and looked back. Each receding pillar was topped with a gray, crumbling fragment of a marble statue.

The road wound, gently climbing up the hillside through the olive groves. Both shoulders were planted with cypresses that flashed past the fast-moving car.

"Is that the house?" she called, pointing to her left. Across the valley, another hill, half a mile away, was crowned with what looked like a rambling yellow stone fortress complete with crenellated walls and towers.

His eyes flicked sideways at her. "No, that is the convent of the order of Our Lady of Peace, the ones who embroider our linen. Our house, or I should say the house of my parents, is directly above us. When the wind blows from the west, you can hear the church bells from the convent.''

The road rose higher, making its way up the hill in an ever-rising spiral. Charlotte-Anne looked down, and between the cypresses she could see the green, gently sloping vineyards and olive groves and villages dotting the valley.

"Look up," he said, pointing. He slowed the car to a snail's crawl and her eyes followed his pointing finger, getting her first glimpse of the ancestral home of the di Fontanesis.

Jutting out above them was a broad, balustraded terrace. The house itself was recessed, half-hidden behind a cluster of cypresses, but even from the little she could see, she realized it was of dishearteningly palatial proportions. Squatting atop the leveled hilltop, it commanded a sweeping three-hundred-and-sixty degree view of the entire countryside.

The central portion of the house, she learned once they came around the next bend, was four stories tall. Three soaring arches on the ground floor created a recessed loggia, flanked by three tall French doors on either side. Directly above that, on the second floor, three massive arched windows mirrored the first floor. The third floor was made up entirely of octagonal windows, except in the center, where the second-floor arches ended. The top floor had three smaller windows; from under the center one a flagpole carried the fluttering crest of the di Fontanesis.

Two long wings, each two stories in height, stretched out from each side of this central pavilion, and with the roofline and the staggered effect of the facade, the palace gave the impression of being a gently sloping pyramid, white everywhere except for the gabled roofs, which were tiled as were all the houses in the region.

Only when the car curved farther around the hill did Charlotte-Anne notice with awe that what she had previously glimpsed was only the tip of the iceberg. All four sides of the palace were identical; the palace was perfectly square, with an open central courtyard. The building was enormous, the size of one of her mother's grand hotels. She took a deep breath and tried to stifle her growing trepidation.

"I grew up here," Luigi said, still driving at a snail's pace. "Of course, this was not my only home. The Villa della Rosa, in which we spent last night in Rome, is where I usually live now, unless I come here to visit my parents. Rome is where you and I shall be living. And then there are the other houses. The neoclassical palace my grandfather built on the shores of Lake Garda, the chalet in the Alps, and the palace in Venice. But this one is my favorite. All the locals call it Palazzo Bizzarro."

"Palazzo Bizzarro? What does that mean?"

"The literal translation is the Bizarre Palace. Its official name, however, is the Palazzo di Cristallo, the Crystal Palace."

She took her eyes off the approaching house long enough to turn and glance at him. "But why? I don't see much glass other than the windows. Why not simply call it the Palazzo di Fontanesi?"

"You shall see soon enough." He smiled mysteriously. "There is, in fact, a Palazzo di Fontanesi. The palace in Venice is called that, but in Venice one simply calls a palazzo a Casa. Ca' for short, so it is the Ca' di Fontanesi."

"I think," she said, staggered, "I'm slightly confused."

"Do not be." He laughed. "You will sort it out soon enough."

"You said that this house is your favorite. Why?"

"Because it *is* the Crystal Palace. And because of its history. You see, this is our ancestral seat, but there is nothing much left of that. My great-grandfather was a little . . . how do you say it? Touched?" He tapped his forehead.

"Touched." She nodded. "Yes."

"The result of too much intermarriage among the other branches of our family, probably. He was our own Mad Ludwig. He had gotten it into his head to raze the original house, which I understand was splendid by any standards, in order to build this one. He had rather strange tastes, as you will see. He traveled a lot in his youth, and the Turkish palace of Dolmabahce on the Bosporus affected him deeply. When he returned, he decided he had to have something just like it. Unfortunately, he tried to outdo the Sultan Abdul Mecid. Building this house, in fact, nearly bankrupted the family. Only the rentals coming in from the villagers and farmers saved my family from total financial ruin, and even that was almost not enough. As a result, although the tenants would now like to buy their properties from us instead of renting them, my family will not hear of it." He shrugged. "At the moment, we are very rich, but who knows? Maybe sometime in the future the rental income will save the Fontanesis once again."

She stared directly ahead now. They had crested the landscaped hill, and in front of her sprawled the Palazzo di Cristallo. It seemed to stare right back at her, its unblinking, dark mullioned windows framed by ocher pediments.

The moment they pulled up in front of the arched loggia, the massive front doors opened. Before Luigi could even switch off the engine, an ancient couple came hurrying down the steps, their faces wide with happy smiles. "Luigi!" they cried in thin, brittle voices.

Luigi hopped out of the car and quickly embraced them. "Cinzia! Marco!"

He turned toward the car. Charlotte-Anne was getting out, the expression on her face one of palpable relief. Perhaps she had worried too much, she thought. Luigi had been right, after all. These people did not look like they would eat her for dinner.

"Your parents look very happy to see you," she ventured with a hesitant smile, when Luigi turned to her again.

He laughed then. "My parents? No, no. Cinzia and Marco helped raise me, but they are not my parents. They are servants."

She blushed crimson, realizing then just how much she had to learn. And until she did, she would be far better off keeping her mouth shut.

"So *this* is why it's called the Crystal Palace," Charlotte-Anne marveled in a bare whisper as Luigi, who had passed his arm through hers, led her inside. Her faux pas of moments ago forgotten, she thrilled to the splendor which greeted her in the main hall. Luigi's great-grandfather might have been slightly mad, but the effect he had achieved was miraculous.

The grand marble double staircase rising before her was U-shaped and covered in deep Oriental rugs. The ceiling of the rotunda, four floors up, was glass, and from it hung a massive cut-crystal chandelier, its countless many-faceted prisms sparkling in the sunlight. But what made the staircase of the Crystal Palace so magically unique was the balustrade, made up of glittering, swirling out crystal, reinforced on the inside with delicate rods of brass.

"There are thirty-two thousand individual pieces of Baccarat crystal in the various staircases alone," Luigi said. "Five hundred candelabra and two hundred chandeliers are scattered throughout the palazzo. That one, however"—he pointed to the chandelier suspended over the landing—"is the most magnificent by far. It is said to weigh more than a ton."

She could only nod, her eyes darting about the cavernous hall. Everywhere, it seemed, marble pedestals held enormous crystal candelabra. The walls were either marble or beveled mirror set into marble. Rare pieces of Roman antiquity looked out from marble niches. The elaborately carved cornices were gilded.

She disengaged her arm from his and took a few steps forward. Gazing up, she saw that each landing of the staircase was lined with marble columns sprouting gold-leafed Corinthian capitals. And the balustrades of sparkling crystal rose four flights up.

It was an icy splendor barely softened by the rich-hued rugs; it hit upon that mad, secret nerve of the fantastic which was hidden deep in every mind.

"Do you like it?" Luigi asked at last.

She turned to him and swallowed. "I . . . I could never have imagined anything like it."

"Neither could I. Only seeing is believing. Now you know why this palazzo has earned both its official and unofficial names. It is crystal, and it is bizarre."

"The most peculiar thing of all," she said, "is that it should be *here,* and not in Rome."

"As I told you, my great-grandfather was quite peculiar. Rest assured, neither my grandfather nor my father nor I inherited his particular madness." He smiled. "Come, let me take you up to our apartment. Marco will carry the luggage upstairs, and you will have a chance to freshen up before you meet my parents."

10

The day was one she had no wish to repeat, ever. They had left Rome in the late morning. Already exhausted by their quick stop in that ancient city, filled with the strange sights, sounds, and smells of a foreign country, and then the long drive through the countryside, she found the overwhelming palazzo almost more than she could take.

Its outlandishness soon became only another nightmarish reminder of just how far removed she was from her own familiar, comfortable world.

Then she had met Luigi's parents. They at least spoke English, but the meeting was formally polite and very cool. They were everything she had imagined them to be: his father stern and aristocratic and his mother meticulously well-groomed and cold. When they learned of the wedding, they had offered no congratulations. His father had ignored the news completely. His mother had simply raised her patrician eyebrows, and had then digested the news in silence.

That evening they ate in the huge dining room on plates of silver, a tablecloth of lace. Everything else, from the candelabra and serving platters down to the stemware and salt and pepper shakers, was, distressingly, of cut crystal. The conversation had been reserved, and immediately after the meal, the Principessa Marcella Luisella Uberti di Fontanesi had pushed back her thronelike dining chair, risen regally to her feet at the foot of the absurdly long table, and smiled coolly.

"Luigi, I am certain that you and your father have much to discuss," his mother had said in the hesitant but excellent boarding-school English she had learned long ago. "We ladies shall retire to the music room to get acquainted while you two go on to the smoking room." She had looked at Charlotte-Anne then, her lips composed in a slight, polite smile, but her eyes were a steely black which held little warmth.

Charlotte-Anne had turned pleadingly to Luigi, but he had only smiled at her and said, "It is a good idea to get acquainted with your new mother-in-law."

The principessa had led the way to a surprisingly small, intimate salon where there was not so much as a stick of crystal in sight, a fact for which Charlotte-Anne was extremely grateful. The room was completely feminine, with fragile French furniture instead of the heavy, ornately carved Italian pieces elsewhere in the house. The decor was all pale tones of light blue with delicate gold striping. A huge grand piano angled out of one corner; a gilded harp stood in another.

"You would perhaps like a coffee?" the principessa asked before they sat down.

"No, thank you," Charlotte-Anne replied.

"Good. I never drink coffee in the evenings. I find it makes it difficult to sleep. Here in the country, we go to sleep very early." She paused, then said, "Please, have a seat." The tiny woman gestured toward the settee and Charlotte-Anne sat down warily, her back erect. She wasn't aware of it, but it was the exact pose her mother would have adopted under similar circumstances.

The Principessa Marcella di Fontanesi was a fine-boned woman of fifty-seven, as beautiful as her tall, balding husband was handsome. It was easy for Charlotte-Anne to see where Luigi had gotten his looks. The long-waisted, well-built body of the athlete which he carried with such ease came from his father, the strong sculptured features from his mother. Diminutive though she was, the principessa did not give off an air of petiteness or helplessness. On the contrary, she seemed bigger than life with her well-groomed head of white hair, her severely tailored black suit, and the single strand of magnificent pear-shaped pearls around her throat. Her eyes were as darkly intense as Luigi's, but larger, more incisive. But Charlotte-Anne soon learned that her stately calm was deceptive: she was a shrewd, tense, and severe woman. From her Luigi had inherited that not-so-subtle air of a panther ready to pounce.

"You are very beautiful, Miss Hale," the principessa began, remaining standing and pointedly looking down on Charlotte-Anne. "I see why my son was attracted to you."

Charlotte-Anne looked up at her and met those piercing black eyes without flinching. "I am no longer a Hale, Principessa," she said softly. "I am a di Fontanesi."

The principessa looked at her and made an irritated gesture. "That," she said directly, "is a matter of opinion, Miss Hale. It was a shipboard romance, a hasty civil wedding. One becomes a di Fontanesi only by being married in, and having the marriage blessed by, the Holy Mother Church."

"That's all you think it is?" Charlotte-Anne asked, shocked. "A lousy shipboard romance?"

"Come, come. Let us not fool ourselves, Miss Hale."

Charlotte-Anne raised her chin stubbornly. "Luigi and I love each other," she said with fierce but quiet pride. "We will love each other forever."

A faint smile hovered on the principessa's lips. "*Really.*" She crossed the room, leaned back against a little writing table, and folded her arms in front of her. The smile never left her lips. "How much do you want?"

Charlotte-Anne looked startled. "I beg your pardon?"

"I said," the principessa repeated patiently, "how much money do you want in exchange for calling off this foolish marriage?"

"You're trying to buy me off?" Charlotte-Anne said with disbelief.

"In whatever currency pleases you. For some it is money. For others it is jewelry, or favors. Everyone has a price. Only the currency differs."

"I don't believe this," Charlotte-Anne said, springing to her feet and crossing the room. She towered over the shorter woman. "I don't think you heard right," she said. "We are already married."

The principessa tilted her head back, her gaze still piercing. "Are you, now? You're certain of that?"

Charlotte-Anne nodded. "Of course I'm certain."

The principessa shook her head sadly, as though trying to get through to a stubborn, recalcitrant child. "You forget one thing. You are now in Italy, Miss Hale," she said in a quiet voice. "The laws here are different. We are a Catholic country. Your shipboard wedding was a meaningless ritual."

Charlotte-Anne narrowed her pale eyes. "Well, not for me it wasn't," she snapped.

"Then you are deceiving yourself. And that is a pity."

Charlotte-Anne's expression did not change. "So what are you trying to tell me? That the marriage isn't recognized?"

"Ah. Now you are getting the point."

"And Luigi . . . he knew it wouldn't be?"

"Surely you cannot think that my son is ignorant of the laws of his country and his church?"

The fight seemed to seep out of Charlotte-Anne. She felt suddenly dizzy. She didn't know if what the principessa claimed was true, but she was frightened.

It can't be true, she told herself silently. Oh God, why do I have to face this creature alone? Why can't Luigi be here at my side now of all times? Her shoulders slumped and her eyes fell wearily.

The principessa seized upon the moment, misinterpreting Charlotte-Anne's desolate pain for defeat. "Leave him now, while there is still time," she whispered hoarsely. She dug her fingers clawlike into Charlotte-Anne's arms and shook her. "You are merely infatuated with each other. But love? What can you know of love? You are too young. When you are older, you will thank me for not letting you make this mistake."

Charlotte-Anne jerked back, loosening the woman's painful grip. Slowly she shook her head, still in a state of shock. She knew now how wrong she had been to underestimate Luigi's parents. She hadn't expected them to welcome her, but even in her wildest nightmares she had not expected a battle such as this.

Defiantly she raised her chin. "Principessa, I think we are

agreed on one thing," she said in a trembling voice. "You do not like me, and I do not like you. So be it. However, I love Luigi." She blinked back the tears which threatened to fill her eyes. "I love him so much that I will fight to my dying day to keep him, and I believe in my heart that he will do the same for me. The way I see it, you have two choices left open to you. The di Fontanesis have power and influence. You will either accept us, and make certain our marriage is recognized, or you will lose your only son. I don't want your money or your favors. I don't care what your twisted mind may come up with, I will never be bought off."

"Call it what you will." The principessa's face was rigid with cold self-assurance. "It is as I have said. Everyone has a price. You need only state yours."

"Damn you, *I won't be bought off!*" Charlotte-Anne exploded in spite of her choked-back tears. "Can't you get that through your head?"

"Do not be so emotional."

Flushed and breathing hard, Charlotte-Anne whirled around and ran toward the door.

"Where are you going?" the principessa cried after her.

Charlotte-Anne spoke without turning around. "I'm going upstairs to pack." She paused, her fingers on the door handle. "And as soon as I'm through, Luigi and I are returning to Rome. I can see we aren't welcome here."

The principessa laughed. "You are bluffing."

"Am I?" Charlotte-Anne let go of the door handle, clenched her hands at her sides, and retraced her steps toward Luigi's mother. "Try me," she challenged. "Besides, we'll be far better off in Rome than in this . . . this museum of an ice palace. You know, I think in your own way, you're as mad as Luigi's great-grandfather. This place is addling your brain." She paused and added slowly, "Believe me, Luigi and I will be happy in Rome."

"And Luigi's career?" The principessa had recovered her momentary lapse into mild fear; her voice was once again smooth and well-modulated. "What about that? Il Duce has let it be known that he has great plans for Luigi."

"What about them? Luigi loves flying and racing; he'd be

content to do that for the rest of his life. So Il Duce wants him in the armed forces. So what? He'll either take him or leave him. And anyway, from what I've seen so far, Luigi'll be a damn sight better off if he doesn't run around with that pack of murdering fascists."

The principessa gasped and her face went ashen. "You fool," she hissed. "You would be best off to keep your political views to yourself. It's not safe to speak that way."

"It isn't, is it?" Charlotte-Anne permitted herself to smile. "Well, in that case I'd better run through this morgue and shout out my opinions before anyone gets the wrong idea. And then I'd better go from village to village, and city to city."

"Please," the principessa urged quietly. "Calm down."

Charlotte-Anne felt like laughing and crying at once. What a farce this was, she thought. She had found the principessa's two weaknesses: her height, which was why she hadn't taken a seat, and, more important, her immense fear of the fascists. Apparently the powerful di Fontanesis were not that powerful after all.

"You may be infallible around here, Principessa," Charlotte-Anne said contemptuously, "but I see I was wrong. You do have more than two choices open to you."

"And what else," Luigi's mother asked, "might there be?"

"Specifically, I will promise to keep my political views to myself. *If* you stay out of our lives and stop trying to meddle."

"And if I do not?"

"Then I'll shout from the rooftops. I'll make the biggest antifascist stink this country has ever seen."

"You would not live for a day!"

"Without Luigi, life is not worth living for me. And believe me, if I go, I'll drag you and your entire family down along with me."

The dark eyes shone with fear. "Please, be reasonable," the principessa gasped.

"No, *you* be reasonable. I think you'll agree that we'd better start accepting each other's presence. I won't have my husband torn between his wife and his mother. Do I make myself clear?"

The principessa stared at her with shocked hatred.

"We'll be polite and civil," Charlotte-Anne continued. "We don't have to pretend to love each other. We'll do our best to stay out of each other's way. And this, Principessa, had better be our last fight. Oh. For another thing, you might as well get used to calling me Charlotte-Anne instead of Miss Hale. Just as I'll have to get used to calling you 'Mother.' "

The principessa cringed.

"Now, I suggest you go and use all your influence to make certain that this marriage is recognized."

And with that Charlotte-Anne stormed out of the music room. She left a quivering Principessa Marcella Luisella Uberti di Fontanesi standing alone, staring at the door.

As she hurried down the cold, gleaming marble corridor lined with crystal candelabra, Charlotte-Anne smiled grimly to herself. The principessa had been both right and wrong, she thought to herself.

Everyone had a price.

Silence, it seemed, was golden. And as such, very expensive.

It had cost the principessa her son.

The moment Charlotte-Anne left the music room, a secret wall panel concealed by the striped blue-and-gold wall fabric swung soundlessly open. His Eminence Giovanni, Cardinal Corsini, the same man Charlotte-Anne had met at her first dinner aboard the *Ile de France*, stepped gracefully into the room, his ankle-length soutane rustling as it swirled around his legs. His thin face with its high, angular cheekbones was impassive. He pushed the panel shut with the palm of his hand.

The Principessa Marcella di Fontanesi turned wearily to him. "You heard everything?" she asked in Italian.

He nodded and slipped into a chair. "She has spirit," he said expressionlessly.

"Spirit!" The principessa snorted. "She is asking to be shot. And she will end up getting us *all* shot. These modern American girls—they think they are entitled to everything. It is true what is said about them. They are interested in only one thing—to marry titles."

His Eminence steepled his bony fingers and held them against his brittle lips. "This one cannot be bought off," he murmured. "I see now that I have misjudged her. I was wrong."

"Yes, you were wrong." The principessa took a seat opposite him, but the fight seemed to go out of her. "However, I am still grateful that you hurried here and warned us about the marriage before they arrived. The church will, of course, receive a sizable donation, as always."

"Whatever charity you find it in your heart to give, Principessa," the cardinal said softly, "the church is grateful for." He stared at her with an expression of hurt. "I did not come because of the donation."

The principessa smiled tightly. "Of course not." She glanced down at her hands as she wrung them nervously in her lap. "It seems we have all underestimated the girl," she mused aloud. She looked back up at him. "How do you suggest we proceed?"

He half-smiled. "With utmost delicacy."

"Of course." She tightened her lips. "Much as I hate to admit it, she has threatened our sole vulnerability. And perhaps she really does love Luigi. Only time will tell."

"Then you wish the marriage to be recognized?"

"Do I have any choice?"

The cardinal shrugged. "Not much. It depends on how serious she is about carrying out her threat."

"The results of which, your Eminence," the principessa reminded him dryly, we cannot afford to even consider."

He nodded gravely. "These are difficult times," he sighed.

"But it is true that their marriage, as it stands now, is not recognized?"

"It depends, Principessa. In the courts of America, England, and Germany, it is official. According to Rome, however, it is not. Prince Luigi and his wife are living in sin. Any child they conceive would be conceived in sin. She is not even Catholic. I discovered that on the ship."

The principessa nodded and pursed her lips. "In that case, I suppose we have no choice. We must make certain this marriage gets recognized with all due haste. Of course," she added delicately, "we will only be too happy to show just how grateful we are for any red tape you are able to cut." She eyed him significantly. "Not for yourself, of course. For the church."

"Of course," he replied, his face still impassive. "I shall put it to the Holy Father at once."

11

The room smelled faintly moist and musky from recent lovemaking. Their labored, anguished breaths had calmed again to become soft, steady breathing. The bright country moonlight streamed in through the open windows. The faint, distant sound of church bells rode over on the cool breeze from the convent on the hill across the valley.

Charlotte-Anne stared up at the dark ceiling of heavy damask canopy covering the bed, her mind drifting. In the moonlight, her face was pale silver and deeply shadowed.

She sensed Luigi's eyes studying her. Then she felt his satin skin against hers as he gently prodded her to turn over on her side. He took deep, appreciative sniffs of her salty skin. "Nobody makes love like you do," he whispered into her spine as he buried his face against her naked back. He made an animal growl, pretended to take a bite out of her flesh, and nuzzled her roughly.

"And nobody makes love like you do either," she retorted, but it was a weak, halfhearted attempt at good humor. The listlessness of her voice gave her away.

"What is the matter?" He shifted on the bed, switched on the silk-shaded nightstand lamp, and lay sideways, supporting his weight on his cocked elbow. He was watching her intently.

"Oh, nothing really." She rolled over and lay flat again, her eyes tracing the swirls of damask. She puffed her cheeks full of air and let go of a deep breath, blowing stray tendrils of hair out of her eyes. "I was just thinking, that's all."

"About what?"

"You. Me."

"What about us?" he asked. "Aren't you happy with me? Don't I satisfy you in bed?"

She couldn't help laughing. "You're perfect. But you know that." It amused her that Luigi di Fontanesi, the notorious ladykiller, should need such reassurances.

"Then what is it?" he asked worriedly. "You look so preoccupied."

"Do I?"

"Yes, you do." He leaned over her face. "When we made love just now, you were so . . . *determined*. It was as though you wanted to use it to forget something." He paused. "I only want you to be happy," he said, kissing her lips. "I want you always to be happy."

"I know that." She smiled faintly up at him.

"And we must never keep secrets from each other. Not ever. Not for as long as we live."

She nodded, feeling ashamed of herself for keeping something from him so early in their marriage. Their *unrecognized* marriage, she reminded herself with a stab of fear, remembering the principessa's icy, self-righteous words. There was nothing she wanted to do more than to confide in Luigi and tell him about her confrontation with his mother, but she knew she would never be able to discuss it with him. What had occurred was between the principessa and herself, and it had to stay that way. She was not about to see her husband torn between his wife and mother.

"Then will you tell me what is disturbing you after such wonderful lovemaking?" He paused. "Was it my mother?"

She gave a start. It was as though he could read her mind. She let out a low laugh which she hoped sounded convincing. "Whatever gave you that idea?"

"You were with her this evening. Afterward when we made love, you were tense. I have never seen you so tense."

"I suppose I *was*," she said slowly, choosing her words

with care, "but that's only to be expected. It isn't every day that a girl meets her in-laws."

"And that's all that is bothering you?"

"Should there be anything else?"

He shrugged his shoulders. "Knowing my mother, who knows? Sometimes she intimidates people without even realizing it."

"Does she now?" Charlotte-Anne regretted the sarcasm the instant the words slipped out.

He nodded. "Yes, she does."

She let out a breath of relief. Luigi's English was good, but the sarcasm was completely lost on him.

He was baffled. "If it is not me or my mother, then what is it?" he prodded. "I do not want us to have any problems."

"I don't either," she said quickly. She turned on her side to face him, her pale eyes glittering. "But, Luigi . . ."

"Yes?"

"Your mother . . . well she . . . she hinted that we might face some problems."

"Problems? What kind of problems?" he asked in a puzzled voice. "Hopefully not any which are insurmountable."

"Knowing you, no problem is unsurmountable." Nevertheless, she bit down on her lip. "It's about our marriage."

"What about it?"

"Your mother is afraid it won't be recognized by the church."

"That *is* a problem." He nodded gravely. "However, I've thought about it and I am not so certain it cannot be worked out. If we must, we will simply get married all over again."

She tightened her lips. "I want us to be married already, Luigi," she said with soft intensity. "I want our marriage to have been official all along. I know it sounds silly, but I want to know that I am your wife."

"Then do not worry." He smiled. "I am a di Fontanesi, and so are you. And God knows, we give enough to the church. Have no fear. Our cardinal will work things out."

" '*Your*' cardinal?"

"Yours, too, now that you are a di Fontanesi."

"But . . . I don't understand."

"You will in time. All the powerful Italian families have a 'family' cardinal, so to speak. It is like having a family doctor or a lawyer. Our cardinal will straighten things out. It may cost us, but then, nothing in life is free."

"Who is this cardinal?"

"You have already met him. On the *Ile de France*."

"You mean, Cardinal Corsini?"

"The very one. So stop worrying. My mother and the cardinal together will move heaven and earth to set things right. My mother is a very determined woman. She always gets what she wants."

Charlotte-Anne nodded.

"Now, wipe that worried expression off your face. I said it would all be fixed, did I not?"

She smiled. "Yes, you did." She bent forward and kissed him deeply. Somehow, just hearing him tell her it was all right made it seem so.

"Now look what you made me do," he accused as he drew away from her.

"What?" she asked, puzzled.

He laughed, flipping off the embroidered sheet and looking down. She followed his gaze and shook her head in disbelief.

The Principessa Marcella moved down the marble corridor on slippered feet. As she passed Luigi's apartment, a perverse kind of curiosity came over her. For an instant she wavered between stopping and continuing on her nightly rounds.

Her curiosity won out. She drew close to the door and pressed her ear against it. Her elegant lips curled with disgust as her acute hearing caught the muffled, urgent sounds of lovemaking. She could hear her son's anguished moans and the cries of passion that the *putana* he had brought home emitted as she urged him on.

Now more than ever the principessa was thoroughly convinced that the girl was the worst kind of tragedy that could be visited on the di Fontanesis. Only an *animal* relished such disgusting acts, the principessa hissed to herself with revulsion. She could not believe that her son could have stooped so low.

For a moment the principessa was reminded of her own youth. How different that had been!

She had married Prince Antonio thirty-one years earlier. He had been young and intensely studious, and she had been the most famous beauty in all Campania, some said in all Italy. And everyone agreed that they made the perfect couple. What they didn't know was that choosing him had been an easy decision for her. She had received countless proposals of marriage, but she had turned them all down in favor of the prince. Not because she had been physically attracted to him. His handsomeness had had nothing to do with it. On the contrary, she had chosen him above the others because he was the least physically demanding of her suitors. She had had the feeling that she could control his passions.

And control them she had. For three decades now she had been the irreproachable chatelaine of the various palazzi, the model hostess, the legendary beauty, and the perfect wife in every way but one. She knew about her husband's mistress of long standing, and she was not at all threatened by her. She was, in fact, relieved that he took those disgusting urges elsewhere to relieve himself of them. She despised having to make love. She had consented to it in the beginning only in the practical interest of producing an heir. After she had become pregnant, she had moved to her own room and never allowed her husband to make love to her again.

She could only wish that her son had inherited her own physical frugality, but from the stories that had found their way back to her, she knew he hadn't. How peculiar that Luigi had come to possess the womanizing qualities she herself found so revolting. He had certainly not inherited that from herself or his father. The prince's discreet mistress was his only bed partner. But Luigi was different. He loved women— *all* women—and that was his great weakness. She wished, not for the first time, that Luigi was quieter and more studious. He reminded her too much of everything she found revolting in a man.

The moist, succulent sounds of lovemaking coming from Luigi's apartment unearthed all the long-buried memories of everything she had found so demeaning. She did not understand what on earth could drive a woman—any woman—to accept it. A man's urgency . . . well, that was understandable. Physically, men were animals. But for a woman to enjoy it? No woman who embraced it with such fervor could, in her opinion, be a lady.

She heard the distant, echoing footsteps of one of the servants approaching from around the corner. Quickly she moved on so she wouldn't be caught eavesdropping.

I wasn't trying to eavesdrop, she told herself as she continued on her rounds down the seemingly endless corridors. I pass this way every night after checking to make certain that everything in this house is in order, she assured herself.

But what, then, a small voice in the back of her mind asked, *prompted you to stop and place your ear against that door in the first place?*

And she answered herself, with an audible snap of her jaw: Just to make certain that I wasn't making a terrible mistake. I had to be sure my initial instincts about the American were correct. And they were. She is everything I feared she was. And worse.

When Marcella reached the apartment she shared with the prince, she went directly to her bedroom. She was about to undress, but she felt so agitated that she wanted to speak to someone. For a long time she stared at the connecting door leading to her husband's bedroom. She had not knocked on his door for years. She hated to do it now, but finally she cocked a knuckle, took a deep breath, and knocked.

"Yes?" His muffled voice sounded surprised.

She opened the door. "Antonio," she said softly. "Are you still awake?"

His room was dark. In the wedge of light flooding through from her room, she saw him sit up in bed and squint. Then he reached across the bed to his nightstand and switched on the lamp. It bathed his face in soft yellow light. "Marcella? Something is worrying you?"

"Worrying?" She laughed as she drew closer to his bed, careful to make sure that she kept at arm's length from him. Her voice held a disapproving tone. "I am happy that Luigi is back. But as for that American . . ."

He nodded. "Did Cardinal Corsini leave yet?"

"No, but I had a chance to speak with him. I put him in his usual guest suite in the opposite wing. He will leave in the morning, before they wake up. They will never know he has even been here. I have warned the servants to remain silent."

He looked at her. "You have had the opportunity to talk to Luigi's wife. What happened?"

"Wife!" The principessa snorted. "She is nothing but a common *putana*. As I passed their bedroom door . . ."

"Yes?" A spark glowed in his dark eyes.

She was so involved in her hatred for Charlotte-Anne that she didn't notice her husband's quickening interest. "You should hear the sounds coming from within the apartment," she spat disgustedly. "You can hear it all the way out in the hall. It's revolting, I tell you."

"Sounds? What kind of sounds?"

"You know . . ." She made an agitated little gesture.

"Lovemaking?"

She blushed and turned away. "That girl is no good. I cannot bear to think of her as a di Fontanesi."

"She will not leave, then?"

She turned back to face him, her eyes flashing. "She refuses. She claims to love him. She has gone so far as to tell me, his mother, that he will stand by her no matter what. It must be our money she's after. Either that or . . . or what they do at night." She wrung her hands in despair. "She threatened me."

"How so?"

She told him about Charlotte-Anne's threat to publicize her antifascist feelings. A tiny smile hovered at the corners of Prince Antonio's lips. No one had displayed the courage to stand up to his wife for many years. The girl had spirit, and silently he applauded her. "As long as Luigi is happy," he said carefully, envying his son, "that is all that matters."

"Perhaps that is all that matters to *you*. Men always stick together. But do you have any idea what it will cost us to have this marriage recognized? And if we don't, think of the scandal."

"There need be no scandal, you know that. Another generous contribution—"

"And another, and then another," she said testily. "I have never seen anything as ravenous as Rome. The Vatican eats up our money. Do you have any idea how much it has already gotten from us?"

"We can afford it," he said mildly. "I don't mind. And besides, you are a good, practicing Catholic."

She raised her chin and nodded. "Yes, I am," she said gravely, his irony lost on her.

"Then it seems we have no choice other than to embrace her into this family."

"Perhaps we have no choice, but I won't embrace her," the principessa growled. "Not now. Not ever. She is merely a whore. It grieves me that Luigi should fall for her. He has always had such cheap taste in women."

"If she makes him happy, so be it."

"Any woman can make him happy, if that kind of gratification is all he seeks."

"She seems quite charming to me," the prince said. "A little shy, perhaps, but under the circumstances, that is understandable. She is very beautiful."

"Yes," the principessa admitted dryly, "she is beautiful. But many women are beautiful."

"You are beautiful still," he said smoothly. "Even more beautiful than you were in your youth."

She stared at him. "That is because I am a lady. I have not allowed physical dissipation to take its toll on me. But she is different. Her beauty will fade quickly."

He felt his own physical needs suddenly rising. Beneath the covers, his phallus throbbed and grew.

"Marcella," he whispered gently, reaching out for her. "*Cara mia.*"

But she had already turned and was walking briskly through the connecting door to her own bedroom. It closed with a soft but decisive click.

The prince sighed and dropped his head wearily back down on the pillow. How long it had been now since their love had died! It had stopped when she was pregnant with Luigi. That had been Marcella's excuse then, and a multitude had followed. In time, he had stopped trying altogether. Perhaps she had never loved him. Or perhaps love did not exist.

He closed his eyes, imagining the sounds of his son and daughter-in-law. Almost without his realizing it, his hand drifted down to his penis. He had a sudden vision of Luigi and Charlotte-Anne naked together, him riding her mercilessly.

Prince Antonio di Fontanesi had barely touched himself when he felt himself explode.

His last thought before he drifted into sleep was that, whatever the price, having the girl in the family would be well worth it.

They soon discovered that even for the mighty di Fontanesis, it wasn't all that easy to appease the powerful Vatican. The laws of the state were one thing, the laws of the church something else entirely. Only after six months could they arrange to have Charlotte-Anne and Luigi's marriage officially recognized by Rome.

During that time, Charlotte-Anne was forced to be as inconspicuous as possible at the Palazzo di Cristallo. Meanwhile, Luigi was in Rome. She was not allowed to accompany him there. According to Cardinal Corsini, this was no time to flaunt an unrecognized marriage before society and the church. Strict conventions had to be observed. This became even more imperative when Charlotte-Anne discovered she was pregnant.

The truce she had worked out with the Principessa Marcella was an uneasy one, and both women did their best to stay out of each other's way. Living under the same roof for over six months was difficult for both. When their paths did cross, they were polite, but no love was lost between the two princesses.

Charlotte-Anne hated being away from Luigi, even if it was only a distance of seventy-five miles. It might as well have been seven thousand. His commission as colonel in the Italian Air Force kept him in Rome, and too often he didn't return to the palazzo for weeks at a time. She was dying to move into the Villa della Rosa with him, but she could only wait. Whenever he came to visit, he would whisper, "Soon now. Just have patience."

It took the patience of Job.

It was January before a final agreement could be worked out between the Vatican and the di Fontanesis. In the end, it cost the di Fontanesis five hundred million lire, along with a donation to the Vatican of three coveted works of religious art.

The day the marriage was recognized, the Principessa Marcella came to Charlotte-Anne's apartment. Luigi was in Rome, and Charlotte-Anne faced her mother-in-law alone.

"Congratulations," the Principessa Marcella said dryly. "You now have the satisfaction of having had one of the most expensive marriages in history. I suggest that, since you have gotten what you wanted, you start packing and leave at once for Rome. Furthermore, I strongly suggest you keep any and all political views to yourself, unless you want to jeopardize your own and your husband's lives. Your car is waiting."

The principessa closed the door without so much as saying good-bye.

But still, the principessa and the church seemed to have had the last laugh. Their child, "conceived in sin," was stillborn. And though Charlotte-Anne became pregnant regularly, she suffered a series of seven miscarriages during the next five years.

12

In the beginning, their life together was a fairy-tale dream come true.

But for her problems with childbearing, Charlotte-Anne considered the next few years as near-perfect as any could possibly be. The moment she finally left the loveless splendor of the Palazzo di Cristallo, she felt liberated as though from a dark, stifling prison into the joyous, brilliant sunshine. It might have taken time and cost a fortune, but finally she really *was* the Principessa Charlotte-Anne di Fontanesi and Luigi *was* officially her husband.

Since arriving in Italy, she had exchanged numerous letters with her mother. The first had been full of explanations, the rest to keep up with what was happening and to fill the loneliness she felt at the palazzo. It had come as a pleasant surprise to her that Elizabeth-Anne held no hard feelings because of the hasty shipboard wedding.

As long as you're happy, darling, her mother had written, *that is all that counts. Hopefully, we'll both be able to travel and visit each other often. I love you dearly, and the only thing which saddens me is that Italy is so far, far away. . . .*

She had felt immense relief when she had read that first letter, and was filled again with that rich feeling of closeness to her mother. The last thing she had expected was her mother's swift blessing. Eventually, she was certain, Elizabeth-Anne would come around, but to have her approval forthwith both amazed and delighted Charlotte-Anne. In this way the thousands of miles that separated them brought her a new outlook on her mother. Her respect for her increased immensely. Elizabeth-Anne Hale was some lady, she realized now. Her only regret was that it had taken her so long to discover it.

Rome quickly became home. Charlotte-Anne fell under the spell of the Eternal City as people had for thousands of years. Her first priority was to transform the formal Villa della Rosa from the haughty palace it was into a warm, comfortable home. She banished the massive carved furniture to storage. In its place she furnished the rooms with the warm honey tones of finely waxed fruit- and nut-wood veneers and the soft glaze of flowered chintzes. She was tired of palaces. She wanted a home where they could raise a family.

As the work progressed, she and Luigi lived in another wing of the villa, and she made him promise not to go and look at what she was doing until it was finished. Then she showed him around, her nervousness highly apparent. She was so afraid he would hate what she had done and would want it all put back as it had been.

He gazed around, silently walking from room to room. His frequent nods revealed nothing of his thoughts.

Finally he turned to her and grinned. "I like it," he said, hugging her tightly. "It is comfortable." Then he kissed her long and hard. "Above all, it is now our *home*."

She knew he had paid her the highest compliment she could hope for. The only note that soured it was his parents' unexpected visit.

"It looks rather plebeian, don't you think?" the principessa asked Luigi. "But then, it's a matter of taste. . . ."

Charlotte-Anne fought to keep her fury to herself. She was only too grateful that her in-laws didn't stay long. And that their future visits were exceedingly rare.

It seemed to her, in those early years, that she and Luigi were as one, except when his long hours working as attaché of Italy's fledgling air force kept him away. But when he was at home, and his time was his own, they spent every waking and sleeping hour together.

Still, she thought, it's not enough. Even if we could spend twenty-four hours together, every day for the rest of our lives, it wouldn't be enough. It was a romance made in heaven, and she was certain it could never end.

Luigi had planned to take a few weeks off so that they could go on a belated honeymoon, but he never found the time. "Il Duce insists he needs me, and I am afraid that things are only going to get busier," he said apologetically.

"I don't care," Charlotte-Anne declared. "With you, Rome is honeymoon enough."

When he had the time, he showed her the city inside and out, until she knew it by heart. She became familiar with the tourist Rome—the lush banks of azaleas rising up the one hundred and thirty-seven stairs of the majestic Spanish Steps, the Colosseum and its multitude of marauding cats, the ecclesiastic splendor of the Vatican, through which Cardinal Corsini personally guided them so that she could view both the public and the private chambers. She and Luigi dined regularly on the Via Veneto, and he took her to the Diocletian Baths and

San'Angelo Castle, where Hadrian's mausoleum was located. Every way she turned, it seemed, there were visible remnants of a civilization long past.

Under Luigi's patient tutelage she came to love Rome. How different it was from the maddening hustle and bustle and grime of New York! She found herself falling under the spell of the monumental panoramas, the splendid ruins, and the wide sidewalks lined with cafés. She loved the contrast of the very old, the merely old, and the new. But most of all she loved the clogged sidewalks, the sweet sounds of tenors singing, the screams of the children as they played in the alleys and on the terraces. Rome was magic and enchanting, and if it hadn't been for the ever-present signs of the military—the precisely strutting fascists parading down the boulevards, the forced civility whenever soldiers were within earshot, and the suspicious glances over people's shoulders—her love for the city would have been complete. She had to keep reminding herself that Luigi, too, was now in the military. And he wasn't a monster.

He took her everywhere and taught her the local customs. Once, when they spent an afternoon walking, they stopped at a sidewalk vendor to buy fruit to eat along the way. Charlotte-Anne had never seen such huge golden peaches, or tomatoes of such a deep, lush red, or bunches of grapes tied with vine. Everything looked inviting, but she settled on a bunch of grapes. She asked how much they were in the halting Italian Luigi had taught her.

The vendor, a thin old crone, told her they were sixty lire. Charlotte-Anne was about to start counting out the money when Luigi stopped her. "No, no!" he cried. "You must bargain."

"But . . . why?" she stammered. "She said they were sixty lire."

"Watch, and listen carefully." He took the grapes from her, held them up to inspect them, then frowned. Shaking his head, he put them back down and picked up another bunch. He squeezed a few peaches, a few plums. Then she watched him wave the bunch of grapes she had chosen in the first place in front of the vendor's face. She followed the conversation only roughly, recognizing phrases here and there that she had learned. "Thirty-five lire," Luigi began.

"Signor!" the vendor protested. "*Bambinis* . . . they starve . . . fifty."

He shook his head and scowled. "Grapes . . . bruised . . . thirty-five."

"Forty-five."

"Forty."

Despite herself, Charlotte-Anne was intrigued. "Enough, enough," the vendor finally mumbled. She shrugged. "So the *bambinos* starve . . . you drive a hard bargain, *signor*." And then the haggling old crone beamed broadly, her gold teeth flashing. Charlotte-Anne counted out the forty lire and started popping grapes into her mouth as they continued to walk on. "That poor woman," she scolded, shaking her head. "How could you do that to her?"

"She expects it," Luigi said. "Anything else would be to rob her of the joy of her trade. Watch."

They halted and looked back. An old man was buying an even bigger bunch of grapes, fiercely haggling with the vendor. He got them for thirty lire. "You see?" Luigi said, smiling. "Things are not always what they seem."

Charlotte-Anne kept her ears and eyes open, and she learned.

But Luigi didn't just show her the tourist sights for which the city was so famous. He took her to the Rome that tourists never saw at all. They dined in a ridiculously cheap restaurant he loved, which was frequented only by the working classes and was located underground in the two-thousand-year-old ruins of the catacombs. He was convinced the chicken cacciatore there was the best in all Italy.

"This is the best-kept secret in all Rome," he told her. "I make it a point never to tell anyone about it. If society were to discover this place, it would be ruined."

Her discoveries of Rome did not cease while Luigi was at work at the Ministry of Defense. She delighted in taking walks through the gardens of the Villa Borghese, whose rambling ancient stone wall comprised the wall of their own backyard. These walks, though without him, were put to good use; she had hired a tutor to teach her Italian, and while she and the tutor walked, she learned her new language. She spent hours on this secret project, which she had begun at the Palazzo di Cristallo to while away her empty hours.

Finally, when she felt she was ready, she met Luigi at the door when he came home one evening and spoke to him in fluent, flawless Italian.

"I'm so proud of you," he whispered back in his native language. And he proved it by showing her off to all his friends.

There were little irritants, too, which she discovered gradually. In the beginning, whenever he had come home, he had changed out of his colonel's uniform and into civilian clothes. But slowly, he started to wear his precisely tailored suits and silk shirts less and less until finally it occurred to her that he had stopped wearing them altogether. It disturbed her, and when she mentioned it to him, he said, "Il Duce wants all his officers in uniform all the time."

"But you're at home now. Surely his orders don't reach into our house."

"So? I'm comfortable."

She didn't go on to point out that when he wore his uniform out their evenings were different than they had been before. People were always so careful of him, civil and polite, their stony faces giving nothing away.

It hadn't been like that in the beginning. Due to his title and his military position, Luigi moved in lofty circles, but he had always been equally at home with common people. She had been both surprised and pleased when she found that he treated everyone equally well, with a total disregard for class or wealth. What amazed her was that everyone seemed to genuinely like him. His easy, contagious laughter, familiarity, and sincerity transcended all social barriers. She had to remind herself constantly that to her he was a husband, but to everyone else he was a national hero of sorts: he had won countless car races, and though his aviation records were not comparable to those of Lindbergh or Earhart, he was, after all, Italy's premier flying ace. But whether he was prince, or sportsman, or the common man's friend, everyone liked him. Until he was in uniform.

In those heady first few years together, several things occurred which marred the otherwise perfect scheme of things, and which, looking back upon them much later, Charlotte-Anne realized should have warned her about troubles to come. But those were such happy and carefree times, and trouble seemed so far away. They were together, invincible, and she believed that nothing could ever come between them. The incidents were spread so far apart that they seemed disparate, and she didn't make the connection until it was much too late.

On one sunny spring Sunday, the first thing occurred which caused her to feel anxious, and told her that everything was not quite as perfect as it seemed.

Luigi drove her to the outskirts of town for a picnic, stopping to point out, in the distance behind them, a low-cost housing project which he explained Il Duce had recently erected.

She was startled by the sudden change in his voice. As he spoke about the dictator's work, she realized just how much Luigi was coming to admire his leader.

Inwardly she cringed. He should never have brought her here, at least not on such an otherwise perfect day. The mention of Il Duce seemed a cloud obscuring the lemon sun.

She was silent for so long that he knew something was wrong. "What is the matter?" he asked her.

"Please, Luigi. Let's go back."

"But why? You look so upset."

She shook her head. "I'm not upset," she corrected him tightly. "I'm confused, that's all."

"Confused?" He looked at her with a perplexed frown. "What about?"

"Please, let's forget it," she pleaded.

"*No*," he said, and she saw the hurt, mingled with anger, which shone in his eyes. "If it concerns the way we feel about each other, I am entitled to know about it." He paused. "Well?"

She waved a hand at the sterile poured-concrete apartment buildings behind them. "I'm confused about those." She gazed at him. "And about you."

"I do not understand."

"You seem to . . ." She tightened her lips, wishing that she'd never started to explain. "Your voice . . . well, it just sounded as though you're starting to like Il Duce." She gazed up at him.

He laughed. "And that worries you?"

"Yes."

"Why should it?"

"Because . . . because he is *bad*, Luigi. He frightens people. Even your own mother let me know how terrified she is of him."

"When was this?"

"That first night at the palazzo."

"She might have been then, but not anymore she isn't. The more Il Duce trusts me, the safer she feels."

She shivered. "And Il Duce . . . he trusts you?"

"More and more, yes." He nodded.

"And you?" She looked at him with a curious kind of defiance. "Do you trust him?"

"I'm beginning to understand him," he said carefully. "He wants what is best for Italy. I see that now. At first I did not believe it, but now I do. Certainly there are things he does which I do not like at all. But he wants a new Italy, Charlotte-Anne. A stronger Italy. An Italy as strong as it was in the times of the Caesars."

She shivered again. There was a conviction in his voice that she had never heard before, and she found it frightening.

"And you, Luigi?" she asked softly. "What do you want?"

"Me? I want what is best for you. For my family. For all Italy." He smiled. "In precisely that order."

But somehow she wasn't sure that was the order of his priorities. He was changing, she realized, changing before her very eyes.

He seemed to sense her fears, and took her hand. "Come, let us not be so serious. It is a weekend afternoon, the sun is shining, and I am off from work. It is time for *amore*, not for worries."

She looked at him, her eyes sweeping over his elegant, hated uniform. She couldn't help thinking: Yes, you are off from work, but why can't I shake the feeling that your work is with you always, that you bring it home in your head? What happened to the dashing Luigi I met? The prince who loved the sport of flying and racing? Now, planes were only weaponry. And cars no longer mattered. There was no more talk of racing.

She pasted a weak smile on her face. "You're right. It's silly to spoil a lovely afternoon. Let's forget it."

And soon she had forgotten about it altogether.

13

It was some months before the next incident occurred which aroused her anxiety.

"We're invited to a formal reception at the Ministry of Foreign Affairs the day after tomorrow," Luigi said casually one evening at dinner.

She had been about to take a bite of veal off her fork; now she put the fork down on her plate. "The Ministry of Foreign Affairs?"

He nodded.

She let out a low whistle. At this point she was used to their burgeoning social life, and although it had intimidated her at first, she had quickly discovered that she was well-liked and admired. But previously their social life had revolved around internal affairs and the military, along with the old-line nobility. That they should be receiving invitations to a reception at the Ministry of Foreign Affairs was an indication that they were being swept into yet another social sphere.

Usually Charlotte-Anne did not like the stiffly formal receptions and dinners with the self-important uniformed officers strutting around on the arms of their gossiping wives, but this time she looked forward to going. She was just recovering from her second miscarriage and, as with the first, she had locked herself away in the villa until she came out of the ensuing depression. While she had been recovering, Luigi had not even mentioned any functions where she was expected to accompany him, and for that she had been extremely grateful. She knew he had waited until now because he sensed that she was finally ready to get out.

"I want you to look beautiful, as always." He smiled across the table at her. "Perhaps you should get yourself a new gown."

"Another one?" She couldn't help laughing. Men were so vain, and Luigi was more vain than most. He loved an opportunity to show her off, and seemed to take a special pride in dressing her.

"I think something sapphire blue would look nice," he mused, nodding. "Yes, very nice indeed."

"But you know I prefer pale colors," she protested. "And besides, two days is hardly enough time for Signora Bella to sew a gown!" She lifted her goblet and took a sip of white wine.

"I don't think she'll mind," he said with a vague smile. "Besides, you've given her enough business that she'd be a fool not to drop whatever she's working on to knock out a gown for you."

Charlotte-Anne knew better than to argue with him. The next morning, as she walked into Signora Bella's little shop, the gray-haired seamstress smiled broadly and brought out a bolt of sapphire-blue velvet. "Your husband had this delivered to me yesterday morning," she said, fingering it between her thumb and forefinger. "It is lovely, no?"

"Yes, it is certainly a lovely fabric," Charlotte-Anne had to agree, despite her anger at Luigi for disregarding her wishes.

"And do not worry, Principessa," Signora Bella said. "You will look absolutely marvelous in it." She made a circle with her thumb and forefinger, and her massive bosom rose and fell as she sighed appreciatively. "It will be *bellissimo*."

"But it has to be completed the day after tomorrow," Charlotte-Anne pointed out.

"So it shall be," the old dressmaker said, her hands tugging at the ends of the yellow cloth tape measure which always hung around her neck. "I have, after all, your measurements on file, so I have gone ahead and cut and pinned portions of the gown together. See?" Signora Bella picked up a partially finished bodice from her paper-clad worktable and held it up. "Now I must see that it fits you to perfection and compliments you. Then, this afternoon at four, I will need you to come in for another fitting, and once again tomorrow morning, when we will see to it that any last-minute adjustments are made. It will be delivered to your villa by three tomorrow afternoon at the very latest."

Signora Bella was even better than her word. At just past noon the following day, the completed gown arrived. As soon as Charlotte-Anne lifted it out of the box, any irritation she had felt toward Luigi seeped out of her. She should have known. Luigi's taste was flawless. The gown was indeed a masterpiece.

He only wants what is best for both of us, she had to remind herself.

She felt strangely exhilarated when her hair was done and she got dressed. Luigi walked circles around her, his hand on his chin as he nodded and smiled his satisfaction. He looked tremendously pleased with himself. "I have never seen you look quite so beautiful," he said. "You are breathtaking. The gown is very becoming."

Looking at her reflection in the tall gilt-edged mirror in the bedroom, she knew he was right. The richness of the sapphire-blue velvet seemed to change the color of her eyes. Instead of their usual pale, unsettling color, they glowed like two rich round sapphires.

"Now for the crowning touch," Luigi said softly. "I have a necklace I would like you to wear tonight." He reached into a pocket of his dress-uniform tunic and took out a long, slender black velvet case and two smaller square velvet boxes. "To show you how much I love you," he whispered.

She stared at him. Then hesitantly she took them from him. First she opened the long, slim case. She let out a startled gasp. Cushioned against the black velvet was a necklace of seventy-nine finely matched pear-shaped diamonds. The pendant

center was a flawless five-carat round blue sapphire as deep
as the moonlit sea.

"Luigi," she gasped.

Without speaking, he took the necklace from her and fas-
tened it around her neck. It felt cool and deliciously heavy
against her skin. She turned to face the mirror. The diamonds
glittered, and the sapphire illusion of her eyes appeared
heightened.

Slowly she opened the lids of the two smaller boxes and
discovered matching diamond-and-sapphire drop earrings. In
the other, she found a ten-carat sapphire ring surrounded by
marquise-cut diamonds.

She felt ashamed of herself for being irritated by the way
he had dictated her choice of clothes and jewels. Of course he
had to pick the sapphire gown—so it would match the jewels.
How ungrateful she was!

"Luigi, they're . . . they're too much," she stammered.
"Far too extravagant."

"When will you ever learn, *cara*?" he chuckled. "Nothing
is too extravagant when it concerns you."

"But . . . it's not even my birthday," she sputtered.

"Does it have to be?" he asked as he clipped the earrings
onto her lobes. "When I saw these, I knew they were meant
for you." He paused and looked suddenly pained. "I know
these can never make up for the loss you have suffered, but
take them as a token of your husband's deep love."

"But what for?"

"For taking in stride the hardships and losses you have had
to endure," he whispered, turning away. "I know how much
you wanted to have our baby, and how much the miscarriage
affected you."

Her eyes filled with tears. "Now look what you're making
me do!" she said in a choked voice as she dabbed her eyes
with a lace-edged handkerchief. "You're making me ruin my
makeup."

The Ministry of Foreign Affairs was not far away, but they
rode there in the chauffeur-driven Daimler, circling the Piazza
del Popolo with its obelisk in the center, and down the Via
del Corso to the Piazza Colonna. During the short ride there

was a nervous energy about Luigi which she found rather peculiar. He was always the very picture of calm, and she wondered what now caused his agitation. She wondered if there were something special about the evening that he hadn't told her about. But she knew it was useless to pry. She would have to wait and see.

The reception began very pleasantly. She had expected to meet only strangers, but there were quite a few guests she knew and hadn't seen since before her miscarriage, and they greeted her warmly. She was introduced to the minister of defense, a sleek, bald man in a well-cut tuxedo who bowed over her hand, kissed it, and introduced her to his plump, shark-toothed wife. And there was a multitude of people she had never seen before but who seemed to know who she was.

She made several new friends that evening. An American who, it was rumored, came from a very wealthy family and had married into one of Italy's most powerful clans seemed to arouse everyone's curiosity, admiration, and respect.

She found herself the center of attention.

And then came the first unpleasant surprise of the evening. Just after the dancing began in the great marble hall, the minister of defense asked her for the first waltz. Then she danced with Luigi, and when he was taken aside for a discussion with the minister and some generals, Charlotte-Anne went over to the white-clothed buffet tables. They were laden with silver trays of imported caviar and salmon, paper-thin slices of prosciutto, and artful little canapés. Domestic wines and foreign champagne flowed freely.

"*Cara*," Luigi said suddenly from behind her. "I believe you two have already met?"

She turned around slowly and drew a deep, startled breath as she found herself face to face with General Kersten. She remembered the German all too well from the crossing on the *Ile de France*, and he looked exactly as he had then, red-faced and meaty, with pinprick blue eyes. She was as instinctively revolted by him now as she had been then, and she remembered how he had cruelly goaded Mrs. Reichenbach and talked so horribly about the Jews. She struggled not to show her distaste. He was not in civilian clothes as he had been on the *Ile de France*. His gray uniform, with its red-white-and-black swastika armband, flared riding breeches, and high gleaming boots, was curiously intimidating. It was only then that she realized how many other guests were wearing similar uniforms. The reception was top-heavy with Germans.

As when they had first met, General Kersten clicked his heels together noisily and kissed her hand. "You look even more charming now than the last time we met," he said loudly. "I congratulate you on your marriage." He turned to Luigi, smiled, and faced Charlotte-Anne again. "It was a most auspicious crossing, *nicht wahr?*"

"Yes, it was," Charlotte-Anne agreed politely, warning herself that she had to be very careful not to let her personal feelings show. This party was too important to Luigi's future.

"And to think," General Kersten continued, "that I have been transferred to Rome. Such a lovely city! We must see a lot of each other. Perhaps you will be so kind as to show me around every now and then?"

"Yes," she murmured, "of course," silently vowing that rather than run into him everywhere she would lock herself up at the villa like a hermit.

"It seems General Kersten and I," Luigi informed her, "shall be working closely together."

"Oh?" She looked startled. "But . . . but I thought you were the Italian Air Force attaché, Luigi."

"So he is," General Kersten boomed. "But things in Germany are now different. Herr Hitler has become chancellor, and his first order of business is to strengthen ties with our Italian brothers. He is an ardent admirer of your Premier Mussolini, you know. The Führer wants for Germany what Herr Mussolini wants for Italy—a thousand-year Reich. And to do that, Germany *must* be strengthened. It seems your premier has kindly lent your husband to Germany for a while."

"I . . . I don't understand." Charlotte-Anne looked at Luigi.

"I only heard about it myself a few minutes ago," Luigi told her. "It seems I'm going to be made a general."

"Oh, Luigi," she whispered, forcing a smile she did not feel. "How wonderful!"

She gazed quietly around the room, at the men in formal wear and dress uniforms, the ladies in their finest gowns and jewels. It was so deceptively peaceful and lovely, and yet she could sense a frightening, invisible undercurrent. It was as though something obscene had entered the marble hall. The talk of thousand-year empires frightened her; she didn't know why.

"Ah, I see that you have already met General Kersten," the minister of defense said as he approached with his wife. He smiled at Charlotte-Anne, then looked at Luigi. "I take it you do not mind if I borrow the lovely principessa for a few minutes?"

"Not at all," Luigi replied. "And I shall borrow your beautiful wife in the meantime."

The minister's wife took his arm, her smile displaying her unfortunately long teeth to disadvantage.

Charlotte-Anne bowed her head and slipped her arm through the minister's, grateful for the opportunity to get away from General Kersten.

"Are you enjoying our little reception?" the minister asked as he led her across the hall.

"It is lovely." She favored him with a smile.

"And you, Principessa, are the single loveliest woman here. I look forward to your adorning more of our functions."

"As you wish." She blushed and inclined her head, expecting him to lead her in a dance. Instead, he took her past the dance floor and out to an anteroom. She looked at him with surprise as he closed the padded door. The music sounded muted and far away.

"I hope you will forgive me for being so mysterious, Principessa," he said as he turned to her, "but I wanted to speak with you in private."

She felt a sudden alarm. "Is something wrong?"

"No, no, not at all," he assured her. "Certainly not. I just wanted to speak to you about your husband's future. And your own."

"I don't think I understand."

"You will, in time. Forgive me if I do not elaborate, but there are forces developing in many countries which will soon change the world as we know it; what these are is unimportant at the moment. What *is* important is that it will be for the better." He paused and smiled. "Your husband is an important man, Principessa. Il Duce is relying on him more and more. He has great expectations for him."

She nodded. She had heard all this before, and she was wondering where it would eventually lead.

"A lovely wife is, of course, a tremendous asset to a man's career, and in that the prince is very lucky."

"You flatter me," she said softly, meeting his eye. "But one thing I do not understand. Sometimes you call my husband 'Colonel.' Other times, you refer to him as 'the prince.' Which is he, Signor Minister? A prince or a colonel?"

"Both, of course." He looked vaguely unsettled; then he said smoothly, "As I was saying, you are a tremendous asset to your husband. And you have the opportunity to be an even greater one. The colo . . . the prince will shortly be made a general, and as you know, even among generals there is a . . . well, to put it bluntly, a pecking order." He smiled wryly. "Your husband can either become a very powerful general or merely one in a crowd. Much of that depends upon you. I sincerely believe that it would benefit this country if he were to become very powerful. Your husband has many attributes that this country needs now as never before. He is a well-respected member of an old and titled family. Il Duce believes that what his government needs to function more smoothly is the support of the aristocracy, who at present do not universally give him the respect he deserves. Times are changing, Principessa. Italy is finally entering the twentieth century as a major power in her own right, and your husband's expertise with automobiles and aviation . . . well, in the near future, that expertise is going to be very important for Italy. It will make the difference between success and failure."

"In what way?"

"That, I'm afraid, I'm not at liberty to say. However, I, and indeed most of Italy, would appreciate it immensely,

Principessa, if you did everything within your power to help your husband rise swiftly within our government. Who knows? Soon he might become second in power only to Il Duce.''

"And how do you suggest I help do this?'' she asked curiously. "By socializing more? By giving more parties, arranging charity functions?''

He smiled. "That, too. But I'm thinking mainly about something else.''

"Yes, Signor Minister?''

"You are still an American citizen, Principessa. In order to help your husband fully and for you to become totally accepted in society and by the government, to gain true credibility for both your husband and yourself, you *must* renounce your American citizenship and become an Italian.''

She stared at him, instantly bitter at his proposal.

"You will do it?'' he asked hopefully.

She schooled herself to speak calmly. "I will certainly consider it, Signor Minister.''

"Of course,'' he said soothingly, "but please . . . do not think about it for too long. For events that are coming . . . well, I cannot overemphasize that speed is essential.''

"But acquiring a country's citizenship takes time, does it not?''

"It usually does.'' He nodded, then smiled. "But in your case, Principessa, I'm certain that the time-consuming steps can be dispensed with. It can be done with much speed.''

"I see.'' She nodded, frowning thoughtfully. "As I said, Minister, I will certainly give it careful but quick thought.''

"I knew you would.'' He paused. "But please, do not take too long to make up your mind.'' Then he bowed, pivoted on his heel, and left the anteroom.

For a long time she remained alone. She wondered if Luigi knew that this conversation had taken place. Or that it had been planned. Perhaps that had been the cause of his uncharacteristic nervousness.

Her hand went to the necklace around her throat, where the diamonds and sapphire felt cold against her skin. What was this necklace, she thought, besides a slave collar? How much choice did she really have about keeping her American citizenship?

She knew only one thing. She loved Luigi with all her heart and soul. She would do anything in her power that might help him, with no questions asked. She had told the minister that she would give his request thought, but she already knew what her answer would be. She would do as he had asked.

Still, she couldn't help thinking that the sapphires and diamonds had been a bribe.

14

Only sometime later did the third occurrence, which was by far the most ominous, take place, and it was then that the previous events took on their true significance. In the meanwhile, Charlotte-Anne went on with her life in the Villa della Rosa with blissful ignorance.

Rome was a social whirlwind. There was no end of private parties and official functions to attend, and everywhere the conversations turned to politics. She had little interest in the subject and her ever-increasing popularity was based, in good part, on the lighthearted, charming, social bantering she preferred. With her, people felt at ease. They didn't have to watch every word they said, or defend their views. The reasoning behind this was simple: when she was around she put a stop to all political talk and adroitly turned the conversation to lighter subjects.

Nonetheless, she increasingly sensed a growing turbulence under the placid surface of Roman society, stemming from the "events" the minister had hinted at, and which were indeed beginning to flourish. There were rumors of unrest, military buildups, and an air of impending war. Overnight, receptions and dinners became military strategy sessions; wives worked the parties, jockeying for their husbands' promotions; generals sought out industrialists and vice versa; favors were exchanged and deals consummated amid the free-flowing champagne, caviar, and waltzes.

Charlotte-Anne sensed the carefree days drawing to an end, but she didn't want to believe what was happening. She tried every way she could not to face it, and for a time she was successful. Europe might have been in the midst of a gathering hurricane, but the power centers, the capitals, seemed to be at the eye of the storm, and were deceptively peaceful. However, eventually her unspoken anxieties grew too strong to ignore. She was terrified that if she mentioned them to Luigi, he would agree that her fears were warranted. His promotions—now coming in quicker succession—would soon make him chief general of the air force. She was increasingly aware of the political turmoil, but tried to tell herself that it was only because of the more powerful social circles they moved in. She wanted desperately to believe that the charged unrest was something she hadn't felt before simply because their sphere of friends and acquaintances hadn't included so many foreigners as it did now. Rome was, after all, filled with them.

Germans were everywhere.

Despite these misgivings, time still seemed to fly past in a blur, and so did the string of miscarriages which truly darkened her life. She was her happiest when Luigi was at her side. Unfortunately, he couldn't be there always. As time went by, she saw less and less of him, and their time together became all the more precious. She wasn't in the least bit interested in what duties he carried out for Il Duce; she cared only for the time he was with her. After their fourth year together, when Luigi was sent on more frequent and lengthier assignments to Germany, she started to become depressed because she felt so alone. Whenever he was not with her, she found herself caught in an emotional limbo.

"I want to go with you," she told Luigi, not for the first time.

He smiled good-naturedly. "I must go alone, *cara*," he replied sadly. "Armed-forces bases are not places for women."

Her face fell, and he urged her to spend the time he was gone at the Palazzo di Cristallo. His parents, he was sure, would look forward to her visit. She shook her head. "I like Rome, Luigi," she said. "Besides, when you return, you come to Rome first. I want to be here waiting for you."

He smiled. "I shall miss you."

"And I shall miss you, too." She paused. "Luigi . . ."

"Yes?"

"Why do you have to go to Germany so often? I didn't think Germany was allowed either an army or an air force after the last war."

"They are allowed a small one of each, but Adolf Hitler is now in power, and he is trying to end all that. He believes Germany must be strong in order to survive." His voice grew more fervent, and his eyes took on a glazed glow. "You wouldn't believe what is happening in Germany, *cara*," he whispered. "The flying! Every weekend, thousands and thousands of weekend enthusiasts take to the air in gliders. It's like the national sport! They're training for when Germany will have a real air force again. Il Duce is lending me to the Germans to help teach them and to point out areas for expansion."

She turned to the window and looked out at their sunlit backyard and its manicured lawn, its oval swimming pool, and the ancient walls of the Borghese Gardens behind it. "What is Adolf Hitler like?" she asked.

He hesitated a moment. It was as though he hadn't yet made up his own mind, and had to collect his thoughts. "He is a very complicated man," he said slowly, "but there's something about him . . . a kind of magnetism he radiates, which draws people to him. I've never seen anything like it. He's very much like our own Il Duce, but much stronger. He seems to throw off an aura of power. When he's at a rally, he can literally drive people berserk. When he's not pleased with something, he rants and raves and throws worse tantrums than a spoiled child. Yet in private he can be exceedingly charming and polite. He's a contradiction, but a fascinating one."

She did not take her eyes off the backyard view. "Do you like him?" she asked.

"I don't really know. I suppose I've never given it any thought."

"Doesn't he . . . frighten you?"

He frowned, then laughed. "Yes, you know, I suppose he does."

She turned around then, not wanting to hear any more. She should never have asked. It was all too frightening. She smiled. "I'd better have Magda press an extra uniform. You won't want to look all rumpled when you arrive in Berlin."

And as she left the room, she felt an ache in the pit of her belly. It wasn't until half an hour later, after she'd calmed down, that she acknowledged its cause: fear. She could no longer lie to herself; she knew that things were not right. She loved Luigi, but hated fascism in all its ugly forms. She would never forget that incident at the border for as long as she lived. But she had made her bargain with the Principessa Marcella: she would never do anything that might hurt Luigi or the di Fontanesis. She loved Luigi too much. She was his model wife, and because of that, he was one of the most envied men in all Rome. Other wives, it was whispered, were known to conduct discreet affairs when their husbands were out of town for any period of time. But Charlotte-Anne would never dream of such behavior. She lived for one thing only.

Luigi.

Often she thought of how she failed him constantly, and she was always trying to find new ways to make it up to him. She knew how badly he wanted a son, and it hurt her deeply, since, after the stillborn child, she failed to carry another to full term.

"Next time, *cara*," he always told her gently. "Next time."

But miscarriage followed miscarriage.

The time Luigi was gone always crawled by. The time he was with her was a blur. Whenever they went to visit his family, or on the rare occasions when the Principessa Marcella and Prince Antonio came to visit Rome, everything was seemingly perfect and polite. On the surface, Charlotte-Anne and the principessa were friends. Over the years, they had perfected the charade. Only when they were alone did the fangs come out.

"I hear you had another miscarriage," the principessa once told her dryly.

Charlotte-Anne stared at her. "Italy is a small country, I see. Word gets around quickly."

"For a di Fontanesi, yes," the principessa said pointedly, hinting that in her mind Charlotte-Anne would never be a real di Fontanesi. "We have ears everywhere."

The next day, Charlotte-Anne changed gynecologists.

A nd then the winds of political change threw their life into a tailspin.

Luigi was gone for longer and longer periods of time, and she saw precious little of him. Slowly, and with growing fear, Charlotte-Anne watched her husband, who had previously been only a token fascist, being converted by the aphrodisiac of power. There was no longer time for the little pleasures of life. Germany had become Luigi's second home.

"I'm very sorry you feel this way," he said one day after she fussed because he was going to be gone for sixty days, "but this is military business."

"Luigi, for God's sake, I'm your *wife*. I don't get to see you for half as much time as those Germans do."

He looked at her with a stony expression. "Please, *cara*, don't whine. It is unattractive."

She stared at him. It was the first time he had ever talked to her in such a condescending tone and she wanted to burst into tears. She managed to remain dry-eyed only by reminding herself that he had many responsibilities weighing on his shoulders. She mustn't add to them by making wifely noises.

The only thing that hadn't changed with his increased hunger for power and ambition was his passion. When he was home, his ardor was as great as it had ever been. But there were times she got the feeling that it was not he who lay in their bed. He looked like Luigi, spoke like Luigi. But increasingly she was under the impression that he was no longer the man she had married.

She wanted the old Luigi back.

The night before he flew to Germany for two months, he took her to bed as usual. He entered her quickly, and rode her hard, bringing her swiftly to orgasm just as he exploded inside her and let out an anguished, drawn-out cry. Then he collapsed wearily beside her.

Like a slap in the face, she realized how much their lovemaking too had changed. Gone from their bedroom was the sensual torture of protracted foreplay. There was a new kind of efficiency even in his sex: he entered her, achieved orgasm, and collapsed. As if there were time for nothing else.

"Luigi," she whispered, opening her eyes.

"Hmmmm?" He was half-asleep already.

"Luigi . . . you said you'd be gone for two months?"

"Hmmmmm."

"Well, it's been ages since I've last seen my family. What do you say I sail for New York and visit with them while you're gone?"

"I don't think so." He yawned.

She frowned and sat up. "Why not?"

" 'Cause . . . you can't go."

She flushed with uneasiness. "You mean you won't let me?" she asked incredulously.

He yawned again. "If it were up to me, you could go anywhere you pleased." Then he rolled over and his breathing came at low and regular intervals. He was already fast asleep.

She stared at him for a long while, then turned off the lights and crawled under the covers. She pulled them up to her chin and lay awake for hours. What did he mean, if it were up to him she could go anywhere she pleased?

She found out the next morning, after Luigi had left. She had gone to the passport office, realizing that since she had renounced her American citizenship she no longer held a valid passport. To date, they'd never had the opportunity to vacation outside Italy, so she'd never bothered getting one.

At the passport office she received the ominous news: she was not allowed to travel outside the country.

She couldn't believe it. There had to be some mistake. Finally she called the minister of defense.

"I am sorry, Principessa," he told her with a soft but final tone of voice. "Things are happening."

"Yes, indeed they are," she snapped. "I can't even travel! I'm a prisoner here."

He laughed soothingly. "No, Principessa. It is just that your husband is handling a very delicate mission, and for that reason the powers that be think it best that you stay in Italy. Please, feel free to travel all you want within this country. There are many beautiful things to see."

"Thank you," she said sarcastically, and slammed down the receiver. She closed her eyes and took a series of deep breaths in order to calm her nerves. For a moment she felt compelled to go to the American embassy, but she realized the futility of that.

She was no longer an American. There was nothing they would be able to do for her.

Whichever way she looked at it, one thing was clear.

She was a prisoner.

The following day, Tuesday, was when the letter arrived. Charlotte-Anne always looked forward to receiving news from home, and went to read it outside under the shade trees beside the pool. As usual, it was written in her mother's slanting, elegant script, but she immediately noticed that the words weren't neatly formed as if at times Elizabeth-Anne's hand had been shaking.

This time, it was a letter which brought pain and shock into her life.

July 21, 1936

My darling Charlotte-Anne,

How I miss you, especially now of all times! And oh, how it grieves me to have to write you this. It's been two weeks now since I've written, longer than any other time between letters, and I know you must have wondered why. Now the bad news must come.

Your sister Rebecca died yesterday. I know you will have to read and reread that terrible sentence again and again before you can believe it. She was hospitalized with pneumonia, but there was nothing they could do to save her. Oh, Charlotte-Anne, what am I going to do?

You, your brother, and your two sisters are everything in my life. A woman's children are the legacy of herself and her husband. It makes this loss doubly painful for me. It was as though not only Rebecca, but your father too, had died all over again. I don't know if I'll ever be able to get over this loss. I know time is supposed to heal all wounds, but I don't know if that's really true. Still today I sometimes relive old wounds I received in my childhood. Nothing ever heals, not completely at least. The scars always remain.

When the hospital called and we rushed over, I could not believe it. Rebecca looked so at peace, so restful. I was certain it was a trick, or some kind of joke. She looked as if she were sleeping.

Larry is so good to me, especially now. It's strange, you know. He isn't your real father, but he feels like a father toward you all. Rebecca's death seems to have hit him harder than anyone else. Last night, when I thought he was asleep, I woke to find him crying.

It is heartbreaking, but just last week Rebecca was starting to make plans to visit you next summer. It would have been so nice for you and she to have seen each other, but I realize that Italy is far away. Do not try to blame yourself for not having seen her in so long. We are all mere mortals, and we cannot see what the future holds for us. There is a power beyond our comprehension, in whose hands our destinies lie.

I know from your painful letters, in which you confided to me about your tragic miscarriages, that all is not perfect with you either. Life, alas, is never perfect. I know now that if you and Rebecca had been able to see more of each other, it would have made no difference over life or death in the end. It just seems such a terrible shame—and hurts so much—that anyone so young can so suddenly be struck down. She was only nineteen! How little we still all know.

Dearest darling, I know how you must feel reading this, but please take heart. Your sister was a good person. I know that she is in heaven and someday we will all be reunited. I don't believe that this is just the hopeful rambling of a woman in much pain. There is a greater design to the world than we know—there must be—and in the depths of my heart I know that no matter how he tests us, God is good.

Perhaps this coming year, if you cannot come to visit us, Larry and I will at least come to Rome. He has business interests in Europe which, due to the international situation, he thinks he might do well to liquidate; perhaps we can combine business with a short visit with you. I would really love to do that. How I ache to see you again and put my arms around you and hug you.

Take care, my darling, for Larry says all is not well in the world right now, and I have learned to trust his judgment. If there is anything we can do to help you, please let me know.

Your loving Mama

Charlotte-Anne let the letter drop to her lap. She covered her face with her hands and wept. It was doubly cruel that Luigi was not at her side to comfort her. She wanted him to hold her, to murmur soothing words, to share some of this burden with her. But he wouldn't be back from Germany for two months. Only now did it occur to her that out of the hundreds of people she knew in Rome, there was not one close friend she could call upon in a time of need.

She had to suffer the burden of Rebecca's loss by herself.

And as she did so, she realized it was more important than ever to get her passport and receive permission to visit with her family.

But even when Luigi returned, that dream proved impossible to attain.

"I'm sorry, *cara*," he told her, his voice gentle and sympathetic, "but they are afraid."

"Afraid? They?" She stared at him, "Who are *they*, and why are *they* afraid?"

"Because of my job. It's highly sensitive, you know that, and with things going the way they are in the world, they are afraid that if I told you anything, perhaps even talked in my sleep, and you let any information slip out, however innocently, great harm could come to this country.''

His words infuriated her, but she knew that there was nothing that could be done.

If a di Fontanesi couldn't pull those kinds of strings, then who could?

15

Elizabeth-Anne and Larry arrived in Rome during the first week of April 1937. Charlotte-Anne was doubly delighted. Not only was she going to see them again at long last, but Luigi had juggled his schedule and managed to take an entire week off in honor of the occasion. That, she well knew, was no small matter, and she was touched by his thoughtfulness. She felt as though it was a combined family reunion and second honeymoon.

Luigi came along with her to meet the train. The moment it chugged in, Charlotte-Anne caught sight of Larry and her mother leaning out the window of a first-class carriage, and tears of happiness rolled down her cheeks. She'd missed them both more than she'd realized. Her mother looked so different, she noticed with surprise. She seemed older, but somehow less distant. Charlotte-Anne had to remind herself that she hadn't seen her mother in six years; Elizabeth-Anne was just forty-two and she was now twenty-three.

"Mama," she sobbed as soon as the train jerked to a halt and Elizabeth-Anne came hurrying down the steps. They fell into each other's arms and held their embrace for a long time.

Elizabeth-Anne was crying too. "Look what a sight we make," she said, laughing through her tears as she dabbed first her daughter's eyes and then her own with a white lace handkerchief. "Oh, darling, let me look at you!" She held her daughter at arm's length and shook her head. "I still can't believe that it's really you. It's been so long.'' She pressed her cheek against Charlotte-Anne's.

"I know.'' Charlotte-Anne smiled and pulled away from her. "And, Mama, this is Luigi.''

He stood tall and dashing in his uniform, then bowed somewhat formally. Elizabeth-Anne broke the ice by kissing and hugging him warmly. Then, as Larry shook his hand and hugged Charlotte-Anne, a porter picked up their luggage and followed them out to the waiting Daimler. The two women walked arm in arm. The men led the way, taking the opportunity to get acquainted.

"I know you invited us to stay at the villa,'' Elizabeth-Anne said, "and we really do appreciate it. I hope you won't be offended that we made reservations at the Excelsior.''

"The Excelsior?'' Charlotte-Anne looked at her with dismay. "But why stay at a hotel? We have plenty of empty guest rooms at the villa.''

"Thank you, darling, but no.'' Elizabeth-Anne smiled. They had reached the car and waited for the chauffeur to fold down the jump seats. Then Elizabeth-Anne ducked inside and waited for Charlotte-Anne to follow. "It's nothing personal, I assure you. I really do prefer to stay at the hotel.''

"Don't forget,'' Larry said as he and Luigi sat on the leather-upholstered jump seats facing them, "hotels are in your mother's blood.''

Elizabeth-Anne leaned forward and slapped his thigh good-naturedly. "There he goes again! He loves to make it sound as though the hotels are all I care about.'' Then her tone grew more serious. "But really, I've been waiting a long time for just this opportunity, and I intend to take full advantage of it. It isn't every year that I get the chance to come overseas to spy on the grand hotels of Europe. I've made up my mind to stay at every one I can, in order to see what needs improving with our own. I can only do that by experiencing firsthand what the competition is offering.''

"In that case,'' Charlotte-Anne said, "I can't very well argue with you, Mama, can I?''

"No,'' Elizabeth-Anne said with a laugh, "I'm afraid you can't.''

*   *   *

After Elizabeth-Anne and Larry got settled into their suite at the Excelsior, Charlotte-Anne sent the car around to bring them to the villa for dinner. She had done herself proud, bringing out the 1878 Ginori china with its cobalt-blue and gilt ribbon edges, the Baccarat crystal, the di Fontanesi heirloom silver, and the heavy linen embroidered by the sisters in the Convent of Our Lady of Peace. The candles cast a soft, flattering light, and everyone had dressed for dinner. She had instructed the cook to prepare a true southern Italian feast made up of the authentic peasant dishes that were her favorites. And what food it was! The generous platter of antipasto and the chilled sliced eel on beds of shaved ice were followed by *pasta alla siciliana*—spaghetti baked with tomato sauce, eggplant, zucchini, and olives. Then came the *saltimbocca alla romana*, "sandwiches" consisting of outer layers of veal and prosciutto, and filled with melted mozzarella cheese. The red wine came from the di Fontanesis' own vineyards, and the fresh-baked bread came straight from the oven, garlicky and steaming hot. For dessert there was a choice of tortoni or ripe fresh fruit, as well as cups of thick, rich black espresso.

"If I eat another bite," Larry announced as he wiped his lips and then placed his crumpled napkin on his plate, "I think I'll burst."

Charlotte-Anne smiled. As she looked around the table, she was filled with joy. Except for Regina and Zaccheus, everyone she loved was seated in her home for dinner. It seemed too good to be true.

"So you are not returning to the United States together?" Luigi asked politely as they headed back into the salon.

"No." Elizabeth-Anne shook her head. "Larry has some business to attend to in Germany, but I'm not going along. He doesn't want me to."

"It's clear Germany is a powder keg right now," Larry said worriedly. "The situation is much too volatile. I don't think anyone should go there unless it's necessary."

Charlotte-Anne glanced at Luigi to read his expression, but his face was studiously blank. He crossed over to the fruitwood sideboard, and while a servant came in with a tray of liqueurs in tiny glasses, he picked up his humidor, opened it, and brought it over to Larry. Larry selected a cigar, sniffed it appreciatively, and rattled it next to his ear before lighting it. Luigi merely selected one at random and lit it. The two men sat down together on facing chairs to discuss politics while Charlotte-Anne and Elizabeth-Anne sat on a couch and caught up on the latest news of family and friends.

"Zaccheus has grown so tall for a thirteen-year-old," Elizabeth-Anne said proudly. "And he's become so handsome. I've brought you a picture of him, but I left it at the hotel. I'll give it to you tomorrow. You'd never recognize your brother. He's the spitting image of his father."

"Has he decided what he is going to do yet?"

"Well, *I* eventually want him to go to college and join the hotel chain, but he's dead set against it." Elizabeth-Anne shook her head in disbelief. "He wants to go to Annapolis."

"The navy?"

Elizabeth-Anne nodded. "He won't let us talk him out of it."

"You're afraid of all the troubles brewing, too, aren't you, Mama?"

Elizabeth-Anne's face wore a strained expression. "Yes," she said quietly, "I am. I'm especially afraid for Zaccheus. If another war does come, and Larry thinks it's inevitable . . ." She shrugged eloquently. "Well, I'm a mother. No mother wants to see her son go off and lay his life on the line, no matter what the reason."

"I understand how you feel," Charlotte-Anne said. "I feel the same way about Luigi. His being in the military . . ." She paused, reluctant to worry her mother with the truth. "Anyway! Enough of this maudlin talk." She sat up. "How's Regina?"

"She sends you her love. Her graduation from medical school was wonderful; we combined it with a celebration of her twenty-fifth birthday. I wish you had been there. She's on her way to being a fine pediatrician, you know. But I must admit I'm not looking forward to her marriage. Her fiancé's orthopedic practice is in San Francisco, so she'll join him there." She looked pained. "It's so hard for a mother to watch her children scatter all over the place. Rebecca is dead, Zaccheus wants to join the military. Now Regina's going to be across the country and you're here across the ocean . . . None of my children want anything to do with Hale Hotels.'' She shook her head. ''And yet I know if you try to keep your loved ones on too tight a rein and don't let them do what they want, you chase them away all the faster.''

''You didn't chase me away, Mama,'' Charlotte-Anne said softly. ''I fell in love.''

''I know you did.'' Elizabeth-Anne smiled and squeezed Charlotte-Anne's hand. Her voice dropped to a whisper. ''And I can see why. Luigi is awfully handsome.''

They both stole a sideways glance at him and smiled, but their good spirits soon faded as they listened to the men's conversation.

''You keep referring vaguely to Germany's problems. What kind of problems,'' Luigi was saying between puffs of blue smoke from his cigar, ''do you think Germany has?''

Larry smiled crookedly, without humor. His one eye watched Luigi intently. ''Hitler.''

''But do you not think the Germans want Hitler?''

Larry sat back, making himself more comfortable. ''The way I see it, they haven't much choice. Not anymore, at least.'' He blew out another thick stream of blue smoke. For a moment he studied his cigar in silence. ''Hitler is now fully entrenched in power. It's too late to do anything about that now. He'll never step down voluntarily. And so far, Germany's economy has been so bad that the people are under the mistaken impression that he's their only salvation. Besides, he's claiming to bring dignity back to Germany by repudiating the Versailles treaty and the reparations agreements, and by remilitarizing the Rhineland. The Germans look upon him as their savior. And why not? They're desperate. And in their desperation, they are unable to see things clearly. They do not see that in the long run, all he can really bring them is despair.''

''I have been to Germany quite often,'' Luigi said casually. ''Il Duce and the Führer are strengthening ties.''

''And both Germany and Italy are supporting Franco, I

know, but I think the only result of the Spanish Civil War will be a compounding of an already tragic situation. Hundreds of thousands, even millions, are going to die.''

"In Spain?" Luigi asked curiously.

Larry shook his head slowly, his expression grim. "I think you know better than that."

Luigi shrugged noncommittally and smoked on in silence.

"In Spain," Larry said. "And in all of Europe. There will be much bloodshed, I'm afraid. Bloodshed like there has never been before."

"But why do you think it will involve all of Europe?"

"I've listened to Hitler's speeches." Larry's voice was quiet but ominous. "Of course, there are those who wave it off as the ranting and raving of a lunatic. And there are others who simply scoff or laugh at him." He sat forward, his body tensed. "Personally, I don't subscribe to either opinion. Or perhaps I would, to both, if the situation weren't so deadly serious. Hitler's out to do what he preaches, you mark my word. And he is a very persuasive personality."

"Then perhaps people shouldn't listen to him so closely," Luigi suggested. "Perhaps he is simply telling them what they want to hear."

"Is that what you think?" Larry asked, staring at him steadily.

Luigi did not reply. For a moment they all sat quietly in the growing, uncomfortable silence.

Charlotte-Anne, ever the perfect hostess, knew from experience just when it was time to change the subject. She sat up straight and clapped her hands together. "I have an idea," she said brightly, intending not only to break the silence but also to keep her mother in Rome longer. "What if Mama stays here while Larry goes to Germany? Then you can both meet here for another week-long stay before returning to the States?"

Elizabeth-Anne shook her head. "Thank you, dear, but no. We've worked out our schedule and it leaves little leeway for extending our trip. We can't stay here that long. We've both got to be getting back as soon as possible. And it's as I said before, I'm keen on seeing what the grand hotels of Europe have to offer. From here I'm going on to Venice to stay at both the Danieli and the Gritti Palace, to Paris for a look at the Georges Cinq, the Ritz, the Crillon, and the Plaza Athénée, and London for the Ritz and Claridge's. Then I'm sailing home from England, and Larry's going from Germany. I think it's high time New York had a world-class hotel of its own, don't you?"

"There are some fine hotels in New York," Luigi commented diplomatically.

Elizabeth-Anne surveyed him with raised eyebrows. "Some fine ones, yes," she corrected him, never one to mince words. "But a truly legendary hotel? No, we don't have one of those. And I intend to give the city one. When we bought the Shelburne Hotel, I had plans for it, and now I intend to see them to fruition. I'm going to renovate the entire building, top to bottom, down to every last room. It will be the flagship of the entire chain, and I'm even renaming it. It will be the Hale Palace."

"Mama," Charlotte-Anne laughed. "You'll never change, will you? Always building, building, building."

Elizabeth-Anne smiled faintly. "What else is there to do in the world? One can either build things, destroy them, or rest on one's laurels and watch the time go by. Myself, I've never been one who was able to sit still."

The seven days flew by so quickly that it seemed to Charlotte-Anne that Larry and her mother had barely arrived before it was time for them to pack their bags and leave again. Larry was taking the train to Germany; Elizabeth-Anne was traveling with him as far as Venice.

"I wish you could have stayed a lot longer," Charlotte-Anne told them regretfully as they all rode to the station together in the Daimler. The late-afternoon shadows were a deep tide of purple creeping slowly across the sidewalks.

"In other circumstances, we would have," Larry assured her, "but with thirty-seven hotels and tourist courts to look after, your mother has become an extremely busy woman. And for my part, I want to get all our business finished here as quickly as possible, and then reinvest the money in the

States. The world is in turmoil right now. It's a time bomb. It won't be long before someone lights the fuse."

Charlotte-Anne shivered. "Don't frighten me, Larry," she said in a low voice.

He looked pained and patted her hand. "I find it frightening too, but I'm realistic. That's the way things are. Fooling ourselves does no one any good. Besides, there are always two sides to a coin. In times of war and turmoil, nations' economies change. Some for the better and some for the worse. It's high time to put some of our money into munitions and aircraft plants in the States. Those are the investments of the future."

"Aren't you forgetting something?" Elizabeth-Anne asked with a sidelong glance at him.

"Of course not." He laughed, breaking the tension. "And the hotels," he said pointedly with mock seriousness, "keep growing."

On the station platform, Larry took Charlotte-Anne aside and held her close. "Listen, if there's anything you want, anything at all, you'll let us know?" She nodded. For the first time she saw him not only as her mother's second husband, but as a father to her too. She stood on tiptoe and kissed his cheek. "Yes, Daddy," she said softly, for the first time not using his Christian name.

He looked deeply touched and hugged her tightly. "You're sure you don't want to come back to the States and sit things out for a while? At least until the troubles here are over? You've always got a place at home with us."

She thought fleetingly how tempting that offer was, but it was no use. And she couldn't admit to Larry and her mother that she wasn't allowed to leave Italy.

"I'm sure," she said, switching on her brightest smile. Then she added softly, "My home is here, beside Luigi. He's my husband, and I love him. But thanks anyway."

She was quiet with sadness now that they were about to leave. It was as though she had a premonition that her life was changing. If Larry was right, the neat order of things was about to be upset. She would no longer be able to govern her thoughts and actions. With marriage, she had crossed a threshold over which she could not return.

"We worry about you," Elizabeth-Anne told her as she took her daughter in her arms.

Charlotte-Anne pressed her head against her mother's breast. "Whatever for?" she murmured. "I'm like you, Mama. Indomitable. And besides, I'm being well taken care of." She pulled away gently, sought Luigi's hand, and gave it a firm squeeze. Then the conductor's shrill whistle resounded down the platform, they all quickly exchanged a few last kisses, and Larry helped Elizabeth-Anne up into the first-class carriage.

Charlotte-Anne and Luigi watched the train as it pulled out slowly. She followed her mother's waving hand, and she waved back with a white handkerchief. Soon the hand and the train disappeared from sight.

"They are very nice people," Luigi observed as they walked back outside to the car. "They love you very much."

Charlotte-Anne nodded. "And they both liked you, even if Larry didn't agree with all your opinions."

"He is a very bright man. Perhaps he did not agree, but he understood."

"He thinks it will all end in tragedy." She stopped walking and stared at Luigi in silence for a moment, gazing into those darkly hypnotic eyes of his. "Do you think that too, Luigi? You never talk about it."

He shrugged. "I can do many things, *cara*, but I cannot read the future."

She laughed then and hooked her arm through his. The visit had done them both a world of good. She hadn't felt so lighthearted and alive in a very long time. And it had been ages since she had seen Luigi for so long without interruption.

"What I still can't get over," she marveled, shaking her head in amazement, "is the fact that it's possible to fly from Germany to New York in a little over fifty-one hours. Larry can get there in two days from Frankfurt, while Mama's crossing will take six or seven days. It's as if the world is shrinking right in front of our very eyes."

"That is nothing, compared to the future," Luigi speculated. "Someday it will be a matter of mere hours."

"Is that the aviator in you speaking?" she teased him.

"It is."

"Well, we'll just have to wait and see. Myself, I can't comprehend that. But someday I *would* like to fly across the Atlantic like Larry's going to do. I think it's exciting."

"And someday you shall."

"Maybe you'll be my pilot."

He made a face. "Not until passenger airplanes can make that trip. I'm an airplane pilot, *cara*. I don't consider those zeppelins to be flying machines. All they are is giant balloons."

"But fast ones."

"You think they are fast? Not compared to airplanes they're not. They are slow and clumsy."

And it was proved on May 6, 1937, that they were unsafe as well.

Exactly one year after regular passenger service was inaugurated between New York and Frankfurt, the *Hindenburg*, while mooring in Lakehurst, New Jersey, exploded and burned. Of the ninety-seven people on board the giant dirigible, there were thirty-six who lost their lives.

Larry Hochstetter was among them.

16

Much later, when she looked back on it, Charlotte-Anne realized that in a way Larry had been lucky. She knew it was often said that death was worse for those left behind, the loved ones who had to face the world, suddenly alone. When she thought of her mother's grief, expressed in Elizabeth-Anne's long and eloquent letters, Charlotte-Anne didn't doubt the truth of that saying. Through the letters, she felt Elizabeth-Anne's pain and disbelief at again having to endure the loss of her husband, just as Charlotte-Anne herself felt the unspeakable devastation of losing a second father. But her mother didn't lose herself in misery long; she steeled herself to her new, lonelier world and threw herself into her work, finding her own kind of comfort and sustenance in running the Hale empire.

But it wasn't only the struggle for recovery that Larry was spared. Difficult as their personal tragedy was, Charlotte-Anne found herself more frightened and overwhelmed by the political drama that was unfolding. For Larry had been right. The bloodshed he had predicted indeed came, enveloping Europe. Hitler was hungry for power and, together with Mussolini, began to swallow up entire lands and peoples. Europe simmered until it finally reached the boiling point.

By 1937 Italy had conquered Ethiopia.

In 1938 Italy followed the example of its ally Germany and adopted anti-Semitic laws.

On March 31, 1938, after four years of the right-wing dictators Schuschnigg and Dollfuss in Austria, Hitler marched in from Bavaria and the resulting *Anschluss* made Austria an integral part of Germany.

In January 1939 Il Duce announced the annexation of Albania, a conscious imitation of the "victories" of ancient Rome.

In 1939 Hitler signed a nonaggression pact with the Soviet Union.

It was quickly broken.

By that time Charlotte-Anne had ceased going to social functions unless Luigi was in town. She could no longer bear to hear the self-congratulatory tone of people's voices or the excited discussions of the new, rising Roman Empire. No one seemed to take into account that the victories had been so easy because many of the conquered had hardly reached the beginnings of the mechanized age. Too often the victory was nothing more than the slaughter of innocent, virtually Stone Age tribes by tanks and machine guns.

And then, between the first and the twenty-seventh of September 1939, the powder keg exploded. Both Nazi Germany and the Soviet Union invaded Poland, dividing a country which had tried to fight twentieth-century battles with the weapons of the nineteenth.

But Hitler's scheming came to its ridiculous but tragic head after he met with the ineffectual British Prime Minister Neville Chamberlain in Munich. Chamberlain and his counterpart in France, anxious to spare their countries from the voracious appetite of the Axis powers, gave the Führer the sanction to dismember Czechoslovakia. France and England promised not to interfere.

As she nervously paced the deceptively peaceful gardens of the Villa della Rosa, Charlotte-Anne could only wonder: *Where will all this lead us next?*

She never answered herself, for the reply was too frightening. She worked hard to keep the world at bay; to her, the walls surrounding the Villa della Rosa made it an oasis from reality.

In the fall of 1940, when Luigi came home from a tour of duty after carrying out yet another of his mysterious assignments for Il Duce, he and Charlotte-Anne had made love in the afternoon. While they lay in silence with the curtains drawn over the late sun, waiting for their breathing to return to normal, Charlotte-Anne put her fears into words. "Luigi," she whispered, "what is happening to the world? What is it going to do to us?"

"Don't worry, *cara*," he said casually, nuzzling her naked back with his lips. "It's all for the best."

She sat up and pressed the rumpled sheet against her breasts. "But only yesterday I saw people beaten in the streets and then herded into trucks. I asked someone what was happening, and he said it was because they were Jews."

"I suggest you don't concern yourself with the Jews," he said darkly.

"How can I not?" she said fiercely. "Hitler's gobbling up Europe like some famished emperor, and he's throwing Il Duce the crumbs. What will happen if this continues? Hitler and Mussolini want to conquer the world! Luigi, what if the United States enters into this?"

"The concerns of Europe are not the concerns of America. The United States has had its fill of war from the last one. You will see. America will wisely stay out of this."

Famous last words, she thought, when on December 7, 1941, the Japanese attacked Pearl Harbor.

It was not long before Japan's allies, Germany and Italy, declared war on the United States.

The United States, in turn, declared war on Germany on December 8, 1941.

And on Italy three days later.

Charlotte-Anne di Fontanesi, born in the United States and an American in her heart, suddenly found herself an enemy of all—other than her husband—that she held dear.

On opposite sides of the Atlantic, Elizabeth-Anne and Charlotte-Anne greeted the declarations of war with equal fear and dismay. Diplomatic relations between Italy and the United States were cut, and mail exchange was no longer possible through normal postal channels. Only through the efforts of Cardinal Corsini, who acted as middleman, did Charlotte-Anne and her mother stay in touch. Vatican intermediaries smuggled their letters, which necessitated going through a lengthy chain of archdioceses. The Vatican was officially neutral, but Pope Pius XII was considered by Hitler to be a pest. Rumor was that the Führer was considering moving the pope and his entire bailiwick to Germany or, God forbid, to Liechtenstein, where the Vatican could be monitored much more closely and be far less influential.

So exchanging letters took time, generally eight to ten weeks, but sometimes as much as five months. Each time a letter got through, Charlotte-Anne seized upon it, pressed it to her heart, and then read it over and over. The news from New York was good, and bad, and bittersweet.

Things are very hectic without Larry, and how I miss him! Sometimes I wonder how I manage to get everything done without him. He was such a terrific administrator—I only realize that now. He's made certain that the empire practically runs itself. . . .

I just added three new tourist courts to the chain. Of course, it being wartime, a lot of the executives are gone fighting, and it's making for a lot of extra work for me. With the men gone, I've had to hire a lot of women, and they're working out just fine . . . .

Zaccheus has been shipped to active duty in the Pacific. He was so excited to finally be part of what he calls the "fighting navy," but he's only eighteen! I worry about him constantly. . . .

I hope everything in Rome is fine. The reports we get here are all so vague. I really don't know what to think, but I know now, with Luigi on the other side, and you there too, how people must have felt during our Civil War, with brother fighting brother. . . .

I'm so devastated. I don't know if I can bear this new tragedy. Zaccheus has been sent home, and he's in the hospital. I don't know what to think or do, other than pray. He's had to have both his legs amputated, and sometimes I fear he's even lost the will to live. . . .

I'm so happy about Zaccheus' nurse, Janet. She's kind and plain, but a sensible woman, and she's nursing him so well. For the first time, Zaccheus seems to be gaining some of his old fight back. . . .

You wouldn't believe it, darling! I cried and cried all through the ceremony. Janet will make him such a wonderful and understanding wife. Only a year after his horrible injury and now they love each other so dearly, and it's heartwarming to know that she can take good care of him. . . .

Janet is pregnant! I'm so overjoyed. At least something good has come of this damn war!

For a while, it was impossible for Charlotte-Anne to guess which side would win. Germany had the support of Italy and Japan, but the Allies consisted of the United States, France, England, and the Soviet Union. Battle after battle seemed to be the turning point, leaving one side or the other in the stronger position.

Since the United States had gotten involved, Charlotte-Anne no longer tried to hide but followed the war avidly. She started going out again, if only to catch up on the latest news.

Charlotte-Anne's circle of acquaintances knew more than most, as they were the power brokers of Rome. Not everyone was as discreet as Luigi, and gossip flowed freely. If the generals and their wives weren't lying, she quickly discovered, then what she read in the newspapers and heard on the radio wasn't the entire truth, not by a long shot. Listening to the official Italian reports, one would have thought that the Allies were taking a devastating beating. At first this was true, but as time went by, Charlotte-Anne learned from her select circle of friends that the Allies were beginning to win. She didn't dare let on how desperately happy this news made her.

And when, on September 9, 1943, the Allies invaded Italy, she sat in the garden of the Villa della Rosa and broke open a bottle of champagne and celebrated quietly by herself.

She had celebrated prematurely; she found that out all too soon.

On September 10, Luigi returned to Rome. He had one night to spend with her before being transferred down to the boot of Italy with an infantry division in order to try to stop the Allies in their tracks. For once, he allowed his worries to show. The fact that Il Duce had put his premier flying ace in charge of mere foot soldiers spoke for itself. Luigi couldn't hide his awareness of the fact that it would be only a matter of time before Italy was conquered.

Charlotte-Anne was more terrified than she had ever been. It was common knowledge that in any war, infantrymen suffered the heaviest casualties. Now she feared for his life so deeply that she berated herself for cheering the Allies on. But she had little time to torment herself. She had to put on her best face for Luigi; after he was gone, she could torture herself with worries all she pleased.

The precious hours flew by. When the staff car arrived to fetch him, she saw him out to the front gate. The night was still, and with one hand she clutched her nightgown around her shoulders. A sliver of moon floated like a white gondola in the sky. He kissed her deeply and urgently, and then he extracted the promise from her.

"Please, *cara*. There is something you must do for me." His voice was thick. "I don't have the time, or I would do it myself. Go to the Palazzo di Cristallo and persuade my parents to come to Rome and stay here until it is all over. They'll be safer here. I'm afraid there's going to be a lot of fighting and bloodshed to the south."

C ampania lulled one into a sense of false security. On the surface, wherever she looked, Charlotte-Anne saw a world at peace. The vineyards were well-tended, the grapes lushly hanging on the vines.

No matter how much she argued, the Principessa Marcella would not allow Charlotte-Anne to persuade her and the prince to travel to Rome. "I wouldn't dream of leaving here," she snapped at her daughter-in-law. "A di Fontanesi never turns tail and runs."

"But it's going to be dangerous," Charlotte-Anne protested. "And anyway, it wasn't my idea. It was Luigi's."

The principessa's dark eyes were hooded. "There is danger everywhere. Even in Rome."

"But Luigi thinks that Campania will become a battlefield."

"Then let it be so. I, for one, refuse to be driven from my home."

"But don't you care about your well-being?" Charlotte-Anne argued incredulously. "Or about living? Must you be so stubborn and selfish?"

"Stop being so melodramatic," the principessa said irritably. "If *you* want to leave and return to Rome, then you're welcome to do so."

And Charlotte-Anne thought: *I would, if only I could. But I promised Luigi that I would see to it that his parents are safe and taken care of. How can I do that if I return to Rome?*

So she stayed on for several more days, and before she knew it the days became weeks. Then she began to feel unwell. At first, when she missed her period, she didn't pay much attention to it. It had happened often enough before.

316

Then each morning, and anytime she smelled food, she began to feel nauseated.

Suddenly she was afraid for more than herself and Luigi's parents.

Even before she went to see the doctor, she knew she was pregnant once again.

As the date of her delivery drew nearer, so did the war, but Charlotte-Anne stayed on at the Palazzo di Cristallo. A promise was a promise, and Luigi, misguided though he might have been politically, was her husband. She could not let him down. If his parents refused to leave, then she had no choice but to stay with them.

Compania became a caldron of speculation. Rumors about the Americans abounded. People said that they were advancing, others that they had been driven back into the sea. Still others whispered that they were committing atrocities.

Charlotte-Anne didn't listen to any of it. She knew the Americans weren't monsters. But she was fearful for her unborn child. Ever since her first stillborn child, she had never carried a child full term. Day after day, she prayed that she would be able to do so this time. Now that the world had gone mad and there was so much death, she wanted more than ever to bring a little joy, a new life into the world.

Each day that passed without the feared miscarriage seemed a miracle.

Months passed, and her body grew swollen. She found it increasingly difficult to walk around. When eight months had passed, she wept silently for joy.

In her ninth month, the Allies had beaten the retreating Germans and Italians to within ten miles south of the palazzo.

Once again Charlotte-Anne pleaded with Marcella, who steadfastly reiterated, "This is my home. I will not leave."

Now when the wind blew from the south, it brought along with it the reverberation of artillery barrages. The night sky began to look like it did back home on the Fourth of July. Then they became aware of the retreating wounded Germans and Italians.

And finally the Allies were two miles away.

It was then that Charlotte-Anne formulated the plan. She knew little of military strategy, but she knew one thing: the hill upon which the Palazzo di Cristallo had been built and the hill on which the convent was located were two of the highest points in the entire region. The Germans and the Allies both would surely try to gain control of them, for whoever was king of these hills could control the surrounding countryside with ease.

She smuggled off one last letter to her mother, informing her that she was now only two weeks from her delivery date, and then she saw to it that a storm cellar was dug in the middle of the vineyards, much like the ones they used to have in Texas in case of tornadoes.

If worst came to worst and she and the di Fontanesis found themselves in the middle of a battlefield, they would be able to hide out there in relative safety.

The shelter was barely completed before she was grateful for her foresight.

17

Charlotte-Anne wasn't sure how long it had been since they fled the palazzo. It seemed days at least since they had hidden out in the vineyard.

There was hardly room for the three of them, and they could barely stretch out all at once. All they had with them were some candles for light, which they used frugally. Above them the hastily contrived trapdoor was a piece of thick wood camouflaged by a huge grapevine which they had pulled over it. The little food they had managed to take with them had run out quickly and now they were hungry, thirsty, and tired. Their nerves were on edge. Charlotte-Anne feared that at any moment they would reach the breaking point, lose control, and turn on each other.

The dark pit of the shelter stank from the bucket they used in the corner and from their own sweat. The battle above seemed to last forever. All they ever heard was the constant roar and echo of artillery barrages, the muffled rat-a-tat-tat chatter of machine guns, the whine of stray bullets. Too often, shells landed nearby, causing tremors in the pit, and stones and earth would come loose and slide down the wall.

Charlotte-Anne was certain they were going to be buried alive.

"Our home!" the Princess Marcella di Fontanesi wept over and over. "All our treasures. Everything we own is going to be destroyed! Generations of—"

"Hush," Prince Antonio di Fontanesi, the father of Charlotte-Anne's husband, hissed at his wife. "At least we are alive."

"Not for long," his wife whined. "You wait and see. We'll all be dead. When Luigi comes back, it'll be to bury us. If he ever finds us down here, that is. We would have been safer staying in the palazzo!"

Charlotte-Anne felt the first pain at the height of the bombing. Several times she started to tell them, but each time she waited for it to subside. Finally there was no way she could deny it.

"I'm going to have the baby," she said.

"What? Now?" The Princess Marcella's voice was a hiss in the darkness. "Here? We have no food to eat, and we've run out of water to drink."

Charlotte-Anne struggled to spread out more comfortably. "I can't do anything about it," she said apologetically. "I know the timing's bad. Please, you must help me."

"You are Luigi's wife. Of course we'll help you," Prince Antonio said. "Won't we, Marcella?"

"If only the battle would let up," the princess wailed. The carefully modulated, cultured tones of her voice had deserted her, and she sounded like any frightened, whining fishwife. "How can we help? We can barely see what we're doing. There is only one candle left. And this place is so *filthy*."

Charlotte-Anne reached out and touched her mother-in-law's arm. "But it's safe, at least for the time being."

Another mortar round landed close by, and the ground

shook crazily. Simultaneously a million hailstones rained down on the trapdoor.

Princess Marcella let out a shriek. "It's the end!" she screamed. "The end!"

"Quiet," her husband said. "We must remain calm."

"Calm!" his wife cried. "How do you propose I stay calm?"

"We *must*. We have a baby to deliver."

The princess began to laugh hysterically. "If it weren't for *her* and her precious *baby*, we wouldn't be in this fix. I'm leaving! I'm getting out of this trap. You two can stay here till kingdom comes, for all I care." Her voice took on a mocking tone. "Ironic isn't it? *Her* countrymen have invaded Italy. It's because of them that—"

The sound of the prince's hand was like a gunshot against his wife's cheek. She let out a shriek and quieted down. Then she began to whimper softly.

About six hours later, as the battle reached its zenith, the angry cries of the baby filled the pit.

"It's a girl," the prince said with soft pride. "The house of the di Fontanesis has another princess."

Princess Marcella laughed. Her voice was shrill. "Another princess! That's just what we need, you old fool, isn't it? Luigi's away in battle, killed for all we know. Who's to carry on our name? It's a *son* our house needs, not another daughter."

Despite her exhaustion, Charlotte-Anne heard the principessa's hysteria and was afraid that the prince would once again strike his wife. Instead his voice trembled with dignified control. "Be quiet, Marcella. Can't you, for once, count your blessings?"

Charlotte-Anne's eyes filled with tears. She had forced herself to hold on, to endure the ordeal for the child's sake. But now the darkness, the filth, the principessa's hysteria and cruelty, her own unutterable exhaustion—it all became more than she could bear. The prince held the child and she let herself slip into dark unconsciousness.

She had no idea of how long she slept, but the baby's cries awoke her.

"I have to feed her," Charlotte-Anne murmured.

Carefully the prince handed her the child.

"Hello, little daughter," Charlotte-Anne whispered, her voice full of love.

"What are we going to name her?" the prince asked.

"I don't know," Charlotte-Anne answered. "We'll wait for Luigi." She was too exhausted to say more, so instead she uncovered her breasts and turned to the child. She laid her near her left breast, where the baby instantly found the nipple and began sucking purposefully. Then fear gripped Charlotte-Anne's heart. The baby suckled, but she wasn't getting any milk. Quickly she moved the child to her other breast, but it, too, was dry.

A cold terror filled her. It was no use, she thought. She had no milk to give the child.

She stroked her baby gently. The infant sucked madly, then began to cry again. Charlotte-Anne's voice was a frightened whisper. "*I don't have any milk.*"

Princess Marcella let out a groan of exasperation. "See? What did I tell you? These modern American girls cannot do even that. I told you, didn't I? Why couldn't Luigi marry some nice Italian—"

"*Shut up, Marcella,*" the prince roared. "For once, will you just shut up!"

A wild kind of triumph crackled in the princess's voice, even above the miserable cries of the child. "But how's the baby going to eat? Eh? You tell me! I suppose we just walk into the kitchen and heat it some milk—"

"Please!" Charlotte-Anne begged, her voice surprisingly strong. "Stop it. You're only frightening the baby."

Outside, the artillery barrage was coming closer, but there was a sudden silence in the pit. Even the baby was quiet, apparently exhausted. But it wasn't long before she began to wail again with hunger.

"Hush, hush, little baby, don't you cry," Charlotte-Anne sang in English, feeling not only fear but also shame for failing in her most basic duty as a mother. The singing did little to quiet the child, and finally Charlotte-Anne wept in misery.

Eventually the infant fell into a fitful sleep, as did Charlotte-

Anne, but it didn't last long. The baby soon woke again from the pain of her hunger. The crying went on for hours, and there was nothing any of them could do.

Charlotte-Anne knew her baby would die.

Finally she could stand it no more. She kissed the baby's soft cheek and whispered, "I'm going to fetch you some food, Miss No-Name."

"You cannot leave," the prince gasped unbelievingly. "Not while the battle is raging all around us. Besides, you are too weak."

"Then who will get milk for the baby?" Charlotte-Anne asked quietly, painfully pushing herself up.

The prince was silent. For once, even the princess did not speak.

"Mama will be back soon," Charlotte-Anne told the baby. She kissed her and then reluctantly handed her over to the prince. "Take good care of her."

"I will," the prince said solemnly.

Carefully Charlotte-Anne rose, lifted the trapdoor, and peered out. It was night, but flashes of hellish artillery lit the sky, and the sounds of shelling were like thunder. She took a deep breath.

"We'll pray for you," the prince said in a shaky voice.

Charlotte-Anne looked down at her in-laws. In the flashes of shell bursts and flares, their eyes gleamed up at her, wide and frightened. Then, without hesitating further, she slowly climbed out of the shelter, struggling for the strength to mount each step of the ladder. At the top, she let the trapdoor slam shut and collapsed. Her nose was filled with the stink of cordite and fire; she was surrounded by the stifling air of hell.

Slowly, torturously, she began to crawl on her belly. Each movement was agonizing, but she imagined she thought she still heard her baby's cries and crawled on.

Before she managed to get fifty yards, she heard the chatter of a nearby machine gun. Two bullets slammed into her arm and her side. She rolled over on her back and looked up at the fireworks sky, feeling nothing so much as surprise. She tried to get up, but she could not move. She was confused, because rather than feeling pain, she couldn't feel her body at all.

Before she slipped into unconsciousness, she began to pray. Not for herself, but for her newborn child, who she feared would starve before the next day was through.

18

The three old crones dressed in tattered black moved slowly through the carnage. Oily black plumes of smoke billowed from various spots around the field. The whole scene seemed like a dreamscape. The intense blue of the cloudless sky, the spires of the tall cypresses, the heat from the fires all around that made everything shimmer, the destroyed weapons, the men lying silent or moaning, the blood-splattered corpses of those who had died or those who would shortly die—it was all unreal and thus, somehow, more bearable.

"It is over," the first of the hunched-over old women whispered in a dry, brittle voice. "All that is left now are the dead."

"And the dying," amended the second woman, clutching her ragged shawl with arthritic claws. Her sharp, pinpoint eyes moved down to the body lying facedown at her feet. It was one of the Italian men. She could tell from the uniform.

With her foot she nudged the stiff body so that it rolled over. The bloody face looked up at her with unseeing eyes.

"Do you recognize him?" hissed the third woman.

She shook her head and gazed all around her. The smell of death was strong in her ancient nostrils. She made a quick sign of the cross. She was an old woman, and death was no stranger to her. She herself had cheated death on at least three occasions. Hadn't she watched the other villagers starve to death? Hadn't she seen relatives and friends lined up against the village wall, shot to death by the firing squads? Hadn't she received letter after letter informing her that her grandchildren and her children were dead? All that was left now were the very old and the very young. And not even many of those.

She heard one of the other old women let out a sharp cry of delight as she spotted the glint of gold on the finger of a blood-encrusted hand. She shook her head, her lips working slackly on toothless gums. Nothing was new, not life, not death. There was simply more death now. But hadn't she predicted this? Hadn't she alone dared hiss aloud her hatred for the fascist pigs?

She continued to work her gums as she skirted the deep bomb craters and picked her way through the destroyed, dismembered bodies. Then she saw it. "Quick, quick," she called out, motioning for the others to come.

They hurried over and looked down. "It is the principessa," the first woman hissed. "In death all are equal!"

"No, she is not dead," whispered the second. "See? She still breathes." She made a swift sign of the cross.

"Principessa indeed," hissed the third. "It is the *americana*. She married him for the title only. I spit upon her!" She sprayed spittle onto the inert body. "Even death is too good for her."

"Do not speak so of the dying," said the first, placing a dry, wrinkled hand on her arm. "Come. We must see if there are any men we know lying here."

"I spit upon you," the third one hissed again.

"Wait," the first said sharply. "Listen!"

They all cocked their ears as they caught the muffled, high-pitched cry.

"It is a child," said the first.

"No, it is just a soldier crying out," said the second. "In death even the men sound like the children."

"Or it is the wind," added the third.

The black apparitions slid slowly out of her line of vision as Charlotte-Anne came to once again. Without moving her head she glanced around, her gaze confused. The white clouds were receding. In their place she could see a vast blueness all around her. She was under water, staring up at the surface. The black apparitions had been people gazing down into the pool in which she lay quietly, like a fish afraid to move and draw attention to itself. She thought she recognized the strange smell which had eluded her earlier and which now seemed more pronounced than ever. She had smelled it once before, many years ago, when she'd been rushed to the emergency room with an appendicitis attack. There had been a highway accident somewhere that night, and she had smelled that same overpowering metallic scent then.

It was the smell of death.

Death? She stared up at the blue sky. No, she couldn't be dead, she thought fuzzily. Not in this curved, beautiful, watery universe, where her entire being felt so pleasantly numb and good.

Slowly, ever so slowly, she turned her head sideways and caught sight of a shattered arm. She frowned to herself. For a moment she couldn't comprehend the sight. Then she felt a dreamy fear growing within her, and it all came back to her in a flash.

The shell-shocking bombs, the whines of the bullets.

The earthquakes that shook the ground beneath her.

The strangely painless numbing of her body as fiery pain after fiery pain flashed through it.

The quivers as things lodged within her.

The quick, powerful roar as her lifeblood rushed to meet the wounds, seeking escape from her body.

The geysers of blood, thick and red, solid streams at the bottoms flowing outward like ruby showers of rich, warm raindrops.

Her mind reeled now with the memory, and fear possessed her. Her heart pumped madly, though she fought weakly to slow it down. She tried to calm her breathing, and take shallow breaths. After a moment her pulse slowed as she felt herself slipping away once again into unconsciousness.

She was dying. The revelation was sudden. Oh, but how beautiful it was, now that she thought about it. . . . The strength seeping out of her, the whirling sensation, like being spun into an ever-quickening vortex. The dimming of everything around her and then the sudden blinding white light, brighter than a thousand suns. How easy it had been to give herself up to that beguiling, dazzling light!

She felt a rivulet of something wet crawling down one cheek toward her lips. She parted her lips and then tasted the salty tear. She was still alive.

Images swirled lazily in her mind, magically becoming fragments of her life. . . .

She was a child, tightening her lips purposefully as she carefully and ever so slowly walked beside her mother, who carried her father's ashes. . . .

She was a child, running breathlessly up the stairs, clutching her report card proudly. . . .

She was half-girl, half-woman, laughing hysterically, the tears running down her cheeks as her best friend, Gina, mimicked the flirtatious walk of a society lady. . . .

She was a sober young woman standing on the deck of the *Ile de France*, on her way to boarding school in Europe, the stone canyons of Manhattan slipping slowly past along the shore. . . .

New York . . . home . . . .

Slowly she closed her eyes, the lids flickering. She was so tired. She didn't want to be underwater anymore. She didn't want to be here, wherever she was. All she wanted was to go back, to long ago. To another world, another time.

The Principessa di Fontanesi, the richest woman in all Italy, born Charlotte-Anne Hale in a small town in Texas and raised in New York, wanted to go back home, where everything had been sane, and warm, and safe, and sound.

Her mind swirled as it reached back to the beginnings of her memory, and her life was a dream rushing upon her, flashing from long ago to the present, a whirlwind of memories, what seemed like a millennium crammed into a few short minutes.

And lost among the moans and cries of the hundreds of mortally wounded lying all around her, there came yet another sound, higher pitched, and more angry, but no less afraid.

It was the cry of her child.

Her baby, whom she had left buried in the shelter underground while she crawled through the raging battle in order to bring it food and water, so that it might live. . . .

19

"Help me. Somebody please help me."

Her cries echoed like thunder in a canyon, bouncing back and forth with decreasing audibility. A radiating heat seemed to burst outward, then contract, then flare again somewhere deep in her right side.

"Help me, please . . ."

The two stretcher-bearers, their white armbands with the red crosses on them splattered with blood, stopped and looked down at her.

"It is a woman!" exclaimed one of them in surprise. He dropped his end of the stretcher and got down on one knee beside her, placing a hand on her forehead. He looked up at his partner. "She is cold as ice."

"Is she badly hurt?"

He examined her side. The moment he saw the pool of gelatinous blood in which she lay, he shrugged impassively. "Everyone is badly hurt."

"There are so many wounded. Do we take her to the hospital now? Or does she wait for her turn? We were told to—"

The man leaning over her tightened his lips. "At sea, it is always the women and children first. I think in battle also. We take her now to the Sisters of Mercy."

Gently they took hold of her and rolled her onto the stretcher. She moaned with the pain, but they seemed oblivious of it. When they lifted the stretcher, each step they took seemed to jolt her insides, causing the pain to flash ever more violently. She screamed and screamed in agony, but she was the only one who seemed to hear it.

After they had gone a few yards, the man leading the way stopped and looked back over his shoulder. "She is so quiet. Is she still alive?"

The other man looked down at her. He nodded. "She is still alive. But she is in great pain. She does not have long, I think."

"Sometimes it is better this way," his partner replied philosophically as he continued walking. "At least in death she will sleep in peace. She will not feel her misery."

She stared up at the bouncing, roiling plumes of black smoke. *You're wrong*, she shouted soundlessly. *Everyone is wrong. Dying is cold and wet and painful. No matter what anyone tells you, it's goddamn* hell.

Everything everybody had ever told her was a bold-faced lie.

She knew that now.

*S*he had not been quite four years old then, and she had been sitting on her father's lap, listening carefully to the fairy tale. The moment he closed the book, she stirred restlessly and looked up at him. "That's all there is?" she asked in disappointment.

Her father smiled and put the book aside. "I'm afraid it is."

"But what happens after it says 'and they lived happily ever after'?"

"It means just what it says. They were happy for the rest of their lives."

Charlotte-Anne nodded slowly. "But when she bit into the apple, she died, didn't she?"

"Yes . . ." her father said carefully.

"And then, when the prince kissed her, she woke up again?"

He nodded.

"What would have happened if he hadn't kissed her?"

"I suppose she would have gone on sleeping forever and ever." Her father smiled reassuringly. "But don't worry

about that. The prince came and woke her up, just like it said he did.''

"Daddy?"

"Yes, dear?"

"I'm not going to eat any more apples."

He laughed. "Oh, I wouldn't go so far as that, if I were you. It was only a fairy story. Things like that don't happen in real life. I'm not so sure people even know how to poison apples."

"Oh." Charlotte-Anne paused. "But people die, don't they?"

"Yes." Her father's voice was soft. "We will all die one day. But you needn't worry about that, either. It's a long, long way off. Why, you were just born."

"But when we die, does a prince come around and kiss us awake? When Billy's mother died, no prince came, and she's still gone."

"What happens, Charlotte-Anne, is that when we've outlived our time, we die."

"Does it hurt?"

"I don't think so."

"And what happens after that?"

"Then a prince comes and wakes us. Only he isn't really a prince. He's God. He wakes up our souls, and if we've lived good lives, then we go to heaven and join him and live happily ever after."

"What do we do once we get there?"

"Oh, I don't know. Whatever makes us happy, I suppose."

"Like baking cookies?" Charlotte-Anne asked eagerly.

"Like baking cookies." He laughed again and kissed her affectionately.

"But . . . God does wake us up? We don't keep on sleeping and sleeping? He doesn't forget about us?"

"No. He never forgets," her father said warmly, enfolding the tiny, inquisitive body in his arms. "God comes and wakes us all up. He's our real prince."

20

The Convent of Our Lady of Peace was built high on a terraced hilltop overlooking the countryside. Only a fluke of military strategy and its proximity to an even higher, more strategically important hill—where the Palladian palazzo of the di Fontanesis, which was now a smoldering ruin, sat—had spared the convent from destruction. The battle had raged for eight days, and now the sweeping view of the countryside through the arched loggias was a vision of hell.

The ancient foundations of the convent dated back to the twelfth century, and it was surrounded by thick stone walls which shut out the world. Inside, the enormous groin-vaulted main hall was filled with cots pushed closely against each other and spilling out into the hall and dormitory. The ancient ceilings and loggias echoed with the screams of the wounded, the murmured litanies of prayer, and a thousand tumultuous foreign sounds. The stench of urine and feces mingled with the copper smell of blood. It was late afternoon, and the steady stream of wounded being carried in had still not slacked off, bringing even more noise and chaos into the usually hushed halls.

Sister Maria Theresa sat on the edge of a cot, sponging the caked blood off the chest of the young soldier. She had not set eyes upon a man for years, and never in her life had she seen one naked until now. She kept her eyes studiously averted, working by feel and the telltale moans of the soldier, rather than by sight. Behind her, stretcher-bearers were bringing in yet more wounded.

"I don't know where we're going to put them all," a female voice whispered from Sister Maria Theresa's right. "They're carrying in more. There must be hundreds."

Sister Maria Theresa turned and locked eyes with Sister Maddalena. Despite the din, Sister Maria Theresa too spoke in a whisper. For seventeen years now she had scrupulously kept her vow of silence, and now that it had been temporarily lifted, the sound of her own voice was hoarse and foreign to her ears. "We ran out of food and medicine hours ago," she hissed. "Most of the water is contaminated. What are we going to do?"

"We shall pray, Sisters," a steady voice intoned from behind them.

Both nuns looked up to see the mother superior, standing staunchly erect, her inner strength glowing despite her weariness of body and soul.

"A cigarette," croaked the injured soldier whose chest Sister Maria Theresa had been sponging. "A cigarette? Please?"

Sister Maria Theresa looked around helplessly.

Wordlessly the mother superior looked down at the soldier. Her eyes hid the compassion within her. She knew he was only a child, seventeen perhaps, and he was another who would not last the night.

The mother superior reached into the blood-caked folds of her once-white gown, now a stiff russet, and sought one of the packages of American cigarettes one of the liberators had given to her. She handed it to Sister Maria Theresa, who took it reluctantly.

"Light one for him," the mother superior said gently.

"Yes, Reverend Mother," Sister Maria Theresa answered. She tightened her lips and fished a cigarette out of the pack, then took the matches the reverend mother handed her. Then she sat still in confusion.

"Well, Sister? Put one in your mouth, inhale as you light it, and then let him have little puffs."

"Yes, Reverend Mother." With shaking fingers Sister Maria Theresa did as she was told. As she lit the cigarette, she broke out in a spasm of coughing. Then she held the cigarette to the soldier's lips. He took grateful puffs.

Sister Maria Theresa handed the pack back to the mother superior.

The reverend mother shook her head. "No, you keep it.

When you run out, see me. I have more. Give one to any of the wounded who request it. If they do not have lung wounds." The mother superior handed another pack and a box of matches to Sister Maddalena.

The mother superior stood there for a moment, watching the two nuns and the soldier. She knew that this was a time of trial, a moment when her faith was being tested as never before. She, too, was confused and horrified by the sights which assailed her, but she knew that she could not succumb to weakness. But there was so little she could understand, so little real comfort she could give. She had devoted her entire life to God and, through him, to man. Ever since she could remember, she had been filled with a deep faith. When she had looked about her in calm times, she had seen God everywhere. In his birds, his heavens, on the very earth she humbly trod. As a young novitiate she was certain that God had things well in hand and was winning. But now she was old, her face parched and creased, her sagging jowls squeezed tight by the wimple that framed her face, the white gown and veil covering her soaked with blood. And now it occurred to her, although she tried to suppress the blasphemous thought, that God was no longer in control, and evil ruled the world.

Two stretcher-bearers approached her. "Where can we put her?" one of them asked.

The mother superior sucked in her breath at the sight of the pale woman, badly wounded and only half-conscious, who lay on the stretcher. She immediately recognized Charlotte-Anne as the Principessa di Fontanesi, daughter-in-law to the family that had always been so generous to the convent. She lifted the sheet that draped the principessa's body and winced at the sight of the shattered arm. Then she noticed the wound in the principessa's side. The kidneys, she thought with despair. Involuntarily she let the sheet drop.

Turning back to Sister Maria Theresa, she said, "Go, show them to the dormitory. Have them put her in my room. In my bed. Do not leave her side, Sister." The reverend mother turned. "Sister Maddalena, find one of the doctors and send him upstairs to see to the principessa. And hurry."

*   *   *

Charlotte-Anne lifted her head a fraction of an inch. Her eyelids felt heavy, but she managed to see out through the haze of her lashes. The world was drifting by as if she were watching it through a scrim. A shadowy white apparition moved stealthily, as in a slow-motion ballet. Everything was white, a hundred different shades of white. All except for the thin ruby-red line staining her left side. Murmured voices seemed to chant incantations in a monotone.

The whiteness and the red line went slowly dark, receding once more into nothingness.

It was a world of white satin and soft acoustics, and she was a princess lying in a huge soft bed. Cut crystal sparkled and flashed fire and ice. Through a white-draped doorway floated her satin prince, coming to wake her with his kiss. She was dead, sleeping her fairytale death of a hundred years, and he was finally coming closer and closer, growing in size as he approached. His face drew near. Asleep, dead, dead, asleep, she seemed to sense the lips that would awaken her, and she responded, her mouth seeming to float up through satin air. She smelled his sweet breath, could visualize those narrow pale lips, his white satin doublet with the puffy sleeves, his legs encased in the soft satin riding breeches of the fascists, tucked into white boots. His skin was smooth and she could see his shiny teeth inside his hollow mouth. She could feel her own lips as they rose and pursed, but before his lips could touch hers, he began to recede as mysteriously as he had appeared, and she felt his life-giving power draining away. He became ever smaller and more distant, and then began to whirl faster and faster as he was sucked into the vortex of a swirling satin dream.

The clouds and white scrim had turned warm and yellow when she awakened again. It was easier to open her eyes now, the lids didn't feel nearly as heavy as they had before. She stared up into space. She could make out a flatness up there.

Without moving her head, she glanced around. Her eyes were a deep greenish blue, filled with a mixture of confusion and wonder. She could make out the flat surfaces all around her. She was in a white box. The warm yellow she had seen was electric light. She was in a box with nothing in it but a giant light bulb above her. It seemed to radiate an awesome heat.

A box? She stared up at the flatness. No, it couldn't be a box, she thought dreamily. It was a square universe, and she was floating in it. The semigloss ceiling was a monotone landscape, topsy-turvy and seen from a hundred miles out in space. A crack of river, held up by gravity, flowed between a valley of mountains. She sighed soundlessly and the light grew tinier and tinier until it disappeared altogether.

She climbed slowly through the clouds, the wisps parting in front of her. The climb was an effort. She was not as strong as she used to be. But then the last of the fog's clinging fingers parted, and she was in a room.

The space was tiny, spare, and white. It was more like a cell than a room. The stone floor was bare, the narrow iron cot was covered with a thin, lumpy mattress, and a single wooden chair was pushed against one wall. Above the bed hung an old polychrome crucifix. There were no curtains at the tiny window. Consciousness came fleetingly and went, came again. Her eyes focused and she noticed a white apparition seated on the chair.

The apparition seemed to sense she was awake. It rose and drifted to her side. Charlotte-Anne stared up at it. It seemed to hover over her, huge and white. It was a beautiful angel.

Then her mind cleared. It was not an angel after all. It was a nun dressed all in white. Only the pink hands and face and the black rosary dangling from her middle disturbed the white of her veil, wimple, bib and gown. Those and splatters of dried blood.

"You are safe, Principessa," the nun said gently, but to Charlotte-Anne the voice sounded distant and hollow, somehow distorted. "No one will hurt you now. The doctor has been to see you. We are doing everything we can."

Something struck Charlotte-Anne as very funny, and she wanted to laugh, but no sound would come forth. Her eyes looked at the nun with an expression of amusement. Why on earth did she need a doctor? She couldn't remember ever having felt better in her life. She was floating on a cotton-candy cloud. Everything was soft and painless. She couldn't feel a thing.

"We ran out of medicine, but the Americans brought some more," the nun explained. "We have given you morphine."

Charlotte-Anne didn't seem to hear her. She knew that there was something important she had to say, but her mind was dulled by the sweet, fuzzy cloud of well-being. Every time the thought drifted close, it seemed to dance away playfully, just out of reach.

"You are going to be fine." The nun smiled reassuringly and steepled her fingers. "We have been praying for you, Principessa. All our prayers are with you."

Charlotte-Anne tried to speak. Her mouth formed the words, but no sound would come. "Do not pray for me," she tried to say as the thought that had been skipping in and out of reach suddenly came close and revealed itself. A tear slipped out of the corner of one eye. "I . . . don't . . . need . . . your . . . prayers . . . Sister. But . . . I . . . know . . . someone . . . who . . . does."

21

S he drifted headlong out of the numb zone.

Despite the constant pain, the crashes of thunder, and the roar of lashing rain, she had managed to slip in and out of sleep. She had no idea how long she had been asleep. Long enough, she realized, to allow the clear sky she had remembered to cloud with a violent storm. The moment she gazed through the haze of her eyelashes, she moved her head slightly to one side. The nun seemed to be right over her, her white-framed scrubbed-pink face glowing in the warm yellow light. Charlotte-Anne smiled weakly up at her.

When the nun realized she was awake, she wiped the worried look off her face and tried to smile reassuringly.

Charlotte-Anne's eyes moved past her. The doctor, who she was vaguely aware had examined her earlier, had his back turned to her. A priest was peering out the tiny window, trying to see through the rain-streaked darkness.

Charlotte-Anne struggled to lift her head. Her face was starkly pale.

"She is dying," she heard the doctor say.

The priest turned away from the window, his soutane swirling around his legs. He shook his head sadly.

"My . . . baby," Charlotte-Anne tried to say. She stared up at the nun. "My . . . baby. Was it . . . found?"

The nun smiled gently down at her. She leaned over Charlotte-Anne and stroked aside a stray lock of her moist hair. "Do not try to speak," she murmured.

Charlotte-Anne gazed at her and let out a thin, reedy moan, convinced her baby was dead.

"She is dying," the doctor said again. "There is nothing more that I can do. It is now in the hands of God."

The priest turned back to the window, his hands clasped behind him.

She is dying.

The soft inflections of that sentence kept floating lightly in Charlotte-Anne's ears. She closed her eyes to try to shut out that voice, but it kept repeating itself, like a recording, the three words playing over and over in her mind.

She is dying.

She is dying.

S ister Maria Theresa prayed quietly, her lips emitting an occasional sibilant whisper.

She was still seated beside Charlotte-Anne's bed in the mother superior's cell. Two and a half days had passed since the principessa had been brought in, and still her condition was unchanged. It seemed a miracle that she was alive at all.

Sister Maria Theresa attributed it to the power of the prayers she offered up to God. She prayed for the principessa, for all the wounded and dead, for all of poor, ravished Italy. After not being able to sleep at all through the days and nights of bombing, and now with caring for the wounded, she was surprised to find that she was still wide-awake. Her body felt heavy and burdened, but she was mentally alert. That too was a miracle. It was as though God had blessed them all with incredible strength to see this tragedy through. Even while she prayed, her eyelids never drooped and her eyes never left her patient's quiet, prostrate form.

The mother superior floated soundlessly into the little cell. She placed a hand on Sister Maria Theresa's shoulder. "How is she, Sister?" she asked softly.

The nun looked up and saw that the reverend mother's usually serene face looked haggard and sad.

"She is unchanged, Reverend Mother," the nun whispered.

"I suppose that is more than we could hope for. She is in the hands of almighty God. Whatever he decides, it is his will." The mother superior nodded and then managed a faint smile. "Would you like to take a few hours and rest, Sister? I can have one of the other sisters replace you. It is going to be a long night and an even longer day tomorrow."

"No, thank you, Reverend Mother. I'm all right. Perhaps later, when I need it."

"Bless you, Sister. I am proud of you. You are very brave."

Sister Maria Theresa said nothing.

The mother superior cocked her head to one side. "What on earth is that noise?"

Both nuns listened for a moment. The faraway chant seemed to be made up of a multitude of voices. Sister Maria Theresa rose from her chair. "It seems to be coming from outside," she said.

Both nuns turned to the tiny window and looked out into the night. They saw a bonfire burning in the middle of the village, the pink glow of which flickered on their faces.

"There are torches everywhere," Sister Maria Theresa said. "And those chants . . . It is as though a celebration is going on." She stared at the reverend mother.

"Either that, or yet another tragedy," the mother superior mused gravely. "Somehow those chants do not seem happy sounds. I hate to think what could be going on now."

*   *   *

A flurry of sounds echoed from the stone-paved corridor outside and caught Charlotte-Anne's attention. A muted roar drifted up from the valley below and filtered into the little room and through her consciousness. She was too weak to speak or to move, but upon waking, her hearing was again exceptionally acute. Every nuance, every rustle, even the faintest faraway whisper, made a loud impression through the thick scrim of her mind.

"The mother superior said so," a hesitant, meek woman's voice said. "There are many more wounded coming in, and there is no more room downstairs. We must put them in our quarters."

"In here, Sister?" It was a much louder, deeper voice. Without thinking about it, Charlotte-Anne realized it belonged to a stretcher-bearer.

"No, no, not in there. That is the mother superior's room. The principessa must be alone."

"Even in defeat, the fascist princess is living like a queen," one of the men grumbled.

The nun ignored the comment. "Here, put him in this room. Line up the cots close together."

There was a loud commotion as hob-nailed boots clicked down the corridor.

"What is going on?" one of the men asked.

Charlotte-Anne recognized what she thought was a familiar voice. She did not know where she had heard it before, but it seemed it had been some time since her foggy consciousness had swallowed her up.

"There is madness in the village!" someone shouted breathlessly. "If it isn't stopped soon, there is going to be an ugly riot!"

"But why? I thought the Allies had moved in. They are supposed to be keeping the peace."

From somewhere far away came the cracks of gunfire. "See? Listen! Even the Americans cannot stop it! The people are angry!"

"I don't understand. I thought it was all over. That the battle had moved to Cassino."

"So did I." The man gave an ugly laugh. "But that's not a battle you're hearing. That is a mob. It seems that Prince Luigi di Fontanesi, Mussolini's right-hand man, has returned to the village. They discovered him trying to make his way back home on foot, disguised as a peasant of all things. They've killed him and hung him upside down from a scaffold in the piazza and . . . and . . . I'm afraid it's not for your ears, Sister."

A nun's scurrying footsteps and swishing robes echoed faintly and then died away.

"Well, what?" another of the stretcher-bearers hissed excitedly.

"They cut off his cock and balls, that's what," the man whispered, "and shoved them into his mouth!"

Sister Maria Theresa, sitting motionless in her chair, overheard the terrible conversation. Her hand flew up to her forehead and she quickly made a sign of the cross. "Oh my God," she whispered, aghast that such terrible things should be discussed in a holy place. Turning quickly to look at Charlotte-Anne, she prayed that the principessa was still asleep.

Charlotte-Anne stared up at the ceiling, her paler-than-pale eyes unblinking. Only much later, when the principessa still had not moved, did Sister Maria Theresa realize that she was dead. Muttering a Hail Mary, she smoothed Charlotte-Anne's eyes shut and pulled the sheet up over her.

"Thank you, O Lord," the nun prayed as she fell to her knees on the cold stone floor and bowed her head. "Thank you for sparing the principessa such terrible news. It is far better that she died rather than hear such an awful thing."

But Sister Maria Theresa was wrong. Only Charlotte-Anne's love for her husband had driven her to cling shakily to life. The instant the brutal words had registered, the fight had gone out of her.

At the awful realization of her beloved's fate, she had allowed herself to drift up, up into that welcoming, peaceful nothingness which was death.

22

The shadows beneath the hill crowned with the convent become long and purple. All around, the incredible destruction seemed out of place against the familiar magnificence of the pink streaks of sunset.

Never in their wildest nightmares had they imagined such devastation.

The principessa's face was tear-streaked and dirty. From more than a week in the storm cellar, and then wandering through the ruins, her clothes had become torn and mud-smeared. She looked more like a haggard peasant than the proud, well-groomed matriarch of the di Fontanesis.

Prince Antonio stumbled after his wife. He had taken off his jacket and wrapped it around the newborn infant in order to keep the little girl warm. He carried her gently, full of fear because the baby had become so listless and quiet. She had not cried for hours, and she lay so still that he was afraid she was already dead.

From somewhere nearby came the distant booms of shelling. The Allied army had moved on to conquer another hill at Cassino. More deaths, more destruction, would follow. The prince shook his head mournfully. Would the nightmare never end?

The principessa sank down on a heap of stones which had once been part of the western wing of the Palazzo di Cristallo. She covered her face with her hands and began to weep noisily. All that remained of the proud palazzo were jagged fingers of wall reaching up into the sky, and mountainous piles of shattered crystal which reflected the setting sun like a king's ransom in diamonds.

"Gone," Marcella whispered in a strangled cry through her tears. "All *gone*."

"Come, come, *cara mia*," the prince said gently. "It is time we moved on."

She turned her face up to him. "Why? *Why* did this have to happen?"

"Because the world has turned insane," he replied with a peculiar, quiet dignity. "Because too many people, our own son included, came to look upon Il Duce as some kind of god, because he promised a return to the times of the Roman Empire. Too few people realized Il Duce was nothing but a mad, power-hungry buffoon." He too started to shed tears, but unlike his wife's, his crying was soundless. "We had to learn the hard way that long ago the twilight of the Caesars marked their end for good. Ghosts cannot be resurrected. It was the scheme of a madman." He paused and wiped his eyes. "Come, while I am talking foolishness it is getting dark. Soon we will not see where we are going. We must find food for the child and a place to spend the night."

"I don't want that child," Marcella whispered numbly. "The whore from America has brought ill luck upon our family. Her offspring is the spawn of evil things."

"Hush! Do not talk such nonsense."

Her eyes blazed. "Nonsense, you say? Doesn't it strike you as peculiar that she should have had the foresight to dig that hole in the vineyards?"

The prince did not reply.

"It was she, Antonio. I tell you, she had her hand in this." She began to wail louder. "She was a spy of some sort. How else could she have been prepared for what has come?"

He took his wife by the hand, pulled her to her feet, and they began to stumble downhill, careful to skirt the treacherous, yawning bomb craters which had opened up the earth. Everywhere, the landscape was pockmarked with them.

The sunset became twilight, and then night fell quickly. It was a dark, cloudy night, with only occasional ghostly patches of moonlight to aid them. It seemed an eternity before they reached the base of the hill. Above them towered the silent ruins where once their proud palazzo had stood sentinel.

"Listen," Prince Antonio said sharply. "I think I hear something."

"What could you possibly hear other than the sound of bombing?"

"No, I do hear something approaching." He listened again, and then his voice grew excited. "It is a horse, I think."

"So?" she hissed. "What good do you think a horse will do us?"

"Perhaps none." He shrugged. "Then again, perhaps everything. But whatever you do, Marcella, this is not the time to play the lady. Say nothing of who you are. We are simply ordinary people who have lost everything and have nowhere to go."

"Why should I want to do that?" she snapped. "I am the Principessa Marcella di Fontanesi!"

"Because," he explained patiently, "Luigi is too well known and too hated for working with Il Duce. Believe me, it is much safer for us this way. Otherwise, God only knows what fate might befall us. There are those who would find great joy in tearing us limb from limb."

And that, he noticed, took the wind out of his wife's sails.

Suddenly he felt the bundle in his arms shifting slightly, and once again he offered up a silent prayer of thanks because the child was, incredibly, still alive.

As the horse-drawn wagon neared them, Antonio di Fontanesi hurried forward to meet it. In the dim glow of moonlight breaking through the clouds he could see that the crude, creaking wagon was packed full of people. As he walked past the horse, it radiated such intense heat that he knew at once it was on the point of collapse.

"Please, help us," the prince begged as the wagon drew to a halt. "My wife is ill, and we have a newborn child with us. Have pity, please. We must get it something to eat, or else it will surely die."

The man sitting on the driver's seat looked down. "We can't take you, you gotta walk. The horse is already half-dead."

"Wait," an authoritative voice said from the back of the wagon. There was a scuffling sound of people moving, and a man jumped down to the road. He moved quickly forward. "Let the woman ride in my place. I can walk." As the man drew nearer, Antonio could make out the dark soutane and the white clerical collar of a priest.

"Thank you, Father, thank you," Antonio murmured gratefully.

Antonio walked Marcella to the back of the wagon, and with his free hand helped her climb up onto it. People shifted to make room for her. Many appraising eyes glittered in the moonlight. Antonio lifted the child up to Marcella, but she recoiled and refused to take her. "You want her," she snapped, "you carry her."

He nodded miserably. He was too hungry and tired to argue with her.

The wagon began to roll on, and Antonio and the priest walked alongside it.

"Where are you headed?" Antonio called up to the driver.

"To the convent," the driver replied. "We hear the sisters have turned it into a hospital. Many of us are hungry, sick, or wounded. They say there's food and medicine there. And Father Odoni says they are probably shorthanded. He's going to offer his help."

Antonio fell silent and hung his head. Despite the overwhelming tragedy and devastation that had befallen everyone, little signs of humanity and caring were cropping up as people tried to cope with their own pain and help others. Sometimes it seemed as though it took a tragedy to bring out the best and the worst in people.

He was ashamed to realize that for both Marcella and himself, it had brought out the worst.

Only by a mere fluke of fate did the di Fontanesis' paths cross with the Viganòs'. In peaceful times, when the lines of society were strictly drawn, the closest they might have gotten to each other was by passing on the road, one family trudging along on foot while the other roared past in the luxurious confines of an expensive chauffeur-driven automobile. They had nothing in common, other than that in years past, Paolo Viganò had at times toiled, along with hundreds of others, in the fertile vineyards of the di Fontanesis.

Until the bombing had started, Paolo Viganò had always considered himself a lucky man. He was hardly rich, being a mere grape picker, but he had always *felt* wealthy. True, at times the meager contents of the kitchen cupboard had to be stretched, but he had never known a day of sickness in his entire life, nor had he known real hunger. In his simple mind he equated hunger with laziness, so he had made certain that he always worked hard. Everyone said that no one knew the grapes like Paolo Viganò, and when he heard the compliments, his chest would swell with pride. He had even been spared the tragedy of leaving his family to fight in the war because of his clubfoot, which was not bad enough to hurt his work but did keep him from being a useful soldier.

His wife, Adriana, was a simple large sun-browned woman with gentle eyes and a quietly pleasant smile. In her youth she had been a great beauty, one of the rare and treasured blond-haired, blue-eyed Italians. But she had never wanted more than her Paolo. The love they shared had only grown with each passing year of their marriage. She helped out at harvesttime, picking grapes in order to supplement their income. Other times she kept the house and tended the kitchen garden and the goats and chickens she raised.

Their six-year-old son, Dario, was turning into a lovely, intelligent child. He was possessed of a quick mind and studious manner, and he filled Paolo with pride. When one day Dario startled his parents with an announcement that he was determined to become a priest when he grew up, both Paolo and Adriana had been filled with warm pleasure, though they regretted the possibility of having no grandchildren. Then, six years after Dario was born, Adriana found herself pregnant again. With that joyful news, Paolo's life was complete. He had felt rich indeed.

Now, waiting by the roadside, he felt neither rich nor blessed. His wife, whom he had half-carried for miles, was resting beside him against a tree, watched over by Dario. Paolo was as devastated as the shelled, war-ravaged land around him. Two nights earlier, at the height of the bombing, his wife's time had come. One moment she was in the kitchen baking bread; the next, she could no longer stand on her feet.

There was no doctor or midwife to be found, and Adriana was sick, burning up with a fever. The child she gave birth to died within the hour. She had been too delirious even to comprehend the tragedy that had occurred. Paolo, sure that she too was going to die, felt frightened and helpless. He could not conceive of a life without his beloved Adriana.

When Paolo heard the horse-drawn wagon approaching in the distance, he held his breath. Was it possible that his luck had not deserted him after all? With growing anxiety he waited for the vehicle to round the curve, then cried out to them.

"Please," he desperately urged the driver. "My wife is terribly sick. I'm afraid she is going to die. Could you find it in your heart to give her a ride?"

"Can't she walk?" the driver asked gruffly.

"No, she is much too feeble. I've already half-carried her for kilometers. She is so sick she can hardly move."

"Then you are in luck," the driver told him. He motioned up to the hill and the convent etched blackly against the weak moonlight. "We are on our way to the sisters. We hear their convent has become a hospital."

Paolo felt a surge of hope. "Then you'll take my wife?" he begged.

The driver hesitated. "As long as someone else who is now riding will walk."

For a fleeting instant Antonio di Fontanesi was tempted to order Marcella down from the wagon, but another woman volunteered. Antonio decided he was just as happy not to have his wife walking beside him.

As soon as room was made for Adriana Viganò, Father Odoni helped Paolo lift the stout woman up onto the back of the wagon.

Only once his beloved Adriana was in the wagon and the party was headed uphill toward the convent did Paolo once again dare consider how lucky he was. Perhaps, just perhaps, things might turn out all right. His sick wife was on her way to the convent. His son had survived the war. His humble home was still standing. And under his coat he had the two loaves of bread Adriana had been baking when her time had come. They had clothes on their backs, there was help at the convent, and he had had the foresight to bring along some food. What else could a man possibly want?

Antonio, Father Odoni, Paolo, young Dario, and the woman who had volunteered to walk went on beside the slow-moving wagon. For a long time no one spoke. Everyone was weary, and the steady uphill climb was tiring. It was Paolo Viganò who finally broke the silence. He had caught Antonio lowering his ear to the bundle in his arm.

He tapped Antonio on the arm. "What are you carrying all wrapped up like that?"

Without losing a step, Antonio parted a portion of his coat. The baby looked pale and lifeless in the moonlight. "She is my son's," Antonio explained sadly. "Something has happened to her mother. Perhaps she is wounded, perhaps she is dead. Perhaps we will never know. The mother's breasts were barren. She left our shelter during the bombing to find the child some food, but she has not returned. Now I am afraid the poor thing is going to starve."

Paolo shook his head miserably. "My wife, too, just gave birth," he said, commiserating. "It too was a daughter, but she died right away." His voice grew choked. "Now I am afraid that my wife will die also. The only comfort is that she is too delirious to know that the daughter she has carried is dead."

"I don't know what I'm going to do," Antonio whispered. "If the sisters have no milk . . ."

Suddenly Paolo reached out for the bundle in Antonio's arms. "Let me have the child," he said excitedly. "Surely my wife, ill though she is, has plenty of milk in her breasts."

Antonio stared at him, then quickly handed the child over.

"Stop for a moment," Paolo called to the driver as he hurried to the back of the wagon, climbed over the tailgate, and bent down over his wife. She was lying on her back, perspiring heavily. When he touched her forehead it felt cold as ice. He opened her blouse and exposed a huge, swollen breast.

Antonio had followed him and now watched as some instinct brought the child to life. Greedily she found the nipple and began to suck the milk from Adriana Viganò's ample breast.

"Just look," Paolo murmured, the tears sparkling in his eyes. He was at once saddened and filled with joy. He wept for his own dead child, and then he dried his tears and smiled proudly that his ailing wife should, without even being aware of it, save the life of another.

God truly worked in mysterious ways, Paolo thought. He had not turned a blind eye on them after all. In the midst of tragedy, he was working his miracles.

From across the room, Antonio watched as Paolo Viganò leaned low over the cot and kissed his wife. The cot was in the makeshift ward that was actually the chapel of the convent. The pews had been carried outside and cots were lined up everywhere. A young nun was burping the baby, patting her on the back. Then she handed the infant back to Paolo. He turned and waved at Antonio, then, with Dario, circled around the sea of cots to where Antonio and Marcella waited against the far wall to one side of the altar.

"Adriana stands a good chance," Paolo burst out as soon as he neared Antonio. "It may be some time until she recovers completely, but the sisters and the doctor are convinced everything will turn out fine. They said she was brought here just in time."

Antonio smiled and clapped a hand on Paolo's shoulder. "I am very glad to hear it."

"I am so relieved," Paolo said, tears in his eyes. Then, almost reluctantly, he handed Antonio the baby. "She *must* have been hungry. She has eaten once again." He shook his head in disbelief. "I don't think I ever saw such a hungry child. She may be tiny, even for a newborn, but she is so beautiful." His face grew mournful and his voice fell to a whisper. "Do you know, for a moment my wife was aware of the child? It was as though the touch of the mouth against her gave her new strength. For an instant she looked at me with total consciousness and smiled and said, 'My beautiful, beautiful baby.' " Paolo bit down on his lip as the tears spilled from the corners of his eyes. He shook his head miserably. "I did not find it in my heart to tell her the truth. Not yet, while she is so ill.''

Antonio nodded. "I understand."

Paolo wiped his eyes with his fingertips, put an arm around his son's shoulders, and drew Dario close. "I'm sorry," he said to no one in particular. "I do not usually cry."

Antonio smiled dryly. "I do not either, but lately I find I've been crying a lot."

Paolo looked at him. "Did you find out about the availability of milk yet?"

"No," Antonio answered, shaking his head. "But we were told to wait and speak to the reverend mother about it. We will see what she can do."

"Should you find it necessary," Paolo said politely, "my wife is producing plenty of milk. It has to be drawn from her breasts anyway."

"Thank you, my friend," the prince said.

"By the way, my name is Paolo. Paolo Viganò."

"I am very grateful for what you have done, signor. My name is Antonio. And this is my wife, Marcella."

"Signora. Signor." Paolo bowed politely, but Marcella merely gave him a frosty smile and turned away.

"There is the reverend mother now," Antonio said. He watched as the mother superior swept through the chapel doors in her bloodstained white robe, every few steps stopping to give words of comfort to some patient.

As she came closer, she happened to look across the row of cots and met Antonio's eye. For a moment her gaze roved on elsewhere; she didn't seem to register him or the principessa in their dirty, changed appearance. Then recognition clicked in her mind and her eyes swept back toward him. She hurried over, still inquiring of various patients, but doing so more quickly.

When she reached them, she gave them a strained smile. "Principe di Fontanesi. Principessa." She inclined her head.

Paolo gasped. "You are . . . the principe? And the principessa?" He stared at them; then his eyes fell and he quickly bowed his head. *"Scusi, scusi,"* he murmured.

"For what?" Antonio asked.

"For being familiar."

Antonio touched him under the chin and raised his head so he could look him in the eye. "I am not sorry. I am grateful for all you have done to help."

The reverend mother cleared her throat and folded her hands. "I'm afraid I have become the bearer of much sad news of late, and now I must bring yet more bad tidings."

"Charlotte-Anne is dead, then?" Antonio asked.

She nodded. "I'm sorry, and you have my deepest sympathies. The stretcher-bearers found her and brought her in, but it was too late. She had suffered too many internal injuries. There was nothing more that we could do, other than make her as comfortable as possible. She was, and is, in the hands of God." The mother superior touched Antonio's arm gently, in a gesture of comfort, and only then noticed the child. Her eyes flared in surprise, and for the first time in days she allowed herself to smile. She bent down to inspect the infant. "A newborn!" She looked back up at him.

"Yes, and now she has no mother," Antonio said bitterly. "Nor is there any milk to be found."

The mother superior tightened her lips. "I'm afraid there's none here."

"And we ourselves don't even have any food to eat," Marcella growled. She looked at the mother superior hopefully. "We have not eaten for days."

"I'm sorry, Principessa." The mother superior's tone was dry. "If we only had some we could spare, I would give you all I could. But the wounded and sick do not have enough. We are waiting for the rations of the Americans."

Marcella grumbled and turned away.

"I have some food, Principessa," Paolo offered, proudly opening his coat. "Two loaves of bread. See . . ." He handed one of the crispy golden loaves to the mother superior. "It is the least I can do, Reverend Mother."

"Bless you," the mother superior said.

He broke an end off the second loaf and held it out to Marcella, who seized upon it greedily. She took a large bite and began to chew as though someone might snatch it away from her at any moment.

"Thank you," Antonio told Paolo quietly. "You have my lifelong gratitude, first for your wife feeding the baby, and now for feeding us." His eyes fell. What had happened to turn his wife into such an animal so quickly? Or had she only needed the opportunity to show her real self? He had never been as ashamed of anyone as he was now of his wife. In mere days, Marcella had taken on all the worst characteristics she had once ascribed to the peasants. And it was the peasants who were now behaving with dignity.

"But the child," Antonio murmured worriedly. "What are we going to do about the child, now that there is no milk and her mother is dead?"

"And her father also," the mother superior said softly. "Perhaps you have not heard?"

Antonio stared at her, his face suddenly drained of all color. "How did he die? Was it here?"

She shook her head. From what she had heard about Luigi di Fontanesi's death, that was information that could surely wait. They would find out about it soon enough.

As the silence continued, the fight seemed to go out of Antonio. As if he guessed the horrible truth of his son's fate, the prince seemed to shrivel and age right before their very eyes.

Marcella finished her hunk of bread and a calculating glint came into her eyes. In her near-madness, she didn't even seem to register the news of Luigi's death. She stared at the rest of Paolo's loaf. "Why don't you take the child?" she suggested in a sharp whisper. "It no longer has a father or a mother."

Paolo stared at her. "I beg your pardon, Principessa?"

"I said, she's yours. For the rest of that loaf of bread, you can have the baby."

"Marcella!" Antonio was shocked. She was haggling like some fishwife bargaining at the market—and using the child as currency. Too much had happened, he supposed. The walk through the ruins of the Palazzo di Cristallo had confirmed the worst of everything to her; it had broken her.

Marcella snatched the child out of his arms and held her up to Paolo. "Look how beautiful she is," she hissed. "An angel. Your wife need never know that she is not of her own flesh and blood. Yours was a day old. This one is not much older. You can have her, substitute her. And see this necklace her mother put around her neck?''

Paolo could only stare down at the pansy charm, numb with surprise.

"The necklace is yours too. I don't want it. You can have her and the necklace! All we want for her is the rest of that loaf of bread." Her eyes gleamed crazily.

Antonio turned to face the wall, the tears streaming down his cheeks. The mother superior had to turn away also. She could not bear to see the ugly expression on the principessa's face.

"Don't you see that it's all for the best this way?" Marcella hissed at her husband. "At least this way the child can eat. And she'll have a mother and a father. And we can have some bread to eat, too."

"You . . . you would do this?" Paolo asked softly.

"Yes, yes," the principessa snapped. "Here!" She thrust the baby into his arms and snatched away the rest of the loaf of bread. "I hated the baby's mother. She was nothing but a fascist *putana*. I knew my son was doomed the moment I first saw her. It was all because of her that he died. Who wants the child of a slut who killed her husband?"

Paolo stared down at the baby. Her tiny, wrinkled pink face was one of wide-eyed innocence. The fluffy, downlike hairs on her head were golden, and the eyes were wide and aquamarine. She was indeed an angel. And his wife would never doubt the child was her own; their coloring was so similar. Paolo looked over at Marcella, who was already walking away, biting off another hunk of the bread. She had not even offered a piece to her husband, who followed after her with a slow step and stooped shoulders.

The mother superior bowed her head and prayed silently. Under ordinary circumstances, she would have tried to intervene, but the situation was hardly ordinary. It would have been useless to challenge the aristocratic authority of the di Fontanesis. Everywhere, there was death and destruction. Better the child live in a family of simple people with loving hearts than stay in the presence of the shrew who was willing to sell her for a loaf of bread.

The mother superior watched as Paolo put one arm around his six-year-old son's shoulder, dropped to his knees to show him his new baby sister, and extracted from him a vow never to tell his mother what he had just witnessed.

Then Paolo looked up. "Reverend Mother, this child does not have a name."

She nodded. "I suppose it doesn't, or else they would have told us."

"What was the mother's name?"

"Charlotte-Anne."

He frowned thoughtfully. "Anna. Yes, we shall call her after her mother. We shall call her Anna."

The mother superior smiled her approval. Yes, it was much better this way.

Somehow, God in his wisdom had seen to it that the child would at least be loved, and she touched the weeping Antonio on the shoulder and told him so.

23

The suitcases lay on the bed, their lids yawning open. Elizabeth-Anne watched in silence as Janet folded and packed their clothes. She glanced over at Zaccheus. Her son had pulled his wheelchair up in front of the window, and he was staring out at the hills of Campania as though some elusive last-minute answer lay hidden in that view. She knew what he was thinking. She was thinking the same thing.

They had come to Italy to find Anna, but had finally had to admit failure. There were so many pieces to the puzzle, and she was afraid that no matter how hard she searched or how deeply she dug, she would never find them all.

She crossed the room and stood behind Zaccheus, wearily placing a hand on his shoulder. For a moment he turned and glanced up at her. Her features were composed; she felt there was no need to show the terrible pain she felt as she stared out at the now-familiar hills.

When she had first arrived, she had imagined she felt closer to Charlotte-Anne here, where she had lived, but she knew now that that had merely been an illusion. These hills could not make up for her loss. Charlotte-Anne was buried in Italy, but her spirit was no longer here. Elizabeth-Anne had to accept that fact and come to terms with the tragedy, just as nature did. In places, the bombed vineyards had already been replanted with surviving vines. There was a lesson to be learned from that.

Life went on, she thought dully. Despite the most tragic devastation ever visited upon the world, life went on.

She steepled her hands and held her forefingers poised against her lips. She knew that her family had not been singled out to suffer. Millions of other lives had been destroyed in the past few tragic years. But the toll the war had extracted from her and her loved ones was high: a son who was crippled; a daughter dead at only thirty, whose very name inspired such loathing that the Italian peasants would spit and curse upon hearing it; a missing grandchild; a son-in-law who had been fallen upon by his people, stabbed to death with pitchforks, and then ignobly hanged upside down and mutilated in the village piazza, because he was the symbol of a government that abused its power and oppressed its citizens. They had taken out their anger on Luigi di Fontanesi because he was a remaining tangible manifestation of a country gone mad.

What had happened to the human race, to turn people into such rabid animals?

She had asked herself that question a thousand times, but there was no answer. There were so many questions, and no answers to any of them.

Slowly she turned around. She decided she might as well help Janet pack. Just moving around in a zombie state did not do anyone a bit of good, least of all herself. They had come here and done all they could, which had amounted to nothing. Now the sooner they were packed, the sooner they could leave. She knew now the best thing they could do was go home and come to grips with their losses. It was time to face the truth. Her granddaughter had disappeared. Like an unwanted puppy or kitten, she had been given to passing strangers by her other grandparents. No matter how far and wide she continued to search for her, Elizabeth-Anne realized that the search would be fruitless. She would never find Anna. The family she had been given to had no doubt heard about her search, because Elizabeth-Anne had had it so widely publicized, and they had disappeared into the night. The worst part of it was, in all her fifty years she had never learned to accept defeat.

She clenched her hands and let out a silent moan of anger and impotence. The many voices and images of the last few weeks seemed to swirl in her mind.

The mother superior, her face sad, her voice torn and tortured: "Signora, the child is happy. You must believe me. It will only hurt her to be torn from the only family she knows and loves. Please, signora. Have a heart. If you insist, yes, I will tell you. But please, signora. It will be a grave mistake."

Her own voice, hollow and faraway: "I have to know. I must. She is my daughter's child."

The mother superior: "Very well, then. Anna. Anna Viganò. Father Odoni himself baptized her."

And the Viganòs' neighbor and landlord: "They left in the middle of the night like thieves running from the law. Who knows where they went? They left owing me two months' rent. Good riddance, I say."

Elizabeth-Anne's heart and soul burned with the pain. She had been so close to finding Anna. Now her granddaughter was once again gone, lost forever. Who knew where the Viganòs had fled to in order to keep the child?

Memories, so many, many memories assaulted her. There was so much that she blamed herself for. So much could have been different if only . . .

If only I hadn't sent Charlotte-Anne to Europe, she might still be alive.

If only I'd spent less time with the hotels and more time being a mother.

If only I'd kept a tighter rein on her.

There were so many ifs.

And so many startling truths that only now came into focus. Charlotte-Anne had been headstrong and rebellious, so very determined to get her way. And that, Elizabeth-Anne knew, was one characteristic inherited from herself. She and Charlotte-Anne had much more in common than either of them had ever wanted to admit. But unlike herself, Charlotte-Anne threw caution to the winds. She never gave any thought to the potential consequences of her actions.

Oh, if only I'd prodded her in the right direction. That was all Charlotte-Anne needed. Why didn't I notice that? Why was I so blind?

But it was too late to dissect the past, to dream of doing things differently. Charlotte-Anne had been tragically killed. She was gone forever, and what Elizabeth-Anne had to do was keep alive the good memories.

Eventually, she knew, she would come to terms with Charlotte-Anne's death. But she also knew she would never understand what the di Fontanesis had done. Nor would she find it in her heart to forgive them.

How could they have given the child away? And for food? Did they think they were the only ones on the point of starvation? Only the arrival of the Allies and their dispensing of rations had kept all of Italy from starvation. But it was love which, despite the scarcity of sustenance and the preponderance of disease, had sustained families and held them together. Perhaps—she dared think—perhaps Anna was better off without such loveless people as the Principessa Marcella and her husband.

Still, she would never be able to come to terms with the fact that Anna was missing. Death was final. Sooner or later, everyone had to die. A grave, at least, was tangible. But a disappearance? No, that was one thing that was truly unacceptable. Not knowing what had happened to Anna would forever gnaw at her. But for now she had to accept defeat, accept the fact that no matter how much effort and money she continued to expend, the child would never be found. She could only pray that whoever had gotten her would lavish all the love in the world on her.

Yes, it was indeed time they all went back home and picked up the shattered pieces of their lives. Janet and Zaccheus' son, Henry, was in the States with the governess, waiting for their return. It was time to concentrate on the here and now, on the living. It was time to take stock and count their blessings.

Wordlessly Elizabeth-Anne moved over beside Janet and picked up a blouse. She folded it carefully, the tears sparkling in her eyes.

The war was over, but the suffering would continue for a long time. But eventually it would be dilute, become more bearable, leaving only memories and sharp little jabs of pain in its wake.

Life had to go on. But that didn't mean that the good memories had to be stifled. She had to open her mind to them, welcome them to fill her, and permit herself to have a good cry.

Despite the tragedies that had occurred, the love for her dead daughter and missing granddaughter did not have to die. In her, the love could thrive as potently as if she were still with them.

And that, she thought, was the key to survival.

But still, she knew there would be those countless days when the nagging thought would creep into her consciousness and wedge there, refusing to budge:

What on earth had happened to Anna?

LOVE-MAKERS

III

Anna

ROME, ITALY
❧

May 22, 1964

1

It was forty minutes past ten by the time the all-too-familiar bus crossed the Cestio Bridge to the far bank of the Tiber. The Roman sky was a sea of calm blue, with a regatta of fleeting gold-tipped clouds sailing across it. But Anna Viganò felt anything but calm.

Of all days to be late! she moaned to herself. Of all days for her brand-new Vespa one-cylinder scooter to break down! She had saved so long, hoarding money she could ill-afford to put aside, hoping the scooter would be a way to avoid the infuriating snail-paced morning rush-hour traffic. And for a while it had. But then, today, the most important day of her life, it had suddenly and mysteriously died. She had tried to get the scooter fixed, but after waiting for the mechanic for an hour, he had pronounced the problem hopeless.

And now she might miss the opportunity she had waited so long for. Her chance to be the one handpicked employee of the Hale Roma sent to the company's management training school in New York and thereby become an assistant manager. It was the opportunity of a lifetime.

Glancing out the window, she saw the bus was finally nearing her destination and pulled the cable to request a stop. As she went to the front of the bus, she snapped at a man who got in her way. How unlike her! She must get control of her nerves. Usually she was the very picture of politeness. Her job required it. It was up to her to smooth over rough edges, to wipe away any irritants in the hotel guests' lives. And she was certainly used to the hustle and bustle of Roman crowds. Having lived here for all but three years of her life, she had had plenty of time to develop patience.

Apologizing to the man with a pleasant smile, Anna got off the bus and hurried down the sidewalk. Time was of the essence. The manager would have a fit if he saw her come in at this hour. Even if someone had tried to cover for her, he had surely found out by now that she hadn't been in yet.

She cringed, just thinking of him. He was a pompous martinet who moved with the speed of lightning and the stealth of a spider. He seemed to be everywhere at once. Nobody had the keen ears and reptilian eyes of Romeo Corvi. Although he was leaving his late forties behind, he certainly didn't show it. All sleekly groomed, with a slightly disdainful, slightly unctuous air, he acted as though he should be behind the counter of Van Cleef or Cartier. She shuddered, thinking of his thick black hair combed straight back and his irritating habit of cocking one dark eyebrow to immense heights while he surveyed one with a look of total contempt. After all she'd been through that morning, having a confrontation with Corvi was something she did not relish.

With that thought, she hurried toward the huge square-block building with its pedimented windows set behind classical colonnaded balconies. On the sloping roof facing her were large gold letters facing outward announcing her destination: HALE ROMA.

Even before she reached the hotel she saw the long line of taxis queued up waiting for the day's before-noon checkouts. As she went by, she pointedly kept her gaze fixed on the pavement directly in front of her, to avoid the cabbies' glances. Nevertheless, she heard an appreciative wolf whistle, which only made her speed up, her heels clickety-clacking a swift staccato rhythm on the pavement.

She fairly flew past the main entrance with its wide red-carpeted steps and gleaming glass-and-brass doors, her destination the employees' entrance around the corner in the cobblestoned side alley. As she neared it, she had no choice but to slow down because of the uneven cobblestones. Her mind only half on the treacherous alley, she lectured herself intently:

Whatever happened today, no matter *what*, she mustn't put her job in jeopardy.

If Romeo Corvi raised a stink about her coming in so late, then she must take his tongue-lashing in silence, be very humble, and above all, *not talk back*.

She mustn't do what she had been tempted to do on a thousand other occasions and what every employee in his secret fantasies dreamed of doing, too: she could not put her hands around that haughty thin neck of his and squeeze the last bit of breath out of him.

Today, of all days, she had to tread carefully. Not only because of the chance of being picked to attend the management training school; even without that, this job was too important to her. Getting it in the first place had been a miracle. It had taken considerable connections. When the Hale Roma had opened a year and a half previously, jobs there had been at a premium. The salaries were high in comparison with those of other hotels, and advancement opportunities were said to be excellent, because everyone had to start from the ground up. Thousands had applied for the jobs, and thousands had been turned away. Only two hundred lucky Romans found employment, and she had been one of them.

Her influential cousin Fabio, who had his fingers in many pies, had been responsible for getting her the initial job interview. But all even he had been able to do was open the door. The rest had been up to her. She'd landed the job and then sailed on with flying colors. In the year and a half she'd been at the hotel, she'd proved her worth time and again, swiftly getting promoted from monotonous hours spent typing in one of the tiny cubicles on the second floor to helping all around: manning the reception desk when things got particularly hectic, filling in for the public-relations manager when she had come down with appendicitis, soothing a hysterical guest and aiding in the tracking down of a lost earring, guiding women to boutiques where silk scarves were to be had at bargain prices or to cobblers who custom-made shoes in three days, finding a suitable baby-sitter for a couple who wanted to leave their child behind while enjoying a night on the town, and searching the city for the one *farmacia* that could fill a guest's rare and necessary medical prescription. And throughout it all, she was always friendly, polite, eager, and patient. She bedazzled all with her ever-present smile, was dependable and went out of her way to be helpful. She made herself indispensable by creating a job for herself where none had existed before; she was an unofficial jack of all trades, summoned whenever there was a need, and she was well-liked and respected by everyone, staff and guests alike.

Everyone except Romeo Corvi.

Just thinking of him was enough to bring her blood to a boil. He looked for fault with everything she did, and she had finally discovered why. She was too naive to have realized it herself, but after someone else had mentioned it, she realized the problem. She was altogether too efficient, and in too many areas. He was afraid that she was ultimately more qualified for his job than he was.

But just as she knew she wasn't one to steal his job, she also recognized there was no way to convince him of that. Confronting him on the issue would only confirm his worst paranoia. It was a no-win situation.

Office politics. *How she hated them.*

Two weeks ago, her troubles with Romeo Corvi had come to an explosive head. The New York headquarters of Hale Hotels had just sent word that the Hale Roma was to submit a list of the ten brightest employees. Each was to be interviewed by an executive officer from New York for a future opening as assistant manager, either in Rome or at the Hale Milano, now under construction. Besides earning regular pay, the chosen candidate would receive an all-expense-paid trip to

New York to take part in the Hale Hotels management training course.

Anna knew that it was the opportunity of a lifetime. Money had always been a problem, and she was determined to overcome it by working her way up through the complicated hierarchy of a major business. She was sure sheer hard work and dedication would take her where she wanted to go. From the beginning, she had faced her qualifications with brutal candor. She had taken stock of her advantages and disadvantages, and knew she had more things going against her than for her. Her education was adequate, but she had only attended public schools. She was young, a woman, and, worst of all, far too attractive for her own good.

At almost twenty, she was possessed of a beauty pronounced and startling. She stood nearly six feet tall in her stocking feet. Her wheat-gold hair was straight, cut to shoulder length in an attractive but no-nonsense style that bounced with her free stride. Her skin was smooth, pale butterscotch in color, and her eyes were arrestingly blue, too deep for aquamarine, too light for sea blue. She had a small waist, generous hips, and long, powerful legs. She exuded health. She strode swiftly, with an economy of movement, as though there was a purpose to her every step. She was a woman in the midst of a man's world, and she was determined to prove her worth. The chance to attend the management training course was manna from heaven.

She'd expected her name to head the list of candidates. In all fairness, it should have. Everyone agreed that she knew the overall workings of the Hale Roma better even than the current assistant manager.

That she had managed to look over the list of candidates had been a total fluke. As luck would have it, Corvi's personal secretary, Gabriella Di Donato, had been out sick. The girl who filled in for her was new and didn't know how to operate the telex machine. She'd asked Anna for help.

"Don't worry about it," Anna had offered. "I'll send it."

She sat down in front of the machine with the typewritten message. The moment she saw that it was the list of candidates, her heart seemed to stop dead.

Her name was not even on it.

Romeo Corvi had seen to that.

She'd been on the verge of tears, when the idea occurred to her. Since *she* was sending the telex, she would simply include herself on the list. The only problem was, New York had specifically asked for a list of ten names. Not eleven. And there were already ten names listed.

She'd sat for a moment, deep in thought, having pangs of conscience about whom to scratch. Then she noticed the seventh name, and she breathed a lot easier. Maurizio Corvi was Romeo's younger brother, who, thanks to nepotism, had only weeks earlier been given his job over many more qualified applicants.

It was no contest. She struck Maurizio from the list and put herself on it instead. After she sent the telex, she filed the copy and waited for Corvi's explosion. Sooner or later it was bound to come, as it was only a matter of time before he would find out what she had done. Her only satisfaction was that it was a *fait accompli*. He would be able to do nothing to change things. Except fire her. If he threatened that, she'd have to be slippery as an eel and wiggle out of it somehow.

Last week, a telex reply had chattered in over the wires from the New York headquarters. It gave the arrival date of the Hale Hotels representative, as well as a list confirming the names of the candidates who should be ready for interviews. Romeo Corvi had been apoplectic with rage. Only his brittle, self-important dignity had kept him from calling her a thousand choice epithets. He had gone so far as to threaten to fire her, but she had wisely pointed out to him that that would look awfully peculiar. After all, one didn't fire an employee who, only a week earlier, had been in such good standing as to deserve a place on the list. He'd gone purple with fury, trembling visibly while he fought to keep his anger in check. Then, after a stern warning, he had stormed off, his chest puffed out, his head held high and tilted back.

She shuddered every time she thought about how close she had come to getting fired. If she had been, there would have been nothing anyone, not even Fabio, could have done to help. Not that she would want any more of Fabio Pegrone's help. Not ever again.

Her hatred for cousin Fabio was second only to her detestation of Romeo Corvi. Ever since she could remember, all she had ever heard was, "We have our cousin Fabio to thank for this," "We have our cousin Fabio to thank for that." Sometimes Anna thought she would scream if she heard another word about having to be grateful to Fabio. Gratitude and niceness, in his case, meant letting him walk all over you.

Fabio Pegrone was a distant cousin on Anna's father's side, and the two men had never been close. Her father came from the poor branch of the Viganò family, while Fabio hailed from the rich Pegrone branch. When Anna had turned three and the Viganòs had come to Rome from Campania, her father had sought out Fabio for help. He'd been given a job in Fabio's construction firm doing mean, manual, back-breaking labor. Her father had never been heard to utter a single complaint, not even on the day he dropped dead of a heart attack.

Nor had her mother ever complained. Not once in all these difficult years.

Ever since arriving in Rome, they had lived in one of Fabio's tenement buildings. For that, her mother always said, they'd had to be extremely grateful. Inexpensive housing was difficult to find, and if Cousin Fabio hadn't let them have the apartment, they would have had to live on the streets.

Only when Anna was old enough to understand the difference between the tenements Fabio owned and the lavish penthouse duplex in the exclusive Parioli district where he and his family lived did the injustice of it all make an ugly, lasting impression. She felt ever more rankled by the lavishness of Fabio Pegrone's life-style, which he maintained by squeezing every last lira out of his tenants. In winter the apartments had little or no heat. Boilers broke down constantly and were not repaired for months. Toilets got clogged and stayed that way for weeks. Rats roamed the dark hallways, biting babies and spreading disease, while cockroaches skittered around the floors and inside the walls. Anna grew to hate the ever-present smells of cooking intermingling with the stench of garbage, the lack of fresh air and light, the squalling of babies, and the huge families crammed into one or two miniscule rooms. When she was seven, and first learned to read, one of the first things she deciphered was the graffiti scratched deep into the walls and doors of Fabio Pegrone's tenements: Pegrone the pig.

She was ashamed to be related to him. And even more ashamed to let anyone know where she lived.

What pained her the most was that when her father died just after she had turned eight years old, her mother had had to take in the Pegrones' laundry in order to make ends meet. The little Adriana Viganò earned seemed to jump right back into Fabio's pockets. It was a vicious cycle, and there was no avenue of escape. Dario was too young to get anything but erratic, low-paying jobs, so it was the laundry that kept the family going. Over and over her mother reiterated that they had to be grateful to Cousin Fabio for letting her do it. Otherwise, they would starve.

Money—or rather the lack of it—was the specter which haunted them ceaselessly. How often had Anna wondered: If she had a lira for every single rat, mouse, and cockroach she saw, how rich would they be? But that was an idle speculation conjured up by anger and helplessness, emotions fed by the continuing injustices she saw as she grew up. The rent for the tenement was often raised without warning. Behind their mother's back, Anna and Dario often went to see Cousin Fabio about it, but all the pleading in the world never did them a bit of good. He sent them to his manager, who insisted they were entitled to no favors just because they were distant relatives of Signor Pegrone.

Somehow, miraculously, they survived. When Dario was old enough, he left home to study to become a priest. It was their mother's fondest dream that he do so, and she refused to even consider that he work to support them instead. At least it was easier with him gone, as there was one less mouth to feed. But Adriana's health was fast eroding, and she found it more and more difficult to do laundry. Anna's job at the Hale Roma literally saved them. It paid far from a splendid wage, but finally set things on an even keel. She continued to live at home in order to help stretch the income; every week, she handed her paycheck over to her mother. She knew it was up to her to give her mother the financial support that had been lacking in the household for so long.

And so it was that her ambition was fueled. Not by greed, but by the lack of basic necessities they had suffered for so long.

If I'm the one who is chosen to go to New York to take the management training course, and if I become assistant manager at a princely salary, then we can finally get out from under Cousin Fabio's thumb once and for all. Then I can finally chase away the bleak ghosts of hunger and wretched despair.

Oh, but everything depended on so many ifs. And there was still never enough money to go around, she thought despairingly.

Sometimes she was under the impression that no matter how hard she worked, it was still futile, as if there was a bottomless drain in the house down which every last precious lira swirled. Not that her mother wasn't careful. Far from it. Adriana Viganò scrimped and saved every last lira till it bled. She mended old clothes, and when they started to fall apart, mended them all over again. She haggled for groceries and bought day-old loaves of bread. But the years of poverty had taken their toll, and now Adriana had fallen ill. Doctors were expensive; specialists even more so. And then, a year ago, just before Anna had started work at the Hale Roma, she herself had had to be hospitalized. All because of Amedeo Battistello.

And the way she had fallen for him.

2

Amedeo.

It had been two years now since she had met him. God, how she had come to hate him! But she hadn't hated him in the beginning. He had dazzled her, and she had fallen head over heels in love with him.

She had been seventeen years old at the time and just finishing her last year of school. It was one of those chance. meetings that could never have been arranged. Every afternoon, when school was over, she would take the bus to Parioli and pick up a bag of the Pegrones' laundry. Every morning, on her way to school, she would drop off the finished laundry, which had been washed, dried, and carefully pressed, then packaged in brown wrapping paper and tied with twine. "As professional-looking as any expensive laundry's," Adriana would say proudly.

Anna had to get up very early to get the deliveries done on time, because the tenement was located far from the exclusive district which was a favorite with industrialists, film stars, diplomats, and the likes of Cousin Fabio. One morning, after she had dropped off the laundry, she rushed out of Cousin Fabio's building, afraid she was running late, and collided with a tall, handsome stranger.

"You're in a terrible hurry," he said, grabbing her by the arms to keep her from falling.

"I . . . I'm sorry, signor," she said hastily, lowering her eyes.

"It is I who should be sorry." He smiled then. "Or perhaps not. It isn't every day that a man encounters such a beautiful young lady."

She stared at him for a second or two, caught off guard by his flashing eyes and the touch of his hands. He was young, tall and broad, and his dark, well-cut suit and white silk shirt were custom tailored. The striped black and tawny yellow tie matched his dark hair and predatory cat's eyes. His nose was prominent, and his lips were soft, sensuous. His gaze and touch set off warning bells in her head, and she quickly pulled away from him and began hurrying down the sidewalk. She heard quick footsteps behind her, and then he was at her side again, easily falling in step with her long-legged stride. He smiled at her. "I have a car. Can I give you a lift?"

She shook her head and kept her eyes riveted on the sidewalk in front of her.

"We should be friends," he said equably. "I mean, we

are, after all, practically acquainted, aren't we? Bumping into each other like that?''

She stopped walking and turned to face him. He was grinning, his teeth perfect and white against his swarthy tan. Off to one side of his upper lip he had a tiny frecklelike mole, odd and dashing. His skin was stretched tautly across his high, almost Slavic cheekbones, and his eyes seemed to reach out into hers, and she felt her mind go blank, then spin with wild thoughts.

He seemed cultured and cultivated but exuded an air of peril and adventure. Although he looked to be in his early thirties, he had an irresistibly easy, boyish charm about him.

"I have to go," she said with sudden vehemence, jerking herself back from that mesmeric countenance. "I'm late."

"Wait." He caught her arm. "I don't even know your name."

She took a deep breath. She could feel the pulse in her temples, the slight clamminess of her hands. He was so close that his face was mere inches from her own. She could smell the sweet perfume of expensive soap and the even more expensive, crisply masculine fragrance of eau de cologne, but she never felt his fingers on the thin tan sweater she wore draped over her shoulders as he tugged loose one of the brass buttons. While he held her gaze, he slipped it into his pocket.

"Really, I must go," she said finally, almost sadly. As she walked away, her low heels clacked an ever-quickening beat until she was half-running. When she rounded the corner she stole a glance over her shoulder. He wasn't trying to follow. She slowed down and let out a breath of relief.

And felt curiously disappointed.

That afternoon, when school let out, she returned to Cousin Fabio's building to pick up the day's bag of dirty laundry. She kept her eyes peeled for the stranger, but he was nowhere to be seen. Again, she felt let down somehow.

That night, lying in the narrow bed in her tiny, humid room, she stared up at the ceiling for what seemed like an eternity. She had trouble going to sleep, but she had no trouble imagining those hypnotic eyes burning into hers, the tiny mole near the corner of his mouth, and those white-white teeth gleaming in the dark. She found herself fantasizing about him until she finally fell into a deep, dreamless sleep.

By morning, she had all but forgotten him. But after she dropped off the Pegrones' laundry and left Cousin Fabio's building to head for school, there he was, leaning nonchalantly against the downstairs door, a crooked grin on his face. He held up a hand, and a brass button caught the sunlight and glinted brightly.

"Oh, you found it!" she cried with delight. "I was wondering where I'd lost it." As she reached out for it, he playfully held it beyond her reach.

"You can have it on one condition."

She looked at him wordlessly.

"You'll come and have an espresso with me."

And so it began.

Amedeo Battistello. How easy it had been to fall for him! He was so unlike any of the young men in her mean, tenement-strewn neighborhood. He was sophisticated, wore well-tailored clothes, and always seemed to have a crocodile wallet full of money. He drove an expensive little Alfa Romeo convertible while the boys in her neighborhood just dreamed of owning cars. They struggled to hold onto low-paying, menial jobs while he worked for his uncle, a producer at Cinecittà, Italy's answer to Hollywood. The boys in her neighborhood had their fun, but were expected to find a nice girl, get married, and have children. Building a family was one of the few things Amedeo never seemed keen to discuss. The one thing he did have in common with the young men around whom she had grown up was that peculiar, hungry look in his eyes.

She found herself rearranging her schedule in order to meet him. She started leaving her books at home and hiding the Pegrones' laundry in her school satchel. She never told Amedeo who she was and he took it for granted that she lived in Cousin Fabio's building. She lied about her age and claimed to have a job. She liked the fantasy of being someone other than poor Anna Viganò, the daughter of a widowed laundress. It was, after all, a harmless deception. Nobody could get hurt by it. Could they?

At first Amedeo took her to sidewalk cafés for espresso and

cake or a cool glass of wine, usually on the Via Sistina, which passed by the top of the Spanish Steps. They sat in the piazzas, walked along the Tiber, or tore recklessly around Rome with the convertible top down. He took her far from the cloying smells of greasy cooking and the infestations of rats. He was glamour and wealth personified, and seemed part of another, more beguiling world. She believed implicitly that he was the most exciting man alive.

Then he told her that he wanted to take her home. But because he lived in the building next to hers, he instead took her to the Hotel Hassler, atop the Spanish Steps. It was there that she lost her virginity.

When he'd signed them in at the reception desk of the Hassler for the first time, the desk clerk had looked at the scrawled registry, smiled politely, and called her "Signora Battistello." She'd blushed proudly, pleased as a genuine newlywed that anyone would even consider that she, Anna Viganò, could belong to someone as extraordinarily handsome and rich as Amedeo Battistello. How many times during the past few weeks had she tested the name Battistello silently on her tongue, savoring the mere sound of it?

But then, everything about Amedeo was wonderful. He brought out a radiant glow in her which seemed to change her entirely. She had always looked mature for her age, but now she seemed positively sophisticated. At first she had been afraid to make love, but with Amedeo it was anything but the lascivious, purposeful copulation about which coarse jokes were constantly bandied about in the tenements. How often, on hot, humid summer nights, with her window open, had she unavoidably heard the grunts and groans coming from the other windows facing the courtyard? But it was never like that with Amedeo. His lovemaking was a graceful, tender ballet full of passion and promise.

That first time, he had led her upstairs slowly, then whispered her name and taken her in his arms. The door was locked and the shutters closed, so that the late-afternoon sunlight streamed through the slants into the semidarkness. She had watched his every move, her heart hammering with excitement while a terrible fear gnawed into the flesh inside her belly. This was her first time, and she knew it was wrong to be with a man like this before she was married.

But the man was Amedeo. How could it be wrong? Theirs was a love so powerful that *nothing* else mattered.

As his strong arms held her, any hesitation she had left evaporated, seemed to drain visibly out of her. Her lips trembled, dry with a mixture of anticipation and dread. She'd heard the stories of how much it hurt the first time, but Amedeo was so kind and gentle and loving, she couldn't believe the stories were true.

He bowed his head to the side of her neck, his lips forming a gentle little kiss, a whisper of desire. His hands caressed her arms and breasts, then coursed down her sides to her thighs. Through her thin cotton dress she could feel his touch tingling across her flesh. She swallowed, shut her eyes, her lips parting. She was unable to resist the surge of passion she felt when she savored the fact that he, Amedeo Battistello, was doing these things to her, bringing such a prickling, intense heat to her body and an ache to her soul.

Slowly, almost reverentially, he unfastened the buttons at the back of her dress and then parted the fabric and pushed it down off her shoulders. It glided, whispering softly, down to her ankles. She stood in silence, her cheap, coarse slip out of place in the soft luxury of the room.

"Anna. Anna." His lips were at her neck again, his tongue flicking moist, warm little circles against her skin. She felt his fingers stroking her shoulders, brushing at the nape of her neck, coiling her long blond hair around them.

"Anna." His voice was a bare ghost of breath as he pressed himself, still fully clothed, against her half-clothed body. She could feel the quickening of his heartbeats merging with her own. She inhaled the intoxicating aroma of his eau de cologne mingling with the ever stronger, more tangible masculine smell of him.

"Anna."

She trembled as he held her face in his hands, kissed her deeply, then paused, to slip out of an item of clothing before kissing her again and helping her shed another piece of her clothing. Finally they stood naked, facing each other.

She averted her gaze in embarrassment, but he took her face back in both hands and whispered, "It is beautiful. Don't be ashamed."

She still could not face him.

"*Look at me*," he commanded sharply.

She forced herself to do so, tears sparkling in her eyes.

"Look," he whispered more gently as he took two steps backward, as straight-backed and proud as a dancer.

As though hypnotized, her eyes swept from his face downward. He was well-muscled, but thin and wiry, and it surprised her. When he was clothed, he seemed broad because of his wide shoulders. He was tanned all over, except for a thin white bathing-suit line; by contrast, her own body was sadly pale. His chest was curly with wiry coils of black hair, making it seem even darker, and the pelt reached down his belly and gathered force at the thicket in his groin. His penis was large and superb, hard and dark red.

"*Anna.*" His voice was a whisper that roared in her ears. She lifted her gaze and stared straight into his eyes. He stepped forward and pulled her into his arms, pressing her fully against his nakedness. His body felt so warm and hard, so unyielding and different from her own. And oh, how the touch of his flesh seemed to sear into hers.

She felt his hot tongue exploring her mouth, filling her with warmth and wild abandon as his penis pressed hotly against her belly. Her nipples grew erect, aching for his hands and his lips, longing for him to take her.

He placed one hand under each of her buttocks, lifted her and carried her effortlessly over to the bed. He laid her down gently, as though afraid she might break, and crawled atop her. His thumbs and forefingers kneaded her nipples while his lips and tongue caressed every inch of her body, bringing the surface of her skin to tingling, vibrating life.

She arched her body and sighed a breathy kind of moan as he began to enter her. Instinctively she clamped her muscles together against the unfamiliar intrusion, but then she began to experiment, to open herself up for him, to welcome him into her most private and precious place. Her eyes stared up at him, wide and luminous.

He pressed his erection more deeply against her, sending little shock waves down her spine, until he met the obstruction of her hymen. He stopped and looked at her in surprise. "You're . . . a virgin?" he asked.

"Go ahead," she whispered, smiling faintly. "I want it. I want you." She reached up with her fingers to stroke his cheek.

He prodded at her twice, but her hymen was unyielding. She tensed in anticipation, and with a hard, brutal thrust he tore into her. Pain exploded in front of her eyes, a searing fireball red in the center and flaring outward into ragged yellow circles. But the starburst gradually faded, and Amedeo transformed it to white-hot desire.

She found herself instinctively raising her hips and working her torso in a purposeful rhythm to meet his own. Her pelvis rose and swayed against him, bringing delicious waves of burning pleasure. She drew her legs up, bending her knees and opening herself wide.

He thrust deeply into her then, drawing out each stroke at an ever-quickening pace so that she sucked in her breath, swallowing the exclamations of surprise as wave after heated wave engulfed her. This was an explosion, a coming *alive* she had never even dreamed of before. She was enveloped in wanting and lust, in hotness and pulsing. For this, she knew, she had been born, just as in every massive thrust there was a little death.

Suddenly he gave a sharp cry. His body arched, and she felt him lunging yet deeper into her as he clutched her and filled her with a throbbing explosion. His head swooped back, his eyes pressed shut, and he jerked uncontrollably.

Both their bodies were coated with a veneer of sweat. He sprawled panting atop her, his breath labored and his penis small. She felt as though her mysterious insides had survived a most delicious assault. The room was dimmer. The glowing, horizontal zebra stripes cast by the shutters had disappeared as outside a cloud scudded in front of the setting sun. Even now that it was over, their thumping heartbeats seemed synchronized.

From somewhere below on the Spanish Steps drifted the faint, muted sound of lovers laughing.

That first time was like no other. It was a time when the joy of discovery and exploration was as intense as the burning of their passions and desires. It was the moment she had stepped over the threshold into womanhood.

Everything had been so beautiful, so filled with pleasure, so softly clean as they lay on the freshly laundered sheets in the late-afternoon sun. She had never even given a thought to pregnancy, then or in the months that followed. She didn't want to spoil what they shared by even thinking about it. Naturally, she had heard whispers about prophylactics. Even if the church forbade their use, they were available. She had never seen one and the only time she had mentioned it, Amedeo had scowled and said he didn't like using them. And besides, who could give a thought to consequences in the midst of such delicious, overwhelming ecstasy?

After that first time, they had met regularly twice a week, always at the Hassler Hotel, and it was on one of those eight heady occasions that their baby was conceived.

She told him about it on a bleak day of thin light and steady rainfall. She had battled with her emotions for weeks, unable to come to terms with her pregnancy or even to tell him about it. Every time she had tried, she lost her courage and instead tried to forget in yet another afternoon of passion.

She was afraid. It was as though by telling him she would be confirming her condition to herself. She knew that the longer she waited, the more irreversible the situation became. But what would it matter? It was irreversible as it was.

Already her mother had noticed that she was putting on weight; Amedeo had too. Twice he'd jokingly called it her "baby fat."

Poor Amedeo, she thought. And poor Mother. If they only knew the truth. She realized that sooner or later she would have to tell them both, and the very idea filled her with terror. She would have preferred to hole up somewhere and die.

On the fateful afternoon when she'd finally broken the

news to him, they had made love as usual. Afterward, when they lay in silence in the dim room, she had stared up at the ceiling with blind eyes. "Amedeo," she had finally said in a soft, frightened whisper.

"Yes?"

She took a deep breath and closed her eyes. "I'm pregnant."

The announcement had all the impact of an explosion. He sat up as though he'd gotten a sizzling jolt of electricity. *"What?"* He stared at her.

She nodded and bit down on her lip. "Don't be angry," she pleaded huskily, turning to him. "Please. I'm scared." She reached out to hold his hand, but he was poking around on the nightstand for a cigarette. She watched tensely as he fumbled with a match and lit the cigarette with trembling fingers. He let the smoke out of his mouth and inhaled it into his nose. "How long?" he asked at last.

"I think . . . three months."

He groaned and let himself fall back down on the bed with such force that the box spring shook under the impact. He lay there and smoked on in silence. Finally he stubbed out the cigarette and sighed deeply. "Of course, you'll have to get rid of it."

She froze then, and her whisper sounded strangled. "I . . . I don't understand."

His laugh was unexpected and bitter. "You don't understand?" He turned to her, his eyes cold. "Do I have to spell it out for you? An *abortion.*" His eyes burned into hers. "Now do you understand?"

She struggled to sit up. With one hand she clutched the rumpled sheet against her naked breasts. She began crying softly. "But . . . it's illegal."

"That doesn't mean it can't be done," he said matter-of-factly. "I know plenty of girls who've gotten abortions."

"Plenty of . . . girls." Her voice trailed off. She wondered how many others there had been before her. She had never given that any thought. She was amazed at her own naiveté. Of course she wasn't the first.

Nor would she be the last.

"Sure." He shrugged casually. "They say it doesn't hurt half as much as having a tooth pulled. It's nothing, really."

"Nothing?" She stared at him. "It's killing. It's wrong."

"Having an illegitimate kid isn't wrong?"

"But it doesn't have to be illegitimate," she said. "We could get married."

"*Married*?" he asked in amused disbelief. "You and me? You're joking."

She shook her head wordlessly and turned away.

"Oh, no. I'm not about to marry anybody. I like things just the way they are. And don't try to argue. I'm not going to change my mind."

Her voice was tiny. "I thought you loved me."

He was silent.

"But you told me you did."

"People always say things they don't mean in bed," he said irritably. "I like you. In fact, I like you a lot. You're a lot of fun."

"Fun?" She stared at him. "That's all I am to you? Fun?"

He scowled suddenly. "That's the trouble with women. Sooner or later all of you start nagging." He sat up, swung his legs out over the bed, and reached for his jacket. He dug into the pocket for his wallet, then handed her a sheaf of lira notes. "The last time, it cost me twenty thousand. Here it is. This should take care of it."

She made no move to take it, and he threw the money at her. It fluttered all around her like confetti. "Arrange to get rid of it," he said grimly. "I don't want to hear another word about it."

"But . . . where do I go?"

"How should I know? I'm not a woman. Ask around."

"Amedeo," she whispered. "I want to have your baby."

"Well, I don't want you to," he snapped. He started getting dressed.

"Amedeo. Please. Don't be angry."

He ignored her. "Why didn't you tell me before? Why did you have to wait three months?"

"Because," she replied truthfully, "I was afraid that when I told you, you wouldn't want me anymore."

His face was cold and expressionless as he buckled his belt.

"Amedeo . . ." She tried to catch his arm, but he was already on his way to the door.

When he reached it, he turned around. "*Get rid of it*," he repeated bitterly. "None of you ever learn, do you? You all think that when you become pregnant, I'll marry you." Then he left, slamming the door behind him. Even across the room she could feel the powerful gust of wind it created.

She sat hunched over, her body and soul aching. She knew she would never see him again. Strangely enough, she no longer felt frightened. It was as though a load had been taken off her shoulders.

She stared down at the money. In a sudden rage she began throwing the notes off the bed. She didn't want his money. She didn't want anything of his anymore.

After a while she dried her eyes and got dressed. She looked in the mirror, hardly recognizing the pale, tear-streaked countenance that stared disconsolately back at her. Slowly she tied her scarf around her head.

Once she got outside, she didn't bother waiting for the rain to subside. As though sleep walking, she trudged over to the front of Trinità dei Monti, the church with its twin bell spires which stood at the top of the Spanish Steps. They were deserted. The rain had chased the hordes of tourists indoors.

She smoothed her belly with her palms, then again wiped the tears from her eyes as she descended the steps. She was moving quickly, starting to feel she wanted to flee, get as far away from Amedeo and all that had happened as quickly as she could. Almost blinded by her tears and the heavy rain, she half-ran down the steps, then suddenly felt her heel slip on the rain-slicked surface.

She screamed as she fell heavily, then somersaulted down the first flight. The stone tore at her skin, battered her bones, and scored her face with its abrasive edges. When she finally tumbled onto the landing, she lay deathly still. Then she was seized by a bolt of white-hot pain in her uterus, and with a scream she curled up and clutched her belly.

*   *   *

In the hospital, the doctor told her she was lucky to be alive, but had unfortunately lost the baby. In addition, he explained, it would now be dangerous for her ever to carry another child. Too much within her uterus had been damaged by the fall. She would probably not survive another pregnancy.

She had closed her eyes, covered her face with her hands, and wept.

She had given Amedeo everything, and he no longer wanted her. She had offered up all of her love with her virginity. Because of him, she would never be able to have a baby. If she did, she would die.

She shut her eyes and sobbed. Even when Adriana came to comfort her, soothing her and telling her that there was no shame, none at all, Anna barely listened. The hatred for him burned terribly within her.

Amedeo.

How she despised him.

3

During the morning shift, Mirella Brino was in charge of the reception desk. The moment she saw Anna hurrying purposefully through the cool, cavernous marble lobby with its wall-to-wall cabbage-rose carpeting, she left her post and cut her off halfway. "Careful," Mirella murmured under her breath as she glanced around. "Corvi's on the warpath. We tried to cover for you, but . . ." She shrugged her shoulders expressively without finishing the sentence.

Anna smiled. "Thanks anyway," she said, giving Mirella's arm a squeeze.

Mirella nodded. "By the way, the Hale representative is here for the management-training-course interviews. They're being held upstairs in the Amalfi Suite."

"What time's mine?"

Mirella tightened her lips across her teeth. "It was the first one scheduled for this morning. When Corvi found out you hadn't come in on time, he juggled the schedule just to make sure you'd miss yours. The bastard."

Anna's heart sank as though weighted suddenly with lead. "Well, I might as well go upstairs and see what I can do. Maybe I can get interviewed later."

"Maybe."

There was something in Mirella's tone that set off the warning bell in Anna's mind. "Why 'maybe?' "

Mirella shook her head woefully. "How come it's always up to me to tell you these things?"

"Mirella, what *is* it?"

"Corvi took the opportunity of substituting his brother in your place."

"Maurizio?" Anna stared at her. "You've got to be kidding!"

"I only wish I were."

"Well, it's worth a try, anyway." Anna squared her shoulders.

"By the way, guess who they sent over to do the interviews?" Mirella's eyes gleamed with secret knowledge.

"Who?"

"Henry Hale. The second in command of the company, would you believe?" Her face held a dreamy expression. "He's so handsome. And so young! They say he's a genius," she sighed. "I think he's just my type. And he isn't wearing a wedding band. I made sure to check."

Despite herself, Anna had to laugh. "You're incorrigible, Mirella! Anything in pants is your type, or haven't you noticed?"

"When you get to be thirty and you're still single, you take what comes," Mirella said morosely. "Anyway, watch out. He's a cold fish. When I met Signor Hale I smiled, fluttered my lashes, and laid on the charm nice and thick. But to no avail." She sighed again. "He's made of stone, apparently. Or maybe I'm slipping."

Anna clapped her friend affectionately on the arm. "Don't worry, Mirella. It won't be long before some man discovers your charms, and you'll sweep him off his feet. If it's not because of your looks, it'll be because of your cooking.''

"Sure," Mirella said, with a weary smile.

Anna took a deep breath. She glanced over her shoulder at the brass-doored elevators. "Well, I've wasted enough time. I'd better get on upstairs. Wish me luck?''

Mirella held up both hands and crossed her fingers. Anna returned the signal. Usually it inspired confidence, but today was one day when she was afraid her luck had run out.

"*Maurizio,*" she swore angrily under her breath. "If he gets sent to New York, I'll break his legs first. I deserve to go, and so does nearly everyone else. But Romeo Corvi's snide little brother? He can't do anything right, but it never seems to matter.''

And with that bitter thought, she strode rapidly past the yawning elevator doors and stabbed the buttom marked "ten."

On the tenth floor, Henry Hale tried to concentrate on the matters at hand, but his mind was wandering. Luxurious though it was, the Amalfi Suite was merely an extension of his New York office. He looked puffy and tired under his clean shave, but he managed to smile reassuringly at the sixth interviewee for the management training course, who was being shown out. Then he told Romeo Corvi to hold off for fifteen minutes before showing in the next one.

When he was alone at long last, he got up from the gold-brocade couch and poured himself a much-needed golden jigger of Johnnie Walker Red. He carried the cut-crystal glass out onto the terrace and surveyed the terra-cotta rooftops of the Eternal City.

He gripped the glass tightly and made a throaty sound of exasperation. He felt both worn down and annoyed. He was long since used to the psychic and physical strains of overloaded work schedules and bone-wearying globe-hopping, so that wasn't the cause of his boiling anger. As a Hale, he knew it was expected of him. Sadly he thought of his parents, who had died in a car accident two years before. He missed them still. He had been raised by a doting mother, and much as he loved Janet Hale, he looked to his father and grandmother as his role models.

He had seen little enough of his father; while Henry was growing up, Zaccheus Hale Jr. was an enigma who seemed to be constantly swallowed up by his work, a remarkable achievement considering he was paraplegic. His father had thrown himself wholeheartedly into his short but brilliant career, perhaps to compensate for his physical disability. Maybe because he had known from the start the lifespan of paraplegics was not long. Little had he expected the sudden death that did take him.

His grandmother's obsessive dedication to the business was legendary, and looking to her and his father, Henry had set stern goals for himself as a child.

He had begun working when he was twelve, hanging around the hotel kitchens during summer vacations and doing odd jobs after school in order to acquaint himself with his legacy. For other children, their hometowns were their world; for him it was the major cities of four entire continents. He loved nothing more than to accompany his grandmother on trips around the world, looking after the sprawling, ever-growing empire. As the only Hale heir (his Aunt Regina had never had children), Henry realized at an early age that he was being groomed for a lifetime of work and dedication, and it had always seemed perfectly natural. By the time he turned sixteen, he was already spending seven days a week hard at work, either for school or for the business. By then it had already been several years since he had enjoyed a real vacation. He graduated from Harvard and Harvard Business School in record time, so that at twenty-three he was ready to step into a senior executive position.

Even now, with the coveted crown of being perhaps the youngest-ever vice-president of a major international corporation, sixteen-hour workdays were the rule rather than the exception. As the most eligible of American bachelors, he was only a frustration to women—he never seemed to find time for them. If anyone were to suggest that he slow down, would he laugh? No, he considered, he wouldn't laugh. He would simply not understand why he should, because he took his career seriously and thought nothing of juggling a hundred duties at a time. And the only thing he asked from others was the same steadfast dedication with which he threw himself into even the most minor chore. Unfortunately, he was quickly discovering that in Rome that was asking for the inconceivable.

The orange rooftops shimmered in the heat, a gently undulating sea reaching all around to the base of the Seven Hills of Rome. Though a city of stunning beauty and splendid history, Rome was not, he was realizing, a city where things got done. At times, he was amazed Rome was still standing and populated. Romans were a breed unto themselves, as different from the northern Milanese or the southern Sicilians as Scandinavians were from Arabs. They were immensely proud of being Romans, and did things in their own sweet time, in their own peculiar ways. There was no changing them.

He sighed wearily and pressed his lips together. Today, he decided, was just not his day. But then, yesterday hadn't been much better.

For starters, there had been the flight from New York, which at best was an uneventful and tiring proposition. However, yesterday's Boeing 707 had developed engine trouble halfway across the Atlantic and had had to hobble crippled into the Azores for an emergency landing. The landing, though hairy, had gone off without a hitch, and the relieved passengers had broken out into enthusiastic applause for their pilot. Nonetheless, it had been an emotionally grueling experience. And as a result of the unexpected, hours-long Azores layover, by the time he reached London his connecting flight to Rome had long since taken to the skies, and he'd had to kill four hours before the next flight. That didn't leave quite enough time to head into London from Heathrow, and yet it was too long a wait to sit patiently around the airport doing nothing. Time was money, and four wasted hours added up to a lot of it.

When he finally arrived in Rome, the limousine which was supposed to have met him at Leonardo da Vinci Airport was not there. When he reached the Hale Roma, Romeo Corvi greeted him effusively, practically prostrating himself as he apologized over and over for the inexcusable limousine mix-up. He had personally shown Henry up to the Portofino Suite.

On the surface, everything in the suite looked fine. Corvi had arranged for a hospitality package, containing a bottle of champagne and a huge formal floral bouquet, as well as a fully stocked bar. Henry, however, had thrown Corvi by refusing to stay in the Portofino Suite and insisting upon the less grand Amalfi Suite instead. Elizabeth-Anne had a firm rule that when she or anyone else in the family stayed at a Hale hotel, rooms and suites were to be switched two or three times a day without advance warning. It was irksome to the staff, but a wise practice, as Henry was now finding. Only in this way could the New York executives keep the thousands of far-flung employees on their toes and get a first-hand glimpse of what could possibly go wrong in a room or suite in which they hadn't been expected. So far, in Rome, altogether too much had gone wrong.

When he'd taken a shower, the drain was sluggish and the tub had filled with water.

When he'd switched on one of the nightstand lights, he'd found the bulb was burned out.

He'd tried to call New York, but the switchboard operator, not yet alerted to who was in the Amalfi Suite, had been slow in placing his call.

He sent his suit down to be pressed, and it had been returned to the wrong room and then gotten lost.

All those problems in a suite for which people paid the equivalent of one hundred dollars per day.

Then, to top everything off, after he'd called Corvi on the carpet and told him he wanted these problems alleviated—*pronto*—it had still taken far too long to fix things. When he'd had to complain about the problems a second time, that slimy little bastard had had the gall to tell him that "in Rome, things are different."

Henry's eyes had narrowed into dangerous slits, and Corvi had finally snapped to it. By 4:30 most of the problems had been smoothed over, but the misplaced suit still hadn't been found. Henry began having doubts he would ever see it again. Instead of waiting, he had changed to another suit and then gone to the car dealer's to pick up a new Maserati he had ordered, which he planned to ship on to New York after he left Rome.

When he'd gotten back to the hotel, that oily, unctuous, self-centered Corvi—whom, as every hour passed, Henry could bear less and less—had been constantly trying to suck up to him. For all of Corvi's efforts, even the interviews today had gone far from smoothly. For some reason, the schedule had been rearranged at the last minute, causing no end of confusion. But worst of all, of the four people he'd interviewed already, there hadn't been one he would not have doubts about recommending for the course.

He shook his head and tossed down the last of his drink. He'd need the fortification. He still had six more employees to interview, and he wasn't at all sure he even wanted to go through with it. Romeo Corvi seemed to employ only morons like himself. Everything considered, Henry thought it incredible that the hotel ran as smoothly as it did. It certainly couldn't be due to Corvi or the employees he'd met so far. He'd have to ask around and find out who kept things running from behind the scenes. Whoever it was would have to be complimented . . . even moved into Corvi's position.

One way or another, Romeo Corvi had to be gotten rid of, and the sooner that was done the better off the hotel, and the entire Hale organization, would be. Nor would only he get his walking papers. Maurizio Corvi would too. His had been the single most unbelievably embarrassing interview of all. The identical last names of the two had not been lost on Henry.

A major shake-up was due at the Hale Roma, but Henry knew he would have to wait a few days. Elizabeth-Anne had a firm rule that no one was ever to be fired unless there was a replacement waiting in the wings. Once one was lined up, then management could proceed with the professional insensitivity of a surgeon.

All in all, Henry thought, shaking his head as he went back inside the suite, the Hale Roma reminded him just a little too much of the Hale hotels in Mexico and Hong Kong. There, too, things had been run in a maddeningly slovenly fashion. That is, until Henry had arrived on the scene to put a screeching halt to all that. For the time being, the Azcapotzalco, Cozumel, and Victoria Hales were running at peak efficiency. For a man his age, he had already become a master at shaking things up. But then, troubleshooting was his job, his talent, just as helping to run the most luxurious hotel chain in the world was in his blood.

Henry was about to call for the next interview when his attention was diverted by a loud voice right outside the suite. "What the hell . . ." he muttered aloud as he crossed over to the double doors and threw them open.

A s the elevator had risen higher and higher, so had Anna's adrenaline. By the time she got off on the tenth floor, she had reached a state of rage.

Corvi, that deceitful, disagreeable, disdainful little *shit*. He didn't miss a single opportunity to trip her up. She had *had* it with him. If he thought she would take this latest scheme lying down, he had a surprise coming, the sorry bastard.

She clenched her hands together and took a deep breath, fighting for control. When she got off the elevator she stopped to check her appearance in the ornate mirror hanging above a gilt console in the corridor. She wore little makeup, and the pulsating anger made her face look curiously hard. It was hardly the way she wanted to face anybody for an interview, but it would have to do. Anger alone would give her the nerve to barge in to see Henry Hale.

She marched down the creamy carpet to the white-lacquered door of the Amalfi Suite, then hesitated only a fraction of a second. Tightening her jaw, she raised her clenched hand to knock and then heard a lisping voice that froze her arm in midair.

"What do you think you're doing, Signorina Viganò?"

Anna turned and found Romeo Corvi rushing toward her. She faced him squarely, by instinct spreading her feet in a fighter's stance.

Steady, she warned herself silently as her heart knocked like a triphammer against her rib cage. Don't lose your self-control. He's going to bait you, and you mustn't rise up to it like a starved fish.

She spoke aloud then, trying to make her voice sound too casual. "I was about to see about my interview."

"Your *interview*?" He smiled an ugly smirk which made his lips and thin nostrils look curiously sharklike. "I'm afraid you're *not* scheduled, Signorina Viganò."

She felt the hairs at the nape of her neck beginning to rise. "I'm going in there," she announced quietly but firmly, "and you cannot stop me."

"I wouldn't try it if I were you," he hissed. The smirk was frozen on his lips.

"And why not?"

"Because the moment you step through that door, you will be fired."

She stared into his face, trying to read the seriousness of his threat. Instead, she saw something that surprised her: fear. He was afraid of Henry Hale. The realization struck her with the force of the courage she needed.

"We'll soon see about that," she said coldly. She grabbed the polished brass door handle, but quick as a cobra, his hand struck out and seized hers. She glared into his face, his eau de cologne cloyingly sweet and overpowering at such close range. "I'll trouble you to let me go," she said, her voice hard.

"You are fired, Signorina Viganò," he hissed. "As of this very moment. Go collect your things and leave at once."

Whether determination or sheer fury caused her to act, she would never know. She feigned to loosen her grip, and he let go of her hand. The moment he lifted his fingers, she moved to open the door again, but he grabbed her by the arms and pushed her roughly away.

"Let me . . . *go*," she cried, fighting to reach the door handle again as he held her back. "Let me go, you . . . you *worm*!"

And at that precise instant the door to the suite was flung open from the inside. Both Corvi and Anna froze in the midst of their struggle, twisted their heads around, and stared at the tall, handsome blond man silhouetted in the doorway.

Anna's eyes flashed. For a split second she couldn't take in that it was actually *him*, that this was how she was to meet her interviewer. Then she slumped, and all the fight seeped out of her.

Henry Hale stared at both of them for a long, silent moment. He couldn't believe the display before him, and was at first disgusted by another one of Corvi's tricks. Then he noticed the girl.

What jumped out at him first were her startling cornflower-blue eyes. He had never seen eyes like that—so radiant, so alluring. But then he realized he had never seen anyone quite like her before at all. She was not just the only woman he had ever really noticed; he was certain she was the most beautiful woman on earth.

All this flashed through Henry's mind in an instant, while Anna and Corvi remained frozen in their ridiculous tableau. Then Corvi seemed to realize suddenly that he was still pinning down Anna's arms. He let go of her, his face glowing red with embarrassment. He yanked out his white handkerchief and dabbed at his forehead as Anna began brushing her arms with her fingers, as though trying to rid herself of the remnants of Corvi's crawling touch.

"Would someone like to tell me just what the hell is going on here?" Henry asked.

Corvi spoke first. "This woman insisted on going in to see you unannounced," he said disdainfully in his thickly accented English.

"Indeed?" Henry's eyebrows arched. "And why should she want to do that?"

"Because," Corvi said, raising his chin, "she is a born troublemaker." He punctuated the word "troublemaker" with a quick, birdlike nod, his eyes glaring at Anna.

"Is this true, signorina?" Henry asked, gazing at her.

Her eyes flashed for a moment, and her fingertips froze in the midst of brushing her arms. "That's a matter of opinion," she answered with all the dignity she could muster.

Henry raised his eyebrows in surprise. Her English was exceptionally good, with little trace of an accent.

"She was fired," Corvi snapped, taking advantage of the moment. "She was fired, but refused to leave. The *gall*." He drew himself up, tucked his handkerchief back into his pocket, and adjusted his silk tie. Anna remained silent.

"And why," Henry asked her, "were you fired?"

"Because she refuses to obey specific—" Corvi began heatedly.

Henry's quiet but sharp voice cut Corvi off in mid-sentence. "I asked the signorina."

Corvi shut his mouth, but stood simmering.

"I was fired," Anna explained as calmly as she could, "because Signor Corvi took it upon himself to rearrange the interview schedule for the management training course, and I wouldn't stand for it. I was unavoidably late and he took the opportunity to stick his brother in my place."

"Maurizio Corvi," Henry said thoughtfully, rubbing his chin with his thumb and forefinger. His expression was grave, but his eyes were now dancing with amusement. Everything was beginning to fall into place.

"Yes, Maurizio Corvi." Anna rolled the name on her tongue with distinct distaste.

"Might I add," Corvi said in a brittle voice, "that Maurizio was initially scheduled? That when the telex went out with the list of applicants, Signorina Viganò herself struck his name off the list and put her own in its place?"

Henry looked at her questioningly.

"I did," she conceded. "But Maurizio didn't deserve to be on it. If anybody did, it was me."

"Be that as it may." Henry turned to Corvi. "Signor Corvi, as the manager of this hotel, you, better than anyone, should know that employees do not fight in the public areas. There are plenty of employees' areas where you can do just that. Our guests do not pay premium rates in order to watch squabbles. We are a hotel, not a colosseum."

Corvi swallowed, his throat suddenly dry.

"And you, signorina," Henry continued in an equally cold voice, "as an employee, should not only be aware of the same thing, but should at least obey the orders of your manager."

Her eyes fell. She felt tears of anger stinging in them, and was ashamed to show it. She was boiling inside, but she knew that this was no time to erupt. She must stand rebuked. The only outward signs of her anger were her tightly compressed lips and the swift heaves of her breasts.

"I think," Henry suggested, "that we would all benefit if we simply forgot this unfortunate incident. You, Signor Corvi, may go back to whatever you were doing."

"But . . . but what about her?" Corvi sputtered.

"The signorina may come inside my suite. That is contingent, of course, upon her temper." He turned to face Anna, his eyes shining.

Anna nodded with relief and slipped past him into the suite. Henry followed her, shut the door, leaned casually back against it, and burst out laughing.

She bristled and stared at him in fury. Alone with him now, she couldn't help but notice how handsome he was with his wheat-gold hair, strong profile, and cleft chin. He was a big man, tanned and expensively dressed, and when he met her eyes with his own surprisingly blue ones, Anna's breath caught. She guessed him to be about her age, but he obviously came from the other side of the tracks—the *right* side. That, on top of the attraction she would have preferred not to feel—that she had believed she would never feel for a man again—and his blithe laughter at her predicament, all combined to make her strike out in anger. "I suppose you think this is all very funny?" she asked as coldly as she could.

"The fight, you mean?" he asked, still laughing.

She nodded stiffly.

But he hadn't stopped smiling. "No, it's not funny. But you are."

"Me!"

"You." With a huge effort he pulled himself together and reassumed his grave, businesslike manner. "I don't believe I've ever met anyone quite as forward or determined as you seem to be."

"I did what I had to do," she replied.

"Of course you did," he said. "You rose to the occasion quite courageously."

Somehow, this didn't make her feel any better.

He cocked his elbow and slid back his cuff to look at his watch. "It's nearly lunchtime." He adjusted his cuff. "You couldn't, by any chance recommend a good restaurant for a business meeting?"

She seemed to shrivel visibly. Apparently he didn't have time for her after all and had only called her into the suite to further humiliate her. "And the interview?" she asked morosely.

He came toward her and placed his hands on her arms. "It is you I want to have lunch with," he said softly.

"You mean . . . I still stand a chance to go to New York?"

"Yes, you do."

She smiled then, her entire face lighting up. She almost couldn't believe it; despite Romeo Corvi, the opportunity toward which she had for so long worked was still within reach. She let out a deep breath of relief.

But Anna would never make it to the management training course; Mirella Brino was the one who finally went. For after lunch, Henry took the rest of the day off and spent it with Anna. Something magical clicked between them, and neither had to delve into their hearts to understand their feelings. Their reaction to one another was immediate and instinctual.

That weekend, they drove to Naples, took the hydrofoil over to Ischia, and spent the weekend together, lying in the sun during the day and making love at night.

Henry Hale, who had never done an impulsive thing in his life, and Anna Viganò, who after her luckless relationship with Amedeo had sworn she would never fall for another man, quietly got married before the weekend was up.

4

For the first time in his life, Henry had done the unthinkable. Those who knew him well were astonished. Henry had never taken a single day off from work, let alone two entire weeks.

"We're going on a honeymoon before heading to New York," he announced to a surprised Anna as they lay together in bed the morning after the wedding.

"But . . . your work," she protested.

"It'll keep for two weeks. Believe me, Grandmother will see to it that nothing suffers."

"What about your family? They don't even know we're married."

"They'll find out soon enough," he assured her. "Right now, I want you all to myself." He gripped her in a gentle bear hug and held her close.

"Where do you want us to go?" she asked.

He kissed the tip of her nose. It had happened so fast, he was still amazed at the happiness he had found with Anna. To love someone so much that he wanted to spend every waking and sleeping hour with her was a joy he had never anticipated. "We'll go wherever you want," he promised softly, "as long as it's far from any Hale hotel. And we'll be alone, just you and me. Name the place, Mrs. Hale."

She tilted her head back and laughed. "I don't have the faintest idea where to go!"

He smiled at the mixed expression of bewilderment and delight on her face. "Never mind. I have an idea. We'll play an old American game. It's called pin the tail on the donkey."

"Pin the . . . what?"

"You'll see." He released her, patted her once on the bottom, and then telephoned down to the reception desk. He instructed the clerk to send up a map of the world. "And also have the gift shop pick out a scarf," he added. "Preferably one of dark silk. Oh, and a brooch as well. Charge them to my suite." When the clerk said she wasn't sure if they had a map, he simply replied, "Then I'm sure you'll be able to improvise something."

Anna was speechless. If fairies and sugar plums were the stuff of childhood dreams, then this was the adult version of the same. The magic that great amounts of money could perform was still unimaginable to her. Being able to pack up and travel at a moment's notice to any far corner of the earth without even having to consider the cost was something entirely foreign to her.

The travel desk wasn't able to produce a map of the world, but the receptionist had sent up a packet of the next-best thing, brochures and pamphlets for tours and cruises the world over. Henry nodded to himself. They would do. They all had maps of one specific area or another, which he quickly tore out. Then he pushed aside a couch, lifted a picture down off the wall, and began taping the maps to the wall in a reasonable facsimile of the globe. He stepped back to inspect his handiwork, and they both burst out laughing. It was a mismatched world consisting of a magnified Mediterranean, a giant Mexico, a small Scandinavia, a tiny East Africa, and only small bits of the Far East.

Henry lifted the scarf out of the shallow gift box and fashioned it into a blindfold, which he then solemnly tied around Anna's eyes.

"Really, Henry," she protested mildly, her hands instinctively touching the blindfold.

"Ssssh," he said, kissing her lips. "Indulge me. Now, here, hold this brooch and stick the needle end of it into the wall. Wherever you stick it is where we'll go. Watch it! You don't want to stab yourself. Now, hold it out . . . this way." He placed his hands on her shoulders and led her toward the map. She moved with cautious steps, uncomfortable with the blindfold. Then he turned her around and around, so that she completely lost her bearings.

"Now pick a spot. Remember, whichever place you pick is where we're going on our honeymoon."

"Henry . . ." She turned in the direction of his voice.

"I'm dead serious. Do as I say."

She nodded obediently and stepped forward, feeling her way with an outstretched hand. She held the brooch out, moved it hesitantly up and down, left and right, and then without further ado stabbed it into the wall.

He slid the blindfold off her and she stared at the wall. "C-Cozumel?" She turned to him, her blue eyes wide.

"Cozumel it is." He smiled.

"But . . . we don't have any clothes for Mexico," she sputtered.

"We'll buy whatever we need on the way, and whatever else we don't have, I'm sure we can buy there."

"Henry . . ." She was starting to cry.

"Aren't you happy?" he asked worriedly, pulling her toward him.

She sniffed and nodded. "Being sad isn't the only reason to cry," she sobbed into his chest.

The two weeks they spent on Cozumel were the happiest of their lives. They didn't stay at any of the big beachfront tourist hotels. Henry called up a friend, a film producer by the name of Schulkin, to see about renting his house. Two years previously, Elizabeth-Anne had invested in one of Schulkin's pictures. Henry had been in on it, and when the picture turned out to be a good investment, they had all become friends. Now, not only did Bernie Schulkin agree to the rental, he also swore on his mother's grave to keep Henry's whereabouts a secret.

"I get it, you son of a bitch," Bernie laughed over the phone. "Making it into a love nest, eh? How many girls you taking?"

"Good-bye, Bernie."

Bernie sighed wistfully. "Sure would love to come along."

"At least two of us here would hate it," Henry quipped, and halfway around the world, Bernie gazed at his white telephone receiver in puzzled astonishment.

He had never before known Henry Hale to crack a joke.

"If anyplace is heaven, this is it," Anna breathed the moment the canopied jeep pulled up in front of the villa.

Far from the big hotels along the beach, the oceanfront estate was made up of multilevel terraces leading down to the sea. The house was sumptuous, but not ostentatiously furnished. Made of rough stone, the villa boasted a proliferation of arches, no two of which were the same, giving the house a unique charm as well as plentiful access to cooling ocean breezes. There were twenty rooms in all, and two swimming pools, one salt water and one fresh. Both pools were made up of craggy rock formations, which had been carefully blasted hollow in order to leave boulders jutting up out of the water. The grounds were tended by a gardener whose job it was to maintain the junglelike patches of palms, eucalyptus, sea grapes, bougainvillea, and passion flowers without making them appear at all manicured. Two other full-time servants staffed the house, while the gardener doubled as the driver and picked up Henry and Anna at the airport.

The estate was a paradise of utter privacy. Each day, Henry and Anna swam, went boating, ate on the loggia, and made love. After a week, they both had even fruitwood tans.

Lulled by the fragrant flowers and tropical breezes, neither Henry nor Anna noticed as their two weeks rushed past in a blur. But as the time approached for them to fly to New York, Anna became increasingly filled with misgivings.

On their last afternoon, they were lying on the chaises under the sun when she said, "Henry, what if your family does not like me?"

He gazed at her pinched expression and smiled. "They will."

"But they don't even know we're married yet. We told no one."

"It isn't such a big family. Two minutes, and they'll all know."

She nodded, but her lips were twisted in a frown. "But still . . . your grandmother . . ." She slipped off her chaise and knelt at the side of his.

"My grandmother." He was silent for a moment, thinking of Elizabeth-Anne. "I wouldn't worry about her if I were you. She'll like you just fine." He took her face in his hands. "Don't be such a worrywart. Nobody's going to bite you. Now, finish your piña colada, and then we'll take a swim and cool off."

"In the fresh water pool. Salt burns my eyes."

"It burns mine too," he agreed with a laugh.

They both turned and glanced at the villa at the same time. Somewhere inside it, the telephone had started ringing. It stopped on the third ring.

"At least it's not for us," Henry said, shaking his head. "I still can't believe how wonderful it is not to be tied to a phone. Still, every time I hear one ring, I feel the compunction to answer it. I'm like Pavlov's dog, I suppose. Conditioned."

"Excuse me, señor."

They turned around, finding the maid had carried out a long-corded telephone.

"What is it?" Henry asked, feeling almost shocked.

"Is for you, señor." She held out the telephone.

"Knowing Bernie, he wants me to do him another favor," Henry told Anna with a smile, despite his own bewilderment. "Trust good old Bernie."

The maid shook her head. "No, señor. Is not Señor Schulkin."

"But no one knows we're here." Now he was truly alarmed.

"Someone does," the maid said gently. "Is Señora Hale."

Anna turned sharply to Henry, who rose to take the phone. For a long moment he stared at the receiver. Then he lifted it to his ear. "Grandmother?"

"Henry, dear!" Elizabeth-Anne's voice floated crisply across the wires only slightly marred by the static. "How's the sun?" She sounded bright-eyed and chipper enough to bring Henry to his senses.

"How did you know where to find me?" he asked sternly.

Elizabeth-Anne laughed. "You left a trail a mile wide. Don't forget, the Hale Roma made the reservations for Ischia, and the hotel there made the reservations for your flight to Cozumel."

"That back-stabbing Schulkin," Henry growled under his breath.

"Bernie? Why, it wasn't him at all. In fact, it took my secretary four hours to track you down to the house, but track you down she did."

"What did you do? Offer her a bounty?"

She laughed. "Perhaps I *should* do that in the future. Anyway, I'm glad you finally took a vacation."

"Don't I deserve it?"

"Of course you do," she said soothingly. "However, you could have let me know where you were." There was no reproach in her voice; it was merely a statement of fact.

"Yes, perhaps I should have."

"Are you enjoying yourself?"

He looked over at Anna and met her gaze. He couldn't help but smile. "That I am," he said into the phone, wondering what Elizabeth-Anne would say if she knew just how happy he truly was.

"Good. Enjoy your last day, then."

"How did you know about . . . ? Oh, I get it. The reservations for the return trip."

"The reservations," she agreed. She paused. "I'll see you tomorrow. Do drop by the Madison Squire after you get in. I'll be home all evening."

"Will do."

"And, Henry?"

"Yes, Grandmother?"

"Be sure to give my best to your bride."

Before he could say anything, the connection was broken. Thoughtfully he replaced the receiver.

"What is it?" Anna asked,

He looked at her with a dumbfounded expression. "She already knows. It's incredible. I don't know how she does it, but she already the hell knows." He smiled wryly and shook his head. "She said to tell you hello."

5

It was close to ten o'clock at night when they arrived at the Madison Squire. Henry didn't announce himself at the front desk; there was no need. Most of the Squire's employees had bounced him on their knees as a child and greeted him with genuine warmth.

Entering the lobby, he was filled with a sense of warm nostalgia. Nothing about the Squire had changed; it never did. Half the staff had spent the better part of their lives with the hotel. Paula Kelley, the head switchboard operator, had been on the staff forty-nine years, and hers was not an unusual case. Many worked well past retirement age. The Squire was their life and joy, and they intended to keep working until the day they died. There was a pride, an esprit de corps, a feeling of being part of the family at the Squire that was sadly lacking in most hotels.

In the same way, Elizabeth-Anne had never allowed the hotel to become ostentatious. She emphasized warm personal service, and rather dowdy luxury, which was kept just this side of frayed so the atmosphere remained nice and cosy. As a result, the Madison Squire had developed a loyal following. More repeat guests stayed here than at any of the other Hale hotels and the Squire employees prided themselves upon re-membering a client's name after his very first visit.

"Everyone seems to know you," Anna observed as they got off the elevator on the penthouse floor.

He nodded, a wistful expression on his face. "I practically grew up in this hotel."

"I like it. It's so . . . so *warm.*"

"Personally, I think it could use a little sprucing up. It's beginning to show just a little more seediness than it should."

"But that would spoil it," Anna cried.

"My sentiments exactly," a crisp voice seconded from the end of the hall.

They turned and found Elizabeth-Anne, bathed in the glow of the wall sconces, looking very stately and beautifully groomed—as always, every inch the lady.

For a long, drawn-out moment time seemed to freeze as the two women's gazes locked. They sized each other up frankly in a split second, the way only two women meeting for the first time, and sharing the love of the same man, can do.

But for Elizabeth-Anne, this meeting was far more than it seemed. Outwardly she appeared to be a composed, hand-somely elegant sixty-nine-year-old with a warm smile and perfectly tailored oyster wool Chanel suit. But her mind was a blur of conflicting emotions and anxious thoughts. Looking at the lanky, poised young woman with blue-blue eyes who stood before her, Elizabeth-Anne felt like a teenager on her first date. She searched Anña's face for the tiniest hints of recognition, and as she peered closely into those clear blue eyes so much like Henry's own, she shivered.

Could it be? she asked herself.

Tears sprang to Elizabeth-Anne's eyes. At first she hadn't wanted to believe it. The startling news of Henry's marriage had shocked her deeply, tearing open the old wounds that had never properly healed. It had started when she tried to call Henry in Rome, and she had been informed that he and Signorina Viganò had left for Ischia.

Viganò.

The name had frozen her tongue, had sent memories of defeat and a thousand dead hopes spinning wildly through her mind. When she finally managed to find her voice, she had haltingly asked for Signorina Viganò's first name.

Anna.

It could not be! she had told herself over and over. It was some sort of cruel trick. It had to be! Anna had been given away, had disappeared. This sudden resurrection was nothing short of miraculous—and Elizabeth-Anne didn't believe in miracles. No, it must be money this bogus Anna was after. She must be a sly, insidious fortune hunter who had somehow found out about Anna and decided to impersonate her. That wouldn't be very difficult to do. After all, no one had ever seen Anna.

Oh, but how devious she must be to manage to worm her way into Henry's affections so swiftly! Henry, who had never looked at a woman twice. Henry, who had never heard the story of Anna, who never even knew such a cousin existed. She, Janet, and Zaccheus had all found the subject of Charlotte-Anne's lost child too painful to discuss, ever; it was taboo.

After Elizabeth-Anne had made the initial discovery about this Anna, she had expected Henry to call at any moment with the news that he had found his cousin. After all, the woman posing as Anna would expose herself to him, wouldn't she? Since it was part of the Hale fortune she was obviously after, that would be the next obvious step in her plan. And Henry, not knowing anything about her, would in confusion call his grandmother.

But the woman obviously wasn't ready to lay her cards on the table, at least not yet. Henry's silence only increased Elizabeth-Anne's inner turmoil. Finally she had been unable to wait any longer, and had placed some calls.

It was then that she found out about the marriage.

The news left her dumbfounded. Henry married? Without even calling to tell her?

But this was no time for hurt. She had to come to grips with this bogus Anna Viganò, and *now*.

What bothered Elizabeth-Anne was that the marriage didn't make sense. Unless, of course, the fortune hunter had found it an unexpected but easier route to the family coffers. Yes, that could be it. Or . . .

Elizabeth-Anne had groaned aloud, not at all wanting to face the other possibility. It was because of the marriage that the new nagging doubt began to form in her mind.

If the girl was really Anna, then she might not even know it herself.

Could she, after all, *really* be Anna Viganò? Miracles did happen occasionally, didn't they?

Suddenly nothing made sense anymore. Elizabeth-Anne knew only one thing. She had to find out who Anna Viganò really was.

So she had had her checked out through a private investigator while the honeymooning couple had been soaking up the sun in Cozumel.

"I want to know her past," Elizabeth-Anne had instructed the detective. "Specifically, who she is. I don't want her personal life dissected. I don't want to have any of the so-called 'goods' on her. I only want to know where she was born and who her family is. Whether or not she was adopted. Nothing else. Is that clear?"

The investigator had been quick and thorough. The news he had returned with had been enough to strengthen Elizabeth-Anne's feeble hopes.

Anna Viganò, she was told, was a nineteen-year-old resident of Rome, who had moved to that city from Campania when she was three. Her father, a laborer, was now deceased; her brother, Dario, was a priest; and her mother had just moved out of the family's ghetto apartment to one in a considerably more fashionable neighborhood. Her new, more comfortable life-style was apparently financed by her daughter, who had recently married quite well. The mother, it seemed, knew her daughter to be nothing but her own flesh and blood, though she admitted to having been ill at the time of her birth, so that her memory of the event was not clear.

It was enough to make the impossible suddenly seem very possible. But Elizabeth-Anne knew that the true and final test remained. She had to see this Anna Viganò herself, for only by meeting her face to face could she decide whether there was anything of her beloved Charlotte-Anne in the girl's visage.

And now, her heart pounding wildly, she saw before her in the young woman's gaze eyes that were heart-wrenchingly familiar. If they weren't Charlotte-Anne's, then they were very, very close. And the regal di Fontanesi nose . . . yes, she saw the girl's father there, too. But what was most important to Elizabeth-Anne was that seeing the girl now, she *knew*. This was Anna.

Her Anna.

These thoughts flashed through her mind in the first seconds of their meeting. Both she and Anna had been momentarily paralyzed as they stood facing one another in the warmly lit hallway. Then, at the same moment, Elizabeth-Anne and Anna found their feet. They hurried into each other's arms and embraced. And it was then that Elizabeth-Anne saw it. Hanging from a delicate silver chain around Anna's neck was the pansy charm that had once been Elizabeth-Anne's own.

"Welcome, Anna," Elizabeth-Anne said softly, the tears slipping down her cheeks. She reached up with her fingertips and gently touched Anna's face. "Welcome. Welcome . . . to your home."

"Thank you," Anna whispered. Tears filled her own eyes as she was overcome with the strange feeling that, in this strong woman's embrace, she truly was at home.

Elizabeth-Anne then turned to Henry. He was smiling broadly, with a light in his eyes that told her he was happier than she had ever before seen him. And it was at that moment that she realized the horrible situation that faced her. *Henry had married his cousin.* He and Anna didn't know—and when they found out, it could destroy their love. And that, Elizabeth-Anne now saw, would destroy Henry.

For now, Elizabeth-Anne forced the radiant smile to remain on her face and turned to embrace her grandson. She would savor this moment, and face its repercussions later.

Henry was overwhelmed; he had never seen his grandmother like this. He held her tightly and kissed her cheek, all the while thinking that although he had hoped that she would like and accept Anna, he had never expected the intense, warm reception she had just given his new bride.

6

Elizabeth-Anne sat stiffly on the apricot couch, wrestling with her conscience. She had been perfectly still for hours, ever since Henry and Anna had left. The silk-shaded lamps cast warm yellow pools of light in the otherwise dark living room of the Madison Squire duplex. Elizabeth-Anne's eyes were locked on the sterling-framed photograph she held in her hands.

The most recent snapshot of Henry captured his face in three-quarter profile. His handsome features were unsmiling, almost stern. She stared at it, remembering the joy she had seen in his eyes earlier this evening, and felt as if her soul were torn in two.

How could she *not* tell Henry and Anna that they were cousins? Marrying a first cousin was illegal in many states. Was it illegal in New York? It would be easy enough to find out, but Elizabeth-Anne wasn't sure she wanted to know.

What, then, about the morality of the marriage? As a Catholic, Anna would see her marriage as incest, the most heinous of mortal sins. How could she live—much less love—with such knowledge?

The power to tell Anna and Henry the truth lay solely in Elizabeth-Anne's hands. And her mind was tormented by the question of what to do. Should she accept Anna as a daughter-in-law or as a granddaughter? Her longing to embrace Charlotte-Anne's child, to find again a little of all that she had lost, was almost overpowering. To do so would be the fulfillment of a hundred buried dreams . . . but they were her dreams, old dreams. What would such an act of selfishness do to Henry and Anna's hopes for the future?

What, then, was her responsibility as matriarch of the family? Could she make a moral and legal choice for Henry and Anna? Telling them the truth would be the "right" thing to do, but it would end their marriage.

And all the happiness they had found together. Henry had always been so serious, so soberly determined to play his part in the Hale empire, to prove himself one of the youngest and most brilliant businessmen in the world. Now, suddenly, he seemed to have learned life was for other things as well, for joy and spontaneity, for knowing and loving a woman.

Elizabeth-Anne had lost Zaccheus' love so long ago . . . then lived through that impossible pain again when Larry died. Hadn't the Hales had their share of suffering?

Could she really, in the name of truth, take this delicate, exquisite flower that was Henry and Anna's love and poison it, crush it with the knowledge of their incest? Could she be so cruel? So heartless? So *righteous*?

Suddenly she knew that they must never, *never* know. It was a secret that must be kept from them at all costs, one that she would take to her grave. They loved each other too much. She could see that just by the way they looked at one another, by the warmth bridging their gaze.

Her frustration and indecision melted away.

Leave well enough alone, she told herself. *Leave them be*.

Besides, she thought with a sudden lighthearted smile, how many grandmothers were there who could love a grandson's wife as deeply as she could?

No, they must never find out. And it was up to her to make sure they didn't.

作 Judith Gould

She sat there for a while longer, then went upstairs to bed, little suspecting she had just planted the seed that would destroy so much happiness for her great-grandchild, yet unborn.

7

When Henry, Anna, and Elizabeth-Anne stepped out of the cool, dark house, they were blinded by the glaring sunshine. Squinting, they made their way down the front steps and skirted the antique yellow-and-black Rolls-Royce that was being buffed by the chauffeur. As they headed across the manicured lawn, Anna fell behind, letting Elizabeth-Anne and Henry talk. They were going slowly, their heads bent forward, and Henry had his arm around his grandmother's waist.

Anna dug her hands into the pockets of her plaid wool skirt, stopped walking, and breathed deeply. How different from the city it was here, how much cleaner and fresher! She could hardly believe this magnificent estate was merely forty-five minutes from midtown Manhattan. Here, only the trills of the birds and the rustle of leaves broke the silence. The air smelled richly of freshly mowed grass.

Turning, she admired the house again. An elegant Colonial, on the crest of a high hill above the waters of the Hudson.

She heard the fading murmur of Elizabeth-Anne and Henry's voices, and hurried down the gently sloping hill after them. When she rejoined them, they were still deep in conversation.

"I know it's *big*," Elizabeth-Anne said, "but you need a large house. After all, Henry, you and Anna have your social position to think of."

"But, Grandmother, this is the last thing on earth we expected for a wedding present."

"I should hope so. I'm not in the habit of giving away houses. Anyway, I know the present was a long time in coming. It took me quite a while to find it. Estates like this one don't come on the market every day."

"It must have cost a fortune."

Elizabeth-Anne turned to him and laughed. "It didn't cost you a penny, so you can stop worrying about it. And you know I can well afford it. It's a drop in the bucket for me, if that much. All you need are a few people to help . . ." She waved her hand casually around the grounds.

"A few! We'll need an *army* of servants just to keep this place up. Several gardeners—"

"So you hire an army," Elizabeth-Anne said flatly, refusing to let him dissuade her. Then she laughed and tugged at his sleeve with mock resignation. "Don't be so impossibly conservative all the time, Henry. For God's sake, if we were financially strapped I could understand your hesitation. But we're not."

"If we're careful," he said stiffly, "we need never be."

"You sound just like a banker," she said irritably. "Still, you must agree that there *are* some investments it doesn't hurt to spend money on. Real estate is one of them." She paused, looked over her shoulder to see if Anna was within earshot, then dropped her voice to a whisper. "And clothes are another. Anna could use a new wardrobe, you know."

"Why? She's happy with what she has. When she needs something, she goes out and buys it."

"When she needs something," Elizabeth-Anne corrected him, "she waits and goes to Gimbels or Alexander's when there's a sale. Really, Henry, don't you think you could take her to Saks or Bergdorfs? I mean, she doesn't need Paris couture. She's very attractive and she can get away with wearing anything. But something nice, heh?"

"She has this thing," he said slowly. "She's been poor all her life, and now she's afraid to waste money."

"No, she's afraid to spend it. There's a difference." Elizabeth-Anne couldn't help the faintly ironic smile that hovered on her lips. When she had first learned about Anna, she had been afraid she was a gold digger after the Hale fortune. Now, looking back, she saw how wrong she had been. If Henry was ultraconservative, then Anna was downright frugal. Idly she wondered if she saved plastic bags and glass jars and reused them. "Haven't you told her we're rich?" she asked Henry.

"She knows that."

"But have you told her just how rich?"

"I have."

"And?"

"She doesn't believe it. She says there can't be that much money in the world."

"Sometimes," Elizabeth-Anne said, thinking aloud, "even I still can't believe it. Two hundred and fifty million dollars!" She shook her head and laughed again. "Anyway. Let's all go back to the house. You're stuck with it. You can't go and exchange it like a table setting from Tiffany's, you know. It's been paid for, and it would be very bad manners to refuse it. It was a present, and it's up to you to accept it graciously."

"You are a dear, Grandmother. But an impossible one."

"You and Anna are my grandchildren. Let me indulge you every once in a while," she growled.

"Then we thank you."

"You already did, over and over." She stopped walking and looked around. "Just think of the advantages of this place. Even commuting to the city is easy. If you like, you can avoid the traffic altogether."

"How?" he asked, mystified.

"By buying a boat. The real-estate agent told me that the last owner commuted to the city in his speedboat. I guess he got the idea from the millionaires who lived up here before the Depression."

He smiled. "We'll see."

"Have we lost Anna?" Elizabeth-Anne asked, twisting her head around. "Oh, you're right behind us." She held out her free arm so that Anna could hook hers through it, and together the three of them began walking the perimeter of the property. "I can't wait till you see the orchard. It's too far to walk today. Altogether, this place is made up of forty-three acres. But they're necessary, and so are the extra bedrooms in the house. A growing family needs space. You *are* planning to give me plenty of great-grandchildren, aren't you?"

Elizabeth-Anne smiled disarmingly at Anna, whose face went pale.

"Is something wrong?" Elizabeth-Anne asked with concern.

Anna smiled, but not before Elizabeth-Anne caught the most implacable, inconsolable look of sadness deep in her blue-blue eyes.

"No, no," Anna assured her hastily. "I was just thinking about something else, that's all."

Anna sat on the bench in Central Park, stonily watching the parade of Fifth Avenue nannies pushing expensive imported baby carriages. It was late morning of a perfect blustery day, and the sun was out in full force. So were her depressed spirits. She couldn't remember ever having felt so miserable.

Until now she had never really taken a moment to stop and think, to sort out her own life and Henry's. Now the prospect overwhelmed her.

Henry. How she loved him! If she had ever been certain of anything in her life, it was that. From the very first, they had been so sure of each other. Neither had felt the need to hesitate or analyze their feelings. How precious little she had known about him then. And how little she still knew. Which was part of the excitement of their love, the joy of discovering each other.

But now all that was over.

Oh God, she thought, her eyes glazing over as she felt the familiar dull ache in the pit of her belly. She had had that ache on and off for days, and knew it would soon culminate in nausea. That was where her pain and misery lived, deep inside her stomach. Whenever she felt depressed, the physical manifestation would show itself there.

Why, oh why, she asked, hugging herself, why hadn't she told him about Amedeo?

But, in truth, she knew she had taken advantage of the fact that she had never been pressed to tell him. From that first time, Henry had known she wasn't a virgin. It hadn't seemed to make any difference to him.

But she knew she owed him an explanation. Because Henry had a right to know that when she had fallen down the Spanish Steps and lost Amedeo's child, she had lost *their* children, too.

Why hadn't she told Henry about that before she married him?

But she had been too happy then. After they had met and made love, she had been selfish and self-centered. She had wanted him all to herself, and the thought of children had been far from her mind. Only now did she realize the magnitude of her mistake. Henry was a *Hale*, the heir to an empire, and as such, he of course needed an heir of his own. A man in Henry's position wasn't free to just fall in love.

She pressed her fingertips to her forehead. Her mind felt numb with guilt and regret. She slowly got to her feet and walked from the bench. She passed a nanny and pink-faced baby playing a game of peek-a-boo. The woman hid her face with both hands and cried, "Where is Rhea?" before parting her fingers and cooing, "*There* she is."

Even as she continued to walk on, Anna could hear the woman and child's laughter. Their happiness seemed to mock her, and she shut her eyes with a heavy sigh. Ever since that day in Tarrytown when Elizabeth-Anne had given them the house, Anna felt she saw children, especially infants, everywhere, reminding her of what her own damaged body could not produce.

She sighed deeply once again, then shook herself. Checking her watch, she saw she had only fifteen minutes to meet Henry at 21 and would have to hurry to get there on time. Squaring her shoulders, she briskly made her way out of the park. No matter what, she promised herself, she mustn't let Henry know how worried she was, or why. It was a problem she had created, and she must find the way out of it. She couldn't burden him with her troubles, not until she decided what to do. She loved him too much for that. He was everything to her. She loved him enough to . . .

She stopped cold, her heart pounding excitedly. Was it

true? The realization, the solution to all her problems, had come so suddenly that it almost overwhelmed her. She took a deep breath to calm herself and reconsider. But there was nothing to think about; this decision was as immediate, as instinctual as her love for him had been. Because it was born of her love for him.

She loved Henry enough to try to give him a child.

She felt suddenly omnipotent with the joy of that knowledge. The weight of her depression slipped away—she felt all-powerful, free, and so *lucky* to have found such love.

But even in her joy, she knew Henry must never know the extent of the gift she would give him. He must never know the risk she would knowingly take, never know that by giving life to their child she was very likely sacrificing her own. Only she could decide to take the chance; he would never allow her to if he knew. But giving life to their love was the only thing that had meaning for her now. Her decision was clear. So she would keep it from him at all costs.

She immediately realized how difficult that would be. There were so many things to consider. Both the family doctor and her gynecologist were the finest in the city, but they were also Elizabeth-Anne's personal physicians. And Anna knew Elizabeth-Anne was on friendly terms with both of them.

Well, she would simply have to find new doctors. That shouldn't prove too difficult. New York City was, after all, not Italy. It was the heart of the most advanced country in the world, a wonderland of physicians and specialists and hospitals. People came here from all corners of the world with their assorted disorders and diseases. Surely it was possible that with such expert medical care she would not only succeed but also survive. It was a dream worth pursuing, an irresistible possibility. Yes, with the power of a love such as hers, anything was possible.

She reached Fifth Avenue and began to rush down the sidewalk in her excitement. Her eyes shone, and every breath she took seemed effervescent. She felt delirious with joy. She practically danced down Fifth Avenue, smiling at everyone she passed—especially the children, the infants!

Yes, now that she had decided, she felt herself tingling with the love coursing through her, felt irresistibly and completely *alive*.

8

Henry and Elizabeth-Anne were in Greece negotiating construction contracts for the Ierápetra Village resort when the call came through. Sotirios Kyrkos, Hale Hotels' Greek resident executive officer, answered the phone in the Pericles Suite of the Athens Hale.

"It is for you, Mr. Hale," he told Henry, covering the mouthpiece with his hand. "It is the New York office."

"I'll take it, thank you." Henry got up from the white couch and crossed the polished marble floor to the telephone table. Elizabeth-Anne remained seated, studying the art boards spread out in front of her. They portrayed the Ierápetra Village, her idea for an exclusive Aegean resort modeled after an idyllic fishing village, right down to the waterfront tavernas and windmills. The instant she caught the sudden change in Henry's tone of voice, she looked up and listened intently.

When Henry finally replaced the receiver, he stared across the room at her, his face white. "That was Dr. Dadourian," he said thickly. "Anna's been hospitalized."

"What?" Elizabeth-Anne jumped to her feet and crossed over to him. "Did he say what was wrong?"

He shook his head. "Only that she stands to lose the baby."

"Oh, Henry!"

He turned away, stepping out onto the sun-drenched terrace. He stared blankly out across the city toward the distant Acropolis, his hands thrust deeply into his trouser pockets.

Elizabeth-Anne followed him outside and squinted in the glare of the Greek sun. She placed a hand on his arm.

"She also stands to lose her own life," he said tightly.

Elizabeth-Anne felt the words plunge into her like a knife. *No, it couldn't be.*

But when Henry turned to her and she saw the cold fear in his eyes, she knew it was. Then it was as if the naked desperation she saw in his face galvanized her. Now was not the time to indulge her own fear, she told herself. No matter how worried she felt, she had to be strong. Henry needed her.

"You stay put, dear," she said firmly. Then she hurried back inside to confer with Sotirios Kyrkos. "Mr. Kyrkos, could you please make travel arrangements for us? We must leave for New York immediately."

Kyrkos didn't know what news the Hales had gotten, but their distress was obvious. "I am so sorry, Mrs. Hale, but there is no afternoon or evening flight. I'm afraid you will have to wait until tomorrow morning."

"Tomorrow morning is too late." She paused briefly to consider the alternatives. "Our only choice is to charter a jet. Could you arrange it for us? I'll take anything as long as it has transatlantic range. Nor do I care what it costs."

"Yes, Mrs. Hale."

"And please ask for a car to take us to the airport right away. We'll wait there until a plane is ready."

"Yes, Mrs. Hale." He gave a polite bow and left the room.

Elizabeth-Anne went back outside. Her face felt tight. "We won't bother with packing," she told Henry. "Either the staff can pack up our things and send them, or we'll get them when we return. All we'll need is our passports. We're leaving right now."

He turned to her slowly, his eyes filled with tears. "I love her," he said in a choked voice. "God, how I love her. If anything happens to her . . ." His voice broke off in a sob.

Elizabeth-Anne took Henry in her arms and held him. She shut her eyes against her own tears, unable to look him in the face and see her own sinking heart mirrored there. "I know that, Henry," she said softly. "I love her too."

More than you'll ever know.

* * *

At half-past two in the morning, they rushed into Columbia Presbyterian. Dr. Dadourian was pacing the lobby, waiting for them. When he saw Elizabeth-Anne and Henry burst in, he hurried forward to meet them.

"How is she, doctor?" Elizabeth-Anne demanded at once, not breaking stride as all three headed toward the bank of elevators.

"Not good, I'm afraid." He punched the button for the elevator and they began an impatient wait for it to arrive. "For the past eight hours she's been in the operating room."

"And the problem?" Elizabeth-Anne looked into his eyes.

The doctor sighed painfully. "She should never have had the baby," he said. "She must have known from the start. I've examined her, and the problem was caused by a trauma years ago."

Henry stared at him. "But . . . she never said . . ."

Dr. Dadourian shook his head sadly. "Nor did I even realize she was pregnant, not until she called today to tell me that something was terribly wrong. I hadn't seen her for over ten months. She called to tell me she had been seeing another doctor, that she was pregnant. But the other man was out of town, and she was terribly frightened."

"She never told me," Henry repeated dully.

"Will she pull through?" Elizabeth-Anne asked.

"I honestly don't know."

"And the baby?"

"Who cares about the baby?" Henry suddenly asked in a sharp, hissing voice.

Elizabeth-Anne and Dr. Dadourian exchanged glances, but before they could speak, the elevator finally arrived.

They rode up in silence. On the fourth floor Dr. Dadourian led them to the nurses' station. The beige corridors were empty and silent, the air heavy with the sharp medicinal odor indigenous to hospitals the world over. Elizabeth-Anne found the atmosphere unspeakably oppressive, but she saw Henry was in too deep a state of shock even to notice.

Dr. Dadourian conferred with the nurse, who told them Anna was now out of surgery, but they would have to wait for the attending surgeon, Dr. Loomis, to learn more. The nurse escorted them to a glass-enclosed waiting room filled with molded plastic chairs.

"Come," Dr. Dadourian said, bringing Elizabeth-Anne and Henry seats. "There's nothing we can do but wait."

Exactly twelve minutes later, Dr. Loomis joined them. He was a tall, distinguished man with silver sideburns and the hands of an artist. His face was drawn, and the green eyes behind the thick glasses were red-rimmed. He had shed his blood-soaked surgery greens; long ago he had learned that the sight of them did little to reassure his patients' loved ones.

"How is she, doctor?" Henry asked, jumping to his feet.

Dr. Loomis sighed wearily. "The good news first. We've managed to save the child. Congratulations." He smiled weakly. "You have a beautiful daughter. She's in the incubator. As you know, she was premature. We had to deliver her by cesarean section. She'll have to stay in there for a few days. You're welcome to see her whenever you like."

"Dammit, man," Henry growled, grabbing Loomis' sleeve. "My wife! How's my *wife*?"

The doctor's eyes dropped. "Not good at all, I'm afraid. We're doing everything for her that we can."

Henry shut his eyes. His face drained of color. He stood motionless but for a slight swaying. It was as if he had become unmoored and stood rocking in a wind. When he opened his eyes again, the effort for control he was making was obvious. "I . . . I would like to see her." His voice came out low, like a growl.

"Of course," Dr. Loomis answered. "This way, please." He led the way back to the elevators and on the ride upstairs explained Anna's condition. "Apparently Mrs. Hale should never have tried to have the child. It seems that long ago her uterus suffered rather severe damage. It's a miracle that she wasn't forced to check in long ago. Or perhaps she did have to, but was afraid for her child. We would have had to abort the pregnancy, and maybe she knew that."

"Will she pull through?" Elizabeth-Anne asked quietly.

The doctor was silent a moment, then said, "Of course, there is always the possibility of recovery. The human body is most remarkable. One never knows its capabilities completely. They change from person to person.''

Elizabeth-Anne met his eyes. "But you think she won't. Survive.''

The doctor met her gaze fully. "In this case, I would say the chances are slim,'' he said gently. "Very slim indeed. I'm sorry.''

Elizabeth-Anne took a deep breath and nodded once, tightly holding onto Henry's arm. Even as all the life seemed to drain out of her, she realized she was supporting him.

Outside the recovery room, Dr. Loomis stopped once again. "I know this is very difficult for you," he said softly, "but please try to be brief. And if she doesn't recognize you or she's still under . . . Well, bear in mind that she's heavily sedated. And very low.'' He opened the door for them. The two doctors waited outside while Henry and Elizabeth-Anne went in.

The nurse on duty avoided their gaze. Elizabeth-Anne held tightly to Henry as they approached the bed. There he fell to his knees, seeking Anna's hand and holding it in his. It felt icy to the touch.

He stared at her in disbelief. He'd last seen her only a few short days before. She had been so healthy, so alive and glowing with the happiness of carrying their child. Now she looked pale and gaunt; for a moment he was afraid she was already dead. But watching closely, he saw the faint movement of her breast as she took in weak breaths. No, not yet. She wasn't gone yet.

He felt dull and empty. How could this still, helpless thing be Anna? Anna, who had always been so exuberant, so bursting with energy. Now, lying in the recovery room with tubes taped to her arms and another coursing out of her nostril, she looked shrunken.

"Anna," he whispered. "Can you hear me, my love?''

He watched her unmoving face desperately, silently, until Elizabeth-Anne came up behind him and put her hand on his shoulder. He turned and looked up at her. He saw what was in Elizabeth-Anne's eyes, but he couldn't face it and almost frantically turned back to stare into Anna's still face. But it was there too. This wasn't Anna, his wife. It couldn't be. It was only a shadow of her.

"Anna." He reached out with one hand, trembling as he touched her soft face with his fingertips. The tears were stinging in his eyes. "Anna," he whispered again.

He did not know how long he knelt at her bedside. Only after the nurse came over and gently pried his hands loose did he realize Anna had slipped away from him.

She was gone. She had never regained consciousness. He hadn't even been able to say good-bye.

Henry collapsed, his sobs shaking his strong body. Elizabeth-Anne took him in her arms and rocked him gently. She too was weeping. "I know, Henry," she whispered, her voice unsteady with pain, her aquamarine eyes glittering. "I know. Don't hurt, baby. Please don't hurt."

Elizabeth-Anne walked stiffly into the seedy, dark bar on the lower level of Penn Station. She made her way through the bar to the tiny booth in the back. Henry was hunched over, both his hands clutching his glass. After the funeral, three days before, he had stalked off white-faced and grim. It had taken her as many days to find him. She had finally done so only by luck. One of Hale Hotels' executives who commuted daily between New York and Port Washington had spied him in that same bar twice in the same day. It was he who had told Elizabeth-Anne where Henry was.

"Henry," she said softly. "Come home, Henry."

He looked up at her, his eyes glassy. When he spoke, his voice was slurred, but he managed his simple sentence. "Leave me alone."

"Henry." She took the seat opposite him and reached for his hands. He yanked them back, spilling some of his drink in the process. She fought her revulsion as she smelled the rancid odor of bourbon emanating from him.

"You can't go on like this, Henry. Come home."

"Home?" He gave an ugly laugh and stared at her. "What home? Yours or mine?"

"It doesn't matter. They're both your homes."

He just shook his head and took another pull at his drink.

"Please, don't make this so difficult," she pleaded. "It's hard enough as it is."

"She's everywhere." His voice dropped to a hoarse whisper. "She's everywhere. I can smell her perfume. I see her clothes. The pictures she bought. She's everywhere."

"She's in our hearts. She'll always be there. Come home with me. To the Madison Squire."

"No."

She leaned across the table. "Look, Henry. We're all entitled to mourn, you especially. But drowning your sorrows in drink isn't the way to do it."

"No?" He scowled at her glassily. "Then what is?"

"You can have a good cry," she suggested.

"I've cried." He took another drink.

"Henry, please listen to me," she urged desperately. "Anna is *dead*! Nothing will bring her back. You can't just drown yourself in alcohol. *Please*."

"Why not, Grandmother? It's my life." He drained his glass, then set it down with a bang.

"Because of the child, Henry," she said quietly. "Your child and Anna's. That's why you've got to pull yourself together."

"I told you before. Don't want that kid."

"Henry, she's your daughter," Elizabeth-Anne said in despair.

"So?" He met Elizabeth-Anne's gaze with hard, glittering eyes.

Elizabeth-Anne sighed. "Come on, Henry. I've got the car waiting upstairs. Let's go." She pushed her chair back, paused, and added softly, "Today's the day your daughter is being released from the hospital. Let's go fetch her, Henry. Let's bring her home. Together, you and I."

"Nope."

She sighed wearily. "But don't you see? She's Anna's too! I thought you loved Anna."

"Yes, I loved her," he said, suddenly ferocious. "I loved her more than my own life. And that baby *killed* her."

"The child did *not* kill her," Elizabeth-Anne hissed harshly. "Anna knew the consequences, but she wanted a child. She wanted *your* child. She wanted it so badly that she was willing to risk her life to give you one." She paused. "Do you want to throw away everything?"

He narrowed his eyes. "You want the baby? You're welcome to her. I never want to see her." He signaled the waiter for another drink, then turned back to Elizabeth-Anne. "Now, leave me alone."

Elizabeth-Anne rose to her feet and went out, passing the waiter carrying an oily glass of bourbon over to the booth.

On the escalator on her way to the street level, she wondered why everyone was staring at her. She didn't even realize it until she got into the Rolls.

She was weeping.

9

The white-uniformed nurse smiled as she handed the squalling bundle to Elizabeth-Anne. The baby was clothed in a christening frock of off-white cotton sprinkled with eyelets and trimmed lavishly with Belgian lace. Elizabeth-Anne had bought it especially for her, and was now touched at how it emphasized the child's angelic sweetness.

Elizabeth-Anne cradled her great-granddaughter in her arms, careful to support the tiny down-covered head with one hand. The child seemed to sense safety and warmth and love, and instantly stopped crying. It was as though they were communicating in a secret language. The minuscule doll's mouth broke out into gurgling, toothless laughter.

"I think you two will get along just fine," the nurse said, laughing and patting Elizabeth-Anne's arm.

Elizabeth-Anne nodded and smiled. She rocked the baby soothingly back and forth in her arms as she studied the tiny face closely. The baby looked so familiar, an eerie image of all four of her children a few days after their birth. But this child seemed even more precious, if that was at all possible.

A hint of tears glistened in Elizabeth-Anne's eyes. The child was so tiny, so blond, so blue-eyed. The familiar features were all there. She was a true Hale.

Just holding the infant pushed Elizabeth-Anne's depression to the back of her mind. Only once she got downstairs and sank into the supple leather backseat of the yellow-and-black Rolls-Royce did she again feel weighed down with despair.

This child. Anna's child.

She was holding more than just her first great-granddaughter. She held in her arms a most precious, living part of Charlotte-Anne, the daughter she'd lost, as well as the child's mother, Anna, her own granddaughter. The agony she had felt over Charlotte-Anne's death and Anna's loss, old pains that had never healed and new ones that had not had time to, now, finally, felt salved. Even Anna's untimely, tragic death, painful though it was, seemed somehow more bearable. She could start to come to terms with it. Because of the child.

She stared thoughtfully out of the side window as the car headed downtown along Riverside Drive. Between the rich foliage of the trees and shrubbery she caught occasional flashes of the wide, silver Hudson.

By all rights I should be taking her in the opposite direction, she was thinking, up the Henry Hudson Parkway to Tarrytown, to her own home. But instead, she's coming downtown, home with me. Not that I don't want her. How I do! But she should be with her father now, not me, no matter how temporary it might be.

Elizabeth-Anne sighed and shook her head morosely. Strangely enough, she felt saddened and hurt rather than depressed and angry. A father didn't just declare he never wanted to set eyes on his daughter and then run off, no matter what the reason. Surely once Henry got over his mourning, he would come to his senses and accept his loss and understand his gain. His daughter was, after all, his own flesh and blood. Wounds took time to heal, but eventually they did.

No one knows that better than I.

But if he didn't, what then?

Her aquamarine eyes narrowed and she thrust out her chin. In that case, she would take care of this radiant child for as long as she had to. She would hire a nanny and juggle her own busy schedule. Somehow, she would find the time to lavish love upon this darling baby until Henry pulled himself together and fought his way out of his depression.

Yes, in the meantime, she would take the baby under her wing. Eventually Henry would accept her. He had to, Elizabeth-Anne told herself grimly. The poor child had lost her mother; she needed her father twice as much.

Who knew what the future might bring? she reflected morosely. To date, she'd put all her hopes on Henry, counting on him to become her successor and head Hale Hotels after her. But she'd never known until now that he was this flawed . . . this *weak*. That's what his reaction to Anna's death showed her. Not just grief, but weakness in blaming the infant. It wasn't the baby's fault that her mother had died in childbirth. Couldn't he understand that?

Couldn't he comprehend that Anna was still alive—in his daughter?

Elizabeth-Anne cooed softly and rocked the baby in her lap. "Don't worry, little darling," she whispered down at her. "I'll love you and look after you, even if no one else will. Everything that's mine will eventually be yours." She leaned down and rubbed the baby's nose with her own. "You are, after all, a *Hale*."

The child stared up at her through solemn wide blue eyes. A look of intelligent understanding seemed to glow in the tiny face—or was it only her imagination?

"And of course we'll have to come up with a name for you," Elizabeth-Anne continued. "I suppose that's up to me now too, since your daddy won't have any part of it. Let me see . . ." She sighed thoughtfully. "Adele . . . no, somehow you just don't *look* like an Adele. Alice? Barbara? No, no. Carla? Dorothy? Yes! *Dorothy*. We'll name you Dorothy-Anne Hale. Somehow it just sounds *right*."

The child broke out into happy, spontaneous laughter, her

fingers reaching up as though trying to grasp the name out of the air.

It was at that very moment that the special bond they would share for the rest of their lives was cemented. And both of them seemed to sense it.

The years would only strengthen it.

"Your daddy will have a change of heart, Dorothy-Anne," Elizabeth-Anne promised. "You mark my words. This won't last long. He's just hurt, but he'll get over it."

But she was wrong.

Henry would never get over the loathing he felt toward his daughter. Not even when she moved in with him in the big house in Tarrytown. To him she would be a constant reminder of everything he hated. Of pain and loss. Of death.

For him, Dorothy-Anne would always be his beloved Anna's murderer.

IV
Dorothy-Anne

QUEBECK, TEXAS

❧

August 14, 1985

1

T he wind howled outside in the rain-lashed groves and the dim light of the single candle left the room steeped in deep shadow. Freddie leaned over Dorothy-Anne as she lay on the bed struggling for breath and sobbing deeply, her body drenched in sweat, her cheeks wet with tears.

Freddie had not been as stunned by her declaration as he was now anxious to comfort her. "Dorothy-Anne, my darling, how could you say such a thing? Your mother died in childbirth. You're not to blame for her death."

"No, Freddie, I am," she answered, struggling to get the words out. "They told me . . . I heard them say it."

"What do you mean?"

"Oh, Freddie . . ." Suddenly her face contorted with pain and she squeezed his hand tightly as a fresh contraction seized her. Her body tensed, her back arched, and for a long minute they did not speak. When it finally passed, she felt her muscles relaxing like melting butter. Freddie saw that she would not be able to fight sleep, and because the contractions would soon be coming closer and closer together, she would need her strength. But her obvious panic had alarmed him and he had to ask, "Dorothy-Anne, what do you mean '*they*' told you?"

She shook her head weakly, her eyes already closed. "My father . . . my father said it . . . he said he hated me . . . on my tenth birthday . . ." But she couldn't go on. She was swimming in a warm black pool far from the Hale Tourist Court. She was receding in time, everything spinning faster and faster until she reached Tarrytown and she was ten years old. Then the spinning abruptly stopped and it was the day of her birthday and she was back in the big house overlooking the river.

She was standing alone in the sitting room. The clock on the mantel ticked noisily. She half-turned toward it and saw it was nearly one o'clock in the afternoon.

She tightened her lips and turned back to stare out through the high French window. The river below was wide, unusually blue-gray and placid. Overhead, the sun shone brightly in a powder-blue sky. Across the river, the hills were blanketed in oranges and yellows. Indian summer, and Mother Nature had decked herself out in all the finery she could summon. But Dorothy-Anne was not enthralled. She felt more miserable than she had ever felt in her life.

She turned away from the view and plopped down onto the couch in front of the fireplace. She avoided looking around. She didn't like the sitting room. Like much of the rest of the house, it was filled with large, stately furniture. She felt inconsequential and uncomfortable, out of place in the only place she could call home.

She sat unmoving for several minutes until her governess came into the room.

"Your father couldn't take the day off," Nanny said gently as she marched into the room with her stately walk. She held an enormous, beautifully wrapped present out in front of her. She smiled at Dorothy-Anne. "But he's left you something very nice."

Dorothy-Anne didn't look up. The empty despair that had been feeding on her for the past two days sat in her stomach like lead. For once, she wasn't even looking forward to seeing her great-grandmother. She didn't want to see anyone or anything. All she wanted was for the pain and loneliness to stop. She wanted her head to be empty, she wanted to wake up and be someone else. She wished . . . she wished she were dead.

"Daddy doesn't like me," she said. "He never has."

Nanny made a sympathetic clucking sound with her tongue. "Now, now, child. Don't be silly. Your daddy loves you."

"He doesn't. He's never around, especially not on my birthdays." Dorothy-Anne continued to sit with a stillness unnatural for a child her age. "Why does Great-Granny always celebrate my birthday with me instead of my daddy?"

"I told you, child, he's a very busy man."

Dorothy-Anne turned to look Nanny in the eye. "Great-Granny's even busier than Daddy," she said flatly. "She owns Hale Hotels and runs them. Daddy only works for her."

"Your father is president of Hale Hotels," Nanny said severely.

Dorothy-Anne still held the other woman's gaze. "And Great-Granny's chairman of the board."

Nanny wasn't a governess for nothing. She knew when she'd lost an argument. Sighing, she set the wrapped box down on a rose-silk-covered footstool. "Aren't you going to open your father's present?"

Dorothy-Anne stared at it. "No," she said with a sudden flash of insight. "Daddy didn't buy it for me. He had somebody else pick it out. I overheard him talking on the telephone to his secretary. He told her to call FAO Schwartz." She paused and closed her eyes. "And he's not at work either. He's in La Jolla. With a woman."

"Now, how would you know that?" Nanny sat down in exasperation and folded her plump white hands in her lap. She looked at Dorothy-Anne. "You've been overhearing a lot of things lately, it seems."

Dorothy-Anne sat in silence, hunched over.

"Ladies," Nanny said succinctly, "do not listen at doors or keyholes."

Dorothy-Anne didn't look up. She knew from experience

what expression Nanny would be wearing. Her pointed features would be severe, her eyes pinched with disappointment.

"I wasn't listening through keyholes," Dorothy-Anne said with sudden savagery. Then she fell silent again.

Nanny did not speak. She knew that the girl's outburst was merely to mask her pain.

Dorothy-Anne bit down on her lip. She could feel the tears threatening to fill her eyes, but she would not let them come. She got up slowly. "I have to go to the bathroom."

"Well, you better hurry up, then," Nanny said. "Your great-granny will be here any minute now."

"Yes, Nanny."

Dorothy-Anne left the room. She did not use the bathroom off the downstairs hall. Instead, she took the staircase up to the second floor, where she glanced around quickly to make sure that none of the servants were about. She slipped into her father's suite and closed the door behind her.

His bathroom was huge and smelled faintly of disinfectant. She got up on tiptoe. She found what she wanted in his medicine cabinet.

And slashed her wrists.

All because the telephone had rung yesterday.

She had been coming down the sweeping stairs when the hallway telephone began to ring. She hurried downstairs to answer it. It was the servants' day off, and her father was busy upstairs in his study. After picking up the ivory receiver, she was about to speak when she heard a second, almost instantaneous click.

"Henry Hale speaking."

She recognized her father's voice and was about to hang up when she heard a cultured, purring woman's voice answer. Something made her stay on the line and listen. Perhaps it was because the caller was a woman.

"Number Two, is that you, darling?"

"I'm not Number Two, Chessy," he growled. "You know very well I'm Henry."

"My, my." The throaty voice held a hint of mocking laughter. "Aren't we touchy this morning."

"Look, Chessy—" he began irritably.

The playful voice changed instantly. "I'm sorry, darling," she said quickly. "You know how I love to tease you."

"Sometimes your jokes aren't very funny."

"Ah, but you don't mind my teasing you nights, do you, darling?" She laughed softly. "But listen, darling, the reason I called was that you mentioned you might be coming out here to La Jolla, and since CeCe's birthday is tomorrow . . ."

Dorothy-Anne brightened. CeCe's birthday? Who was CeCe? Was that a nickname for her that she didn't know about? After all, *her* birthday was tomorrow . . .

"Oh, shit," Henry broke in harshly.

Dorothy-Anne held her breath and tried to keep her heart from pounding. Had she made a noise. Had her father discovered she was listening?

"What is it, darling?" the woman asked. "Is something wrong?"

"No, it's nothing. I just remembered my daughter's birthday is tomorrow too."

"Oh, Henry. I am sorry. I didn't mean to take you away from your little girl. You've got to be there."

"No, Chessy, it's all right. I'll be happy to join you in La Jolla. There's no need for me to be here. In fact, I'd rather not."

"Henry, how can you say that? She's your own daughter—"

"I prefer not to think of her that way."

"Henry," the woman said, shocked by his words, "you sound as if you hate the poor thing." She laughed tentatively, uncomfortable with the turn the conversation had taken.

Henry paused for a minute, then spoke in a strangely expressionless voice. "I do. I can't stand to be around her. You see, tomorrow is also the anniversary of my wife's death. I do hate that child. Especially on the anniversary of the day she killed my wife."

She first became aware of invisible angels humming softly all around her. The cool currents stirred up by their wings caressed her face. She heard faint, ethereal whispers. She listened closely, but they made no sense. A pecu-

liarly buoyant, floating sensation held her in its spell. It was
not at all unpleasant. Rather like floating lazily in a swimming pool. The water felt soft and warm and smelled vaguely
of chlorine. Through half-closed eyes she tried to look around
her. Big, soft white shapes moved gracefully in ever-so-slow
swirls. Wherever she was, she had never been to this place
before. She couldn't understand what was happening. Nor did
she really care. The buoyant feeling felt so good. So good. . . .

She closed her eyes and let everything recede as she gave
herself up to that pleasant nothingness.

Next she noticed that her sense of smell was heightened. A
sharp, medicinal odor seemed to emanate from within her. It
seemed to come and go in waves, teasing her nostrils.

She lifted her head a few inches. Her eyelids felt heavy,
but she managed to see out through the haze of her lashes.
The world was drifting as if she were watching it through a
white scrim. Shadowy white apparitions moved in a dream-
like slow-motion ballet. Everything was white, a hundred
different shades of white. All but the thin ruby-red line which
rose from her arm to be swallowed up by all that white.
Murmured voices seemed to chant incantations in a monotone.

The whiteness and the red line went slowly dark, receding
once more into sleep.

The clouds and white scrim had turned warm and yellow
when she awakened again. It was easier to open her eyes
now; the lids didn't feel nearly as heavy as they had before.
She stared up into space. She could make out a flatness above
her.

Without moving her head, she glanced around. Her eyes
were a deep green, confused. The clouds were receding. In
their place she could see more flat surfaces all around her.
She was in a two-toned box. The top halves of the walls were
white, the bottom half bilious green. The warm yellow she
had seen was emanating from an electric light. She thought
she recognized the strange smell which had eluded her. She
had smelled it once before. Three years ago, when she'd had
her appendix taken out. She was in a hospital.

A hospital? She stared up at the flatness. No, it couldn't be
a hospital, she thought dreamily. The semigloss ceiling was a

monotone landscape, topsy-turvy, seen from a hundred miles out in space. A crack of river, held up by gravity, flowed between a valley of mountains. She felt a peculiar longing. She didn't want to be in outer space. She wanted to be home.

She turned her head sideways and caught sight of a small pale hand, bandaged at the wrist. Her eyes widened. For a moment she didn't understand. Then she could feel a tightening in her chest as it all came back to her.

The metallic-gray razor blade, paper-thin and yielding easily from the pressure of her fingers. So thin she almost bent it.

The strangely painless parting of her soft flesh as the blade sliced into it.

The pop as the artery was severed.

The mighty, pulsating roar as her blood rushed to meet the wound, seeking escape from her body.

The geyser of blood, a thick, powerful stream at the bottom spraying outward like a ruby fountain, the droplets falling all around like warm rain.

Her stomach churned with the memory, and a flash of heat engulfed her. The moment she tasted the bile starting up, she lunged forward and held a hand to her mouth. She swallowed, breathed deeply, desperately.

Bit by bit her head cleared. She remembered every painful detail. Now she knew why she didn't have a mother like other children. Because she had killed her. She didn't ask herself how or why. She never even remembered seeing her mother. But Daddy had said she killed her, so it must be so. And he hated her so much for doing it that she had tried to kill herself.

And failed.

The breath hissed out of her as she sank back down. The mattress was hard, the sheets starched and scratchy. They weren't her own sheets.

She *was* in a hospital.

She closed her eyes, feeling helpless, ashamed. She couldn't bear to face anyone. Not after what she had done.

Death. Oh, how peaceful it had seemed. . . . The falling sensation, like being sucked into a slow, powerful maelstrom.

The darkness that first engulfed her becoming blinding light, brighter than a thousand suns. How easy to give herself up to that beguiling, dazzling light!

She felt a moistness sliding down her cheeks toward her lips. She tasted it with her tongue. The tears were salty. Suddenly she was glad she was alive.

She heard a door opening. A mannish-looking nurse in uniform came toward her, stopped, turned on her heel, and went right back out. The door sighed closed, opened again. She heard the faint squeak of pneumatic tires. She struggled up. The nurse was holding the door wide and Nanny was wheeling Great-Granny into the room.

Except for the wheelchair, Great-Granny hadn't changed a bit since Dorothy-Anne's earliest memory of her, though Dorothy-Anne knew she was now over eighty. The erect, regal posture, the sterling-silver hair perfectly coiffed; even the wrinkles at the corners of her eyes didn't seem to have changed at all. The only thing that was different was how Great-Granny got around. She hadn't let that slow her down either.

Dorothy-Anne was relieved she wouldn't have to face anyone but her great-grandmother. If anyone could understand, she would.

Elizabeth-Anne was the only person in Dorothy-Anne's life who had ever truly shown how much she loved her. She was the only one who understood her, who was there when she needed someone. Yes, she was glad she was alive, if only for Great-Granny's sake. They had had a special rapport all Dorothy-Anne's life, as if they had recognized even when she was an infant how alike they were.

These thoughts flashed through Dorothy-Anne's mind in the moment that passed before Elizabeth-Anne raised her right hand and said, "This is far enough. Please leave us now."

Nanny nodded. She cast a worried glance at Dorothy-Anne but left the room, shutting the door behind her. Elizabeth-Anne placed her hands on the wheels of the chair and negotiated her way to the bedside.

Elizabeth-Anne smiled at her great-granddaughter. "Good

evening, Dorothy-Anne.'' She reached out and took the girl's bandaged hand in her own. "How are you feeling?"

Dorothy-Anne looked at her sheepishly. "You're not angry with me, are you, Great-Granny?" she asked in a tiny voice.

"No, I'm not angry," she answered. "But I am disappointed. If something was troubling you, you should have come to me."

Dorothy-Anne bit down on her lip, preparing herself to be chastised. But she had forgotten one thing; Elizabeth-Anne Hale was some lady. She knew her priorities. Smiling conspiratorially, she reached under her cashmere lap blanket and produced a stack of comic books. "I know for a fact that Nanny doesn't allow you to read these, but just this once, I thought we could break the rules. What Nanny doesn't know won't hurt her, eh?"

Dorothy-Anne was awed. "How did you ever manage to sneak them in past her?"

"I sent Nanny on an errand while Miss Bunt wheeled me into the bookshop." Elizabeth-Anne shook her head in marvel. "I picked them out myself. My, my, you can't even find a simple Superman comic anymore. Just those ghastly creatures like Hydraman and Granite Woman. Brrr!" She made a production of shuddering. "Hide them under your blanket. Nanny will be in a little later." She paused as Dorothy-Anne slid them under the covers. "Do you hurt?"

Dorothy-Anne shook her head. "No. But I feel kind of . . . weird."

"I should imagine. Probably the result of blood loss. I talked to Dr. Sidney. He assured me you'll be out of here in no time. Thank goodness Nanny and I found you in time. Otherwise you might have died." Elizabeth-Anne paused, bowed her head, inspected her hands. "I've always been of the opinion that there can't be effects without causes. Some people say certain acts are never justified, but I'm not one of them. People usually do things for a good reason." She lifted her head and gazed at Dorothy-Anne. "Do you want to talk about it?"

Dorothy-Anne shook her head. "You . . . you wouldn't understand." A look of hurt came into Elizabeth-Anne's eyes. Dorothy-Anne felt instantly contrite. "I didn't mean it that way, Great-Granny," she said. "I know you would understand. It's just that . . ." She took a deep breath, frowned, then shook her head again. "It's just that *I* can't talk about it. At least not yet."

Elizabeth-Anne cocked her head to one side. "I've lived a good many years, you know, and one of the few things that I have learned is never to coop up any hurt inside you." She paused. "You just concentrate on getting better. Just remember, I'm not advising you to do it, but if you feel you don't want to talk about it—ever—well, I'll understand that, too." She smiled gently.

Dorothy-Anne returned the smile, her eyes moist. "Thank you," she whispered.

Elizabeth-Anne rearranged her lap blanket. "Well, I'd better be going before the nurse charges in here and throws me out. Five minutes, I was told, and no longer."

As if on cue, the door opened and the mannish nurse poked her head in. "Five minutes are up, Mrs. Hale," she said.

"I'm going, I'm going." Elizabeth-Anne shook her head. "To several thousand people I may be the boss, but when it comes to doctors and nurses, *I'm* the one who gets pushed around." She laughed, maneuvering her chair back to the door. "You just make sure they take good care of you," she warned. "After all, you're a Hale. I didn't set up an endowment for a new wing here for nothing."

"Great-Granny?"

Elizabeth-Anne stopped wheeling the chair. "Yes, dear?"

"Why are men the way they are?"

Elizabeth-Anne started; then a veil seemed to drop down over her eyes. She moved the chair around so that she faced the bed. "I honestly don't know, dear," she said. "That's one question I haven't been able to answer."

"And Great-Grandfather? What was he like?"

"Zaccheus?" Elizabeth-Anne steepled her fingers and raised them to her lips. Her eyes held a faraway look. "He was sweet. And I loved him."

"Was he like Daddy?"

Elizabeth-Anne's eyes flashed. So that was it. Henry had

driven his daughter to this, caused a mere child to reach for solace in death. As stunned as she was, she wasn't surprised. She had always admonished him to do more for his daughter. Yet what was more impossible to fake than a love that was not there?

"Your daddy doesn't mean to be cruel," Elizabeth-Anne said. "It's just that he's still hurting from something that was no one's fault. He's angry that he couldn't control things."

Dorothy-Anne paused for a long minute, then asked, "Are all men like that?"

"No, my love, not all men. Someday you'll see. Just be patient, and someday you'll see."

The day Dorothy-Anne was released from the hospital, her great-grandmother had to leave for Tokyo to inaugurate the newly completed Hale Imperial Palace. The most ambitious hotel in the Hale chain, the Imperial Palace rested amid an ancient rock garden of lakes and cherry trees. It boasted every modern luxury but also respected traditional Japanese design. Elizabeth-Anne had been applauded for insisting that the authentic design also spoil as little of its ancient setting as possible. "Art," Elizabeth-Anne had told reporters at a much-publicized press conference before the hotel was built, "must be respected and preserved, no matter the price."

The price had been a million dollars more than anticipated.

"There's been so much fanfare that I've got to be there." Elizabeth-Anne explained when she stopped by the hospital to visit Dorothy-Anne before leaving. "The press will be there, and so will the American ambassador, as well as an emissary from the emperor. I've spoken to Dr. Sidney. You're to go home this afternoon. Nanny will have my car at her disposal and she'll come to pick you up. Also, I've spoken to your father. He should be home this evening."

Dorothy-Anne nodded. She had been in the hospital for two days, and that had given her plenty of time to think. She had been hoping that when her father got back and was told what she had done, things would change. At least she knew why he hated her. That was a start. She promised herself that she would try her best to make things up to him. Perhaps, in time, if she tried hard enough, he would find it in his heart to forgive her for killing her mother. They would get along better together. He might even learn to love her. He'd celebrate her birthdays with her. Take her out to dinners. Even to his office, where he would probably introduce her to his associates.

But now that the time to face him was nearly at hand, Dorothy-Anne wished that she didn't have to see him. She had counted on Great-Granny being there, giving her support. Without her, the dreams of reconciliation vanished. Much as she needed to, she knew she would never be able to explain to her father why she had tried to kill herself. Worse, she felt like a stupid, weak bungler for having tried it. She knew how her father despised weak people.

She felt miserable during the drive home. Once she got there, she stayed in her room until her father arrived and Nanny came upstairs to get her.

She was surprised when she entered the big sitting room. Four people were there: her father, a beautiful woman she had never seen before, and two girls about her age. The woman was tall and blond, a combination of femininity and virility, elegant but athletic. She studied Dorothy-Anne with wide blue eyes set in a tanned face. The two girls were mirror images of her, smaller, but just as self-assured.

Her father cleared his throat. "Dorothy-Anne?"

She stepped timidly forward, hugely conscious of her bandaged wrists. She hid her hands behind her back. "Yes, Daddy?"

"This is Chessy," he said, gesturing at the beautiful woman. "And these are her daughters CeCe and Diane." He indicated the two girls.

Dorothy-Anne stared first at the woman, then at the girls. She didn't understand why they were there. She looked stupidly at her father.

"Chessy and I stopped in Las Vegas this morning and got married," Henry Hale said. "Aren't you going to kiss your new mother?"

Dorothy-Anne stood stock-still. For a moment she couldn't believe her ears. It was too much to bear. "You're not my mother!'' she shouted angrily. ''You'll *never* be my mother!'' Then she burst into tears, ran upstairs to her room, and locked the door.

Chessy got to her feet to follow her, but Henry Hale waved her back. ''Leave her be,'' he said sternly.

Chessy looked at him dubiously, but sat back down.

''He didn't even ask why I did it or how I was,'' Dorothy-Anne sobbed, clutching the pillow to her. ''He couldn't have cared less if I had died.''

She wept all night long, long after no more tears would come. She was still sobbing when morning came. Her face was red and tired, her eyes swollen, and the nubby pink bedspread was rumpled and damp. But the good cry had done her good. It had anesthetized the hurt.

Sitting up slowly, she wiped her fingers across her eyes. During the endless night, the answer had come to her. She was too sensitive and vulnerable. Hurting herself did no one any good, herself least of all. Instead, she would arm herself with her own defenses. She would be stoic. Poised. She would never again show emotions, never let on how hurt she was.

She would be just like Great-Grandmother Elizabeth-Anne.

2

Freddie took a last drag on his cigarette. The ash glowed red in the dim room, then he stubbed the butt out in a saucer. Reaching for the cup of coffee Mrs. Ramirez had brought him, he looked up at her. ''Thanks,'' he said gratefully, taking the cup with both hands.

''De nada.'' Felicia Ramirez nodded toward the bed. ''Your wife. How is she?''

''Resting.'' He blew on the hot coffee, then sipped it carefully. It was thick and bitter, but it would help keep him alert. Help him do what he now realized he had to do.

Mrs. Ramirez drank from her own cup, then said quietly, "I try the telephone while I make the coffee."

He looked at her with raised eyebrows.

"It still does not work," she said.

Freddie glanced at his wristwatch. The dial glowed pale green, showing past ten o'clock. He had thought it was much later; the minutes seemed to have crept by like hours. He looked up at Mrs. Ramirez. "Do you think I should go outside and see if a car passes?"

Mrs. Ramirez shook her head. "No one but the locals use this road anymore. They know better than to travel in this storm. The bridge down the road sometimes washes away."

Freddy looked over at Dorothy-Anne, who slept quietly. "She'll need a doctor."

Mrs. Ramirez laid a hand on his arm. "We must wait until the storm is past."

He shook his head. "It may be too late then."

Felicia Ramirez stared at him, her face pulsating in the flickering candlelight. She knew it was true. The contractions were coming more frequently and still the young woman burned with fever. "What do you suggest?"

Freddie tightened his lips. "I'll walk into town. You give me the directions and I'll come back with the doctor."

"The best way is through the groves." Her eyes clouded over. "You may get lost. It is a long way."

He met her eyes. "I'll have to take that chance," he said softly. "I have no choice."

Minutes later, Dorothy-Anne struggled to rouse herself. When she opened her eyes, everything was at first a blur. Then her vision cleared, and she saw Freddie at the foot of the bed, shrugging himself into his jacket. Mrs. Ramirez handed him a black rain slicker, saying softly, "Here, you will need this." Freddie took the slicker, his expression grim.

"Freddie?"

He looked up sharply, then forced a smile. "Hi, honey," he said cheerfully. "Feeling any better?"

"Yes, a lot." Dorothy-Anne hesitated. "Where are you going?"

"To get us some doughnuts." He came toward her, sat on the edge of the bed, and took her hands in his.

"No, I mean really," she said, smiling weakly.

"I'm going to see about a doctor."

"But—"

"Ssh. It's just a short walk across the groves into town." He glanced over his shoulder. "Mrs. Ramirez told me the way."

Dorothy-Anne's voice was thick with fright. "But I don't want you to leave me."

"Don't you want to have a healthy baby for us?"

She nodded solemnly.

"Then you'll have to trust me. You do trust me, don't you, honey?" With one hand he smoothed her glossy forehead.

"Yes," she whispered, "I trust you."

A particularly sharp gust of wind tore at the tin roof above them; the roof buckled inward and then snapped back, like tin shaken for theatrical thunder.

"I love you," she whispered urgently.

"And I love you too."

"You'll be careful?"

Taking her hand in his, he pressed it firmly against his cheek. "Of course I'll be careful."

"I wouldn't . . ."

"You wouldn't what?"

"I wouldn't want . . . in the wind, anything could happen."

"Don't you worry your pretty head about me." He leaned forward and kissed her, then got to his feet.

She looked up at him. He seemed so tall, so strong and in command. She was awash with gratitude, with love for him and the child of his she carried. "I love you," she whispered again. "I've loved you ever since the first time I saw you."

He smiled at the memory and whispered, "And I've loved you, Dorothy-Anne."

They stared at each other in silence, the memory a visible bond between them.

* * *

Octobr 17, 1983, was a windswept autumn afternoon in Chicago. The giant skyscrapers stood out in sharp relief against the sparsely clouded sky. One could smell the tang of the lake, a mere three blocks away. The beaches along Lake Michigan were chewed by the breakers, and the sun peeked out from behind the clouds as Dorothy-Anne got out of the rental car.

She tilted her head back, squinted up at the large grimy building, and shook her head in despair. It did little to inspire her. Still, her great-grandmother had sent her to scout out the work of Freddie Cantwell, so scout it out she would. Although she couldn't for the life of her see why she was doing it.

Slamming the car door shut, she picked her way gingerly across the debris to get to the planks coursing up into the high dark doorway of the building. The stairs had been removed. The sidewalk was torn up, and the sand was thick and deep. She would have to cross ten feet of it in order to get to the planks.

As soon as her feet sank into the soft sand, she was irritated. She had spent a hundred and fifty dollars on the Maud Frizon shoes, and now they would be ruined. She hadn't anticipated such a mess; it was the last time she would ever wear good clothes to a construction site she wasn't familiar with. But she hadn't had a choice. She had flown in, rented the car, and she'd have to fly back to New York again this very evening. There wasn't time to go to a hotel and change.

Suddenly her left ankle twisted sideways and she let out a short cry at the sharp pain. Bending down, she massaged her ankle gingerly.

A burly black construction worker in a silver hardhat and sleeveless T-shirt hurried over to her. "You okay, miss?" he asked.

She tilted her head to look up at him. No, I'm not all right, she wanted to snap, but she nodded, bit down the pain, and refused to show either it or her irritation. "Yes, thank you. I'm fine."

"You sure don't look it. I mean, you look right sharp in

that outfit, but it's all wrong for this place." He tilted back his hardhat and scratched the front of his gray, woolly scalp. His face held a puzzled expression. "What you doin' here, anyway?" He eyed her keenly. "Are you from the bank?"

She straightened and shook her head, her wheat-gold bangs and pageboy cut swaying gently. "I'm afraid I'm not."

"Good." He grinned with relief. Then, as she took a few tentative steps, he automatically reached out to help her.

"Thank you." She smiled at him faintly. "Do you work for Freddie Cantwell?"

He grinned widely. "Sure do. Wouldn't want to work for anyone else, either."

"Oh? And why's that?"

" 'Cause he's a genius. He can take an old building like this one, gut it, and make it better than anything ever been built. Better-looking too. He can cut corners and costs, but he knows where to cut them." He grinned even more broadly. "But most of all because he hires folks like me." He saw her puzzled expression. "You see," he explained, "I ain't got much of a chance to work. Neither have many of the others. We've all had troubles in the past, jail, drugs and stuff. Cantwell's the only person who gives us a chance."

"I see."

"You want to see him."

"That's what I came for."

"He's up there." The black man took off his hardhat, leaned his head way back, and squinted as he pointed toward the roof of the building. A crane was lifting a pallet of bricks skyward, and then swung its cargo gracefully out of view.

"Fine. Just lead the way."

"That's the way up." He gestured at the crane. "But we got to wait till the pallet puts down empty."

"You mean . . ." Her voice faltered. "That's the *only* way up?"

" 'Fraid so. We ain't got no money for nothing else." He smiled apologetically. "But I'll go up with you. I won't let you fall, don't worry."

Sooner than she would have liked, Dorothy-Anne found herself clinging to the big black man's arm as the two of them rose gracefully into the sky, perched on the pallet. She groaned in dismay as she glanced down between the wide gaps in the pallet wood and saw the ground sink swiftly away. She glanced sideways at her companion, who casually held onto the cable.

"Old Sepp, he's the operator," the big man said admiringly. "Handles this baby smooth as silk."

Dorothy-Anne nodded and forced her eyes to look up. She hated heights, but she didn't say a word. A minute later, the pallet swung gently toward the roof and set down without a quiver.

"See? What'd I tell you? Smooth as silk."

She smiled gratefully. "You'll help me? On the way down?"

"Sure will. You just signal for me. My name's Luther. And over there, that's Mr. Cantwell." Luther pointed to the far end of the roof.

Dorothy-Anne's gaze followed his pointing finger. A man was kneeling on the roof with his back to them. Spread out before him were sets of blueprints weighted down with a brick at each corner.

"Hello? Mr. Cantwell?" Dorothy-Anne called out.

The man didn't appear to hear her. She narrowed her eyes, squared her shoulders, and made her way toward him.

"Mr. Cantwell," she said sharply, when her shadow covered the blueprints. "I'm Dorothy-Anne Hale, of Hale Ho—"

He turned around then, and suddenly, for no explicable reason at all, she lost her voice.

Perhaps it was his smile, or maybe the magnetic, bottomless depths of his eyes, or even the easy charm that emanated from him. Dorothy-Anne had the sensation of suddenly tumbling into a vacuum, of somersaulting through airless space, of being drawn in slow motion into those hypnotic eyes.

In that instant her mind seemed to snap, clicking a sharply focused photograph of such impossible intensity, such surreal clarity, that she knew it would be frozen in her mind forever. She had captured his face, been drawn into the inescapable image of his pale gray eyes with amber flecks and fine, thread-thin streaks of emerald. She would never forget his soiled sleeveless T-shirt which showed off his thick muscular shoulders, tapering down to a slim, tight waist. His stormy good looks were dark, and his face tanned and rugged, but with laugh lines sculpted deep around his eyes. Even close-cropped, his hair was blue-black, his chin strong and cleft, his mouth generous and sensual.

One instant he had been a stranger, and the next she could think of nothing but his touch, his hands holding her against his powerful chest.

One instant she was a young lady, a mere girl just out of school, and the next she was a woman, a full-grown woman with a desire that shook her to her very core.

In that instant, all the frustration she had felt over soiling her shoes and hurting her ankle evaporated. Instead, she saw him, and knew with an uncanny certainty that he was just as keenly aware of her. For a long moment he locked eyes with her.

She felt the blush creeping up into her face. "I have come all the way from New York to see you, Mr. Cantwell," she said, her voice curiously unsteady.

"Have you, now?" His eyes appeared to be laughing at her.

"I have," she said a little too sharply. She swallowed, trying to regain her calm. "I'm here as a representative of Hale Hotels. We're interested in your work. You have a reputation not only for coming in under budget but also for renovating and designing buildings which . . ." Her voice trailed off under his unblinking gaze. She felt acutely uncomfortable.

"Yes?" he asked quietly.

Suddenly she was burning with anger. She was not used to being treated like this, to being thrown off kilter so completely by a perfect stranger. He was obviously not only aware of her discomfiture but also relished watching her flounder. She knew then that he wasn't about to come to the aid of her faltering monologue.

"I have come," she said between clenched teeth, "to see some of your work firsthand."

"But most of all," he added shrewdly, "to see if I can be bought by the Philistines?" He winked at her.

441

She ignored the wink and the gibe. "Well? Are you going to show me around?"

He placed his hands on his lean hips and grinned disarmingly. "No," he said matter-of-factly.

Her eyes widened. "And may I ask why not?"

"Because," he said without taking his eyes off her, "it's way past lunchtime, for one thing."

"Then I'll take you to lunch."

"Sorry." He shook his head. "I can't take the time. I've still got too much to finish today."

She growled in exasperation. "Mr. Cantwell," she said curtly, "I've flown all the way from New York just to see you."

"Something which neither I, nor anyone else here, asked you to do," he reminded her.

She inclined her head. "Granted." Then she raised her face, her stubborn chin jutting outward. "Under the circumstances, I should think you would be only too happy to see me and show me around."

"Oh? And why should that be?"

"I happen to know for a fact that you're financially strapped. You've put everything you have into this project, and it's still far from completion. It'll be a miracle if you ever finish it."

"Ah. So you've been checking up on me. How deeply did you happen to delve into my resources, Miss . . ."

"Hale. Dorothy-Anne Hale." She shrugged. "We checked you out perfunctorily. But we know you need money, and lots of it."

"And you can provide it, I take it? As long as I join your organization?"

"Perhaps."

"I don't want it."

"I haven't offered it yet."

"But you will, won't you?" He gazed at her intently. "Why else would you have flown all the way out here?" He paused. "The answer is no."

"You mean you won't show me around?"

"I mean, I don't want your money. I happen to like my independence. I don't want to work for anyone but myself. It's nothing personal, you understand."

She smiled grimly. "Oh? Then what is it?"

He smiled disarmingly. "I just don't happen to think it's healthy for a husband and wife to work together."

She looked startled. There was a quiet intensity to his voice which turned her knees to jelly. Then she recovered her composure. "Mr. Cantwell," she said quietly, stressing every syllable, "I do not appreciate jokes. I take my business very seriously. And my time happens to be precious."

"And so is mine." He reached out and took her hand. He smiled hugely then, and his unexpected touch sent a tremor through her.

"Let's . . ." She took a deep breath. "Let's be serious, Mr. Cantwell."

"Freddie," he corrected her calmly. "You should call me Freddie. After all, this isn't the Victorian age when husbands and wives call themselves by their formal surnames."

"Stop joking," she said in a whisper.

"I'm dead serious."

"But . . . you don't even know me," she sputtered. Suddenly she couldn't face him, and looked down at his hand. He was still holding hers.

"I know enough," he said confidently.

There was a long silence then. In the background, the sounds of construction equipment sounded distant and unreal. From somewhere below she could hear a workman's harsh, clipped voice yelling, and then she heard the clearing of her own throat. She was aware of Freddie's gaze softening, the gray-and-black limpid pools of his eyes surveying her tenderly, his teeth even and white and flashing as he smiled good-naturedly, his natural, instinctive charm in brilliant evidence as he said, "Naturally, I don't expect your reply right now. You've got to think it over first. And for that I've got all the time in the world."

"You're persistent, aren't you?" she said with grudging admiration. She smiled, her coolness thawing.

"That I am. And like I told you, we've got time. Lots of it. Because before I get married, I intend to finish this project. Without any help."

"And why's that?" she found herself asking. "It might be a year. Even two."

"I wouldn't want you to get the wrong idea." He smiled. He let go of her hand.

"What do you mean?"

"I wouldn't want you to think I'm after your money. It's like I said. I'm independent. Now, since that's settled, can I buy a lady a cup of coffee?" he asked.

And like a fool, Dorothy-Anne blushed a bright crimson and found herself sputtering, "Yes, thank you . . . I mean . . . if you really want to . . ."

"I do," he said gently, hooking his arm through hers and leading her toward the pallet. His words echoed in her mind. She couldn't believe this man meant to offer those words to her as a promise.

Do you, Frederick Cantwell, take this woman to be your lawfully wedded wife, to honor and cherish her, through sickness and through health, until the day that you die?"

"I do."

I do. Tiny, simple words. Huge, grave words of responsibility. But they were uttered only a short year later. Meanwhile, Dorothy-Anne and Freddie lived together on weekends. During the workdays of those many, many weeks, he was in Chicago, and she traveled constantly on business. Until the building he was working on was finished, without any help from her, he refused to tie the knot.

For the time being, there was her flight back to New York, a smooth flight through soaring emotions she would never forget. The day seemed to billow and sail, along with her spirit, and her thoughts were filled with the image of Freddie Cantwell's eyes. Only when she arrived back in New York and met Elizabeth-Anne at the airport did she remember what day it was. And even then, Elizabeth-Anne had had to tell her.

The night in New York was clear and star-studded. Traffic on the Long Island Expressway was light and moving along at a swift clip. Elizabeth-Anne unsnapped her large Bottega Veneta handbag and rummaged through it. She took out a thick vellum envelope. "Dear?" She held it out to Dorothy-Anne.

"Yes, Great-Granny?"

"Please. Accept this graciously."

Dorothy-Anne took the envelope and switched on the reading lamp on her side of the Rolls. She looked down at the envelope, frowning in puzzlement as she stroked a stray lock of hair out of her eyes. The left-hand corner of the envelope was embossed with a blue return address: Shatzkin, Morris, Bernstein and Bidgood, P.C., 666 Fifth Avenue, New York, N.Y. 10019.

Slowly she tore the envelope open. She unfolded a sheaf of legal papers, held them up to the light, and then turned to Elizabeth-Anne. "But . . . but it's a deed," she murmured in surprise.

"Don't you think I know that?" Elizabeth-Anne said with mock crossness.

"But—"

Elizabeth-Anne held up a hand, gloved palm facing outward, as if to ward off an attack. "No buts, dear. We've waited a long time for this day."

"What do you mean?"

"Don't tell me you've forgotten!" Elizabeth-Anne eyed her great-granddaughter shrewdly. "Dorothy-Anne, darling, it's your eighteenth birthday. Don't you remember? Today the Hale Palace Hotel, which has been held in trust for you since your ninth birthday, is officially *yours*."

"Oh Great-Granny, I *had* forgotten. But . . . I thought that maybe . . ."

"Maybe what?"

"Well . . ."

"When I give someone something, I give it to them for keeps." Elizabeth-Anne smiled faintly.

Dorothy-Anne threw her arms around her great-grandmother just as, in the distance, far beyond the Silver Lady hood ornament, they could already see the distant winking skyline of Manhattan pushing up over the industrial buildings and factories of Long Island City.

A flash of lightning lit the little room like a strobe and the scene became a frozen tableau. The past merged with the present, and Dorothy-Anne returned to the

Hale Tourist Court outside Quebeck, Texas. She looked up at Freddie. Her eyes were solemn and her face pale.

"More pains?" he asked.

She shook her head and breathed deeply. "Freddie? I don't want you to go out into that storm."

"It'll be all right, hon."

"You'll be careful?"

He grinned and held up a hand, palm out. "Scout's honor."

"You were never a scout," she said weakly. He smiled, but she was still worried. "Freddie?"

"Hmmmm?"

"I'm afraid."

"Don't be." He smiled down at her. "All I'm going to do is go get a doctor. Remember what you used to tell me? As a child, whenever you heard a siren wailing, and you were frightened, what did your great-grandmother tell you?"

"That it doesn't mean that something bad has happened," she whispered. "It means that help is on the way."

"That's right. Just keep that in mind." He paused and flashed her his most enigmatic grin. "Who loves ya, baby?"

This was an old game between them. She smiled faintly. "Kojak," she whispered.

He kissed her forehead. "Atta girl."

And he was gone.

Dorothy-Anne had drifted into a restless sleep, and woke easily when she heard Mrs. Ramirez come back into the room. She struggled to sit up. "How long has he been gone now?" she asked anxiously.

Mrs. Ramirez checked her watch. "It hasn't been that long," she lied softly. She turned away and busied herself blowing out one of the candles that had nearly burned itself out. She stuck a new taper into the candlestick, then lit it before setting it back down on the dresser.

Dorothy-Anne stared at the ceiling and listened to the drumming of the rain. It seemed to be coming down even heavier now. "The storm's not letting up," she said tremulously.

"No, not yet," Mrs. Ramirez said. "But soon."

"It seems to be getting worse."

Mrs. Ramirez cocked her head and listened. She nodded.

"Sometimes it is at its worst right before it ends," she said reassuringly. She reached behind Dorothy-Anne and fluffed the pillow. "You just rest. And stay covered." Mrs. Ramirez leaned over her and patted her hand. "You will need all your strength." Then she smiled and lowered herself onto the chair she had pulled up alongside the bed. "Do not worry," she said gently. "I will not leave you alone."

Dorothy-Anne nodded gratefully. Then she sighed and let her head drop back down on the pillow. She shut her eyes and listened to the violent drumming of the rain. It was coming down heavily, as it had done on the day of her fifth birthday.

It had been raining cats and dogs then, too.

That had been in 1970. Outside, the thunderstorm had raged and flashed. Inside the sitting room of the big house in Tarrytown, it was warm and cozy. A fire crackled in both of the two big fireplaces.

Dorothy-Anne had been seated on the tiny Louis XVI children's chair, working the giant jigsaw puzzle Nanny had given her for her birthday. She kept frowning at the picture of the giant Mickey Mouse on the cover of the box, wondering how on earth to recreate it. Opposite her, Nanny was seated very erectly on the gold brocade sofa, watching her intently but giving Dorothy-Anne no clue as to where to place the puzzle piece she held in her hand. Dorothy-Anne knew better than to ask for help. Nanny was a great believer in letting one figure out problems by oneself.

Nanny seemed to sense rather than hear the bald black butler come silently into the room. She turned around. "The car has arrived," he announced.

Nanny nodded. "Thank you, Franklin." She rose to her feet and smoothed her dress. "It's time we left, Dorothy-Anne."

Dorothy-Anne looked up at her, the puzzle piece still in her hand. She looked sorely disappointed. She didn't want to leave. "I'm not done yet," she said unhappily. "Can't we wait?"

"I'm afraid not," Nanny answered firmly.

Dorothy-Anne sighed and pushed herself to her feet. Nanny came toward her, knelt down on one knee, and adjusted the collar of Dorothy-Anne's party dress.

"I want you to look very nice," Nanny told her. "Your great-grandmother is a great believer in neatness. And so," she added pointedly, "am I."

"Why isn't Great-Granny coming here?" Dorothy-Anne asked.

"She would have, I'm sure, but she called to say she's very busy today," Nanny explained. She straightened and took Dorothy-Anne by the hand. "Come, child. It's time we left." With her free hand Nanny scooped up Dorothy-Anne's shiny red plastic raincoat.

Dorothy-Anne eyed the raincoat with disgust. She didn't like it. It made her feel hot and sticky. "I don't want to go to the city!" she announced suddenly, withdrawing her hand from Nanny's. "It's too noisy and there are so many people." She shivered and rubbed her arms. "It frightens me."

"You have nothing to worry about," Nanny assured her, giving her an affectionate squeeze.

Dorothy-Anne stared up at her.

"Besides, your nanny will be there, won't she?" Nanny asked. "And so will your great-grandmother. You want to see her, don't you?"

Dorothy-Anne nodded solemnly.

"I happen to know for a fact that your great-grandmother is going to take you to a very special place."

Dorothy-Anne's eyes glimmered with anticipation. "She is?"

Nanny nodded. "She is. But I can't tell you any more. It's supposed to be a surprise."

Dorothy-Anne's face broke into a grin. She tugged at Nanny's hand. "Well?" she demanded. "Let's *go*."

The rain didn't let up even after they reached the city. During the drive down, Nanny had explained that the average thunderstorm lasted only about twenty minutes, so there must have been several thunderstorms piled up, and passing over New York one after another. Dorothy-Anne listened in fascination, watching the rain bead up on the windows of her father's sleek black limousine. She snuggled farther into the corner of the gray velour seat. With one hand she wiped the foggy side window clear. It felt cold and wet to the touch.

The world outside was blurry and gray. Timidly she glanced sideways at Nanny.

Nanny held out her arms. Quickly Dorothy-Anne scrambled over to her. She let herself be enveloped in Nanny's protective warmth.

"We're almost there," Nanny said as the car turned on to Seventy-second Street, then entered Central Park. Ten minutes later, they pulled up alongside the tall steel-and-glass building on Park Avenue and Fifty-first Street. "Here we are," Nanny said. She handed Dorothy-Anne the raincoat. "Put it on or you'll get soaked."

Dorothy-Anne made a face.

"You'll have to wear it," Nanny said firmly. "Otherwise we'll drive right back to Tarrytown."

Scowling, Dorothy-Anne shrugged into the coat. The chauffeur opened the passenger door and held an umbrella over them as they hurried through the driving rain to the big revolving glass doors.

Once inside, Dorothy-Anne looked around the cavernous marble lobby with awe. The ceiling was so high and there seemed to be marble everywhere. "Is this one of Great-Granny's hotels?" she asked as Nanny held tightly to her hand. They were walking through the crowded lobby toward the elevators.

Nanny shook her head. "No, this is not a hotel. It's an office building. Many people work here, including your great-grandmother. You see, her hotel business is so big that she has to have separate offices just to run everything. She owns hotels all over the world."

Dorothy-Anne nodded sagely as she digested this. "And this whole building belongs to her?" she asked as they waited in front of an elevator door.

Nanny chuckled. "Lord no, child. But as far as I know, she rents two entire floors, which is a lot of office space, believe me."

Dorothy-Anne looked up at her. "Does Daddy work here too?"

A mask seemed to slide down over Nanny's face. "I'm not

really sure,'' she said quickly. ''You'll have to ask your great-grandmother.''

Dorothy-Anne's face fell. ''Nobody ever tells me anything about him,'' she said quietly. ''Every time I ask, I get told to ask someone else.''

Nanny looked at her with a sad sympathy Dorothy-Anne was too young to recognize. ''That's because it's good manners to mind your own business,'' she said lamely.

''But what Daddy does *is* my business, isn't it?'' she asked with the damning, incisive insight of the very young.

Nanny was saved from answering by the arrival of the elevator. After they stepped inside, Dorothy-Anne watched as Nanny pressed a button marked ''32.'' The moment Nanny's finger touched it, the number lit up. Dorothy-Anne's eyes grew big. Tentatively she reached up and fingered one of the numbers. She squealed with delight as it lit up. She pressed another, then another.

Nanny slapped her hand lightly. ''Stop that,'' she scolded. She looked apologetically at the other passengers, but no one returned her smile.

Stung by Nanny's slap, Dorothy-Anne tightened her lips. For a moment she thought she would cry, and she tried very hard not to. And then the doors were sliding open and Dorothy-Anne found herself face to face with an entirely new world.

''Is this where Great-Granny works?'' she asked as they got off.

Nanny nodded solemnly. ''It is.''

Dorothy-Anne felt a strange pride at the thought that all this belonged to her family. The reception area was lavishly furnished in a style that spoke of opulence, grand comfort, and a solid financial footing.

The walls were paneled in mahogany and the carpeting was a delicate oh-so-pale pink. The sprawling sofas and chairs were masterpieces of the art-deco artist Andrew Groult, and worth a small fortune. The huge marble fireplace was artificial, but looked as if it belonged. The only hint that this was not the lobby of a luxury hotel but instead the headquarters of a vast business empire was a discreetly engraved gold plate facing the visitor from atop the receptionist's Persian desk. The plaque read merely, HALE HOTELS, INC.

The receptionist was young and blond. She seemed startled to see a child, but she recovered her composure with a cool smile. "May I help you?" she asked Nanny.

"We'd like to see Mrs. Hale," Nanny answered.

"Do you have an appointment?"

Nanny sniffed. "We do."

"And who may I say is here to see her?"

Nanny smiled down at Dorothy-Anne and gave her hand a squeeze. "Miss Dorothy-Anne Hale," she announced

The name worked magic. The receptionist's professional smile thawed. "If you'll have a seat for just a moment, someone will be right out," she said with new warmth. She picked up an ivory telephone as Nanny led Dorothy-Anne over to a sofa. Before they had even settled down, the tall French doors leading down a long pink-carpeted corridor opened and an impeccably dressed woman with raven hair strode toward them.

"Miss Hale?" she asked, leaning down and smiling at Dorothy-Anne. "I am Mrs. Goldstine, Mrs. Hale's secretary."

"How do you do?" Dorothy-Anne asked solemnly as they shook hands, but inwardly she winced. Mrs. Goldstine's hand was cold and dry.

"I'm fine, thank you." Mrs. Goldstine smiled, turned to Nanny, and shook her hand also. "Please," she said, gesturing elegantly. "If you'll follow me?" She led the way through the tall doors, walking briskly so that Nanny as well as Dorothy-Anne had to hurry to keep up with her.

The hallway seemed impossibly long. They passed countless closed doors, then turned the corner and faced a wall of glass that looked onto a huge windowless room crowded with rows of desks.

"That's the typing pool," Mrs. Goldstine explained.

"That's where I want to work when I grow up," Dorothy-Anne announced. "Because of the pool." She craned her neck. "But where *is* it?"

"It's only an expression. It's called a pool because it's where a lot of people work together in one spot."

"Well, maybe I *don't* want to work there after all," Dorothy-Anne mused thoughtfully.

"I think," Mrs. Goldstine said, "that when the time comes, your great-grandmother has bigger plans in store for you than the typing pool."

A little farther on, they passed another, almost identically glassed-in room.

"Another pool?" Dorothy-Anne asked brightly.

"That is the accounting department," Mrs. Goldstine explained. "The people you see in there take care of all the money your great-grandmother's hotels bring in from all around the world."

Dorothy-Anne nodded. "But don't you ever get lost here?" she asked as they continued walking.

Mrs. Goldstine laughed. "I *was* a little confused in the beginning," she confessed, "but you get used to it very quickly." They turned another corner. "Here we are."

The first office was Mrs. Goldstine's. It had a big Renaissance desk and the chairs were upholstered in genuine brocade. The office beyond was Elizabeth-Anne Hale's. They faced two huge, tall French doors with beveled glass windows and opaque blue curtains.

Mrs. Goldstine knocked, then swung one of the doors open. Dorothy-Anne stood in the doorway, Nanny's hands on her shoulders, and gazed across the room at her great-grandmother.

Elizabeth-Anne was standing beside a sofa, speaking on the telephone. The moment she glanced toward the door, she quickly said something and hung up.

Ever since she could remember, Dorothy-Anne had been immensely impressed by her great-grandmother. Elizabeth-Anne always looked so imposing and in command, with never a spun-silver hair out of place. She stood tall and slender, and looked much younger than her seventy-five years in her classically styled peach woolen suit. A single strand of matchless South Seas pearls encircled her neck.

"Great-Granny!" Dorothy-Anne cried, and she dashed headlong toward Elizabeth-Anne's outstretched arms.

"Mrs. Goldstine," Elizabeth-Anne called over Dorothy-Anne's head as she embraced her, "please hold all calls."

Mrs. Goldstine nodded and smiled.

"I'll wait outside," Nanny said discreetly, and then the French door closed soundlessly and Elizabeth-Anne and her great-granddaughter were alone in the room. For a moment they held their tight embrace. Then Elizabeth-Anne held Dorothy-Anne at arm's length and gazed deeply into her eyes.

"Is this office all yours, Great-Granny?" Dorothy-Anne asked in wonder.

"It is," Elizabeth-Anne replied. "Do you like it?"

Dorothy-Anne twisted around. The room was huge, with floor-to-ceiling windows looking out over Central Park, the huge apartment buildings lining the West Side, the wide silver breadth of the Hudson, and all the way into New Jersey. The rainswept view was gray, but no mere gloomy weather could dampen the plush comfort, and the office was at once warm and cozy. The furnishings were similar to those of the reception room, but dominated by rich peacock blues and warm wood. Elizabeth-Anne's desk was a large, ornately carved Italian piece facing two plush armchairs. Dorothy-Anne thought it beautiful, but felt comfortably at home at the same time.

Elizabeth-Anne's aquamarine eyes glanced toward the rain-streaked windows. "It's still coming down," she said, "but that's all right. The car is waiting for us, so we won't get wet."

"At least the thunder's stopped," Dorothy-Anne said softly. "It frightened me."

"I can understand that. I was the same way when I was your age."

"You were?"

"Of course I was." Elizabeth-Anne strode toward the telephone and placed a call. She did not refer to the caller by name, nor did she have to identify herself. Her crisp, clear voice was unmistakable. "I'm ready to go to lunch now," she said. "We'll meet here in my office." She hung up the telephone and winked conspiratorially at Dorothy-Anne.

"Who was that?"

Elizabeth-Anne smiled secretly. "You'll find out soon enough."

"Nanny said we're going somewhere special."

"And indeed we are." Elizabeth-Anne came forward, patted Dorothy-Anne's shoulder, and turned as she heard the door opening.

Dorothy-Anne turned around too. Her eyes bulged in disbelief. Seeing her father in the flesh was more than a minor miracle. Although she lived under the same roof as he, their paths rarely crossed. She was too young to realize that this was purposeful, that unlike her, most children saw their fathers daily, and that hers tried his best to avoid her. Dorothy-Anne could hardly know that after hiring Nanny, her father had told the governess that her job was not so much to provide child care as to act as a guard. He had explained to her that he wanted to see as little of his daughter as humanly possible. Nanny had disapproved of this thoroughly, but upon seeing Dorothy-Anne's sweet elfin face, she had been unable to refuse the post. The child had clearly needed someone.

Luckily, although Dorothy-Anne mourned the fact that her father was elusive, she did not think his behavior at all strange, because it was all she had ever known. She loved him unquestioningly and with all her young heart. To her he was the most handsome man in the world, and now, looking across the room at him, she was filled with love for him.

"Daddy!" she squealed, racing across the deep blue carpet toward him. She flung her arms around his thighs and hung on for dear life.

Henry drew a deep breath and seemed to recoil. He clenched his hands at his sides and his face went dark as he glowered across the office at Elizabeth-Anne. "*This* is the luncheon appointment?" he asked in quiet disbelief.

Elizabeth-Anne raised her chin. "It is, Henry," she answered. "Need I remind you that it's her birthday today?" Her clear eyes glared at him challengingly.

But he matched her gaze without wavering. "How can I ever forget?" he asked. "It's the fifth anniversary of her mother's—"

"*Henry*." Elizabeth-Anne's warning tone cut him off. She came over and, taking Dorothy-Anne in her arms, carried her away from her father. "Be a good girl and wait outside with

Nanny and Mrs. Goldstine, dear,'' she said in a strained voice as she took Dorothy-Anne to the door. "Your father and I have something important to discuss in private. It won't take a minute, I promise." Elizabeth-Anne attempted a smile, and hoped Dorothy-Anne didn't notice how false it was.

Dorothy-Anne's face fell. She didn't understand exactly what was going on, but she could tell Elizabeth-Anne was tense, and that was something she had never seen before.

Dorothy-Anne's small shoulders slumped as she stepped out of the room and the doors closed behind her. The moment they clicked shut, she heard voices raised in anger from behind her. Helplessly she gazed over at Nanny, who was seated on one of the gold brocade chairs facing Mrs. Goldstine's desk. Behind it, Mrs. Goldstine busied herself by beating furiously on her sleek red typewriter, obviously attempting, though unsuccessfully, to muffle the tirade seeping through from Elizabeth-Anne's office.

"Goddammit, Grandmother," Henry Hale said bitingly, "can't you the hell ever stay out of anything? Do you always have to meddle in *all* my affairs?"

"You're my grandson," Elizabeth-Anne replied with calm. "Dorothy-Anne is my great-granddaughter. She's also a minor, and as such, needs someone to protect her interests. I don't think I should have to remind you that she's your daughter, Henry. Your much-neglected daughter."

"You think I don't know that?" Henry, usually the cool, composed executive, found himself losing control. His face was red and his neck cords stood out in bold relief. "You *dare* stand there and tell me who is or isn't related to me?" he shouted. "You *dare* tell me how I should treat that child? I suppose the next thing you'll try to tell me is how I should forgive her and forget it all, isn't it? After all the pain and heartache she's caused?"

Elizabeth-Anne was angry, but she did not allow herself the luxury of succumbing to her emotions. "Henry," she said, "what happened was a tragedy, but it was not Dorothy-Anne's fault and you know it. If anyone was to blame, it was

Anna. The doctor warned her, but she ignored him. Nor did she even tell you the danger she was in."

Henry made a sharp, dismissing gesture and turned away from Elizabeth-Anne. "I don't believe you could say such a thing," he said with angry disgust.

"What do you mean?"

"How could you speak of Anna like that . . . blame *her*! You act as if she's nothing, as if all you cared about were that child!"

"She's all that matters now, Henry," Elizabeth-Anne answered sadly. "She's your daughter and my great-granddaughter. She's our living legacy. Everything else was yesterday. Dorothy-Anne is *today*. She's all we have. Don't waste it, Henry, don't live in the past. What's gone is gone. You've got to leave it behind you."

"Sure." He laughed bitterly. "And kiss her at bedtime. Tell her stories. Tuck her in."

"Yes, Henry. That's exactly what I mean."

"Never," he answered, his voice cold as ice. "And this . . . this is one thing I can do something about."

The odd words, and the ugly vehemence behind them, caused the terrible truth to sink in. Elizabeth-Anne shook her head and compressed her lips. She was aghast with the realization that Henry would never change. He couldn't. He didn't just ignore his daughter, he wasn't just indifferent to her; he detested her. Somehow, in the grief-twisted state he had been in just after Anna's death, he had turned Dorothy-Anne into some kind of villain in his mind. And now he clung to that belief as the bedrock of his sanity. It was his lifeline, as if he couldn't face the world, couldn't live with his loss, unless he blamed it on someone, on the inhuman devil that he believed his child to be.

And now Elizabeth-Anne understood why. To Henry, Dorothy-Anne was not just a symbol of death, but a living proof of his own mortality. He had believed himself invincible, a match and master for any challenge. But the one battle that had really mattered was the one he had lost, the one that cut him down to mortal size. Death had won out, and he blamed the child.

"Henry," Elizabeth-Anne begged softly, "can't you find it in your heart to forget the past?"

"Forget?" he answered in disbelief. *"Forget."* He turned on her again, his eyes blazing with a light that frightened her, that took the heart out of her struggle. "Just remember one thing, Grandmother," he spat out. "You may pull the strings around here, but I won't let you do it in my home. Your power stops right here, at Hale Hotels. My life is my own." He turned and strode toward the door, and with his hand on the doorknob spoke again in a chilling voice. "And as far as *that child* goes, you can have her. I would prefer it if I never saw her again."

With that he was gone, striding through the outside office without a backward glance.

Elizabeth-Anne dropped her head to her hands. She looked terribly old, as if all the years she had lived had suddenly caught up with her.

Dorothy-Anne twisted her head around and gazed after her father's departing figure in confusion. She glanced over at Nanny, but her face was stoically expressionless. Mrs. Goldstine kept right on typing, as if trying to pretend nothing unusual had happened.

Finally Nanny pushed herself to her feet. "Come, dear," she said gently, reaching for Dorothy-Anne's hand. "Let's go see your great-grandmother again."

Together they headed back into Elizabeth-Anne's office. But once they saw Elizabeth-Anne, Nanny frowned and let go of Dorothy-Anne's hand. Elizabeth-Anne was swaying unsteadily on her feet and Nanny rushed forward to catch her as she collapsed in slow motion. Nanny stretched the old lady out flat on the floor and loosened the constricting collar of her blouse.

"Mrs. Goldstine!" she cried over her shoulder. "Quickly, call for an ambulance!"

In the outer office, the machine-gun typing stopped abruptly as Mrs. Goldstine jumped up from her chair. She peered around the corner of the doorway, her hand poised on her breast, and then lost no time in snatching up her telephone.

Dorothy-Anne stood quietly, a jumble of fleeting images

flashing through her mind. She did not know what was happening, only that Great-Granny and Daddy had had an awful fight.

And now Great-Granny was lying motionless on the deep blue carpet.

Dorothy-Anne was filled with a black, chilling fright, and began to cry soundlessly.

3

While they waited for the ambulance to arrive, Mrs. Goldstine got busy on the telephone. Elizabeth-Anne hadn't hired Natalie Goldstine, trained her over the years, and raised her income to the princely amount of fifty-five thousand dollars a year for nothing. Elizabeth-Anne considered it a small price to pay for the services Natalie Goldstine was capable of providing. And, right now, she was proving her worth.

First she called Elizabeth-Anne's physician of many years, Dr. Vartan Dadourian, who didn't waste a moment of precious time. "Make certain they take her to Columbia Presbyterian. I'll meet you there." He hung up before Mrs. Goldstine could thank him.

Next, she tried to get hold of Henry, which proved to be more difficult than she could have imagined. In the scant minutes which had passed since he had stormed out, he had already disappeared from the building.

"He went to lunch, and he doesn't have any meetings scheduled this afternoon as far as I know," Ruby Schaber, his secretary, told her. "I don't know when he'll be back."

"Call all the restaurants where he might have lunch and have him paged," Mrs. Goldstine said testily. "And if that doesn't work, start calling around town. Tell him it's an emergency. We'll be at Columbia Presbyterian."

"But when he walked out, he looked so . . . so angry," Ruby Schaber stammered uncertainly. "I don't know if I should bother him . . ."

Among her other talents, Natalie Goldstine was a woman who knew how to collect gossip and when to use it. "Miss Schaber, if you value your job, you'll do everything within your power to locate Mr. Hale as quickly as possible. And that includes calling the numbers in his little black book, which you have so indiscreetly let everyone know you have access to."

With that, Mrs. Goldstine hung up, but even Miss Schaber's fear-inspired efforts failed to turn Henry up by the time the ambulance arrived.

Mrs. Goldstine, Nanny, and Dorothy-Anne followed the stretcher-bearers down to the lobby. They knew Elizabeth-Anne was gravely ill, but decided not to call her sole surviving daughter, Regina, who had lived alone in California, ever since her husband's death, until they reached the hospital and conferred with the doctor.

"I'll ride with Mrs. Hale," Mrs. Goldstine told Nanny as they reached the ambulance. "You two follow in Mrs. Hale's car and we'll meet at the hospital."

Nanny looked hesitant, loath to let Elizabeth-Anne out of sight. If she should die, perhaps she would come to first and want to see Dorothy-Anne.

Mrs. Goldstine seemed to read her thoughts. She laid a hand on Nanny's arm. "I don't think the child needs to be exposed to the horrors of an ambulance ride just yet, do you?"

Nanny shook her head and Mrs. Goldstine climbed up into the back of the ambulance. The paramedics ducked inside, slammed the door, and the ambulance nosed into the thick traffic, siren wailing.

Nanny led Dorothy-Anne by the hand to Elizabeth-Anne's familiar yellow-and-black Rolls-Royce, which was double-parked a few yards away. Nanny's sharp eyes did not miss the fact that Henry Hale's limousine, which they had taken into the city, was gone. He had obviously used it for his escape.

They caught up with Mrs. Goldstine in the Hale Wing of Columbia Presbyterian. "Any word on her condition?" Nanny asked as she and Dorothy-Anne joined Mrs. Goldstine in the waiting room.

Mrs. Goldstine shook her head. "None yet. It's too early to tell, I'm afraid. Dr. Dadourian is in the emergency room. We'll just have to wait and see."

They sat down and began their impatient vigil. The busy sounds of the hospital's emergency waiting room—the hurried comings and goings of doctors and nurses, the cries of patients and the worried whispers of their loved ones—all seemed to be taking place at a great distance. Dorothy-Anne was lost in another world of fear and confusion.

Nanny's face was pinched and set in an expression of tight anxiety. Mrs. Goldstine kept fidgeting, constantly consulting her tiny gold wristwatch, and jumping up to use the pay telephone.

"Did they get through to him?" Nanny asked the first time Mrs. Goldstine returned from calling Miss Schaber.

Elizabeth-Anne's secretary had shaken her head morosely. "Nobody knows where to reach him," she said, "and the mobile phone in the limousine isn't being answered. This just isn't *like* him."

Thereafter, each time Mrs. Goldstine returned from using the telephone, she merely shook her head in a negative response to the hopeful question in Nanny's eyes.

"I'll get us something to drink," Mrs. Goldstine said finally, needing desperately to keep busy. She brought back three Styrofoam beakers from the vending machine, but she and Nanny didn't take more than one sip from their coffee before putting their cups down. Dorothy-Anne finished off her hot chocolate. It was not at all rich and creamy like the cocoa the cook made at home, but the sitting and waiting in the big airless room for so long had made her thirsty.

After what seemed an eternity, Dr. Dadourian pushed open the swinging doors of the waiting room to see them. He was a large, burly man with bushy salt-and-pepper eyebrows. As soon as they caught sight of him, Nanny and Mrs. Goldstine sprang to their feet, but Dorothy-Anne, whose experience with Dr. Dadourian had been limited to countless childhood inoculations, tried to make herself look as inconspicuous as possible. She sat swallowed up in the big green vinyl chair, her feet sticking straight out in the air in front of her.

"Mrs. Hale has suffered a severe stroke," Dr. Dadourian said heavily in his thick, guttural accent.

"Can we see her?" Nanny asked eagerly.

"Not just yet, I'm afraid."

"When *can* we see her?"

Dr. Dadourian sighed. "Perhaps tomorrow, but I'm not certain you'll want to."

Nanny looked at him in alarm. "Why not, pray tell?"

Dr. Dadourian looked at Nanny and Mrs. Goldstine, then at Dorothy-Anne. His eyes fell. "Mrs. Hale won't respond to you," he said quietly. "She's in a coma."

Dorothy-Anne didn't hear what he said, but she saw Nanny's and Mrs. Goldstine's faces turn white. After a moment, Nanny came over to her. "Let's go home," she said quietly.

And that was what Dorothy-Anne remembered of her fifth birthday.

4

The storm had worsened considerably. Flashes of lightning were followed by deafening peals of thunder as the wind-slashed rain hammered fiercely against the corrugated roof and the windows. Shrieking drafts of wind found their way inside the house, mocking the delusion of human shelter and threatening to throw the sheltered world into darkness. Dorothy-Anne felt it all swim before her eyes like a live creature.

Elemental chaos.

Angry gods.

Fear.

And pain.

Pain which was more than she could endure.

She was lying perfectly still now, her face shockingly white. She had no strength left to move. This contraction seemed the worst yet, seemed to take over her entire body with all-encompassing pain. Chills slashed up and down her spine, while deep inside her something that struggled to get out, whose time had come, was wedged unnaturally.

Was trapped.

Mrs. Ramirez sat in frightened silence. For a long time now she had been thinking, studying her memory, looking for some half-remembered answer. Long-forgotten tidbits were recalled from the dark depths of her mind. A story told once surfaced slowly and rippled the pond of her memory.

But then it was gone, and her mind again was blank. I must remember! she told herself again.

She crossed herself, then glanced at the young mother-to-be. Dorothy-Anne's eyes seemed lost in foggy thought, so far, far away.

Felicia Ramirez wondered where the young woman was, and what she was seeing.

Faraway.
    Another time.
    Another place.

The private recovery room of the Hale Wing of Columbia Presbyterian Hospital.

It was a week after Elizabeth-Anne had come out of the coma. She had been unconscious four months and three days. Upon awakening, the first visitor she had summoned was her grandson, Henry. She had warned him to be prepared. She expected a detailed report of business matters.

He was surprised when he walked into her room. She was confined to the bed, her legs rendered useless by the stroke, and he knew the prognosis was that she would never walk again. Fortunately, the doctors had said, she had suffered no other serious long-term damage from the stroke. They promised she would eventually fully regain her strength and be able to carry on with her business.

Elizabeth-Anne, typically, wasn't about to sit around and wait for this to happen. She had never been sick in her life and was determined not to bow to illness now. If her strength was to be regained, she would see that it was in the shortest possible time.

Although the hospital continued to enforce a recuperative schedule, Elizabeth-Anne persuaded Dr. Dadourian that she was at least well enough to visit with her grandson. And for that she would have to look her best.

After applying light makeup earlier that morning, she had made a fuss until her hairstylist from Kenneth's was allowed to come to her room. During the coma, her hair had grown considerably and turned completely white. Now she had it tinted its usual shade of sterling silver and set in a permanent.

By the time Henry walked in, Elizabeth-Anne had never looked better. She was sitting up straight in bed, wearing not a hospital gown, but a beautifully embroidered bed jacket. She was surrounded by piles of business-related reading material—back issues of *Forbes, Fortune,* and *Business Week,* as well as the *Wall Street Journal* and the business sections of the New York *Times.* On the nightstand beside her, a pot of water was kept heated on a hot plate, and a silver tea service, along with a can of herbal tea, was within easy reach. The room was a mass of flowers, with the more formal arrangements, sent by friends and acquaintances, hidden behind forests of pink peonies. She hated formal arrangements, and she had done her best to hide them from sight.

Henry bent down to kiss her cheek. "You look," he said pointedly, shaking his head in disbelief, "like you're vacationing on the Côte d'Azur."

She smiled at him. "Thank you, Henry dear. But a forced vacation, I'm afraid, is really no vacation at all."

"How are you feeling?"

"I'll feel a lot better," she answered, "once I know what's been happening at Hale Hotels over the past four months. Pull up a chair. I suggest we begin at once."

They were at it for two hours. After the nurse insisted Henry leave, Elizabeth-Anne sent for Dorothy-Anne and Mrs. Goldstine. She napped before they arrived, but they were allowed to visit for only fifteen minutes. Elizabeth-Anne had little intention of respecting this directive, and finally Dr. Dadourian had to come personally to escort Miss Goldstine and Dorothy-Anne out. He wasn't surprised or annoyed by the chore; Vartan Dadourian had been a personal friend of Elizabeth-Anne's for years and knew her stubbornness. He wasn't even taken aback when Elizabeth-Anne pleaded to have Dorothy-Anne stay a minute more.

"For God's sake, Vartan, I just want to look at my great-granddaughter. After all, I haven't seen her for four months. You're not going to begrudge an old woman that, are you?"

He studied her chart. "And since when do you consider yourself an 'old' woman?"

She raised her chin stubbornly. "When it suits me."

He glanced sideways at her. "I thought as much."

Dorothy-Anne was allowed to stay, and what she witnessed was an extraordinary battle of wills. Because in one thing Dr. Dadourian was determined to have his way, and he was insisting that Elizabeth-Anne plan an extended stay at one of the European spas. She was equally dead set against such a plan.

"Vartan, I'm *not* sick. Perhaps a bit disoriented and weak, but that's not surprising, considering I feel like Rip Van Winkle must have after he woke up. I need a little time to catch up on things and gather my wits. But that's all." Her years of stubborn pride would not allow her to admit she needed coddled care, and her bright eyes flashed like cold steel. "I'll be damned if I'll allow myself to be hospitalized around sick people."

"Those spas aren't exactly hospitals," Dadourian corrected her.

"Well, as far as I'm concerned, they are." Her eyes were steady. "And don't tell me they're fashionable resorts. You know how I *hate* resorts of any kind. I *despise* programmed days and nights. I refuse to sit around water fountains in parks or take part in group therapy. And I *don't* need to take any curative waters, thank you very much. The water that pours out of my faucet at home suits me just fine."

He sighed. "You do try my patience sometimes, you know."

"Vartan, if you didn't have me to spar with, you'd be bored to death."

"You really do need rest and professional care," he insisted gently. "You need time to readjust, I repeat, *readjust* to life as it is experienced awake, as well as to adjust to the fact that you're paralyzed from the waist down. You need a period of *transition*." He permitted himself a rare smile. "Don't forget, you're not a spring chicken anymore."

"No one knows that better than I." Her lips smiled at him, but her eyes looked at him hard and long. He was a fine doctor, the finest there was. As well as the most expensive. But, most importantly, he was a decent man who had been a friend to her for years. Perhaps if he thought she needed therapy and rest, it was for the best. But not at one of those dreary dress-up spas where patients strolled around in minks. She didn't want it, and she wouldn't have it.

Suddenly she remembered what Henry had first said to her and she had an idea. "Vartan . . ." she said thoughtfully, "you know, maybe you *are* right after all. Perhaps a *vacation*"—she stressed the word—"would do me some good. God knows, I haven't had one in decades." Her lips tightened. "But I don't want anything remotely smacking of hospitals and clinics and sanatoriums."

He nodded slowly, suspiciously.

"And I won't go alone," Elizabeth-Anne added. "I'd be bored to tears and get far too restless." Her eyes twinkled mischievously as she glanced across the room at Dorothy-Anne. "I don't really want to go at all. I want you to know that for the record. But I'm not adverse to it—under one condition."

Dadourian sighed wearily. "And what is that, pray tell?"

She smiled at her great-granddaughter. "That Dorothy-Anne accompanies me."

Dadourian turned around and stared at the child. Under the circumstances, Elizabeth-Anne's five-year-old great-grandchild could only be a liability. What his old friend and patient needed was rest and therapy. However, the child did have a governess. Perhaps having company would even do Elizabeth-Anne some good. That too could be therapy of sorts. Especially since the old woman and the young child were such fast friends. He turned back to Elizabeth-Anne. "I suppose you'll take her whether I like it or not," he said at last.

"I knew I could count on you, Vartan."

Elizabeth-Anne settled upon the south of France. A real-estate broker was called, and he combed the Maritime Alps until he found a suitable villa to lease. A local doctor was contacted who would drop by daily and keep his eye on her. Meanwhile, Henry had come up with a pride of private nurses who would accompany Elizabeth-Anne. There were three of them. The first, Miss Hepple, Elizabeth-Anne hated on sight. She was short and stout, a no-nonsense middle-aged woman who was gruff and tight-lipped. Miss Hepple and Henry got along all too well for Elizabeth-Anne's liking. She could sniff out a spy when she saw one. She suspected that the woman had been instructed to report the slightest infraction of Dr. Dadourian's orders to Henry. She knew she would have to be careful. She wasn't planning on just lying around on chaises and sunning herself. She and Natalie Goldstine were going to be doing a lot of business over the telephone, contrary to doctor's orders. But she liked the other two nurses, Miss Bunt and Miss Kinney, and she sensed at once that they weren't very fond of the dour, overbearing Miss Hepple either.

The trip was planned swiftly. The Hale jet would fly Elizabeth-Anne, Dorothy-Anne, her nanny, and the three nurses to Paris, and then on to Nice. From there, hired cars would drive them to St. Paul de Vence.

The morning of the departure, Vartan Dadourian paid Elizabeth-Anne a last visit. "You won't have to worry about a thing," he assured her. "Miss Hepple, Miss Kinney, and Miss Bunt are fine nurses. I've also arranged for a Fräulein Ilse Lang to meet you in St. Paul de Vence. She comes highly recommended. She's reputed to be the finest physical therapist in Europe."

"And I suppose you'll tell me next that if anyone can help me walk again, it's she?"

He made a gesture of irritation. "No, I won't. You know better than that. I've never kept anything from you in the past, and I'm not about to start doing that now. It's possible, of course, but none of us think you'll walk again. There has been too much damage.''

Elizabeth-Anne nodded. ''Thank you, Vartan. It's cruel of you, but I need to know the truth, not a bunch of lies.''

He eyed her sorrowfully. ''If I could—''

''I know you would.'' She held his hand and smiled. ''And I'm grateful, really I am. Perhaps the vacation will even do me some good.'' She bit down on her lip. ''If only Miss Hepple weren't coming,'' she murmured.

''You don't like her?''

She met his eye. ''Not a bit. Henry chose her for me because she's his spy. I can tell. She'll report to him on everything I do.''

''I could recommend another nurse.''

She shook her head. ''Don't bother. Knowing Henry, he'd make sure she was another Miss Hepple. At least I know whom I need to watch out for.''

Dadourian squinted his eyes dangerously. ''This doesn't mean you've lied to me, does it?''

''Lied to you?''

''Just remember what I told you. You're to do absolutely no work. At least not yet.'' He paused. ''*Absolutely* none.''

Elizabeth-Anne was not one to lie, even for convenience. She simply nodded vaguely, which she felt he could interpret any way he chose. She had extracted a solemn vow from Mrs. Goldstine to phone her regularly to keep her posted on any and all important business developments. She had a feeling that the transatlantic telephone wires would be buzzing. She knew all too well that if she, the center of power at Hale Hotels, was out of touch for too long, Henry could simply take over without anyone's knowing it. He could fire the staff that was loyal to her and replace them with his own people. Elizabeth-Anne alone could prevent this from happening. She knew once she lost control she would have difficulty regaining it.

Henry was her grandson, and she loved him dearly, despite his faults. But he was hungry for power. Far too hungry, and with her gone, his appetite could be sated far too easily.

Somehow she would have to manage to keep him at bay.

The alternative was too frightening.

5

The villa was named La Fleur de Matin, the Flower of the Morning, and it was a picture postcard come to life. Nestled on a wooded hillside high above Cannes, the original portion of the house dated back to the thirteenth century. Fortified, renovated, and expanded many times since, the villa was now an odd conglomeration of rambling buildings. It ranged from one to four stories in height, while a certain homogeny and a guarantee of privacy were provided by high walls surrounding the entire six-acre property.

Upon arriving, Elizabeth-Anne stared up at the house as the driver lifted her out of the car and gently set her down into her wheelchair. She let out a sigh of relief, seeing at a glance that she would be more than comfortable here. This was a dream house, a fanciful collection of dark-stained wood and sturdy stone surrounding a colonnaded, groin-vaulted terrace on three sides. Through the huge arches of this terrace, one could see for miles, and directly below it lay the villa's courtyard and garden, a sumptuous collection of cleverly clipped plane trees and lush vines.

While the drivers, supervised by Miss Kinney and Miss Hepple, unloaded the mountains of luggage from the three cars, the real-estate agent showed Elizabeth-Anne and Dorothy-Anne around. The grounds were lushly planted. There were green oaks, their thick, short trunks clad in grayish black bark. There was a grove of olive trees. Under the olive trees, clumps of deep blue, velvety violets flourished as ground cover. There were pistachio trees with their red berries which would ripen to brown.

Spring would obviously bring paradise to its headiest full bloom. There were nine hundred rose bushes altogether, clumps of daisies, countless jasmine vines, delicate mimosa trees, and masses of trumpet flowers which would burst forth into riotous color, and then August would bring the fuchsias, the fragrantly sweet oleanders, the dazzling bougainvillea, and the pale blue morning glories after which the villa had been named. Even before they were shown the inside of the house, both great-grandmother and great-granddaughter were enchanted. This was their paradise, their own secret garden.

The inside of the house posed few problems for Elizabeth-Anne's wheelchair, as she would live entirely on the ground floor. This arrangement was essential to her fierce pride in self-sufficiency and need for relative freedom of movement. All in all, the villa afforded beauty and comfort and privacy.

But even paradise has its drawbacks.

Despite days filled with Ilse Lang's therapy exercises, Dorothy-Anne's company, and hours spent on the phone with Natalie Goldstine (who called under the code name "Alicia" to throw off the prying Miss Hepple), Elizabeth-Anne found herself growing increasingly restless. She was sick and tired of constantly sitting, sitting, sitting. She came to despise her wheelchair. It was at once her mode of transportation and the symbol of her affliction.

But worst of all, she despised doing nothing. The therapy, the games, the telephone calls—it was all make-work. That was the worst part. She had spent a lifetime building and creating, managing and expanding. She ached for the thrill of accomplishment, the tension of even an average business day. There were only so many games one could play before one tired of them.

She felt as if she had been put out to pasture.

She would sit in the fragrant, shady courtyard, and a single thought would enter her mind and fester there.

If only there was something to do.

It started out as a game.

It turned into Les Petits Palais, an entirely new string of ultraluxurious small hotels operating under the Hale Hotels banner.

One early afternoon, after finishing lunch in the courtyard, Elizabeth-Anne and her great-granddaughter were in the midst of one of their usual, now lackadaisical games. Dorothy-Anne would toss a huge inflated beachball at her great-grandmother, who would catch it, toss it back to her, and then move her wheelchair around a tree to another position. Dorothy-Anne soon tired of it, for which Elizabeth-Anne was extremely grateful. It was a game that was boring beyond endurance and taxed her energies severely.

"Now we'll play hotel," Dorothy-Anne announced out of the clear blue.

Elizabeth-Anne felt tired. She eyed her great-granddaughter sadly, then closed her eyes for a moment. "If only we could, darling," she said. "But this isn't a hotel."

"Yes it is!" Dorothy-Anne nodded emphatically, secure in her childhood knowledge. A house was more than just four walls. It could be a cottage, or a castle, or even a hotel. "We'll *pretend* it's a hotel. Anything's what you pretend it is." She began to skip toward the house. She turned around and motioned excitedly for her great-grandmother to follow.

Shaking her head, Elizabeth-Anne pushed on the wheels of her chair. "Where are we going?"

"Out front to the parking lot. We'll pretend we just got here, and we've got to unload our suitcases. That's the first thing that happens at a hotel, right?"

"It certainly is, young lady." Elizabeth-Anne regarded Dorothy-Anne with warm affection, delighted by her eager imagination. But Elizabeth-Anne wanted to play this new game even less than she'd wanted to play ball. It would only emphasize how far she was from her empire, from the heart of the passion that made her tick. But she was determined not to disappoint her favorite little girl; and besides, without Dorothy-Anne's company and vivacity, life would be completely unbearable.

So Elizabeth-Anne followed Dorothy-Anne up to the house along the gently sloping ramp that had been constructed over the raised threshold, and then through the cool, dim downstairs halls and out to the large raked-gravel parking lot outside the walls. She looked at her great-granddaughter curiously. "Well? What do you suggest we do now?"

Dorothy-Anne's eyes sparkled. "I'm riding in a car. See?"

She raced to the end of the long drive, dwarfed by the two facing sentinel rows of cypresses lining the smooth expanse of gravel, oblivious of Elizabeth-Anne's cries of caution. Then she spun around and came rushing back the way she had gone, but her demeanor had changed. She was pretending to drive a car, her hands clasped around an invisible steering wheel. She pulled up beside Elizabeth-Anne with a pretended screech that drove Elizabeth-Anne to clap her hands over her ears.

Dorothy-Anne sneaked a tiny sideways flick of an eye at Elizabeth-Anne. "Now I'm getting out, getting my luggage," she explained.

She mimed it to perfection, a wealthy dowager stepping out of the car, nonchalantly slamming the door and unlocking the trunk. She lifted out two enormously heavy invisible suitcases and lugged them up to the front door.

"Wait," Elizabeth-Anne called quickly. Despite herself, she was getting caught up in the game. "A porter has to come running and get the suitcases for you. A lady never needs to carry her own luggage. Not at a fine hotel!"

"Oh yes! Here he comes now." Dorothy-Anne quickly set down her imaginary luggage and placed her hands on her hips. "You're late, young man!" she chided threateningly, parodying someone she'd once heard. "This is no way to earn a tip." She glanced at Elizabeth-Anne. "What do I do now?"

"You tell him you have a reservation."

Dorothy-Anne held her head high with regal hauteur. "I have a reservation," she announced importantly.

The game continued for an hour. Dorothy-Anne "checked in" at the "front desk," a refectory table in the hall behind which Elizabeth-Anne quickly wheeled herself, pretending to be the concierge. Dorothy-Anne was then led by an invisible bellboy to the nonexistent elevator. She rode upstairs to her room (which was really still on the ground floor), and then she had lunch in the courtyard.

And as Elizabeth-Anne watched the fantastic game, something slowly began to stir in the back of her mind.

A small lobby with a desk, precisely where the refectory table was located.

The image flashed through her thoughts, and she closed her eyes.

All around her, the building seemed to come to life. She could almost hear the sounds of clattering dishes in the courtyard, the murmurs of earnest conversation, the lighthearted tinkle of silvery laughter. She could almost feel people gazing down from the colonnaded terrace above her.

The quiet, whispering feet of bellboys.

The ringing of the concierge's bell.

The scraping of suitcases on the tiled floor.

Startled, she opened her eyes and gazed around. Lithe, dancing fingertips prickled up and down her spine. A powerful surge of excitement billowed through her, and her eyes glittered with feverish excitement.

"Great-Granny!" Dorothy-Anne called urgently. "What is it? Is something wrong? You didn't bring me my drink!"

But Elizabeth-Anne didn't hear her. She was lost deep in thought. She was in another world. The very world Dorothy-Anne had described to her earlier.

Anything's what you want it to be.

Yes! It could be!

Slowly she spun her wheelchair around and gazed up at the immense, rambling house. The more she thought about it, the more she realized that it *could* be more than a villa. It really could! It could be . . .

A hotel.

A small, intimate luxury hotel in the heart of Provence. From what the help had told her, there were countless bedrooms upstairs.

The farmhouse next door was deserted; a gallery could connect the two buildings.

The courtyard would be the dining area.

She glanced up at the colonnaded loggia. The loggia would be yet another dining room.

An elevator would have to be installed.

A staff found.

More bathrooms put in.

But the kitchen was big enough. She had seen it.

The thoughts raced through her mind, one upon another.

Suddenly she reached out and pulled Dorothy-Anne close. "Darling!" Her whisper was solemn and intense, but her face was radiant. "How would you like to turn this house into a hotel? A *real* hotel?"

Dorothy-Anne stared at her. "Oh, Great-Granny," she breathed finally. *"Yes."*

"But it's got to be a secret," Elizabeth-Anne warned. "No one must know."

"Oh, I can keep a secret. I promise."

Elizabeth-Anne raised her chin with satisfaction. She had found something to do.

Now came the logistics.

Buying the property, as well as the one next door. *If* they were for sale.

Finagling finances; her banks were located three thousand miles away. Large sums of money would have to be transferred to a local bank. She couldn't use Hale Hotels money; Henry would get wind of it immediately. But she had millions of her own tucked away.

Hiring a contractor. And a handpicked staff.

And while all that was going on, she had to be certain Miss Hepple was far removed from it all. For now, she would change her to the night shift. And . . . something else hadn't escaped her sharp eyes. She had noticed the dour woman staring at the young live-in gardener. She hated to do it. She was a businesswoman, not a pimp. However, no one knew better than she that special circumstances required special solutions.

A thousand francs changed hands. The gardener began to speak to Miss Hepple, who was icy and insulting. And intrigued.

The real-estate agent who had leased Elizabeth-Anne the house was sent to Paris, where he successfully negotiated its sale.

Two million dollars was wired from New York to the local bank.

The deserted farmhouse next door was soon hers too.

Another thousand francs was paid to the gardener. Miss Hepple was thawing, and soon he was taking her on long drives around the countryside. His instructions were specific: to keep the nurse away for as long a period of time each day as was humanly possible. Miss Hepple quickly became an authority on the local landscape and customs.

Soon the time was ripe. Elizabeth-Anne gave the gardener twenty thousand francs and the promise that his job would not be jeopardized. He then lured Miss Hepple into an upstairs bedroom, where he and the unsuspecting nurse were "accidentally" discovered making love. The gardener was "fired" on the spot, and Miss Hepple was sent home in disgrace. Elizabeth-Anne called Henry and assured him that two nurses and one therapist were quite adequate. Besides, she insinuated, after the incident with Miss Hepple, she could no longer trust his judgment when it came to hiring nurses. The young gardener was immediately rehired.

Money spoke. And spoke.

As the renovations on the villa progressed and Elizabeth-Anne immersed herself in other arrangements, she came to glorious life. She had never felt better or looked better. She supervised every step of the villa's conversion. It was a game—a game that cost millions—but even Ilse Lang agreed that it was the best therapy Elizabeth-Anne could have had.

She was building another hotel, but one so vastly different in concept from the others that it was a true challenge. And she was doing it all behind Henry's and Vartan Dadourian's backs. She relished simply pulling it off and proving to herself, once and for all, that a wheelchair-ridden old woman need not stop living or working. But best of all, the conversion of La Fleur de Matin from villa to hotel became a labor of love for everyone involved, and that was the key to its subsequent success.

Never had Elizabeth-Anne known so many people working hand in hand. The construction workers became her fast friends; two of them in particular, Bertrand Delacroix and François Bricteux, became not only her protectors but also her co-conspirators. Early in the morning on certain days, they would lift her, wheelchair and all, into the back of their open truck, tie the chair securely down, and then hoist Dorothy-Anne up beside her great-grandmother. Then the truck would rumble off, with Elizabeth-Anne in her throne in the back, holding a parasol, while Dorothy-Anne gazed out over the tailgate. It was a sight that made her famous in all Provence.

But these extraordinary outings did not merely serve as entertainment for an eccentric old woman. Elizabeth-Anne was on a mission. Bertrand and François drove her all over Provence and the neighboring provinces of Dauphiné and Languedoc, scouring the countryside for anything that would embellish their jewellike little hotel.

Their frequent searches for art and antiques paid off handsomely. Invariably they returned to La Fleur de Matin at night loaded down wth precious finds. For instance, at a fifteenth-century château that was being demolished, they haggled for an ancient fifteen-foot-high baronial fireplace mantel. They scoured far and wide for more fireplaces; every room was to have one. They bought antique Provençal beds and chairs, and then they discovered the richest, most unexpected find of all—a huge marble pre-Christian-era sarcophagus that was to become the famed bar in the courtyard. After they transported it back, it was discovered that it was too huge to fit through the gates. Undaunted, Elizabeth-Anne ordered a section of the wall ripped out, and the sarcophagus was moved in.

The villa was connected to the neighboring farmhouse by a two-story arched gallery and the buildings became one. The new structure was even more rambling, and thus charming, than the last. The colonnaded loggia overlooking the courtyard became the protected dining terrace Elizabeth-Anne had envisioned, and she spent hours there, thanks to the elevator she had installed, which gave her freedom of movement throughout the four floors.

Elizabeth-Anne decided that the staff of this tiny hotel must be exceptionally gracious, and she handpicked everyone from the concierge to the chef, whom she lured from a three-star restaurant in Dauphiné. Small wonder, then, that La Fleur de Matin became an exclusive club of sorts. Everyone said that staying there was like staying with friends. Which was,

Elizabeth-Anne congratulated herself, exactly what she had set out to do in the first place.

However, even she had not dared to predict the hotel's phenomenal success. It had been a therapeutic labor of love, and because of that, she'd have been content to underwrite a losing proposition. Instead, she found herself most pleasantly surprised. Although, with its mere twenty-five guest rooms, it was the smallest of all the Hale hotels, La Fleur de Matin quickly became the most famous in the entire chain, and one of the most celebrated inns in the world. Within its very first season its standing as the favorite haunt of internationally known artists, writers, and film stars was firmly established. It was at once forbiddingly expensive, terribly exclusive, and overwhelmingly casual—but on the intimate, lovely, and friendly scale that few first-class hotels ever achieved.

As the years passed, Elizabeth-Anne was to create other Les Petits Palais, the small palaces, as she called them. They were all conceived along the same lines of exclusivity and beauty as La Fleur de Matin, and were all just as hugely successful. The second was a Tuscan villa with muraled rooms and formal gardens that overlooked Florence. Next, Elizabeth-Anne found a turreted white, fairytale château on the Loire which overlooked the farmlands and river from within its one-hundred-acre wooded park. Then a fifteen-story stucco villa rising from the beach up an entire hillside in Puerto Vallarta, each floor boasting its own tiled swimming pool overlooking the Pacific Ocean. And the list went on from there, each more fantastically beautiful and warmly charming than the last.

These were Elizabeth-Anne's pride and true passion; with Les Petits Palaises her role of the innkeeper as hostess was brought one step closer to her lifelong ideal. She became the chatelaine of far-flung palaces and villas, as well as friend and confidante to the world's most celebrated guests. Even heads of state were drawn to these private hotels, many to write their memoirs, some just to relax in their rarefied, enchanted atmosphere. Selectivity was the key to the success of Les Petits Palais, for they were the very essence of the life-styles of the rich and famous. They quickly became one of the worst-kept secrets in the world.

6

Although no one knew it, as 1985 began, the last days of Elizabeth-Anne Hale's life were drawing to a close. There were some things Elizabeth-Anne told everyone, some things she confided only to her nearest and dearest, and a few things she kept to herself and never told a soul. The cancer was one of the things she kept to herself. She didn't see any reason to upset her family and friends by telling them about it. Everyone would know soon enough, anyway.

Above all, Elizabeth-Anne didn't want Dorothy-Anne to know. She and Freddie were too happy. Bad news traveled fast. Too fast, she thought as the big yellow-and-black Rolls-Royce sailed sagaciously through the thick New Jersey rain.

Elizabeth-Anne rested her chin on her hand as she stared out the rain-streaked window. The tires hissed and the windshield wipers thumped steadily, tossing aside the heavy, thick sheets of rain.

Suddenly Elizabeth-Anne pressed the button that lowered the glass partition between her and the driver. With the sterling head of her cane, she rapped on the slowly descending glass. "Faster, Max," she said urgently.

Max hesitated, his eyes glancing at Elizabeth-Anne in the rearview mirror. She seemed so strong, so sure of herself. But her usual imperturbable calm had for once deserted her. "We're already going the speed limit, Mrs. Hale, ma'am," he said politely. "The road's slick. Everybody else has slowed down."

"My vision is still excellent, thank you," Elizabeth-Anne replied crisply. "Perhaps those people are not pressed for time." She paused deliberately. "I *am*. And you might bear in mind, Max, that I am *not* everybody else."

He took a deep breath and tightened his grip on the steering wheel. This was the first time she had ever chewed him out or told him how to drive. He let out the deep breath slowly. "Yes, ma'am, Mrs. Hale."

"Well? Then step on the gas!"

Elizabeth-Anne sat painfully forward and craned her neck so that she could see the speedometer inching upward until it reached seventy-five miles per hour. The car was a tank, nearly three and a half tons of fine-tuned machinery, and once momentum was achieved, it surged majestically forward through the rain.

A satisfied expression came into Elizabeth-Anne's blue eyes. She sat back in her seat and pressed the button; the glass partition rose soundlessly.

She pushed up the cuff of her white silk blouse to glance at her wristwatch, then sighed. Rush or no, the watched pot never boils. She decided to try to get some work done, hoping that, once immersed, she would lose all track of time.

Still, she couldn't help wishing that she weren't so vain. Flying to Baltimore would have been much easier, but Max would have had to carry her from the car on board the plane, and upon arriving, a virtual stranger would have had to carry her off. She couldn't bear the thought of it. Then, too, Max was the only person she trusted to keep mum about her whereabouts. Anyone else was bound to talk. It was still too early to let anyone know why she was visiting the Johns Hopkins University Hospital.

As long as the car ride didn't take much more than four hours, she preferred driving to taking a jet anyway. A lengthy car ride was difficult enough. She always had to plan in advance, cutting down on her fluid intake twelve hours before each ride so that rest stops were not necessary. Something as simple as going to the bathroom was no longer simple. Oh, how she hated this infirmity! Her fierce independence was rankled no end by her powerless, atrophied legs. She despised having to use the wheelchair. She'd been in it for years, and she still hadn't been able to get used to it. She was only grateful that at least she had enough money to be able to employ people to compensate for her legs.

She sighed angrily. All her life long she had despised people who felt sorry for themselves. The last thing she needed now was to join their ranks.

Without further hesitation, she reached for the Vuitton attaché case on the seat beside her. The sturdy miniature suitcase had served her well for decades; just the sight of it reassured her now.

She placed the case on her lap, flipped it open, and reached for her small Ben Franklin–style reading glasses. Perching them on her nose, she snapped on her reading lamp and took out a three-inch-thick report bound in clear plastic. She gazed down at it. Printed at the top-right-hand side of the page was a letterhead:

Hale Real Estate Acquisitions Board
Empire State Building
350 Fifth Avenue
New York, New York 10001

The logo at the top-left-hand corner of the page was the emblem of Hale Hotels, Inc., a blanket corporation and the parent company of the sprawling empire Elizabeth-Anne had built. The symbols of her home state, Texas, were artfully intertwined: a stylized pecan tree, a mockingbird, and a blue-bonnet inside a Lone Star outlined in blue. On either side of the Lone Star were two smaller red stars, four altogether, symbolizing not only the state where her empire had had its roots, but that rarest of the rare in the hotel business: a conglomeration of five-star hotels worldwide.

COMPILED FEASIBILITY STUDY
*Potential Conversion
of Central Park South Site
into
Mayfair Hale Hotel*

And under the title were typed the legends:

Property Still Open for Negotiation
Other Known Bidders: None
Suspected Secret Bidders: None
Hotel Possibilities Previously Explored by: •Best Western
                                               •Helmsley
                                               •Sheraton

Elizabeth-Anne's face creased into a frown. She would have to check into just why the other three hotel corporations had turned down the site. But she was gratified to see the red ink stamped onto the title page and onto each of the subsequent 526 pages within. The single word warned: CONFIDENTIAL. Smaller red letters, also stamped, further warned: ORIGINAL ONLY COPY IN EXISTENCE; UNDER NO CIRCUMSTANCES MAKE COPIES OF ORIGINAL. The melodrama was, in fact, necessary. Elizabeth-Anne had long ago learned that corporate espionage was rife even in the hotel business. Furthermore, when it was learned that Hale Hotels had its eyes, however lazily, on a certain piece of property, she could count on the real-estate price invariably, greedily, skyrocketing. To counter this, once the Hale Acquisitions Board had recommended that a certain property be bought and she had endorsed it, the sale was slyly negotiated through a third, secret party.

She opened the report and began to read.

The feasibility of the new hotel, indeed all the possible pros and cons which could be imagined, had been discussed in scrupulous detail. The report started by cold-bloodedly reducing the property and its existing, sweetly gaudy Belle Epoque–style building to their value in dollars and cents, then projected the future worth of the property alone under various depressed and inflated financial climates. It had also predicted the cost of converting the building into a hotel, as opposed to the staggering fortune necessary to raze the structure and start from scratch. It then went on to project the number of rooms versus the years the hotel would have to operate at various vacancy percentages in the red before it could be turned around to operate in the black.

The legal department had studied that essentially New York phenomenon: the effects a potentially outraged citizens' group would have upon the razing, or even conversion, of the existing building, if it decided to fight to protect the structure by seeking landmark status for it.

An independent marketing survey rated existing New York hotels and had sent out fifteen thousand questionnaires to regular Hale business customers, whose addresses were on file in the central Hale data bank. The return-postage-paid questionnaire sought answers as to what, in particular, enticed travelers to any one hotel.

The creative department had mapped out the potential hotel's particular style: from ballroom, to theme restaurants, all the way down to the last napkin ring.

The managers of the existing Hale hotels reported on what essential services all worldwide hotels offered, what significant services were offered exclusively by Hale hotels, what was lacking in any one hotel, and what, in particular, would make the projected new Hale hotel more desirable than any other hotel in the city and, indeed, the world.

The in-depth coverage of all possibilities was mind-boggling.

Elizabeth-Anne felt overwhelmed by it. Nothing had been like this in the beginning. No longer was the slightest, most seemingly inconsequential item left to acumen, instinct, chance, and a galloping maverick gambling spirit. It made her feel somehow useless, as if she were a lone dinosaur plodding through the modern world. And she wasn't at all certain that she liked the way the business world had changed. In the age of computers and surveys, she had no choice but to bow to the report writers. But that didn't mean she had to like it. Everything was so . . . so cut and dried. The chances for error were greatly reduced. But somehow that had taken all the *life* out of it.

She felt a tinge of regret, and a stirring of gratitude . . . gratitude that she had been born when she had, at a time when a person could still have vision and spunk and fulfill his dreams on nothing but faith and hard work.

She closed the report, marking her place with her thumb. Taking off her glasses, she pinched the bridge of her nose, then stared out the rain-streaked window. The visibility was even worse than before, and the tattoo of rain on the roof was a muffled but constant drumbeat.

With an abrupt gesture she slammed the report back into her attaché case. She had been a fool even to open it. She was in no mood to deal with work now. She couldn't simply distract herself from the mental anguish that plagued her. There was no turning away from the inevitability of the truth. Perhaps when the trip was over, when her mind was once again fresh and at rest, reassured about her own future, she could pick up the report again. But not until then.

Not until the tumor inside her, of which no one but she and the doctors were aware, was cut out, exorcised from her body.

The doctors had assured her that her chances were good, despite her age.

Why, then, did she feel so darkly convinced that she was dying? That this was the beginning of the end?

7

These memories. There were so many of them.

Time seemed to have become frozen, and the minutes stopped ticking.

She felt something soft and deliciously cool against her forehead. She opened her eyes and smiled wanly up at Mrs. Ramirez. "I'm scared," she whispered.

"Do not be." Mrs. Ramirez smiled with gentle reassurance. "It will be fine. Everything will turn out fine. See?" She stopped wiping Dorothy-Anne's head, reached into the front of her blouse, and held out a tiny glittering medallion hanging from a thread-thin gold chain. "It is the medal of the Blessed Virgin. I wear it all the time. José, a nephew of mine, he and his wife went to Fatima. They brought it back." She paused. "It has been blessed." On an impulse, Mrs.

Ramirez put down the cloth, reached behind her neck, and unclasped the necklace. Then she hung it around Dorothy-Anne's neck. "You wear for now. The Blessed Mother, she look after me. Now she look after you, too."

"Thank you," Dorothy-Anne whispered.

She watched Mrs. Ramirez rinsing out the cloth in a bowl. Then the big woman crossed the room, stopped in the shadows near the doorway. "I see about the telephone. Maybe is already fixed."

Dorothy-Anne suddenly heard Mrs. Ramirez's voice, but the face did not seem to belong to her. Suddenly the face she saw was a handsome one with a stubborn chin and angular cheekbones, head of silver hair, and arresting aquamarine eyes with a wise, all-knowing expression.

Dorothy-Anne sighed softly and shut her eyes. "Great-Granny," she whispered, although she knew it could not be. Not here. Not today. Not ever again.

It had been the last time she had seen her great-grandmother alive.

Three short days ago, a lifetime that had spanned the better part of the century had ended.

It had been the night of Elizabeth-Anne Hale's greatest triumph, the crowning touch to an empire forged out of nothing.

The crowning gem: the Hale Castle.

It was Elizabeth-Anne's shining achievement, a lasting monument to herself and her family, to her dream.

Only now that she looked back on it did Dorothy-Anne realize that the day the Hale Castle had been conceived had been the beginning of the end. She should have realized it at the start—that the grandest of all the grand hotels would be Great-Granny's last achievement. But how could she have known? Great-Granny had always been building and expanding. It had been her lifeblood. Only after it was all over, and Elizabeth-Anne was dead, had she realized the truth.

Elizabeth-Anne Hale had been secretly battling the cancer for years, but had never let anyone know. She had sent her loved ones away on business trips or vacations, or had disappeared herself, supposedly to relax, but in truth to enter the hospital for surgery or treatments. She had done it all quietly, behind everyone's back. And while the cancer was eating deeper and deeper, and her time was running out, she had gone on to build her greatest achievement of them all, and had fought to live until the day it was completed.

It only proved to Dorothy-Anne how little she knew of the remarkable woman to whom she had been so close all her life.

All those years together—and yet in the end Elizabeth-Anne hadn't confided her deepest secret.

Oh, how could I have been so blind?

For three long and sleepless days and nights she had been torturing herself with that same question.

Even on that last night, I didn't realize she was at the point of death.

But how could she have known? Even on that last night of Elizabeth-Anne Hale's life, during the inauguration of the newest star in the hotel chain, the old lady had gathered the last remaining vestiges of her strength and had given the illusion that all was well with the world and with herself.

The inauguration had been more than just that. It had been Great-Granny's farewell party to all she held near and dear.

And no one had known it until after it was over.

The grand ballroom of the Hale Castle had been filled to capacity. Two thousand guests had been invited, and more than eighteen hundred had shown up. At Elizabeth-Anne's request, Dorothy-Anne stood on the right side of the wheelchair on the dais, Freddie on the left. They each held one of Elizabeth-Anne's hands. Behind the chair, Miss Bunt stood silent with grim decorum, an expressionless sphinx whose eyes alone gave away her impatience with Elizabeth-Anne's insistence on attending what she considered a senseless event. Off to one side were Henry and Chessy. Regina had not traveled all the way from California for the event.

The pride glowed in Dorothy-Anne's face. She didn't think she had ever seen her great-grandmother looking quite as beautiful as she did on this particular evening. There was something regal about the way she sat poised in her wheelchair, as though it were a throne. And why shouldn't she be such a commanding presence? Dorothy-Anne asked herself. Elizabeth-Anne was, after all, the supreme ruler of an empire that dotted the globe, and she looked every inch the royal sovereign.

At ninety, her eyes were lively and sparkling, and her aquamarine silk gown lent her a delicate, luminous beauty. Her face wore an expression of ceremonial amusement, as though she were being entertained by an army of court jesters. Occasionally she would tilt her head sideways and look up at Dorothy-Anne through her hooded eyes, a sly twinkle saying, "See? See what we've done together, you and I? All is revel, merriment, They kowtow to me and tell me what they think I want to hear, but deep inside they all hate me. And you know why? They're wondering how we've done it, that's why! But we'll never tell them the secret. Vision and hard work, daring to dream, and putting every last bit of energy behind it—that's all it took, and the fools don't even know it! They all think it was some kind of luck or magic, or, worse yet, a talent of mine! Oh, if they only knew the truth, how disappointed they'd all be."

Dorothy-Anne saw all this in her great-grandmother's gaze and, squeezing her hand, she nodded happily as tears shone in her eyes. Beneath the voluminous folds of her maternity gown her child was approaching the time for delivery. A new child was soon to be born, the first of Great-Granny's great-great-grandchildren. "I hope it's a girl," Elizabeth-Anne had confided to her only a few days earlier. "In this family it's the *women* who make the difference. Oh, don't get me wrong. The men have done their share. But the women— they're the strength, the backbone! Oh yes, I *do* hope it's a girl! What more could a silly old woman want?"

A great-great-granddaughter.

And the Hale Castle, conceived and built against all odds, completed at long last.

Yes, what else indeed?

No wonder she looks so happy, Dorothy-Anne thought. *This is her moment to bask in the sun. And she deserves it, by*

God. She deserves every last accolade, every bit of comfort, every outpouring of love and respect. Ninety, going on ninety-one this week, and she's still not resting on her laurels.

Instead, she had built the Hale Castle. All told, the cost had come to more than a quarter of a billion dollars after the price of the property, design, construction, and decor had been tallied. It was said to be the single most expensive structure in the entire world.

It towered seventy-two stories above Fifth Avenue in midtown. Just to accumulate the entire square-block property had taken several years of patient, secret bidding. Dozens of real-estate agents, none of whom were aware of the identity of their client, had bought up the individually owned parcels of land, one by one. Then the existing buildings had been razed, the rubble trucked off, and the foundations dug. Elizabeth-Anne had hired one of the nation's preeminent architects to design the Hale Castle. Not for her one of those carbon-copy steel-and-glass boxes. She wanted something that would add an extra cachet—her own—to the New York skyline.

Dorothy-Anne had sat through many of the countless meetings between client and architect, and she had followed every phase of the progress closely.

"You have carte blanche," Elizabeth-Anne was fond of telling the architect, half in jest, half in seriousness, "as long as I end up with what *I* want.'

The architect had laughed, but Elizabeth-Anne's vision had been specific and he found himself inspired by it. She wanted a modern building of medieval style. The plaza would be graced by a modern version of a medieval drawbridge and a moat with a narrow reflecting pool. She wanted the public rooms to be imposing, "baronial" in scope. And the top was to be crowned with turrets and towers, like something out of a childhood fairytale.

The architect had managed to achieve all this brilliantly. From the moment the plans were first made public, the building became the focus of a raging achitectural debate heard round the world. Some critics praised the daring design concept combining the fifteenth and twenty-first centuries; others denounced it as an abomination.

Elizabeth-Anne knew she had made her statement.

She was delighted. The furor only fueled everyone's excitement, and it was the sort of publicity that no amount of money could ever have bought.

And, once the luxury castle had been completed—ready for occupancy by the hotel, as well as condominium buyers and office-space renters—Elizabeth-Anne had further amazed her staff. "Charge through the nose," she had instructed. "Make it as expensive and exclusive as it can possibly be."

And, as she knew it would, the Hale Castle had snared the rich, the famous, and the powerful. One Arab businessman bought three entire floors of condominiums and combined them to become what was probably the largest and most expensive triplex—including indoor swimming pool—in all of New York, possibly the world. Even before the building had opened, all but two of the ninety condominiums had been sold.

Now, watching Elizabeth-Anne closely, Dorothy-Anne reveled in the excitement of the glittering event before them. Their guests had come from near and far. The mayor, governor, and vice-president were rubbing shoulders with Supreme Court justices, society dowagers, businessmen, tycoons, members of the press, novelists, and film stars. All the movers and shakers had come out in full force to celebrate the grand opening.

It had all the makings of a Hollywood premiere, down to the red carpet on the sidewalk and the searchlights crisscrossing the sky.

By ten o'clock the reception line had long since fizzled out, a fact for which Elizabeth-Anne was extremely grateful. The palms of her hands were sweaty. She was feeling tired, and wished the party were already over, but she had the determination of a last wish, a last goal to achieve to carry her through. Once she had done what she had come to do, then she could have her rest. A long and final rest.

She glanced over at the orchestra and caught the conductor's eye. At a signal from her, he added a few flourishing final notes to the dance music and then moved straight into a pulsating rendition of "If You Wish Upon a Star."

"This is it." Elizabeth-Anne turned to Dorothy-Anne. "Wish me luck."

Dorothy-Anne smiled, leaned down, and kissed her great-grandmother on the cheek. "Good luck, Great-Granny. Though I'm sure you won't need it. You never do."

"Flattery," the old lady said crisply, "will get you everywhere." She twisted her head around to look up at Miss Bunt. She gave a regal nod, and the ever-faithful nurse wheeled the chair forward to the edge of the dais. As soon as the music came to a crescendo, the lights dimmed and a single white spot bathed Elizabeth-Anne in its startling, silvery glow.

The ballroom became very quiet. People pushed their way forward and faced the dais. A gray-haired man in tuxedo was setting up a microphone in front of Elizabeth-Anne.

She smiled her thanks to him. Then she cleared her throat and spoke in her precise, ringing voice. "Ladies and gentlemen, I thank you all for coming and making the inauguration of this building such a success. And I thank you even more for taking a few minutes out to listen to the ramblings of an old woman." After some polite laughter, she went on.

"As you all probably know, many said it couldn't be done. Not a building like this." She waved one hand in a dramatic gesture. "Not one combining stores, offices, rental apartments, condominiums, and a hotel. In fact"—she broke off and allowed herself a nervous laugh—"for a while there, I wasn't quite so sure it could be done either." She pretended to let out a deep breath of relief, and the crowd again laughed good-naturedly.

"Nevertheless . . ." She clapped her hands together. "What is done is done, and I'm glad it's finished. The New York skyline has changed a little bit once again, and that is what gives this marvelous city its magical excitement and its character. I love the constant state of flux, of things always changing. I'm proud to have been part of it for so long. I love this city. I came here in 1928, and I've been here ever since.

I've been proud to call myself a New Yorker. This city has been good to many of us, and to no one so much as myself."

She paused again as a murmur of approval rippled through the crowd.

"However, to show you just how much times change, and without taking too long, I would like to read you an advertisement that Hale Hotels ran recently in the New York *Times*."

She turned around and held out her hand. Miss Bunt produced a pair of reading glasses and a newspaper clipping. Carefully Elizabeth-Anne put on the glasses.

"I should warn you that I wasn't even aware that this advertisement had gone in. Of course, why should I be? Hale Hotels has become so big that I really can't know what's going on in every department. Anyway, I saw this advertisement and I read it. Now I would like to share it with you.

" 'Technical Support Analyst. Hale Hotels Corporation has an immediate opening for a data-processing professional to handle new software releases, evaluate software packages, troubleshoot program inefficiencies, system-tune the IBM 38, and provide procedures and standards for a group of programmer analysts. The ideal candidate will have a college degree, at least three years of RPG III experience, and in-depth knowledge of the IBM 38.' " She took off her glasses and folded her hands in her lap, then stared out at the sea of upturned faces. "What the *hell*," she asked with a wry smile, "are 'troubleshoot program inefficiencies,' 'system-tune,' and 'RPG III'?"

There was a roar of laughter, and thunderous applause.

She nodded. "My sentiments exactly. It just goes to show how much times change. Why, for heaven's sake, I started Hale Hotels without even graduating from high school! However, I'm too old and cantankerous and much too set in my ways to start changing now. So, in light of this, and in light of the fact that I'll be turning ninety-one this week—"

A burst of thunderous applause cut her off. She had to wait for it to subside before continuing. She inclined her head. "Thank you, thank you," she said crisply. "However, longevity itself does not deserve applause. Nor does success which is directly due to longevity. As *Forbes Magazine* quoted me as saying in a recent interview, anyone can get where I've gotten. You've only got to live long enough.''

There was more applause and laughter.

"Now, down to serious business. Since I've finally grown up and decided to join the ranks of senior citizens, I might as well start collecting my social security. Therefore, I would now like to appoint my successor. Lord knows, everyone has waited long enough for this moment. Well, it is finally that time. *At long last.* I think I could use a little peace and quiet. After all, I'm no longer as young as I used to be.''

There was more hearty applause; the orchestra broke into a few stanzas of "Auld Lang Syne."

Elizabeth-Anne held up her hands to silence the guests. "It is possible,'' she said with typical candor, "that when you *first* see whom I've chosen to succeed me, you'll say to yourself, 'Well, the old girl's finally flipped her lid.' '' She smiled patiently, shook her head, and wagged an admonishing finger. "Believe me, I haven't. I built this corporation when I was a single mother raising four children, and though I'm not the spring chicken I once was I *am* of sound mind and body. Furthermore, as the advertisement I have read to you indicates, it is indeed time for young blood to take over.'' She paused and took a deep breath. "Ladies and gentlemen, I am proud to introduce my successor, the new, and probably the youngest-ever chairman of the board of a corporation of this size, Dorothy-Anne Hale Cantwell.'' And with that Elizabeth-Anne held her great-granddaughter's hand in hers and lifted it high.

Dorothy-Anne stared down at her great-grandmother open-mouthed. Tears were welling up in her eyes. "Me?'' she asked in disbelief.

"Yes, you,'' Elizabeth-Anne answered. "You will succeed me as head of the Hale empire I have built.''

There was thunderous applause as Elizabeth-Anne was wheeled back a few feet on the dais, holding Dorothy-Anne's hand in her own.

"Like me when I first started out, you are soon to be a mother,'' Elizabeth-Anne told her great-granddaughter. "But that is beside the point. Women are just as capable of running a business as men, and mothers as capable as single women. It's up to you to prove that and clear out the myths." She smiled. "Believe me, darling, nobody is as well suited, or as talented, to run Hale Hotels as you. Nor do I trust anyone else as implicitly. You've been living in hotels ever since you were a baby. Do you remember?"

Dorothy-Anne looked as though she was going to burst out crying. "Do I remember?" she whispered. "How can I ever forget?"

She laughed then, feeling the tension break, and wiped her eyes. Leaning down as far as her swollen belly allowed, she embraced Elizabeth-Anne. Then Freddie kissed both their cheeks in turn. The other members of the family stepped forward to offer their congratulations to Dorothy-Anne. Only Henry did so perfunctorily, a cold, fathomless look in his eyes. For an instant Dorothy-Anne felt a pang of regret. She knew her father had always thought he would be the one to step into Elizabeth-Anne's place when she retired. At forty-one, this could only be a bitter disappointment to him. But she knew there was nothing she could do. They had never mended the open wound between them. Dorothy-Anne couldn't reach out to him now.

Elizabeth-Anne took a deep breath, the tears shining in her still-bright eyes. "And now," she said softly to Dorothy-Anne, "you'll have to excuse me. I'm a little tired. It's way past my bedtime, and tonight I can rest easy. Hale Hotels is in good hands. The papers have already been drawn up, and I've done what I came to do. Now I plan to go home, relax, and enjoy myself. Right now, with a good night's sleep, and tomorrow, with breakfast in bed. Maybe I'll even get a chance to watch some television." She raised her voice. "The rest of you stay and enjoy the party. But you'd better listen to my great-granddaughter when she breaks it up! She's a tough cookie. Like me." And with that she leaned back wearily, her face clenched as if she were in pain.

"Great-Granny," Dorothy-Anne asked worriedly, "are you all right?"

Elizabeth-Anne opened one eye and glared at her with an expression of amusement. "Of course I'm all right!" she snapped in pretended irritation. "Why shouldn't I be? Doesn't a retiree get any peace?" Then she turned around and raised one hand, the fingers making a fluid forward gesture. "Home, Miss Bunt!"

Sniffling noisily, Miss Bunt wheeled Elizabeth-Anne down the ramp. The crowd fell back to make a path, and throughout the ballroom, the music and applause were deafening.

The queen had abdicated. A new queen had been crowned.

When they returned to the Madison Squire, Elizabeth-Anne told Miss Bunt, "I think I'd like to sit outside on the terrace by myself for a while, if you don't—" Her voice was soft, but she was cut off by a wave of pain that arched her back like a cat's and contorted her face. Miss Bunt recognized the symptoms; over the past few months she had grown familiar with them.

"Has your painkiller worn off?" Miss Bunt asked thickly. "Shall I get you another pill?"

But the attack had passed, and Elizabeth-Anne now only breathed somewhat heavily in its aftermath. Her spirit was still strong. "Now, why should I want that?" she asked irritably.

The nurse knew there was no point in arguing with Elizabeth-Anne, even about this, and dropped her gaze.

"Good." Elizabeth-Anne sat back, her lips a grim line. She had never discussed her cancer with the nurse, but knew the medication, the furtive visits to the hospital, and the recent bouts of surgery all spoke for themselves. After all, Miss Bunt was a trained nurse. Elizabeth-Anne was grateful for her silence and discretion, her respect for her employer's obvious desire not to let her condition become known. It was a relief not to have to explain—even to Miss Bunt—how completely the cancer had spread. The surgery had never cut it all out. It had been impossible to do that, and now it was everywhere, gripping her vital organs in a tight, unyielding vise.

"The terrace, Miss Bunt," Elizabeth-Anne said softly.

Miss Bunt nodded and took Elizabeth-Anne out through the

French doors. She set the hand brake, then gently tucked a plaid lap blanket around her.

Elizabeth-Anne chuckled, then snapped with good humor, "Now leave me alone, for God's sake. I'm not a child."

Miss Bunt hesitated. "Do you . . . would you like me to stay out here with you?"

"No, I'd really rather be alone." Elizabeth-Anne reached for her nurse's hand and held it, smiling faintly. "Faithful Miss Bunt," she said softly. "Whatever would I have done without you?"

The nurse shook her head. She appeared to be on the verge of tears.

"No, don't cry," Elizabeth-Anne whispered sternly. "Tears are for those with regrets. I have none. None at all. I've lived my life to the fullest." She paused. "I've left you well provided for. You can finally retire. You've been good to me, and I thank you."

Miss Bunt nodded silently, beyond words, and turned to leave.

"I have one last favor to ask you."

"Yes?" Miss Bunt's voice was husky.

"Do not come out here to check on me. Leave me here until morning. Don't call anyone. Is that a promise?"

Miss Bunt couldn't turn to face Elizabeth-Anne and only whispered, "Yes."

"There's no use ruining everyone's party. They'll find out soon enough. Let them enjoy themselves tonight." Her voice rose. "Now leave me be."

Miss Bunt hurried inside, not quite shutting the tall French windows.

Elizabeth-Anne sat motionless in the wheelchair, her clear aquamarine eyes scanning the city that for almost sixty years she had called home. The clear August night was humid, but the breeze that rippled past was delightfully cool against her face. All around her, the monoliths of Manhattan glittered with jewellike sparkle. Peering above them, she could see out to the floodlit towers of the Hale Castle.

She took a deep, satisfied breath. The roses in the redwood planters perfumed the air, and the breeze rustled through the birch trees. It was a velvety night, a perfect night, and far below on Madison Avenue, through the iron railing of the terrace wall, the dark asphalt was ruby with the taillights of traffic.

How good it felt to be alive! How fabulous this city was, this pulsating behemoth which had the power to create or destroy with equal swiftness, the power that had granted her the greatest opportunity under the sun.

Hearing the drone of an overhead jet, she watched its flashing lights float past.

She smiled to herself. How this terrace had changed in the decades since she had first moved to the Madison Squire penthouse, before there had even been jet planes. How the trees had grown, the trunks thickening with every passing year, and how the wisteria and ivy she had planted so long, long ago now crept up the brick walls, cloaking them completely with heavy green. She had watched the seasons change from here many, many times. How often she had smiled at the gray, thin winter sun, the spectacular spring sunsets over New Jersey to the west, the bright lemon mornings of summer. And how often the terrace plants had shed their leaves, only to renew themselves the following spring.

She had traveled so far and wide in her long life, seeing to her far-flung empire, but had always been overjoyed to return here to her beloved sanctuary. How long now had she lived and fought, built and traveled, watched her children being born and dying? And how short the span of years had seemed at times. How much pain, and joy, and bittersweetness she had encountered. How good it was to be alive! And oh, how good, too, it would finally be to rest. To shut her eyes a final time.

It was time to stop fighting and bow to the inevitable. She had lived long and full and well. Her empire was in order, and so were her personal effects. Her last will and testament had long since been prepared, signed, and witnessed. It was safely locked away in her lawyer's vault. How lucky she had been to have had the time—and forewarning—to put everything in order. To provide for her descendants. To install Dorothy-Anne at the head of the empire.

And what an empire it was. The hotels and motels, the investments and the treasures. And most of all, Dorothy-Anne, pregnant with child.

The greatest gift of all.

She sighed happily, wondering why now, of all times, as she felt her strength sapping slowly from her, she should feel such contentedness. She would never for the life of her understand why people were afraid to live, and afraid to die. Life and death had to be experienced to the fullest.

She leaned her head back and stared up into the star-filled sky, imagining that each winking light in the firmament was a living soul. Up there were her parents, her aunt, Zaccheus and Janet, Rebecca and Charlotte-Anne, her beloved Larry, her much-mourned Zaccheus Jr., and Anna, the unexpected treasure. They all seemed to beckon to her, calling her silently to join them.

She closed her eyes, savoring the imagined music of their voices as she felt the strength slowly ebbing from her body. She knew the pain was rising, but somehow didn't feel it. Instead, she leaned her head back, and the faint enigmatic smile was frozen on her lips as she lost consciousness. In the morning, she would not wake. That smile would be frozen there forever.

8

Lightning flashed, followed by the peal of thunder and then the eerie silence, filled only with the machine gun staccato of the rain. The rich smell of burning wax from candles filled the room.

The contractions were close together now, racking her body with bursts of pain, squeezing her into white-hot flashes, billowing outward, radiating to her extremities. Through her closed eyes she saw firelike patterns, showers of sparks.

Pain.

And regrets. So many regrets. They circled in a frenzy through her mind. Regrets for a thousand things she could have done for Great-Granny and didn't. Things she had always wanted to tell her and hadn't. Regrets for not staying home and waiting until the baby was born before coming here. But how could she have known? How could she have held back with Great-Granny waiting, with the vision of her anxious, tired eyes before Dorothy-Anne's own fogged, exhausted mind?

Regrets. For foolishness and selfishness. But how could she know?

She hadn't this morning, when they had boarded the Hale Hotels' Boeing 727-100. Twenty thousand feet over the Gulf of Mexico, the jet engines had changed pitch as the plane had swung around in a miles-wide semicircle and slipped into its landing pattern. Even then, there had been time to change her mind, but she had never even considered it.

The plane's interior had been constructed to look like a living room, with oversized beige plush couches and bolted-down easy chairs. She and Freddie had sat side by side in intense silence. He was holding her hand, but he did not speak. He knew that physically she was beside him, but mentally she was not. Her mind was wandering elsewhere, besieged by the tidegate of memories opened when Great-Granny died.

He squeezed her hand to reassure her that she was not alone. She turned to him, nodding gratefully, her lips smiling a sad, tired smile; then her eyes filled with tears. They took on that distant look as wave after wave of remembrance washed over her. There were so many of them. And they were all good.

She closed her eyes as she heard distinct voices, both recent and from the past:

Great-Granny, on her ninth birthday: *"The Hale Palace is yours, and yours alone."*

Mr. Morris, the ancient gray-haired senior partner of the law firm, reading from Elizabeth-Anne Hale's last will and testament: *"The bulk of my estate, which includes all prop-*

erty, both real and personal, the entire chain of hotels and motels, I bequeath to my beloved great-granddaughter Dorothy-Anne.''

Freddie, gazing at her with shining eyes during the cremation: ''She'll never be dead, Dorothy-Anne, not really. Not as long as we keep her memory alive. Not as long as a single Hale hotel remains standing.''

Dr. Danvers, every inch the well-meaning pediatrician: ''Dorothy-Anne, I have known you since you yourself were a child, and you've always listened to my advice. Please do so now. Wait to travel. Your time is too near.''

And Great-Granny's last wish, spoken through the brittle, impersonal voice of Mr. Morris: ''I wish to be returned to Texas, my ashes scattered where those of my first husband, Zaccheus Hale, were scattered so long, long ago.''

Her eyes were sparkling with tears.

Elizabeth-Anne Hale was returning home at last.

9

The rain slashed at Freddie's face, stinging his skin with the force of needle-nosed bullets. He staggered on, his torso hunched forward as he kept his face down. A flash of lightning crackled, illuminating the blackness all around with a silver strobe of pulsating light.

He took the opportunity to look around and get his bearings. He was in the middle of the grove. Straight rows of citrus trees extended into the distance all around, each row looking just like the last. The leaves were being torn off the trees and the fruit rained down from the flailing, wind-whipped branches. Every direction he turned, he saw identical rows of trees.

He could only hope to God he didn't lose his sense of direction.

He stumbled on, keeping his face down. The wind shrieked with the high-pitched, agonizing screams of death. The wet ground sucked at his feet. Every step was an effort. In his mind, he repeated his words of determination like a litany: He couldn't fail. He couldn't lose his way. He had to get to town and find a doctor.

Thoughts of death bombarded his mind from all sides. Dorothy-Anne's pain-tensed face . . . the baby within her . . .

Death was primordial. It was everywhere. It had always been, and always would be.

It was up to him to keep the grim scythe-bearer at bay.

He fought on, his eyes closed against the wind until his feet caught on something. His arms shot out, he flailed the air as he fought to retain his balance. One foot met nothing; for a moment he seemed suspended in midair. Then he crashed down into the water, chilled even though it was lukewarm.

He had fallen into an irrigation canal.

The water closed in over his head, and his feet touched the sludgy bottom. Sputtering, he surfaced, shook his head, and waded to the bank. He clutched at the mud and pulled himself out. Slowly he got to his feet. He stared all around, waiting for a flash of lightning to show him the way.

But when it came, he only stood in confusion, trying to remember which way he had come. Where was he headed? He couldn't even tell if he had crossed the canal, or had returned to the side he had fallen from. The rows of trees were so damned identical, everything the same in every direction, each tree seeming a carbon copy of another, and another, and another.

He had no idea which way to turn.

He hesitated only a moment. There was no time to lose. If he was wandering off in the wrong direction, the sooner he found out about it, the better.

It was all up to him now. His wife needed a doctor. The unborn baby needed a doctor.

It was up to him. He alone could keep death from his family's door.

The wind shrieked its carnival barker's message: *Hurry! Hurry! Hurry!*

*   *   *

Silently Mrs. Ramirez cursed the largeness of her hands. They were working hands, thick-fingered and thick-wristed. What she needed was tiny, delicate hands with narrow, tapered fingers and very thin, elegant wrists.

"I am no midwife," she muttered, disgusted with herself.

Dorothy-Anne sucked in her breath, biting down against the pain for as long as she could. The scream, when it came, seemed to shatter the night. Her back arched as she tried to pull away from Mrs. Ramirez's probing touch. The fingers felt rough and foreign, alien protrusions inside the soft safety of her womb.

"Please, please," Mrs. Ramirez gasped. Her dark skin gleamed with beads of sweat. She was unused to this position, half-kneeling and half-lying between the young woman's splayed legs in order to see inside her. She was much too old for this kind of acrobatics. "Your pains. They come every thirty seconds now. We *must* move the baby! You understand?" Her eyes glittered.

"But Freddie. He's going to bring help."

"There is no time. By then it may be too late. Think of the baby! Please, you must listen to me!"

Dorothy-Anne looked at her with fear-widened eyes.

"I am not going to hurt you. You must believe that."

Dorothy-Anne nodded as best she could.

"Is tiring, I know. But you must be brave. You must breathe deep, and push." Mrs. Ramirez' huge breasts rose and fell as she demonstrated. "You can do?" She narrowed her eyes.

Dorothy-Anne squeezed her eyes shut, imitating the short barks of rhythmic breathing.

"There. Is fine. Now, let me try again," Mrs. Ramirez said soothingly. As gently as she could, she once again began to poke the fingers of one hand up inside the moist warmth of Dorothy-Anne's vagina. With her other hand she felt along the outside of the abdomen.

Defeated, Mrs. Ramirez withdrew her hand.

"Is it all right now?" Dorothy-Anne asked hopefully.

Mrs. Ramirez stared at her, then shook her head. "No,"

she said softly. "It is impossible." She got up and moved over to the enamel basin on the nightstand and began wearily washing her hands. Suddenly she froze and let out a sharp cry. "Oh, now I remember!" She smiled broadly, then even laughed out loud.

"What is it?" Dorothy-Anne whispered.

Mrs. Ramirez' voice rose with excitement. "There is a way! Now I remember." Suddenly the story she had been searching for came back to her, the one that had teased her memory all night. Jorge, her second-oldest nephew, had also been in a difficult position. The doctor had insisted that her sister Mariana have a cesarian section, but the local Mexican midwife had managed to shift the baby around without it. All night she had tried to remember *how*. And now she had! It was so simple.

"Let's do it," Dorothy-Anne, gasped, struggling to sit up.

"Do not move." Mrs. Ramirez paced the room, rubbing her chin. "There is only one problem." She bit down on her lower lip. "I will need help."

"Help?"

"I need someone else. Someone to help me with you." She lowered her voice, repeatedly shaking her head. "Now, why I not remember this before I let that poor man go off in to the grove. *Estupida*!"

F reddie squinted through the silver sheets of rain and let out a strangled cry.

The pale lights in the windows had drawn him to this house, had given him a surge of renewed hope. He had run toward the lights, and in his haste collided with the metal hulk in front of him.

A car.

He stared at it, stunned. The big Lincoln Continental was all too familiar.

He shut his eyes, dropping to his knees beside it. He let out a keening moan of self-disgust. How stupid could he be? He had gone off and gotten lost and ended up right where he had started.

As if to reinforce this tragedy, a flash of lightning lit up the tourist court. The sloping galvanized roofs and the sagging porches throbbed silver-white, and then were once again lost in blackness.

Sighing, he staggered to his feet and leaned against the hood. His mind was in turmoil. He could either continue, trying once again to cross the grove, or else he could waste precious moments by going inside and seeing Dorothy-Anne.

She was so close. Just across the road.

He hesitated only a moment more. Then he ran across the asphalt toward the tourist court.

T he moment Felicia Ramirez heard heavy footsteps pounding on the porch boards, her heart gave a hopeful leap. So the Blessed Mother had heard her prayers and had answered them. Just when she needed somebody, somebody had come.

She crossed herself thankfully and rushed toward the door. But when she flung it open and saw Freddie, her face fell. "No doctor?" she asked.

"No. I got lost." He took a deep breath and leaned wearily back against the wall.

She shook her head. "Is all right. I need you. I remember something."

He gripped her arm before she could rush off. "How is she?" he asked, the fear obvious in his eyes.

"The same." Mrs. Ramirez sighed softly. Then she smiled. "But I think maybe we can do something. Come. We have no time to lose." She gestured impatiently.

He saw the hope shining in her dark eyes, and hurried after her.

"Freddie," Dorothy-Anne moaned in an exhausted whisper as soon as he came into the bedroom. She lay pale and drenched, barely able to move. "You're back. I'm glad."

"Hi, honey." He held her hand tightly in his, trying to give her a reassuring smile.

"I need your help to change her position," Mrs. Ramirez said without further ado. "We *must* get her on her knees."

"I'm so tired," Dorothy-Anne protested weakly.

"Later you can rest," Mrs. Ramirez said harshly. "Right

now we have work to do." She nodded once at Freddie.
"You stand on that side of the bed. I remain on this side."
She flipped off the sheet, and Dorothy-Anne shivered in the
sudden chill. Except for her magnificently swollen belly, she
looked gaunt, bony, and haggard. Her teeth chattered. "I'm
cold," she whispered.

Mrs. Ramirez ignored her. "Now, when I say so, we
move her over to her left side. Then we make her kneel."
She raised her eyebrows questioningly. Her expression made
it clear that any argument was useless. "You ready?"

Freddie nodded hesitantly.

"Good. Now we both hold her and rock her gently."

Slowly they both pushed on Dorothy-Anne, rolling her
over on her side. She let out a muffled scream. Freddie
cringed and went pale.

"Now we get her on her knees." Mrs. Ramirez leaned
close into Dorothy-Anne's ear. "We need your help also.
Help us. Support yourself on your elbows."

Dorothy-Anne clenched her jaw as Freddie and Mrs. Ramirez
helped her get into position. It wasn't an easy maneuver, not
in her state of exhaustion and with the clumsy, swollen belly
getting in the way. When she finally was on her knees,
Dorothy-Anne let her head sag down between her arms, her
triangular shoulder blades jutting from her naked back like
two shark's fins, her limp hair hanging down over her face.

"Good. Very good." Mrs. Ramirez, ignoring Dorothy-
Anne's apparent collapse, sounded pleased. She knelt beside
Dorothy-Anne, pressing the outside of the abdomen ever so
lightly with the palms of her hands. The skin was stretched
tautly against the pear-shaped belly. "Is better?" she asked.

"I . . . I think so," Dorothy-Anne whispered in surprise.
"It . . it doesn't seem to hurt nearly so much now."

Mrs. Ramirez nodded with satisfaction. "Is because of the
pressure. The little one no longer pushes on the wrong spot."
She gestured to Freddie. "Now, move her back and forth.
Gently. Like so. Like she is on a boat." She made a cradle of
her arms and demonstrated a steady rocking motion with her
hands. "Meanwhile, I feel for the baby. Now, do it!"

Freddie began rocking Dorothy-Anne, holding onto her very gently, yet firmly, so she would not collapse on her side.

Suddenly Dorothy-Anne sucked in her breath.

"What is it?" Freddie cried with concern. "Did I hurt you?"

"No. It's the baby." Dorothy-Anne looked sideways through her curtain of limp hair, her voice taking on a tone of wonder. "It's . . . it's *moving*. I can feel it *move*." Her back arched and tensed, and she lifted her head slowly, staring in wide-eyed amazement first at Freddie, then at Mrs. Ramirez.

But Mrs. Ramirez was not looking at her. She had eyes only for the sagging belly. Even from the outside, she could see that the bulging outline which was the child was percepti-bly shifting from one side to another.

Mrs. Ramirez held her breath. "A little bit more," she whispered under her breath, wiping the tickling sweat off her mustached upper lip. "A little bit more."

The bulge stopped shifting. Then, after a moment, it con-tinued to move.

Mrs. Ramirez let out a short sigh of relief. "Stay like that," she commanded as she changed her position on the bed so that she could insert her fingers into Dorothy-Anne's va-gina. For a moment she felt around, then squeezed her eyes shut and heaved a massive sigh.

"What *is* it?" Freddie whispered.

Mrs. Ramirez slowly withdrew her hand. Suddenly she burst out into laughter. "The head! I feel the head! It is now down at the opening where it should be. *Dios mío!* We have done it. *We have done it.*" Tears of relief flowed from her dark eyes. "Now, quickly. We must turn her over."

"You mean . . . it's all right now?" Freddie asked in disbelief.

"Is fine, is fine." Mrs. Ramirez' head bobbed happily up and down. "*Quickly*, get her on her back." Then in a softer voice she added, "It will still hurt, but it will be a normal hurt . . . and now we can deliver. Do you hear?" Her eyes gleamed triumphantly. "We can *deliver* the little one. We have done it!"

GENESIS

QUEBECK, TEXAS
&

August 15, 1985

Dorothy-Anne had never known anything so glorious, so filled with amazement and wonder, as the moment she heard the first cry of her newborn baby.

"Look, a beautiful girl!" Felicia Ramirez cried happily. "You have a perfect little daughter."

Tears filled Dorothy-Anne's eyes, but they were tears of pure joy. The awful pain of the long night of labor was over, gone with the storm that had crashed and howled as ferociously as she herself had cried out. But that was all a memory now. The morning sun broke through the small bedroom window and lit the room with a warm glow like the happiness in her heart.

Freddie sat beside her, tears coursing down his own cheeks as he cradled their child in his arms. Dorothy-Anne savored the sight of them, then let her eyes wander to the Buccellati urn still standing atop the dresser. It gleamed brightly in the morning sunlight.

She took a deep breath. She felt immensely drained, but she was exhilarated, too. She could hear the sounds of the birds and crickets returning, and Mrs. Ramirez making little cooing noises over the infant. And she could smell the moist, damp freshness mingling with the scents of citrus. A choked feeling came up in her throat, and she could feel a tear of sadness roll slowly down her cheek. She stared at the urn. It seemed to fade as the first ray of sunlight hit it directly, throwing off a blinding glare.

Great-Granny's voice was a dry whisper. "Look up, Dorothy-Anne!"

She leaned her head way back, her eyes following Great-Granny's finger, as it pointed up, up, to the Hale Palace. The thousands upon thousands of tons of pale limestone looked buttery soft and weightless, and the sunlight bathed the windows and turned them into silvery mirrors. The ornate twin towers scraped the fast-moving clouds that scudded across the Wedgwood blue of the sky.

How could one adequately express thanks for such a gift, for the flagship of an empire that took a lifetime to build? How could one repay such a legacy as Elizabeth-Anne had left her?

Suddenly she knew. The night had passed, and a new day had begun. Today was August 15.

Elizabeth-Anne Hale's birthday. She would have been ninety-one.

Dorothy-Anne turned around and reached out with her hands. Freddie gently laid the child in the crook of her arm.

Dorothy-Anne looked down at her tiny daughter and smiled. She was so lively, and looked so tiny and fragile. An almost angry scowl was on her face, as if she were protesting the indignity of her birth. Her tiny hands were smaller than a doll's, and she kept clenching and unclenching them, grasping at air. Like a true Hale's, the child's few silky strands of hair were gold, and her large, inquisitive eyes were aquamarine.

Dorothy-Anne held her daughter close. She glanced up at Freddie. "Elizabeth-Anne?" she asked softly.

He nodded. "Elizabeth-Anne it is," he agreed, "though I warn you, it won't be easy for her to follow in her namesake's footsteps."

"Not easy, no," Dorothy-Anne said pensively. Then she smiled. "But she'll do it."

And then Dorothy-Anne's lips moved slowly, soundlessly. So soundlessly that even Freddie couldn't hear.

"Happy Birthday, Great-Granny."

From *The Forbes Four Hundred Fall 1988*

Dorothy Anne Cantwell

Inheritance, Hale Hotels, investments. New York. 24. Married, 3 children. Raised by great-grandmother, Elizabeth-Anne Hale. Served as youngest-ever U.S. CEO with great-grandmother's company. Family-oriented. Lives quietly. Noted for N.Y.-area philanthrophies, otherwise intensely private. No photos, no interviews, execs keep mum if they value jobs. Despite motherhood, expanding superluxury hotel empire and lately investing in vacation "villages" begun by Elizabeth-Anne Hale projected at $500 million over 5 years. Already spent $100 million upgrading current hotels. Refuses to go public. Reported annual income of $83 million. Took great-grandmother's place as world's richest woman. Certainly is the youngest. Husband Freddie expanding Hale conglomerate interests in real estate, apartment complexes, resorts, restaurants, travel agencies, banks, mineral mines around the globe. Refuses to confirm net worth of $2.6 billion, or income. "I'm well fixed, that's all."